A Wizard's Fury

Sophie only turned away, carrying the Dragon's Egg back to Erik's hoard. He waited for her to return, his thoughts swirling.

If Alex Madison was the Wizard, then she was the one who had taken the initiative that would save humans from the repercussions of their own deeds. And if the old legend was true, she would mate with the Warrior. They would lead the *Pyr* to victory.

Donovan. The best candidate to become the Warrior had to be Donovan, the *Pyr*'s greatest fighting machine—and the *Pyr* most reluctant to make a commitment of any kind. What if the Warrior and the Wizard didn't consummate their firestorm? What if Donovan didn't allow himself to be transformed into the Warrior? What if this Alex Madison didn't want to be involved? Erik winced and shoved a hand through his hair.

He decided that he hated portents and prophecies.

ALSO BY DEBORAH COOKE

Kiss of Fire

KISS OF FURY

A DRAGONFIRE NOVEL

DEBORAH COOKE

A SIGNET ECLIPSE BOOK

SIGNET ECLIPSE
Published by New American Library, a division of
Penguin Group (USA) Inc., 375 Hudson Street,
New York, New York 10014, USA
Penguin Group (Canada), 90 Eglinton Avenue East, Suite 700, Toronto,
Ontario M4P 2Y3, Canada (a division of Pearson Penguin Canada Inc.)
Penguin Books Ltd., 80 Strand, London WC2R 0RL, England
Penguin Ireland, 25 St. Stephen's Green, Dublin 2,
Ireland (a division of Penguin Books Ltd.)
Penguin Group (Australia), 250 Camberwell Road, Camberwell, Victoria 3124,
Australia (a division of Pearson Australia Group Pty, Ltd.)
Penguin Books India Pvt. Ltd., 11 Community Centre, Panchsheel Park,
New Delhi - 110 017, India
Penguin Group (NZ), 67 Apollo Drive, Rosedale, North Shore 0632,
New Zealand (a division of Pearson New Zealand Ltd.)
Penguin Books (South Africa) (Pty.) Ltd., 24 Sturdee Avenue,
Rosebank, Johannesburg 2196, South Africa

Penguin Books Ltd., Registered Offices:
80 Strand, London WC2R 0RL, England

First published by Signet Eclipse, an imprint of New American Library,
a division of Penguin Group (USA) Inc.

First Printing, August 2008
10 9 8 7 6 5 4 3 2 1

For all the readers who wrote to me about their love of dragons and their enjoyment of this series. Thank you for your enthusiasm! I hope you enjoy this dragon's story just as well.

Prologue

August 28, 2007

Erik Sorensson was tired, but the ritual with the Dragon's Egg always exhausted him. He and the other members of the high circle of *Pyr* had met in Samoa earlier in the day. Beneath the full lunar eclipse, they had received the portent that the next firestorm would occur in Minneapolis.

Would it be his? Erik thought not.

He hoped not.

He'd worry about the details later. For the moment, he just wanted to sleep in the solitude of his lair. He replaced the Dragon's Egg in the most secure area of his hoard and yawned.

"It is more than the journey that fatigues you," said a woman in close proximity.

Erik jumped and pivoted.

Sophie waved her fingertips at him. "Surprise."

She lounged on one of his two black couches, looking as ethereal as ever. Her fair hair fell loose over her shoulders and she wore a dress made of sheer layers of silver and gray. She could have been a stray beam of moonlight.

Erik checked, but his protective smoke was still thick around the perimeter of his lair. It resonated with the clarity of an unbroken territory mark.

"How did you get in here?"

"I am the Wyvern," she said without interest. "I know many tricks, both magical and mundane." She glanced around his home, which was in a converted warehouse. The old hardwood floors gleamed and the furnishings were modern and few. "Nice lair. I like the smell of brimstone. It's a fitting touch."

Erik strode across the floor to check his locks. He knew his tone was sharp and he didn't care. "It's not brimstone. It's sulfur. I store the pyrotechnics in the back room." The locks were exactly as he had left them. He faced Sophie without troubling to hide his irritation.

She held his gaze. "Aren't you going to ask why I've disturbed your solitude?"

"You're the prophetess. You tell me."

"I'm not the only one with the gift of foresight."

Erik muttered something uncomplimentary under his breath and Sophie smiled as he perched on the couch opposite her. He might as well hear what she had to say, as enigmatic as it was likely to be. "All right. Tell me why you've come."

"Surely you can guess."

"Maybe I don't want to. I'm tired, Sophie, and need some sleep."

She shook her head, her gaze knowing. "Sleep isn't going to fix what ails you."

Erik ignored that. "Why did you come?"

"I had a portent to deliver, of course."

"The next firestorm will be in Minneapolis," Erik said, even though he expected that Sophie already knew as much.

The firestorm was the mating sign of the *Pyr*, the sign that a *Pyr* had met the mortal mate who could bear his child. A firestorm could happen at any time in any place, but those of critical importance to the *Pyr* were signaled by total lunar eclipses.

"Do you know whose firestorm it will be?"

Sophie closed her eyes and leaned her head back against the couch. Her long hair spread across the dark fabric like a veil. Erik remembered the sight of snow on coal, felt a pang for the past; then her chanted words brought him back to the present.

> *The Dragon's Tail demands recompense*
> *Owed the land for man's violence;*
> *Both human and* Pyr *must sacrifice,*
> *To earn the chance to make matters right.*
> *A portal has opened to the past*
> *Making possible what has been lost;*
> *Time to muster forces for the final battle,*
> *In which* Pyr *and* Slayer *learn their mettle.*

"That sounds like a warning," Erik said when she fell silent.

She opened her eyes and smiled sweetly at him. "It is."

Erik felt a surge of frustration, one he often felt in Sophie's presence. "I know there will be three total lunar eclipses, which follow the change of the moon's node to the Dragon's Tail. And we've known for centuries that a total lunar eclipse is the mark of a firestorm of particular import to the *Pyr*, like the firestorm the Smith indicated by the last eclipse."

Sophie continued to smile.

"So, this one, this firestorm that will occur in Minneapolis, must also be important. But how? The Smith is already mated and Sara carries his child. What is significant about the next firestorm, or about the *Pyr* who will experience it?"

"Three total eclipses in rapid succession," Sophie mused, staring at her three outstretched fingers. "Three *Pyr* of critical importance who will feel the firestorm." She looked at

Erik. "Three firestorms that must succeed, if the *Pyr* are to survive for the pending battle."

"We must ensure them all or lose the war before it begins?" Erik was incredulous, but Sophie was serene. "Can't you tell me any more than that?"

"I brought you the prophecy."

"But it tells me nothing!"

"On the contrary, it tells you everything you need to know."

Before Erik could argue, Sophie unfolded herself from the couch and drifted across the room. She seemed to float, to not be bound by gravity. She disappeared into Erik's hoard and he forced himself to stay put.

They were on the same team, after all. He *should* trust her.

She returned with the Dragon's Egg. He was offended to see anyone else handling it. "I just put that away. . . ."

She halted before Erik with the obsidian orb cradled in her hands. "Look," she said.

Erik knew better than to argue. He looked.

The Dragon's Egg gleamed. Sophie's tune began low and soft. Erik couldn't hear the words, couldn't anticipate the rhythm, but he knew he was hearing an ancient charm. The surface of the stone seemed to swirl, as if it were covered with clouds of gray.

Storm clouds.

He'd never seen the Dragon's Egg respond to anything other than the light of a total eclipse. He stared and marveled.

Sophie's song grew louder and the clouds became darker, ever darker. They churned and boiled on the surface; then abruptly they cleared.

Erik was looking into a dark mirror, one as clear as glass. It reminded him of deep water and he wanted to recoil, but he forced himself to keep looking. His own past wasn't important, not now.

Sophie leaned over the stone, her brow almost touching his. "Tell me what you see," she urged in a whisper.

"An office," he said, watching with excitement as the shapes became clear. "At night. There's somebody there, working on a computer. I see the screen but no other lights are on."

He glanced up in confusion.

"Yes. Look deeper."

Erik did more than look. He used all of his keen *Pyr* senses and felt the scene. He became a part of it. He was there, in the moment, experiencing the events. He saw shadows separate from the walls, heard the snick of an alarm wire being cut. He sensed a threat sliding into the quiet building and was aware that he looked through the eyes of another.

But who?

"There are others, breaking in," he murmured. "They don't know there's anyone there."

"Don't they?" Sophie said quietly.

Erik felt a heart race and knew the person who watched events unfold was afraid. "When will this happen?"

Sophie's tone was resolute. "Look."

Erik knew the crime had to somehow be important to him and the *Pyr*. He looked. He saw chairs being flung and desks overturned. Files were dumped and computers were thrown at walls. "They're destroying the place. Where is it?"

Sophie didn't answer.

Erik fell silent when he saw the dragonfire erupt, its orange flames devouring the carpet, cubicles, files, and walls. Its hue and power were unmistakable. He watched more closely, knowing what he would see. His heart sank all the same when he spied the silhouettes of his own kind in the flames.

He felt the viewer's palms grow damp with terror. He heard the scream of another human being injured and felt the viewer catch his or her breath. He heard malicious laughter and knew what he was witnessing.

The old battle had moved to new ground.

"*Slayers*," he said to Sophie, hearing the hatred in his

own voice. "Why this place? What are they trying to destroy? Whom are they hurting?"

Sophie blew on the Dragon's Egg. The flames on its surface burned brighter, then disappeared, as if she had extinguished them. The Dragon's Egg was so black that it might never have been otherwise.

"When will this happen? Where?" Erik demanded, his frustration rising when Sophie didn't reply. "Can it be prevented? Can the victim be saved? Why are they injuring a human?"

Sophie bent and kissed the stone with reverence, and Erik sensed that she was thanking it for its aid.

Then she glanced up at him, her eyes clear and bright. Their remarkable turquoise shade always startled him. "We cannot save humans on our own. They must make reparation themselves for the injury they have done to Gaia—they must initiate change within their own society. Then and only then can we fight for their survival."

"These humans were targeted by *Slayers* because they took that initiative," Erik guessed. Sophie's smile was fleeting, but he knew by the glimpse of it that he was right.

"You have seen through the eyes of the Wizard," she said.

Erik caught his breath at her assertion. "The Wizard and the Warrior. It was once said that together they could build an army and lead it to victory."

Sophie smiled again.

"But that's just an old story, Sophie, a myth that has no root in truth—"

"A myth?" she interrupted him with a laugh. "And you are not a myth come to life?"

Erik was impatient. "There's never been a Wizard, not that I know of. . . ."

Sophie spoke as if he hadn't. "Alex Madison will survive this attack," she said with force, then met his gaze. "You cannot stop the attack, but you can help her." Her words silenced Erik's protestations.

"Alex Madison is the one who was working there, the one

who was afraid," Erik guessed, but he knew the answer already. He was shocked that he knew the name of the woman who would experience this firestorm—Sophie had never been so forthcoming. A cold shiver of dread slid down his spine. Were their prospects that grim? "And she's the Wizard."

Sophie's smile left him hungry for more.

"When will this happen? Or has it happened already?"

Sophie only turned away, carrying the Dragon's Egg back to his hoard. Erik waited for her to return, his thoughts swirling.

If Alex Madison was the Wizard, then she was the one who had taken the initiative that would save humans from the repercussions of their own deeds. And if the old legend was true, she would mate with the Warrior. They would lead the *Pyr* to victory.

Donovan. The best candidate to become the Warrior had to be Donovan, the *Pyr*'s greatest fighting machine—and the *Pyr* most reluctant to make a commitment of any kind. What if the Warrior and the Wizard didn't consummate their firestorm? What if Donovan didn't allow himself to be transformed into the Warrior? What if this Alex Madison didn't want to be involved? Erik winced and shoved a hand through his hair.

He decided that he hated portents and prophecies.

He paced as he waited, his impatience rising with every moment.

Sophie didn't come back.

Erik finally pursued her into the hidden warren of his hoard. The Dragon's Egg was precisely where it belonged, nestled in its black velvet sack. The doors to his lair were still barred and locked. His smoke was still undisturbed.

But Sophie was gone.

Erik was alone once more. He swore, returned to the main room, and booted up his laptop.

Fortunately, the Wyvern wasn't his only source of information.

Chapter 1

Minneapolis
The following October

*H*ell had swallowed her world.
  Worse, there was nothing Alex could do about it.
  The flames raged from every side, their orange tongues greedily devouring files, walls, carpeting. It was impossible, improbable that the lab should erupt in fire now. Mark had run through the flames into the lab, but she feared for his life.
  Alex was about to go after Mark when someone laughed.
  More than one someone.
  For once in her life, Alex was cautious. She held a damp cloth over her mouth and listened. Her heart pounded and her palms went damp. She heard the intruders fling open file drawers, heard the flames crackle as fuel was added to the fire. She heard computers crash and screens shatter. She heard the fire alarm ringing insistently as the smoke got thicker.
  The laughter became louder, closer, meaner.
  Then she heard them smashing the Green Machine in the

lab. The sound infuriated her. Alex had worked years on this project and was within an increment of loosing it on the world. She had forfeited everything; Mark had mortgaged everything; they had begged and borrowed, and it was within a single hair of paying off.

But someone was trying to destroy that dream.

Alex wasn't going to let that happen. She ran out of her office and her first breath burned her lungs. The carpet in the corridor was in flames. The file room had become an inferno.

None of it stopped her. She ducked her head, darted into the fire, and headed for the lab.

Mark screamed. It was a wrenching cry of pain, a sound unlike anything she'd ever heard him make before.

Alex ran faster.

The laughter grew louder, more malicious. Alex rounded the last corner in the corridor, confronted a wall of flames, and braced herself for the worst.

But what she saw in the lab was beyond any vision of hell she could have imagined. . . .

Alex awakened abruptly. Her heart was galloping and there was a cold trickle of sweat running down her back.

She wasn't at the lab.

She was in a cold and unfamiliar room. She was lying in an elevated bed and the lighting was low. Darkness pressed against the large window to her left. The walls of the room were a pale mint green and the furniture was stainless steel.

There were no flames.

She looked again, then exhaled shakily. Judging by the darkness outside the windows, it was the middle of the night.

But what day was it?

An IV hung at her side, the needle buried in the back of her left hand. There were bandages on her palms and she could feel her skin sticking to the gauze. She was sore, as if she had been bashed and bruised all over.

But she was safe. Alex forced herself to breathe slowly. She was safe.

There was no fire.

Even better, there were none of *them*.

Alex surveyed the unfamiliar room. It looked like a hospital. There was a band on her right wrist with her name and the name of a doctor she didn't know.

Mark was dead. Alex knew that with complete certainty, although she didn't want to think about why or how she knew. And the hidden lab of Gilchrist Enterprises, the focus of her life for the past five years, had been destroyed by fire. The Green Machine had been trashed, right before its big moment.

The fire hadn't been an accident.

That made her furious. Only someone evil could have destroyed something so good. Only a truly awful person could care more about money than the planet itself. An image of that evil rose in Alex's thoughts, but she shoved it aside.

She might be down, but she wasn't out yet.

Before she could look for a calendar or chart, Alex heard voices approaching. She did what she had always done when there was trouble brewing: she feigned innocence. She closed her eyes and pretended to be asleep.

"She's had a quiet day today, at least," an older woman said, compassion in her tone. "Although she usually has her nightmares around three in the morning."

"Every night?" asked a man. There was no real interest in his tone.

"Every night," the woman replied. Alex felt a stroke on the back of her hand. "It's wearing her out, poor thing."

"It says here that she talks about dragons," the man said, and Alex's breath caught at the word.

Dragons. Her breath hitched and she struggled to remain impassive. The hair was prickling on the back of her scalp.

Dragons.

"She does," the woman said softly. "She screams and

thrashes, and she shouts out for Mark. Then she cries." The nurse stroked the back of Alex's hand. "It's terrible to watch."

"Well, she needs sleep to heal," said the man crisply. "We're going to kick up the dosage on the sedative. Put it in her drip tonight and see if we can avoid tonight's nightmare." Alex heard him scribbling. "And I'm going to move her over to Psych for observation."

"But you can't transfer her to the psych ward! She's just traumatized, and who wouldn't be—"

"When I want your opinion, Nurse, I'll ask for it," the man interrupted. "It's the twenty-eighth already. Her burns are healed and we need the bed."

It had been October 14 when she and Mark had driven to the lab and found it burning. The fire had happened on a Sunday, the first Sunday they'd taken off in years.

Alex knew sabotage when she saw it.

She'd lost two precious weeks. If this was midnight on the twenty-eighth, there were only three full days left before the Green Machine's big chance.

She could make it happen.

A piece of paper tore and Alex heard footsteps as the man walked away. "Who's next?"

"Poor thing. I would have given you another couple of days." The nurse gave Alex's hand one last pat. Then she strode after the doctor, the soles of her shoes squeaking on the linoleum floor.

Alex had seen enough movies not to be thrilled about a move to the psychiatric ward. She wasn't going to be able to get anything done when she was drugged up and tied down, and she sure wasn't going to be able to make her presentation from a big padded room.

The best way to avoid the transfer was to leave, and to leave when her move was least expected.

The nurse was getting more sedative to put in her drip.

Now looked like a really good time.

*   *   *

Donovan strolled the quiet corridors of the hospital, striving to look as if he belonged there. He was wearing green scrubs and there was a fake identification card pinned to his pocket. He tried to mimic the resigned exhaustion of the other staff he encountered in the ward, tried to look purposeful but not agitated.

He was looking for room 767. Erik had gotten the room number and a status report from the hospital computers that very afternoon. The *Pyr* had been waiting for Alex to be healed enough to leave the hospital, watching vigilantly for intruders who might have plans similar to their own. There had been nothing suspicious, not a whiff of smoke.

Donovan didn't trust the silence. He was on full alert.

After all, the *Pyr* had found the secret lab of Gilchrist Enterprises one day too late. The *Slayers* hadn't killed Alex in their attack on the lab, even though she'd been there.

Which meant they had a two-phase plan.

The sooner she was in the *Pyr*'s protective custody, the better. Donovan sauntered down the corridor of the seventh floor and hoped Alex didn't have a roommate. It would make his job simpler.

He also hoped she was sedated.

He snagged a gurney as if he'd been sent to fetch it and mumbled a few words in Spanish to the other orderly loitering by the elevators. He eased down the hall and began to whistle tunelessly.

Room 767 would be on the window side of the hall. He counted the doors and narrowed his eyes to check the number from a distance.

That one. Unfortunately, the room was near the nurses' station and three nurses were doing their paperwork at the desk. The older one glanced up and Donovan hid his trepidation. She looked like a rule keeper.

"You're new," she said with suspicion, and he shrugged.

He mumbled something in colloquial Spanish.

"Figures," she said under her breath to the younger nurse

beside her. "All the good-looking ones are illegal." The cute nurse bit back her laughter, then winked at Donovan.

He winked back. Some things were universal.

A couple came out of room 767 just then and he halted to stay out of their way. The nurse followed the doctor in his lab coat, both of them taking notes.

"Have her transferred to Psych before the shift change," the doctor said. "Call so they know she's coming. They can watch her for the rest of the night."

"It's tough to get a gurney during the night." The nurse spoke with a disdain that revealed her opinion of the doctor. "Lots of morgue traffic this month with that flu."

The doctor gave her a look so poisonous that another woman would have flinched. This nurse, though, just looked right back at him. Donovan pretended to need to tie his shoelace so he could keep his head down.

"There's one right there," the doctor said, pointing to Donovan and his gurney.

"Where's that going?" the nurse asked Donovan.

He decided he spoke only Spanish, and was inclined to be quiet. He shrugged, as if it wasn't his problem.

"Solved," the doctor said with satisfaction, and turned away.

The nurse sent the dark glance this time, aiming it for the doctor's back, then called to the station. "Maria? Can you finish up for me? I'm just going to get this patient transferred." The cute nurse left the desk, smiling at the doctor.

The one who had accompanied the doctor meanwhile beckoned to Donovan. She indicated that he should take the gurney into room 767, then gave him instructions in Spanish. He nodded his head, shuffled his feet, and hoped like hell that it was Alex they were planning to move.

If not, he would have to make a mistake.

Maybe he was illiterate, too.

*   *   *

Alex's scheme was foiled before it began. Within moments of deciding to escape, she was strapped to a gurney, still pretending to be out cold, and gliding down the corridor.

This was so not a part of her plan.

Even worse, she didn't feel well. There was a sizzle of heat beneath her skin, one that had started when the attendant had moved her to the gurney. She felt feverish and excited and agitated, as if she were burning up.

And aroused.

This was not good.

What was she going to do? Her situation was only going to get worse. She had to act now. But could she even walk? She didn't remember being on her feet at all—she was probably weak and might be dizzy.

That eliminated the chance of running.

Or at least, of running and not getting caught.

The nurse remained behind, only the attendant with his strong arms escorting her. Alex felt as if her blood were humming. Was it the drugs? Or was it an effect of shock? She didn't like it, either way. The gurney was guided into an elevator.

"Main floor?" asked someone else.

"*Sí,*" agreed the attendant. It was the first sound he had uttered and Alex was surprised at the deep resonance of his voice. It seemed to vibrate within her and awaken a desire she hadn't felt in a long time.

She opened her eyes a slit and caught him studying her. Her heart skipped and she closed her eyes again.

He had auburn hair and green eyes.

He was tall, muscular, and handsome.

And he knew she was awake. She could tell by the glimmer of mischief that had danced in his eyes. She could have sworn that if she'd kept looking, he would have winked.

Alex tried not to panic. He'd tell them in Psych that she was conscious, and they'd give her a sedative immediately.

She'd never get out of here in time, and those who had destroyed the Green Machine would win. Alex couldn't let that happen.

Even if she wasn't sure what she could do about it. She wasn't good at standing aside. Alex liked to solve problems, fix things, leap in and do her best to change the course of the world. Her hand clenched on the rail of the gurney in her frustration.

To her astonishment, the man steering the gurney stroked the back of her hand with a fingertip, as if to reassure her, although Alex didn't know why he'd bother.

She also couldn't understand why heat emanated from his touch, making her skin sizzle. She let her hand fall limp in her surprise. Her breath caught in her throat just as the elevator dinged for the main floor, covering the sound of her dismay.

The other passenger left the elevator first and strode to the right. The attendant pushed the gurney to the left.

How far was it to the psych ward?

Could she trust him to help her?

Could she ask?

She wished suddenly that she'd learned Spanish.

Alex peeked through her lashes to find that they were leaving the lobby. He turned into a quieter corridor and picked up speed. Alex couldn't see anyone in this hallway and it didn't look as if it went anywhere important.

Did they lock the psych patients in the basement? She gripped the railings again.

"Just stay cool and don't move," he said through his teeth. Alex was shocked by his vehemence and his words. He *did* speak English. "Leave everything to me. I'll get you out of here."

Before Alex could say anything, he tossed a sheet over her face, then turned another corner. Alex couldn't believe what she had heard, but when they got into another, smaller elevator, she smelled formaldehyde.

Then she knew where they were going.

She caught her breath and her apparent savior tapped one fingertip on her shoulder in silent warning. She felt the sizzle of a spark, heard him swear under his breath, but knew what he meant.

She shut up. Corpses, after all, weren't known to be chatty.

Was he really going to help her?

The elevator doors opened and the air was cold. Alex refused to shiver. He moved faster then, pushing her down a narrow corridor. Alex had a vague impression of other gurneys parked on either side; then her driver was challenged by someone else.

He explained himself rapidly in colloquial Spanish.

She was sure there were some cuss words in his response.

He didn't slow down while he talked, compelling the interrogator to run beside him to continue asking questions. Alex could hear the other man's footsteps. His voice rose in protestation, her driver's assurances seeming to fall on deaf ears.

Alex held her breath.

There was a squeak of hinges and a waft of cold air that smelled of freedom. Her attendant kept talking, his tone low and persuasive. Alex heard a car door open—no, it was bigger than a regular door. A gate on a truck maybe.

Another man joined her attendant, the two of them unlocking the stretcher from the gurney. She slid horizontally and guessed that she'd heard the back gate of a hearse.

The interrogator began to shout.

"Madre de Dios," muttered Alex's attendant.

"Beguile him," commanded the other man, his voice even deeper.

Alex felt her gurney driver turn away, felt the absence of his attention as if she'd turned her back on a fire. His tone was low and urgent, yet strangely melodic.

The other man argued with him persistently.

The deep-voiced companion meanwhile pushed the

stretcher all the way into the hearse. Alex heard him walking around the vehicle. She eased back the edge of the sheet
as he got into the driver's seat of the hearse and started the
engine.

She could see through the back of the hearse that the hospital employee was more agitated.

Alex's auburn-haired attendant shook his head curtly.
"That's it," he muttered, and the other man fell silent in surprise at his English.

"But . . ."

Her attendant decked the smaller hospital employee, who
disappeared from Alex's view. Her ally bent over the fallen
man, before giving his companion a thumbs-up.

"He'll have a shiner, that's all. And we're out of here."
His confidence did dangerous things to Alex's equilibrium.
He reached for the gate to the hearse.

"What's going on?" she asked, her words coming slowly.

He grinned and winked at her, the gold stud in his earlobe
glinted wickedly. Her heart skipped a beat at the sight.

"We're saving you, Alex Madison," he said, his eyes
filled with dangerous lights. "Saving you and the Green Machine. Hang on." He slammed the back gate with a decisive
gesture as his companion put the hearse into gear.

He knew who she was.

He knew about the Green Machine.

Alex knew she'd gone from the frying pan into the fire.
She was being kidnapped, probably by two men working
with the ones who had torched the lab.

Dragons. Her mind shied away from that last image of
Mark.

Alex worked her hands free beneath the sheet and pulled
out the IV drip. She willed herself to wake up.

She wasn't kidnapped yet.

Erik had set him up.

Donovan seethed with the realization. Erik had chosen

Donovan to capture Alex because Erik knew that she would
be Donovan's destined mate. He didn't know how Erik
knew, but he was convinced he did.

Well, Donovan wasn't going to fall for the manipulation
of the leader of the *Pyr* as easily as that.

It was a dangerous and daring choice—exactly the kind
of thing Donovan might have done—but a plan that could
have gone badly awry. He'd been startled by the firestorm. He could have made a mistake. He could have been
unlucky—instead of glancing up to find the nurse too ab-
sorbed in her charts to notice the spark dancing between
himself and her patient.

And he needed to work on his beguiling talents. He was
jangled at the abrupt arrival of his firestorm, infuriated that
Erik had set him up, and had only just barely gotten them
out of there without serious trouble.

He and Erik would have to have a talk.

It wouldn't be a friendly one.

Rafferty ignored Donovan's sour mood, which could
mean only one thing. Donovan's mentor was complicit.
Donovan folded his arms across his chest and glared out the
windshield.

It didn't help matters that he was strongly attracted to
Alex. She was precisely the kind of woman he most admired: tall and athletically built. Dark hair was his particular favorite and he had a weakness for clever women. The
inventor of the world's first eco-friendly car couldn't be anything less than brilliant.

The hearse had mushy suspension and lousy acceleration.
Donovan was impatient with its stately progress. The windows were tinted, so no one would be able to recognize
them, and Donovan had smeared mud on the license plates.
There was a barrier between the front seats and what Donovan thought of as a cargo bay, but Alex would be safe
enough there until they got to Rafferty's car.

She seemed to still be sedated, anyway.

She was his mate.

Donovan tried to avoid the truth, but the truth wasn't having any of it. He could still feel the spark that had leapt between his fingertip and her shoulder in the elevator, could still feel the heated shimmer of his body awakening to her presence as he moved her to the gurney in her room. He was still simmering, just because she was mere feet away from him, and his protective urges were redoubled.

His firestorm.

Defiance boiled within him, and his mind churned to create an alternative plan. He wasn't designed for settling down with one mate for the duration, for commitment and parenthood. He wasn't like Quinn and he wasn't like Rafferty.

Donovan liked running solo just fine.

"It went well," Rafferty murmured in old-speak, his words the barest rumble in Donovan's thoughts.

"You knew, too," he accused, replying in kind.

Rafferty shrugged. Donovan appreciated that his mentor didn't lie to him, but he didn't like that Rafferty thought it had been necessary to deceive him.

"No excuses?" he demanded, his tone harsh even for old-speak.

"You won't believe anything I tell you about serving the greater good," Rafferty replied. He stopped at a traffic light and looked directly at Donovan, a yearning in his gaze. *"Is it true?"*

Donovan nodded. Rafferty exhaled with obvious disappointment. He put his hand on Rafferty's shoulder. *"It should have been yours. You're the one who wants a firestorm, not me."*

"The Great Wyvern has wisdom beyond ours," Rafferty said with a conviction that Donovan didn't share.

"The Great Wyvern likes to jerk us all around," he retorted, just before the back door of the hearse flew open. He heard the click, saw the warning light on the dash, felt the draft.

Donovan pivoted. In the light that poured into the rear of the hearse, he saw a woman in a backless hospital gown.

Running away.

"Shit!" he shouted, and flung himself out of the hearse. Rafferty stopped, but Donovan was already running in pursuit of his mate.

"Stop!" he shouted.

Alex didn't.

She made directly for the ER entrance, her steps wobbly but determined. She was faster than he would have believed. A pair of people turned to watch as she hobbled up to the lit entryway barefoot, her gown fluttering around her hips.

Donovan halted with reluctance. He couldn't exactly follow her there and snatch her up. Donovan reminded himself of his failure to beguile the other orderly. There would be even more witnesses by the time he caught Alex and carried her off.

"Let her go," Rafferty counseled, pulling the hearse to a halt beside Donovan. "We'll follow her and wait for a better moment."

Donovan flung himself into the passenger seat, watching Alex intently. A taupe Buick was parked in the curve of the entryway, its engine running, and she headed straight for it.

Alex opened the driver's door and slid into the car as if it had been her destination all along. She must have said something to the people there or smiled, because they shrugged and turned away.

The Buick roared as she rocketed out of the Emergency drop-off.

"Follow her!" Donovan cried, wishing that he was driving, that he had his Ducati instead of this limping excuse for a vehicle.

"I thought she was sedated."

"So did I. She's taking a right there."

"I'm on it," Rafferty acknowledged. "Relax." The silence

between the two *Pyr* crackled, Donovan aware only of his own irritation.

It was Erik's fault. He should have told Donovan about the firestorm, should have warned him. Surprise was ruining his game.

But then if he'd known he'd be stepping into his own firestorm, he'd never have accepted the assignment.

"Usually you're the one who bolts," Rafferty observed. "Around for a good time, not a long time, as you like to say."

"She took another right," Donovan said tightly. He'd been angry before, but it was beyond unthinkable that his destined mate should flee from him and his protection.

Women did not run away from Donovan Shea.

Ever.

It was rude of Rafferty to remind him.

"You still think the Great Wyvern doesn't know how to plan a lesson?" the older *Pyr* mused.

Donovan barely kept himself from doing injury to his old friend. "I don't want to think about lessons and plans," he snapped.

"Maybe you should. Maybe this won't go well until you do."

"Just drive." Donovan sat back and forced himself to think calmly. "Where do you think she's going?"

Rafferty mused as they took another turn. "I'll put my nickel on that lab of Gilchrist Enterprises."

"Me, too. Exactly where the *Slayers* will look for her." Donovan snarled in his frustration. He might not want a firestorm, but having one meant that Alex Madison was his responsibility—never mind that he was to take her into the protective custody of the *Pyr*. "I thought she was supposed to be a genius."

Rafferty was unruffled. "Then she must have a good reason for going back there."

"Maybe she's one of those brilliant people who don't do real life that well."

"Maybe. In which case, she's a perfect match for you."

"She's not going to be my match. . . ."

"Is that so?" Rafferty murmured.

Donovan gritted his teeth as Alex took another turn in the direction of the industrial park where the lab was located. "Miss the turn," he said impulsively. "Let her think she lost us."

"And?" Rafferty asked as he did what Donovan suggested.

"Ditch the hearse and wait for me at Erik's hotel suite."

"But what about Alex?"

Donovan spoke with grim determination. "I'm not that easy to ditch. Stop along here and let me out." He slanted a glance to Rafferty. "You can tell Erik that I'll bring her there safely."

Rafferty pulled to a halt at the side of the road and Donovan reached for the door handle. When the door opened, they both caught their breath at the scent.

"Slayer," Rafferty said softly, his nostrils flaring. Donovan stepped out of the car and Rafferty leaned across the seat. "And no one I know. You sure you want to do this alone?"

"Yes." Donovan was using all of his keen senses to identify the threat to his mate. The *Slayer* was old, but younger than he was. He was alone and unfamiliar. He wasn't that close.

"He might not be alone. Boris can disguise his presence."

Donovan was dismissive. It would take a herd of *Slayers* to bring him down. "She's my mate and my responsibility."

Donovan ignored the quirk of Rafferty's lips at that. Doing his job was not the same as committing himself to one woman for the duration, but he suspected that Rafferty wouldn't see things that way.

"You'll need help," Rafferty said in old-speak.

Donovan glared at him. *"My firestorm. My problem."*

Rafferty frowned. *"But—"*

"You and Erik lied to me. I'll do this alone." Donovan

could tell that Rafferty was offended, but he didn't care. He was offended that he'd been tricked.

"Suit yourself."

Donovan nodded once at his mentor. *"Go. I'll be fine."*

He strode down a quiet side street without looking back. He heard the hearse move away.

His only regret was that he didn't have the gloves Quinn had made for him. He'd left them at Erik's hotel, afraid their metal talons would trigger an alarm in the hospital. Now he felt vulnerable without them.

Especially as there was a *Slayer* around.

Donovan found a dark alley, stepped into its shadows, and shifted shape immediately. He leapt into the sky and flew toward the lab.

And Alex.

If he got to her first, the *Slayer* would have a bigger fight on his talons than he expected.

Gilchrist Enterprises smelled of smoke and destruction. Given a choice, Alex would have gone anywhere else in the world, but the first thing she needed was here.

She just had to get it fast.

If she could have disappeared without coming here, she would have. The only good thing was that her brother, Peter, had given her that dare.

And she'd followed through.

Alex punched in her access code and held her breath until the light flashed green. She hauled open the steel door and ducked inside. The lab was dark. Alex could smell ash and melted plastic; broken glass crunched underfoot.

She would not go into the lab itself.

Alex didn't believe for a minute that the guys in the hearse really had lost track of her. Did they know where she was going?

Alex didn't intend to linger and find out.

She found her office by feel and by memory, and tapped

the code into the security panel of the fire safe. The drawer rumbled open, making far too much noise in the silent building.

Alex held her breath, but there was no sound of pursuit. All she could hear was the pounding of her own heart, which was loud enough to hide a lot. She reached into the dark drawer, relieved when her fingers landed on a big Ziploc.

Her stashed package was there and still sealed.

Alex snatched the package and ran. She bolted back down the corridor and out of the building, without glancing to either side.

She was in the stolen car, hitting the gas even before she had the door fully closed, the Ziploc on the seat beside her. She squealed the tires, caring only that she got out of there ASAP.

She heard the sirens in the distance and told herself it was just a coincidence. The police couldn't be after her for leaving the hospital without her doctor's authorization, although someone might have an issue with her having stolen the Buick.

On the other hand, anyone who had left a car idling at the entrance to the ER probably had bigger problems in the short term. Her gaze fell again to the key tag, which pronounced the vehicle to be the possession of Archibald Forrester, WWII vet.

She really hoped Archibald was okay.

She'd stolen a car. Alex couldn't even believe it herself, but what else could she have done? Too bad she hadn't thought to grab a pair of latex gloves at the hospital. Her fingerprints would be all over Archibald's car by now.

A lifetime of being honest hadn't prepared her for recent events—or for what she was going to do about it. Alex was going to have to lift her game if she was going to be a successful survivor.

Like Harrison Ford in *The Fugitive*.

Alex gripped the wheel. She could do that. Alex glanced in the rearview mirror and nearly had heart failure.

The hunky gurney driver was in the backseat.

He waved at her and cast her a smile that made her heart go thump. "Hi, gorgeous. Going my way?"

Chapter 2

A lex swerved and came close to putting the car into the ditch. When she was back in her lane on the empty road, she looked in the mirror again.

He was still there, still smiling at her with confidence.

Even worse, he was better looking than she'd thought.

Maybe that said something sad about her recent social life. Admiring the looks of a kidnapper didn't count as the smartest thing she'd ever done.

He was broad shouldered and tanned. His hair was wavy and auburn, his jaw square. His eyes were very green—or maybe the hospital scrubs made them look more green—and Alex felt a familiar heat start low in her belly.

Maybe she was experiencing side effects from whatever had been in her IV drip. She wasn't dead, but she wasn't stupid, either. Alex decided to take command of the situation.

It wouldn't solve anything if he knew she was terrified.

"Get out of the car," she said with authority. "Right now."

"Tell me what you took from Gilchrist Enterprises first. Was it this?" He reached for the Ziploc on the front seat and Alex swerved the car hard. He fell back in the opposite corner of the backseat while the car fishtailed down the road.

"Where'd you get your license?" he asked with indignation as he sat up and straightened his jacket. "Out of a cereal box?"

Alex glared at him in the mirror. "Get out of the car."

A glint of challenge danced in his eyes and she knew he wasn't going to be so easily daunted as her brother, Peter. He reached for the Ziploc again and Alex hit the brakes hard. The car almost stopped on its hood.

She'd hoped he'd go right through the windshield, but her move had precisely the wrong effect. He catapulted over the bench seat, taking advantage of his own momentum, braced his hand on the dash, and landed elegantly right beside her.

He was an athlete, then, or a gymnast. Just her luck.

He bumped shoulders with her and a spark danced between them. Alex stared at it in shock, then hit the gas.

A spark? There couldn't have been a spark.

But she'd felt that heat before.

They'd put hallucinogens in her IV drip. That had to be it. Side effects were the only possible explanation for the way she was tingling. He was close beside her, close enough to bump thighs, close enough for her to see how well the scrubs emphasized his muscled legs. He must be tall, taller even than she was.

Alex told herself that she didn't want to know.

She probably shouldn't be driving.

She accelerated and wrenched the wheel hard to the left. He was flung against the passenger door. "Maybe you got that license mail order," he said, rubbing his shoulder and wincing. "Take it easy, would you?"

"I told you to get out of the car." Alex snatched the Ziploc and dropped it down the neck of her gown.

He straightened and pushed a hand through his hair, watching her all the while. His smile should have been classed as a lethal weapon. "Now things are getting interesting."

"Don't even think it." Alex kept the Buick spinning in a tight donut of a turn. The wheels squealed against the pavement, but the g-force kept him at the other end of the bench seat.

"Or what? You'll drive even more recklessly?"

"This is defensive driving."

"Don't tell me you're defending yourself against me."

"You see any other would-be kidnappers in the vicinity?" Alex straightened out the wheel and accelerated, going over a curb so hard that he smacked the back of his head on the headrest.

He winced, rubbed his neck, then turned his glittering gaze upon her. Alex's mouth went dry. He eased along the bench seat toward her, his voice dropping to a purr.

"Let's just understand each other," he murmured, and Alex shivered. She made the mistake of glancing his way and couldn't tear her gaze away from his. "I don't snatch what I want from women. I don't have to steal. They give it to me, willingly."

"Before or after you hurt them?"

His eyes flashed with anger. "I've never hurt a woman. Ever." He spared a glance out the windshield. "Although you might hurt both of us." He made a grab for the wheel.

"What?" Alex looked to find a truck closing fast. She turned right, rocking the car on its shocks, and passed within inches of the truck. The truck driver honked as Alex took a shaking breath.

"Just drive," her companion suggested. "I'll stay over here. Promise. I won't even go after the Ziploc."

Alex couldn't keep her tone from turning scornful. "Because you think I'm going to just give you whatever you want?"

"Because of this." His words were low enough to make her shiver again. He reached out a hand and before Alex could flinch, a spark leapt between his fingertip and her shoulder.

It was harder to deny it the second time.

She certainly couldn't deny the heat of arousal slipping over her skin. Her mouth went dry, her breath caught, and she was achingly aware of how long and tanned his fingers were. His hands looked strong and sexy; the auburn hair on his arm contrasted with the stainless steel of his watch. It was too expensive a watch for an orderly. Who was he? What did he really want?

Why was she even wondering about it?

Alex was very aware of how masculine he was, how close his hand was to her shoulder. Or to her breast. It was easy, too easy, to imagine how he would persuade a woman to do whatever he wanted.

He'd move slowly, purposefully. Alex forced herself to watch the road. He moved his hand away and looked grim.

She needed to find out what kind of stuff had been in her drip, in case she ever wanted to feel this hot and uninhibited again.

Assuming that she lived long enough to have the choice.

"Get out of the car."

"First tell me what you stole."

"Nothing." It was true: the Ziploc was her own possession, therefore not stolen.

"That's a big bag of nothing in your gown."

Alex had to ditch him *and* the car. There was something wrong with Archibald's car. It was a crisp October night; she was barefoot in a backless cotton hospital gown; the heater was off and she was melting.

Maybe it would have been more accurate to say that she was sizzling. She was far too aware of her lack of underwear, as well as the allure of her attacker.

This was why she never took drugs.

"Why don't you slow down a bit?" he suggested.

Alex ignored him and pushed the gas harder. She made a two-wheel turn onto the main road that led into the industrial park. She felt his gaze upon her and could have named the moment he saw that she wasn't wearing a bra.

Alex couldn't keep herself from blushing. To her mortification, her nipples were tightening and she hoped he couldn't see them. No luck. She looked down and their peaks were unmistakable.

He turned to stare out the window, his throat working before he spoke. "You seem tense," he noted. "Your first stolen car?"

"First time someone tried to kidnap me," she snapped, and he laughed.

He had a good laugh, one that tempted her to laugh with him.

As if.

"If it's any consolation, this is my first attempted kidnapping. How am I doing?" He turned that wicked smile on her and Alex was drowning in desire again.

Did Stockholm Syndrome happen this fast? Why did she want to trust this man? It was irrational and Alex was not irrational.

"Lousy. Get out of the car right now." Alex poked at the temperature control to turn down the heater, but it was already off. Obviously Archibald's car needed service.

"No, we're in this together now."

"No, we're not. Just tell me what you want."

"Sparkling conversation; good champagne; peace on earth." He shrugged and settled back against the seat with a sigh. Alex wasn't fooled. She knew he'd move fast if she did anything unpredictable. "What everyone else wants, pretty much, which must be why there's never enough of any of the above."

His smile must have been intended to weaken her resistance.

It worked beautifully. Alex liked how his eyes sparkled. She liked that the scrubs stretched across his chest, and she even liked the single gold stud he wore in his left ear. Alex could believe that he didn't have to take whatever he wanted from women.

She was in big trouble.

At least, things couldn't get worse.

Something heavy landed on the roof right then, landed so hard that the car bounced. Alex lost her grip on the wheel for a moment.

"What the hell was that?" Her companion leaned forward to peer out the windshield.

A large tail hit the glass with a resounding thwack at the very same moment.

"Shit!" Alex's companion put one arm over his own face and one over Alex's as the windshield cracked into a thousand shards. Alex couldn't see a thing—because she had her own eyes squeezed shut, too—but she didn't lift her foot from the gas.

She knew what kind of tail it was.

"Dragons!" she shouted, and swerved hard to one side. The Buick went over the curb, nearly giving both of them whiplash, then bounced across rough terrain.

The hunk swore again. "You're going to kill us!"

Even though he'd moved his arm and she'd opened her eyes, Alex still couldn't see. The safety glass had done its job, breaking but staying in place. There was no light other than the meager bit cast by the Buick's headlights. She must have broken one of them. Alex was going too fast, but she wasn't going to stop the car and become dragon chow.

She would not think about Mark.

"What's wrong with dragons?"

"What's *right* with dragons?" Alex winced as the dragon tail hit the windshield again, hard enough this time to take out the safety glass completely. Cold air rushed in.

It was an amber-colored dragon tail.

One of Mark's tormentors had come after her.

Alex didn't need to ask why. Gleaming silver dragon talons appeared on the edge of the roof. Alex screamed.

Her companion reached for the wheel. "I think we're going fast enough."

"No, we're not." Alex pushed him aside. "We're not going *nearly* fast enough." She put her accelerator down to the floor, not caring that the car was completely out of control.

The amber dragon leaned over the edge of the roof just then, the sight of his many teeth making Alex's heart stop cold. He opened his mouth, exuded a puff of smoke, and Alex knew she was toast.

Maybe the psych ward would have been the better choice.

Donovan blamed the firestorm.

He didn't want a firestorm. He had tried to reassure Alex and had missed the scent of the approaching *Slayer*.

Alex screamed and held up her bandaged hands in front of her face as the *Slayer* inhaled to breathe dragonfire. The car raced toward a stand of trees and Donovan had nothing left to lose.

"Hey, do you know Boris?" he asked the dragon on the roof. "Because I haven't seen him for a while. Is he doing okay?"

The *Slayer* blinked, shocked into not loosing his dragonfire. "How do you know Boris?"

That moment was the only advantage Donovan needed.

He leapt through the windshield, changing shape en route. It was a smooth move. He reared back, flying above the car in dragon form, and felt the awe of his opponent. The car bounced across the field, losing speed. Alex must have taken her foot off the gas.

"You'd better believe it," Donovan said. "I was hoping to kill him, but the sneaky bastard got away."

"You're *Pyr*," the *Slayer* hissed with hatred.

"The real thing," Donovan said. "In living Technicolor." He breathed dragonfire on the infuriated *Slayer*.

The *Slayer* was the golden hue of amber, his scales patterned as if they held bubbles and leaves of prehistoric plants. His talons were silver and ornate.

Donovan had never seen him before.

The *Slayer* ducked and twisted under Donovan's assault, taking off quickly. Donovan ascended behind him and seized his wings. They locked claws and wrestled, tumbling end over end through the air.

Donovan wished again for his steel claws as he tried to rip open the *Slayer*'s chest. The *Slayer* exhaled smoke and Donovan ducked it, slashing at his attacker with his tail. The *Slayer* took the hit and fell bonelessly toward the earth.

The Buick, meanwhile, was leaping across the field. Alex couldn't be intending to crash the car, could she?

Donovan flew in pursuit and landed on the roof of the car. He reached through the windshield to grab her.

Alex recoiled from him in terror, releasing the wheel as she lifted her hands in front of her face again. "No! Don't touch me. You're a dragon—"

"And in five seconds, you'll be dead. Choose your poison, gorgeous."

Alex gaped at him, obviously recognizing his voice.

"Yes, I'm the dragon," he said impatiently, not needing a replay of that scene from his past. "Come on!"

She looked at the trees, closing fast, then looked at him and fainted.

"Good choice." Donovan snatched her arm and hauled her right through the broken windshield. He snatched her precious Ziploc from the seat, then ascended as quickly as he could.

A heartbeat later, the car hit the first of the trees. It rolled and exploded, sending a tongue of flame into the night sky.

So much for Archibald Forrester's Buick.

Donovan turned and watched the amber *Slayer* fly away. Boris had to be in the vicinity, if not others as well. Once again, the *Slayers* had let Alex live. It wasn't a coincidence, although Donovan didn't know their plan.

He flew for Erik's hotel suite. He looked down at Alex and his heart tightened. She *was* gorgeous, as well as tough and smart. Spunky even when terrified, she could have been specially ordered just for him, the precise kind of woman he liked best.

But Donovan wasn't going to have a firestorm.

All he had to do was tell Erik as much, and that wasn't likely to go well. On the upside, his mate was probably going to be good with his decision, given her fear of dragons.

Funny, but that didn't make Donovan feel any better.

Alex awakened in a strange room.

Again.

She kept her eyes closed. It smelled more like a hotel room than a hospital room. She didn't hear anyone else in the room, didn't feel the presence of anyone else, either.

She felt less woozy and cooler. The drugs were wearing off.

Alex opened her eyes cautiously. She was lying on a regular bed in a darkened hotel room. Actually, it was a pretty nice bed, a king-sized bed with high-thread-count linens.

Not a dumpy hotel, then. The door to an adjoining room was ajar. As far as she could tell, she was untouched. She still had bandages on her hands, still felt bruised, but was pretty sure there was no new damage.

She was not going to think about dragons.

There were men arguing in the adjacent room. Alex could hear the rumble of their voices. She heard the cadence of a familiar voice and knew that the hunk who had tried to kidnap her was close by.

So, he had succeeded and, as a bonus, he was irritated.

Another rumble sounded like his laconic older partner, the one who had driven the hearse. The third man had a faint British accent and Alex was sure she didn't recognize his voice.

She wasn't going to speculate on their plans for her.

It was time to go.

The door with the dead bolt must lead to an outside corridor. Her Ziploc was on the desk by the phone. There was a small backpack on the chair and a leather jacket hanging over its back.

Alex eased from the bed and grabbed her Ziploc. She was relieved that it seemed to be exactly as she'd left it. She peeked into the backpack and saw a T-shirt and sweatpants. She decided they could be her spoils of battle. She dressed quickly, feeling warmer and less like a flasher. The sweats were too long and the T-shirt was too wide, but she'd live.

Alex ran a hand over the shoulder of the black leather jacket and knew it was *his*. She tingled when she remembered how he had looked at her, as if she were the sexiest woman alive.

He'd tried to kidnap her. He'd hidden in the back of her stolen car. He'd challenged her and charmed her, and Alex was more attracted to him than was healthy. Sparks had shot between them.

She realized she was caressing his leather jacket.

He had changed shape, too. He'd become a dragon. She hadn't imagined that.

The men's voices rose slightly and someone was pacing in the next room. Alex's heart leapt at the deep sound of *his* voice—she knew that she'd be in deep trouble if she saw him again, if he smiled at her, if he winked at her, if he laughed.

The green scrubs were discarded on the carpet. There was a helmet on the desk, a set of keys tossed beside it.

Alex stared. She couldn't possibly be so lucky, could she?

The key tag had a Ducati Monster logo. Alex knew that was a kind of motorcycle, an expensive Italian kind: she remembered Peter wanting one desperately and arguing with their father as only a teenager can argue for his heart's desire. Peter—no surprise—had lost both the battle and the war.

He'd never been good at getting what he wanted.

Alex remembered her brother's astonishment when she'd shown him her own motorcycle license shortly afterward.

She picked up the keys, ensuring they didn't rattle. There couldn't be two Ducati Monsters in the parking garage, and if there were, she'd steal the one that the key started.

There was a pair of black leather boots beside the desk: she took them, pulled on the jacket, and carried the helmet. Alex crept to the door and eased the dead bolt open.

The men continued their dispute in the other room. Alex turned the knob and was very appreciative of the maintenance people in this particular hotel.

The hinges didn't make a sound. Alex slipped out the door. She pushed her feet into the boots. They were too big, but would be better than riding barefoot. She put the Ziploc into the inside pocket of his jacket. The elevator was in the direction opposite to the room where the men argued.

Alex didn't linger long enough for her luck to change.

Donovan paced the main room of Erik's suite. It wasn't enough that his mate was safe in the next room. It didn't appease him that the smoke the *Pyr* had breathed together was deep and thick, protecting them from *Slayers* as surely as if they had been in a permanent lair.

He had been deceived, and his mate could have easily paid for it.

Rafferty tented his fingers together as he watched Donovan, waiting for trouble to erupt. Erik was at the desk, using his laptop, trying to ignore Donovan.

Donovan wasn't ready to be ignored. "You sent me to my own firestorm!" he charged. "Without one single word of warning. You *lied* to me, Erik!"

"Not exactly," Erik said mildly, typing without glancing up. His British accent was more pronounced, as it always was when he was annoyed and pretending not to be. "Unless you count a lie of omission."

"I do!"

"Lead with anger and follow with remorse," Rafferty murmured.

"What are you talking about?" Donovan demanded.

"It's an old saying," his mentor explained mildly. "One that I've endeavored to teach you for several hundred years without success. You need to harness your anger."

"I need friends who don't lie to me."

At that, Erik glanced up. "And if I had told you the truth, would you have gone to collect her?"

"Of course not. I don't want a firestorm. You know that."

Erik returned his attention to his laptop. "Precisely my point."

"You won't compel me to act upon the firestorm."

"I don't think you have a choice."

Donovan strode to the desk and leaned his weight on it, compelling Erik to look at him. "I'm not going to consummate a firestorm. I ride alone, always have."

"You don't have to commit yourself to her forever," Erik said. "Quinn's solution is not necessarily that of every *Pyr*."

"What then?" Donovan challenged. "I should have sex with her, get her pregnant, and walk away? No kid needs to live my story again. Keir didn't do me any favors."

"Your father's choices don't have to shape yours." Erik frowned at the display.

"I decided years ago that history wouldn't be repeated," Donovan informed Erik. "No child of mine ever will repeat my history, because there will never be a child of mine. Understand?"

"Not even for the firestorm?" Rafferty asked, and there was yearning in his voice. Donovan understood then that his mentor disapproved of his failure to embrace his good fortune. Rafferty had waited centuries for his own firestorm and it must seem unfair to him that Donovan didn't want his.

Not that Rafferty's feelings would change Donovan's choices.

Only Alex could do that. Donovan thought of her, the way she moved with athletic ease. He liked her determination and he liked how she'd fought to get rid of him. Her short haircut and lack of makeup should have made her look boyish, but instead only made her look more feminine. It was her long lashes, he was sure of it, and the way her eyes tipped up at the outer corners.

Or maybe it was their brown hue. They seemed to be full of shadows and secrets. Mysteries left for him to solve.

Even the hospital nightgown hadn't disguised that she had curves in all the right places—or that she hadn't been wearing a bra. He'd seen the silhouette of her nipple tightening right after the spark had lit between them.

It had distracted him, and put them squarely into danger.

And there was another problem with this plan.

Erik was impatient with Donovan's logic. "You're being emotional about a practical matter. We *Pyr* can ensure that your child is not abandoned, even if you choose not to be involved. . . ."

"Be serious. You can't be advocating for me to breed and forget about it."

The leader of the *Pyr* pushed to his feet, his gaze steely. He changed to old-speak, so his insistence would echo in Donovan's own thoughts, perhaps even meld with Donovan's own thoughts. *"We must breed. You must breed. We must consummate each firestorm."*

"I won't do it," Donovan retorted, speaking aloud. "You can't make me do it."

Erik glared at him for a moment, then pivoted to pace the room himself. The silence in the room was charged with restless energy, but Donovan wouldn't back down. Erik took a deep breath, then spoke quietly. "Think about what you just said to me."

"What about it?"

"You accused me of deliberately sending you to your firestorm."

"And you didn't deny it."

Erik turned to face Donovan, a challenge in his eyes. "How did I know the name of your mate?"

Donovan and Rafferty exchanged a glance in the silence that followed. "The Dragon's Egg ritual?" Donovan guessed, but he knew that wasn't right.

Erik shook his head. "That tells us the location of the firestorm."

"The Wyvern has been to see you," Rafferty suggested.

Erik stared down at the carpet, his hands on his hips. "The Wyvern is forbidden to reveal the name of the human who will experience the firestorm. Sophie learns the name of the woman during the eclipse ritual, but she is charged to keep it secret."

"She knew Sara's name," Donovan reminded his leader.

"And she only confessed it to the *Slayers* under torture."

Rafferty caught his breath. "You didn't . . ."

"I did not injure the Wyvern!" Erik snapped. "That, too, is forbidden among our kind."

Rafferty mumbled an apology, his neck turning red. "But then, how did you know?"

"How do you think? Sophie *offered* the name to me," Erik said tersely. "She came to me and she told me Alex's name, of her own volition." He paused, looking between the two *Pyr.* "Do you understand what that means?"

"It means we're in deep shit," Donovan guessed.

"It means that something is happening, that a threat that we have not yet discerned conspires against us." Erik shoved a hand through his hair. "Sophie is not inclined to be of assistance if she knows we can surmount a challenge ourselves. I fear that she knows we are about to have a setback. A major one."

"But that makes no sense," Donovan protested. "It was the *Slayers* who had heavy losses in the fight for Quinn's mate."

"We lost only one," Rafferty agreed, and Donovan refused to think of that one loss, so horrific had it been for him. "One too many but far fewer than the four *Slayers* we killed."

Erik stared out the window, his hands shoved into his pockets. He was reflected in the glass, superimposed on the city lights. He looked even more grim than usual. "I have dreamed of a dark academy, a place so foul that it has no name." His low words sent shivers down Donovan's spine.

"What kind of academy?" Donovan demanded. "What do they teach?"

"I don't know," Erik said, turning and looking weary. "I sense only that crimes are committed in the shadows. There is evil, I know as much, but I can't see into its murk. The dream fills me with such loathing that I can't look deeply." He sighed. "Not yet, but I continue to try."

"Can you do it without injury to yourself?" Rafferty asked, concern in his tone.

"I am not sure." Erik shuddered. "It is a wicked place, more wicked than ever I believed could exist."

The hair prickled on the back of Donovan's neck.

"While I have dreamed of teeth," Rafferty said with a smile, clearly trying to lighten the mood in the room. "Dragon's Teeth, in fact." He cast a glance at Donovan. "Do you still have it, or did Olivia have that treasure from you in the end, as well?"

It was Erik's turn to look perplexed.

Donovan felt his lips tighten. What had happened with Olivia was done. "She had no more and no less from me than she deserved," he said, hearing dismissiveness in his tone.

Rafferty didn't let the matter go. "Yet still you can't say her name. Did you give her the Dragon's Tooth?"

"Of course not. I still have it." Donovan tapped his chest. "Quinn used it to repair my armor after the eclipse."

Rafferty arched a brow. "There is an irony in that."

Donovan glared at his mentor. "What do you mean?"

"In using the Dragon's Tooth to repair the wound that Olivia inflicted upon you." Rafferty had that bemused confidence that was so annoying. He liked to think he knew Donovan's secrets.

"It has nothing to do with Olivia. The Tooth was just the best piece of treasure in my hoard."

Erik glanced between two of them, following the conversation but clearly not understanding all of it.

"Uh huh." Rafferty's skepticism was clear.

His mentor's response irritated Donovan even more. "We don't need to review the past in order to live the future."

"Don't we?" Rafferty mused, his gaze steady. "I thought we would have to address the fears of the past to embrace the future."

"We are not going to talk about this," Donovan said.

Rafferty watched him knowingly. "Seems to me that Olivia's shadow is sufficiently long that we *do* need to talk about her."

"All right. Who was or is Olivia?" Erik asked.

"A dead woman." Donovan changed the subject before Rafferty could answer. "I don't need to be manipulated by the two of you," he said with impatience. "I am not going to consummate this firestorm, no matter what you say, so just leave it alone."

Erik arched a brow. "No matter what I say?"

"No matter." Donovan folded his arms across his chest.

"Not even that we are doomed as a race if we do not successfully negotiate the three firestorms immediately following the change of the moon's node?"

"This is the second of the three that begin the journey of the Dragon's Tail," Rafferty said.

"That's not true," Donovan protested. "How can three firestorms be so important?"

"They can be if they are foretold firestorms," Rafferty mused.

Erik's gaze was fixed upon Donovan. "Sophie said it was true."

Donovan looked between the two older *Pyr*, seeing the determination of one and the yearning of the other. "I don't believe it. Sophie says a lot of things that aren't true, or that mean something other than what they appear to mean. I think you're trying to persuade me to do what you want."

"I don't care whether you believe it," Erik retorted. "You must act upon your firestorm—"

"I won't do it," Donovan said, interrupting his leader. "Alex is in our custody and safe now: you can defend and protect her. I don't even need to see her again."

To Donovan's surprise, Erik smiled. "I don't think you have a choice," he said softly, then held up a finger when Donovan might have argued with him.

Donovan heard the distinctive rumble of a familiar motorcycle engine.

Fading.

"Sounds like she knows how to get your attention." Rafferty settled back into his chair with a satisfied smile. "Only your destined mate would have the nerve to steal your bike."

It couldn't be true. Donovan ran for the room where he'd left Alex sleeping.

She was gone.

So were his keys, his boots, his helmet, and his jacket. There was a terrible sound of a bike engine losing its rhythm as gears were changed badly, and the three *Pyr* winced in unison.

"Second to fourth, I think," Erik said with a grimace.

Donovan swore. It didn't make him feel any better. He flung himself out of the suite after Alex and his bike, unsure what he would do when he found her.

Strangling her was probably not the right choice.

Donovan took the stairs to the roof three at a time. He raced across the roof of the hotel, then leapt into the night, shifting shape in midair. The only good thing was that he had the gloves Quinn had made for him and he had time to pull them on before he shifted shape.

This time, he was ready for anything.

Donovan spun in the air, caught his mate's scent, and

flew in pursuit. She missed a gear again, the sound making him cringe to the tips of his scales.

If she messed up the Ducati, he'd definitely have to kill her.

Firestorm be damned.

Chapter 3

The Ducati was different from the old Yamaha Alex had ridden for her motorcycle classes. It was for racing, nimble and powerful, designed for someone who was in perfect union with his machine.

As Alex didn't happen to be.

She shifted badly twice, but learned from her mistakes. She found herself leaning over the bike, urging it to greater speed, liking its efficient purr.

She needed some different clothing. A bra. Boots that fit. It was time to find out whether the fake credit cards worked.

Alex stopped at a bank with automated teller machines, one with a drive-through lane so she wouldn't have to leave the bike. It was the bank for which Peter did contract security work, and she wondered whether he'd be the one watching the video of her in the morning.

The name on the card would tip him off. Would Peter send the police after her? Alex knew the answer to that, given that her brother was the straightest straight arrow on the planet.

She wasn't the only one who knew nothing about a life of crime.

The helmet proved to be an asset, as the camera in the ATM wouldn't get a good shot of Alex's face through the tinted visor. It wouldn't even know how tall she was.

Ha. The fictional Meredith Maloney would remain hidden.

Alex punched in the personal identification number. It seemed to take an eternity for the card to authorize.

Maybe the machine was calling the cops. She glanced casually down the road in both directions, seeing only a long line of gas stations and fast-food restaurants. There weren't very many cars driving on the road, and certainly no police lights.

Nary a dragon to be seen.

That worked for Alex.

The machine beeped and spit out a fistful of twenties.

Ha! Alex was tempted to call Peter and *nyah nyah* at him—Peter had been so sure that his new antifraud program was infallible that he deserved no less—but anyone following her would expect her to call Peter for help.

She was going to think like a felon now.

Alex put the money away in her Ziploc and closed the jacket. It was a nice leather jacket, supple and yet thick enough to keep out the wind. Alex had always wanted a biker jacket, but hadn't thought it would go with her practical image. Changing her look might help her hide, though.

Maybe it was time to release her inner biker chick.

First she had another collection to make.

Alex revved the bike and put her foot on the tread. Alex would have pulled onto the road, but a large blue and gold dragon landed right in front of her.

A *dragon*.

Alex's mind stalled, then skipped ahead, as if she'd mentally missed a couple of gears. There was a dragon in front of her.

He could have been jeweled, the way his dark blue scales gleamed in the sodium lights. He looked like he was made of lapis lazuli stones, set in gold. He was more than twice as tall as she, a serious piece of bling, and his tail coiled a long way across the asphalt. The only part of him that wasn't lapis lazuli and gold was a massive pearl that looked like it was mounted in the center of his chest.

He was also familiar. Alex felt a tingle in his presence, and it was easy to remember how her body had responded to the kidnapper/orderly's smile.

Except that now he was furious. Alex could tell by the light in his eyes. Oddly enough, he hadn't been angry about her foiling an abduction or stealing a car or their being attacked by a dragon.

Stealing his bike, though, had ticked him off. It was hard to believe that this fuming dragon was the one who had saved her.

Maybe he was having second thoughts. He reared up to his full height, opened his mouth, and she knew that nothing good could come out. She flinched, expecting flames.

"Get off the bike," he growled instead.

"I don't think so," Alex said.

He took a step closer and Alex felt the pavement vibrate. "Get off the bike now," he said. Something about his manner put Alex in mind of fire, destruction, and a dead partner.

"It's a good thing you're a figment of my imagination," she said, and gunned the bike, driving straight at him. She was so frightened that she missed second gear, but Alex didn't care.

The dragon did. She could tell by the way he screamed.

He leapt out of her way in the nick of time, taking flight as she zoomed past him. She felt him flying right behind her, practically incinerating the back of the jacket. Fire and brimstone had nothing on the heat of his breath. The little hairs on the back of her neck were singed.

And she was ridiculously turned on.

What had been in her drip?

"Stop the bike," he commanded. "Now."

Alex didn't answer, just kicked it up a notch.

This corner of Minneapolis was asleep. There were a couple of tractor trailers pulled into the gas station by the interstate, but the drivers were probably asleep in their cabs. The road was an empty black ribbon, unfurled in front of her. There was no one for her to hit, if she had to employ evasive maneuvers.

There was also no one to help her, much less save her from a furious dragon.

"That's my bike and you've stolen it," he fumed. "You're going to return it now."

As if Alex was going to stop.

"Why don't you just call the cops?" she suggested, and heard his grumble of frustration. She could believe that the police wouldn't be hot to take a stolen vehicle report from a dragon.

She hadn't thought he'd be able to hear her talking, what with the visor down on the helmet, but he could. And she could hear him as clearly as if he whispered in her ear. Alex thought about the spark that had lit between them and wondered what was going on.

Maybe they'd been giving her the really good stuff in the hospital.

Experimental stuff.

"Pull over. I'll drive you to wherever you're going."

"I can drive. You can follow. It's working for me."

"You can't drive."

"Yes, I can!"

"I have three words for you," he muttered. "Archibald Forrester's Buick."

"What happened to it?"

"It crashed and burned."

Alex felt herself blush, even as she thought she didn't have to worry about her fingerprints anymore. With any luck, Archibald had good insurance. "Well, that was extenuating circumstances. I was attacked by a dragon."

"And who says you won't be again?"

Alex spared a glance to the night sky, which glinted with stars. She changed gears to accelerate and heard his satisfaction at how smoothly she'd done it.

He *had* saved her from the other dragon. Were there good dragons and bad dragons? It seemed too complicated, given that a few weeks ago, she hadn't thought there were any real dragons at all.

Considering how many dragons had shown up in her life recently, it might be handy to be on good terms with one inclined to defend her. Alex had to think about that.

Later.

When she was alone.

"Pull over *now*." His anger made her reluctant to comply. She glanced up and he bared his teeth.

That wasn't what made Alex's heart leap in fear.

It was the other dragon right above him and closing fast. "Look out!" she shouted.

Her dragon pivoted right in midair, and she was impressed by his agility and strength. He was like a piece of over-the-top jewelry—or the Romanov egg of action figures, fit for a czar. It was hard to believe he was real. He raised his tail and his claws, then exhaled fire.

The flames were very real. Alex heard them crackle in the night air and felt their heat.

"Come on, don't be shy," he said, beckoning to the amber dragon with that confidence she found so attractive.

His claws looked like retractable knives. Alex wouldn't have rushed to fight with him, but the amber dragon dove toward him without hesitation. It was the same dragon that had attacked them earlier.

The same one that had held Mark down . . .

Alex tore her thoughts away from the memory. The two dragons collided overhead with a crash, sounding like mailed knights in combat. The earth jumped at the impact.

Some instinct for self-preservation urged her to get out of there right then and there.

But it didn't seem right to abandon her dragon, not after he had defended her earlier. Alex wasn't sure what she could do to help, but there had to be *something*. She pulled the bike over to the curb, but left it running when she got off.

Just in case.

It took everything in her to hold her ground and watch the dragons fight. Meredith Maloney had taught Alex a long time ago that the only way to conquer fear was to face it squarely. Alex hadn't managed to watch dragons up close and personal earlier that evening, but that wouldn't keep her from trying again.

She just hoped they stayed really high.

The amber *Slayer* was already weakened from their earlier fight. Donovan was surprised that he engaged again so quickly, but he knew there had to be a reason.

Slayers were sneaky. Donovan couldn't catch a scent of another *Slayer*, but he wasn't going to make assumptions. He'd learned the previous summer that Boris, the leader of the *Slayers*, could disguise his scent. Maybe the others could as well.

He remained watchful and alert, even as he turned his attention on the amber *Slayer*. If the *Slayers* thought they could take Donovan easily, they could think again. The presence of his mate sharpened Donovan's instincts and made him more determined to win than usual.

That was saying something.

The amber *Slayer* was big and old, and again Donovan was surprised that they'd never met. Donovan locked claws with his opponent, who sent them both tumbling with his momentum. The *Slayer* aimed dragonfire at Donovan's chest as they spiraled through the air.

Donovan twisted away from it, striking at the *Slayer*'s belly with his rear claws. The *Slayer* hissed and tried to retreat, but Donovan held tightly to his front claws. The *Slayer* winced as the metal talons bit deeply into his claws, and Donovan saw his surprise.

"Don't go yet," Donovan said. "Not when we haven't been formally introduced."

"I know who you are," the *Slayer* snarled.

"Then return the favor. I like to know all of my dance partners by name."

The *Slayer* growled. Donovan struck the *Slayer* with his tail, as a reward for his poor manners, then kicked his opponent as he loosed his grip. The *Slayer* grunted and fell toward the pavement.

Alex gasped far below, but Donovan knew she was okay.

The *Slayer* snarled, recovered, and raged upward. Donovan was waiting. He struck the *Slayer* across the face three times in rapid succession, making his head whip from one side to the other. The *Slayer* roared and snatched at Donovan; his teeth tore at Donovan's chest; his tail lashed Donovan's back. Donovan took a hit to his shoulder and a scratch to his chest. He spun in the air and fried the *Slayer*'s left side with dragonfire.

The *Slayer* arched at the pain and bellowed.

"Tyson is my name," he said, his eyes glinting with malice.

"Delighted to meet you," Donovan said.

Tyson watched Donovan as they circled each other. "Surely you know who I am."

"Sorry, but your reputation hasn't preceded you."

"It should have. I was famous as a candidate for Warrior, until I left the field." Tyson's eyes narrowed. "I stopped fighting, at least until Everett died."

"Everett?" The *Slayer*'s confession gave Donovan a bad feeling. Donovan had been one of three *Pyr* who had killed Everett just a few months before.

"My student," Tyson hissed. "I mentored him for centuries."

Donovan chose not to comment that Everett had been born with both the cruelty and stupidity that were his distin-

guishing characteristics. Did that say more about Tyson's
tutelage or Everett's thickheadedness? Better not to ask.
"So, this is personal?"

Tyson chuckled and attacked.

Donovan was surprised that Tyson wasn't challenging
him to a blood duel. The two grappled for supremacy again,
each raining blows on the other with his tail.

"Nothing like a firestorm, is there? I find it gives a little
extra spice to the meat." Tyson laughed, then pivoted to
pounce on Donovan's mate.

Alex was already leaping onto his bike. Donovan liked
that she didn't just wait to see what happened. All the same,
she'd never get away. Even his bike wasn't fast enough for
that.

He sprang his retractable claws, bellowed, and attacked
Tyson from behind. He sank the claws Quinn had made for
him into the *Slayer*'s wings and ripped the tendons. Tyson
screamed and spun, struggling to keep himself airborne. He
turned to fight, bloodlust in his eyes, but Donovan caught
the *Slayer* across the chest, leaving four long wounds.

Black blood fell on the pavement far below and sizzled.
Tyson twisted and ascended, then turned to leave. Alex
gunned the bike and rode away. Donovan hovered between
Alex and the departing *Slayer*, ready to finish the fight.

But Tyson kept flying. Were his wounds sufficient that he
knew he'd be defeated?

Or was there a trick? Donovan turned to follow Alex,
fearing he'd been distracted on purpose. He heard a rush of
air, then was attacked from behind himself.

"Hello, son," his assailant breathed in old-speak.

Son.

Donovan's heart stopped cold. He shook off his assailant's grasp, fearful of what he would see. He spun and
the sight of a silver and peridot dragon shook him to his
core.

It *was* Keir.

And he wasn't dead.

Anger replaced surprise with lightning speed. Donovan had never seen his father in dragon form, but he recognized the selfish glint in his eyes. Keir had the same easy grace in human form, even when he was stone drunk. "Don't call me your son, Keir Shea."

Keir laughed. "Denying it will change nothing. Why don't you acknowledge what we have in common and join the winning team?"

Donovan replied with an onslaught of dragonfire.

Donovan had seen his father only once, when he had sought his *Pyr* parent far and wide. He would never forget the drunken wreck he had found in the tavern in Tortuga. Making what coin he had by piracy, infested with lice, indifferent to anything beyond his own pleasure, the reality of Keir Shea had been a crushing disappointment to the young Donovan.

Keir Shea hadn't been a *Slayer* then, but Donovan wasn't surprised by his father's change of loyalty. Rafferty always said that the true allegiance of a *Pyr* could be found in his heart.

If the *Slayers* thought Donovan wouldn't kill his father, they could think again.

He owed Keir less than nothing.

He was ready to render the balance due.

Quinn could feel the firestorm. He didn't know whose it was, but the heat was fierce and its power drew him closer.

He also sensed the presence of *Slayers*. He drove past Erik's hotel, then parked around the corner. "Go to Erik's room immediately," he said to Sara, and flung himself out of the truck. "Let the valet park the truck."

"What's happening?" Sara moved into the driver's seat.

"A firestorm."

"The one we came for."

"But there are *Slayers*." He met her gaze for a moment,

knowing she understood the risk. She herself had been captured by *Slayers* trying to stop Quinn's firestorm. "Erik will protect you."

She nodded and he felt her pulse skip in fear. He kissed her quickly, knowing he couldn't leave her undefended.

"Wait," he murmured, his gaze slipping over the windows. Quinn sensed that the leader of the *Pyr* was close at hand.

"Help Sara," he urged in old-speak, hoping Erik would hear him. *"I'm going to the firestorm."*

"It's Donovan's." Erik replied immediately.

He saw the silhouette of Erik on the roof a heartbeat later; then an onyx and pewter dragon descended to the side street. Quinn felt Sara's relief when she saw Erik. The leader of the *Pyr* shifted shape on the sidewalk, then strode toward the truck. He got into the passenger seat, sparing Sara a smile.

"Go," he said to Quinn, his eyes flashing.

Quinn didn't need to be told twice.

Keir took the dragonfire on one side but didn't flinch. Donovan smelled his father's scales burning, but his father didn't seem to be aware of his injury.

Donovan couldn't understand it. Only the Smith could endure dragonfire and emerge stronger. Keir wasn't strengthened, though—he was injured but oblivious to it.

How could that be?

Keir roared and, claws extended, dove at Donovan. They locked talons and rolled, thrashing and biting. Donovan pulled one claw free and slashed at Keir, ripping open his shoulder.

Again, Keir didn't notice the wound.

And he didn't bleed. There was neither red *Pyr* blood nor black *Slayer* blood emanating from the wound.

Donovan felt a trickle of fear.

What had his father become?

Keir smiled with a vestige of what had been a rakish

charm and spoke in a brogue as thick as Donovan remembered. "Deny it as you will, but you are my son—blood of my blood, shard of my talon."

"You might have planted your seed in my mother's belly, but you were no father to me." Donovan struck his father with his tail, following that with a slash of his front claws. The metal talons struck so deep that Keir's left arm was dismembered.

It fell to the ground, but his smile never wavered. There still wasn't any blood. "You cannot deny what you are, Donovan—devil's spawn. Better to embrace it."

"Is that what you told my mother? That you'd come from hell to seduce her?"

Keir smiled. "The slut was willing enough, once the firestorm started. I saw no reason to abandon my own pleasure."

"Although you were quick to abandon her. Did you even stay until morning?"

"Why bother? There was no spark after the firestorm was sated." Keir glanced down, just noticing the loss of his arm, and chuckled as if it were irrelevant. His eyes shone with new malice when he looked at Donovan again. "You're not one to linger, either, are you? I suppose the spark never falls far from the blaze."

"We have nothing in common!"

Keir laughed. "Don't we? How long will it take for you to recognize that you're really a *Slayer*? The truth lies within, and your heart sings the same chorus as mine."

"Liar!" Donovan dove at his father, determined to silence his lies forever.

Alex was hyperventilating, but she was getting better at driving the bike. She felt guilty about leaving her good dragon behind, but everything had a limit.

Three dragons had made appearances this evening in rapid succession, each more splendid than the last. She didn't doubt that the others could also change into men, like her dragon did, which meant the world was a whole lot weirder than she'd previously believed.

How many dragons were there?

How many of them were hunting her?

Alex passed under an overpass and the amber dragon ambushed her. He streaked out of the shadows, appearing suddenly on her right, and Alex nearly tipped the bike in her terror. He tried to snatch at her, his extended talon passing over her head.

She accelerated, knowing the bike was nearly out of control. A curve in the road loomed ahead and she feared that one way or the other, she'd be dead very shortly.

She'd rather miss the curve than share Mark's fate. The dragon inhaled and Alex knew he would breathe fire next. She gritted her teeth, sure that she was taking her last breath, and felt a presence behind her. The world lit with flickering orange flames, but Alex felt nothing.

Maybe she was dead already.

Maybe this was a nightmare.

"Just keep driving," a man said, his low tone reassuring. "I'll be right back."

Alex glanced up to see a sapphire and steel dragon engage with the amber one. A fourth dragon. They locked claws and fought, the amber one exhaling fire on the sapphire one. This new arrival laughed, seeming to get bigger under the fire's touch.

The amber dragon fell back in shock, his chest wounds still dripping dark blood. The sapphire dragon went after him, thrashing and snapping and spewing fire of his own. The amber dragon yowled and retreated, finally flying high to leave the fray.

Alex kept going, even though she was shaking. Had she found another good dragon? The sapphire and steel dragon flew beside her, his manner vigilant.

"He'll leave it now," the sapphire dragon said, his words

surprisingly clear to Alex. "Stop the bike before you crash it."

Alex was trembling right to her marrow and had that light-headed feeling that hinted that she was going to pass out again.

Four dragons.

Sedatives in her drip.

Two weeks of bed rest followed by one crazy night. She didn't think her body could take any more.

And she didn't blame it. Perhaps her chances of survival were better if she stopped the bike. This dragon had saved her from the murderous amber one, after all.

She stopped but kept the bike running, only one foot on the ground. She dipped her head, wishing she could put it between her knees. She'd have to get off the bike for that, though.

The dragon didn't land. "Turn around," he said with quiet force. "We have to go back and help Donovan."

"There's another dragon there."

"Yes. A *Slayer*. Donovan won't let him touch you."

"Why not?"

It was as if the sapphire dragon smiled. "The firestorm," he said with such conviction that Alex believed him. "It's his duty to protect you because of the firestorm." That made about as much sense as anything else she'd heard that night.

But the lapis lazuli dragon *had* protected her already.

Alex turned the bike around and followed the other good dragon back toward her dragon.

Donovan.

Alex saw immediately that her dragon must have taken a hit, because there was blood on his chest. Donovan kept on fighting, though, as if untroubled, his claws flashing as he fought. Sparks seemed to fly from him in his fury. The fire he breathed burned hot and red against the night sky and Alex felt a bit overwhelmed.

She put her feet on the ground, but kept the bike running.

She concentrated on breathing in and out at regular intervals. She couldn't do a damn thing about the ringing between her ears or the racing of her heart.

Donovan rained blows on the green dragon, pummeling him until he should have been limp. He'd already lost one foreleg and the opposite wing. It didn't seem to matter to him. The sapphire and steel dragon joined him and they fought grimly together, anticipating each other's moves.

Even with two fighting against him, even with his wing and leg gone, the light green dragon didn't give up. The two good dragons exchanged a glance and Donovan began to take their opponent apart.

If Alex hadn't seen dragons do what she'd seen them do in the lab to Mark, she would have had a harder time watching the fight. There was a rumble, like distant thunder, and the flashing signs at the mall seemed like a beacon from another world.

There was no blood, which just made the scene more surreal. Alex stared, her numb mind unable to make sense of what she witnessed. Donovan was dismembering the light green dragon one limb at a time. Alex could sense the good dragons' distaste for the battle, as if they did an unpleasant job that needed doing.

When the green dragon's legs and wings were gone, they tossed him out of the sky. His remains fell heavily, then kept twitching. The two good dragons gathered the other limbs and tossed them on the mangled body; then the sapphire one breathed fire. Alex smelled the burning flesh and forced herself to watch the destruction of a bad dragon.

He became a bonfire in a parking lot.

Through the glimmer of the flames, Alex saw that he shifted shape. She had a glimpse of a man with salt-and-pepper hair. He was handsome in a roguish way, and he looked as if he had thoroughly sampled all of life's pleasures.

Then his body was devoured by the flames, the fire crackling as it leapt high.

That was enough. Alex got off the bike, her knees shaking, and sat down on the curb. She put her head in her hands and then between her knees. She told herself that none of this was real and didn't believe it for a minute.

It would have been nice to pass out again, but Alex knew she didn't have that luxury. There were too many dragons around.

Alex glanced up as the two good dragons landed in unison on the pavement. They shifted shape so quickly that Alex couldn't discern the change. One minute, they were massive dragons descending toward the earth; the next, they were two men.

Handsome, built men. They shook hands, like old friends who had worked together. There was nothing left but cinders where the other dragon had fallen. Alex's mind wobbled a bit in its conviction of how the world worked.

What she needed was some sleep.

The sapphire and steel dragon had become a dark-haired and broad-shouldered man who moved with deliberation. He was more muscled than her dragon and his manner was more thoughtful.

"No water," he said inexplicably, then spared a glance to the clear sky overhead.

Donovan grimaced, then stopped beside the pile of ash. He spat on it, then turned away. "That'll take care of that," he said as he turned toward Alex, his gaze simmering. She saw then that he bore a passing resemblance to the fallen man and wondered at it.

"Subtle," the new arrival commented with disapproval, and Alex's dragon man shrugged.

"But effective."

"Are you sure?"

"I don't care. What's past is passed," he said grimly.

"You knew him?"

"You could say that." Donovan spoke without emotion,

his words sending a shock through Alex. He surveyed her, as if uncertain what she would do. On some level, Alex thought that was funny—she was the predictable one in this company.

"Are you going to pass out again?" he asked, and there was a teasing undertone to his voice.

"I don't faint," Alex said.

He smiled and her heart skipped a beat.

"Okay, maybe I'm still deciding."

Both men smiled then. "Quinn Tyrrell, Alex Madison," Donovan said. "Quinn is the Smith," he added, and Alex nodded as if that made sense to her.

It didn't, but then neither did much else.

"Let me see," Quinn urged, his expression expectant.

"This isn't a freak show," Donovan protested.

Quinn shook his head. "That's the last thing it is. I can feel your firestorm. Let me see it."

Donovan arched a brow, managing to look both seductive and skeptical at the same time. He tugged off a pair of gloves and held them in his left hand, while he stretched his right toward Alex, his palm up.

Alex recoiled.

He frowned. "Just touch my fingertips. It won't hurt."

Alex was unconvinced.

Donovan smiled. "Quinn wants to reminisce about his own firestorm. It's a small favor for his showing up to help us."

Us.

"No fast moves," she said, and Quinn tried to hide his laughter.

Donovan held her gaze, his own so hot that she couldn't look away. "I told you: that's not my strategy."

Alex hesitated. What could go wrong on a public thoroughfare?

In the middle of the night, with no one else around, after dragons had attacked three times without warning and her two companions were also dragons.

A *lot* could go wrong.

But being afraid never solved anything.

Alex stood up and walked unsteadily toward Donovan. She wanted to see the spark again herself, to verify that she hadn't dreamed it. He simply stood and watched, letting her set the pace.

She liked that.

He was handsome, maybe the best-looking guy she'd ever seen. A simmer began deep within her. It seemed to get hotter as she got closer, as she could see the bright green of his eyes, the faint shadow of a day's whiskers on his chin, the slight upward curl of the corners of his firm lips. He had a good smile.

Desire simmered inside her.

But then, she had always had a thing for strong men who knew how to fight, confident men who knew they were sexy, and hunks who knew what to do about both.

The heat grew with every step. Alex felt warm, right to her toes, warmer than seemed reasonable on a fall night. She was aware of his scent on the jacket she wore.

She barely knew him.

And what she knew about him should have sent her running.

A trickle of sweat eased down Alex's back and she licked her lips. It was hot, maybe because a dragon had been incinerated so close by. The pavement felt cold, though. The heat seemed to be within Alex and it was more than a thermal response.

It was a sexual one. She looked at the strength of his neck and shoulders, his long fingers outstretched to her, the russet arch of his lashes. She eased closer, reached out, and touched his hand quickly. His skin was warm.

The spark that danced between them was unmistakable.

"The firestorm," Quinn whispered with satisfaction.

Alex swallowed; then her breath caught in her throat. That mischievous glint lit Donovan's gaze and he smiled. He shoved a hand through his hair and nodded once at Quinn. Alex knew he was as affected as she was.

His smile made her go all shivery.

"Hey, gorgeous," he said, indicating the bike with a jerk of his chin. "Going my way?"

With those five words, Alex recovered her senses and wanted to bolt.

Chapter 4

A lex was afraid.

Donovan couldn't blame her. His mate had been exposed to two dragon fights in rapid succession. He respected that she had returned, even at Quinn's urging.

She had guts. He liked that.

He also liked the soft curves he could see through his own T-shirt. He liked her crisp scent, which teased and tempted him, making him think of better ways to get to know each other. He liked how she looked both disheveled and purposeful.

He liked that she surprised him.

He could hear the soft whisper of her breathing. The heat rose between them, gaining momentum as they stared at each other. Donovan heard her pulse, felt his own heart match its pace to hers. She licked her lips, running her tongue across her bottom lip nervously, and he watched it avidly.

He could think of lots of activities that involved tongues.

She caught her breath, her eyes widening slightly as she glanced away. Her lashes were dark and thick, the line of her jaw enticing. He liked how primal his body's response to her presence was, and couldn't help thinking that the sex would be great.

But then, she'd conceive a child.

Donovan was not going to make that kind of commitment.

There were shadows under her eyes and fear lurked in their chocolate depths. He was shocked by how sexy she looked in his clothes. She wasn't wearing much underneath, though. A pang of desire shot through him at that realization and he forced himself to look away from some very intriguing shadows. He reminded himself that he wasn't having any part of his firestorm.

Even if his body greeted the idea with enthusiasm.

Quinn spoke quietly to Alex. "You'll need to come back to the hotel with us."

"Excuse me?" Alex took a step back.

"You've been attacked by *Slayers* twice tonight," Donovan said, leaving the issue of the firestorm for the moment.

"*Slayers*?" Alex folded her arms across her chest.

Donovan didn't blame her for being skeptical. "Dragon shape shifters intent on eradicating humans from the planet."

She nodded as she digested the information. To Donovan's surprise, she didn't question it. Her gaze did flick to Keir's ashes, then back to meet his. "Right. How do you come into it?"

"We're *Pyr*," he said. "*Pyr* are dragon shape shifters intent on protecting the earth's treasures, of which humans are one."

Her eyes took on a tentative sparkle and the sight made Donovan's blood boil. "I like that philosophy better."

"Most people do." Donovan said, and she smiled slightly. "Donovan Shea," he said, offering her his hand.

She hesitated only a moment before putting her hand in his. Heat flared between them, sending an inferno through his veins. Even though he expected it, desire nearly took Donovan to his knees.

She pulled her hand away. Her cheeks burned red and he could see that her nipples were taut again. "Alex Madison." She swallowed. "But you knew that already."

"True."

"Why were you trying to kidnap me?"

"To keep these *Slayers* from getting to you."

Her dark gaze danced to the pile of ash again. "One got away."

"So you need to come with us." Donovan saw immediately that Alex didn't agree.

"I think we should part ways," she said. "Divide and conquer. Thanks for taking out those dragons, and here's your helmet. . . ."

"Twice in one night, Alex," Donovan said flatly. He didn't take the helmet from her. "If there's a third time, do you want to be facing them alone?"

The color drained out of her face. Donovan sensed her indecision and didn't know what to say to persuade her.

Quinn knew. "Come with us. My mate, Sara, is at the hotel. Four months ago, she didn't know anything about us, either."

"There are female dragons?"

"Sara is human, just like you." Quinn smiled. "An accountant who owns a bookstore."

Alex blinked. "That sounds normal."

"She is," Quinn said, his affection for his mate clear in his expression. "If you want, she'll stand guard while you sleep."

Alex still hesitated.

"There's no safer place for you to be." Donovan watched as Alex's gaze trailed for a third time to the pile of Keir's ashes.

"He didn't bleed," she said, her voice shaking. "I don't think he felt any pain. Why not?"

Donovan frowned. "I don't know."

"Do any of you feel pain?"

"We all do. We all bleed, except *Slayers* bleed black." Donovan found himself staring at the cinders that had been his father. The wind gusted and they began to scatter across the pavement. "I don't know what he had become."

"A new development," Quinn said. "And not a good one."

"Are you sure he's dead, then?" Alex asked. Donovan glanced at the blowing ashes, then exchanged a glance with Quinn. He didn't want to lie to his mate and he wasn't sure.

Quinn looked away, evidence of his own uncertainty.

Alex watched, then shuddered. "Okay," she said with obvious reluctance. "Okay, I'll go with you, then, and stay with Sara."

Donovan wanted to reassure her. "One condition," he said in a teasing tone, holding up a finger. "I drive back to the hotel."

"But you're hurt."

"Scratches and bruises," he said dismissively. He grinned then, wanting to prompt her smile. "Remember: three words."

Alex did smile then, the mischievous sparkle in her eyes taking Donovan's breath away. "You're not going to let me forget about that Buick, are you?"

"Not a chance." Donovan laughed, liking that she laughed with him.

It had been a bad idea to let Donovan drive, because that meant that Alex rode behind him.

There was no escaping the strength and sinew of him, not when Alex's legs were around his hips. She kept her hands on his shoulders, not wanting to make his injuries worse, but that didn't help at all. Her breasts collided with his back; his hips bumped against the inside of her thighs.

She was aware that Quinn flew high above them, that he was acting as a sentry even though the two friends hadn't said anything aloud. Strangely enough, Alex felt a little bit safer being in the custody of two good dragons.

And more aroused than she would have believed possible under the circumstances. Even the bandages on her hands didn't keep her from wanting to caress Donovan. She wanted to feel him up, right on the bike. He was hard and muscled, so buff that it was hard to imagine that he did anything other than work out.

The heat between them was inescapable. Alex couldn't stop thinking about it. It was easy to imagine his muscled chest bare, her hands running over his shoulders and chest, his strength beneath her fingertips. She wondered about the rest of him—how he would kiss, how he would feel inside her—and had to lean the helmet against his shoulders to catch her breath.

The scent of his skin didn't help. She shouldn't have been able to smell it, not with the helmet on and the visor closed, but she could. It made her sizzle with desire.

She changed position and hung on to the back of the bike's seat instead, resisting the urge to rub her hips provocatively against him. Stress obviously was making her forget who she was and how she usually behaved. The thrum of the bike, the vibrations from the engine, seemed to make her body yearn even more.

In one way, Alex wanted the ride to last forever. In another, she wanted it over immediately.

Before she did something she might regret.

Finally, they got to a hotel parking lot. Donovan pulled the bike into the same parking spot. Alex got off the back quickly, wanting to put some distance between them. She pulled off the helmet and shook her hair, then shoved the helmet at him.

There was something between them then, a barrier of some kind, even if it was just a helmet in her outstretched hands.

He was watching her, his arms folded across his chest. His T-shirt was stretched taut; his jeans clung in all the right places, leaving nothing to the imagination in terms of his build. His expression was thoughtful. "Where'd you learn to ride a bike?"

"I took a class."

"Why?"

Alex looked around the concrete parking garage. If she was going to make any attempt to sound coherent, she had to stop ogling him. "Because of my brother. He wanted to get a bike, but Dad said no."

"Why?"

Alex smiled. "Dad's an orthopedic surgeon. He always calls them *donor cycles*. He took Peter down to the ER one night when a motorcycle accident came in, but Peter still wanted one. Finally, Dad just said no."

"But he let you take a class?"

"Of course not!" Alex laughed at the idea. "I took it anyway. I was eighteen; Peter was twenty. He spent the summer moping about Dad not letting him do what he wanted. I just went and did it."

Donovan's eyes narrowed. Having his undivided attention made Alex's mouth go dry. It made her feel more sexy than she usually did.

"You wanted a bike, too?" he asked.

Alex wasn't sure whether he was seeking common ground between them, but she wasn't going to lie. "No. I wanted Peter to see that you can't wait for people to give you permission to live your dreams. I wanted him to understand that if you really want something, you just go get it."

Donovan smiled crookedly. "And did he believe that?"

Alex sobered and shook her head. "No. I think he waits for his wife Diane's permission for everything now, instead of Dad's."

"That's not much different."

"No, it's not."

"Disappointed in your pupil?"

It was Alex's turn to smile. "I'd make a lousy teacher."

"But maybe a good example."

Alex was going to have to think about that. Donovan took the helmet from her and their fingers brushed, the spark making them both jump. Donovan frowned and indicated the door to the stairs.

Alex wanted him to give her a story about his childhood in exchange. "What about you?"

His expression became guarded. "What about me?"

"Do you have siblings?"

He shook his head. "No. I had a cousin who might as well have been my little brother."

"Did you teach him to ride a bike?"

His smile turned wicked. "Among other things."

"So you were a good teacher?"

Donovan chuckled. "And a bad example."

Alex could believe it. She smiled. "Do you still hang out together?"

"No."

His sudden change of mood told Alex that there was a story there, one he was unlikely to share. "Where is he now?"

"Dead." He jingled the keys to the bike. "Let's get upstairs."

Alex was intrigued by the glimpse of his vulnerability. "Will you answer a question for me first?"

Donovan shot her a look. "I did that already."

"Another one. A pertinent one." Alex took a deep breath. "What's the firestorm? What does it mean and what causes it?"

Donovan stopped outside the door to the stairs. This time, he surveyed the parking garage as if he were collecting his thoughts.

His gaze collided so suddenly with Alex's that she caught her breath. His eyes were a vivid green, the intensity of his expression making her wary. His voice was low, as if he were sharing a secret with her, and Alex tingled. "No one knows what causes it, or where it comes from, or why it comes when it does. Some *Pyr* think it's fate; others think it's dumb luck."

"What about you?"

He shrugged. "I've never thought about it enough to decide. It doesn't really matter, does it? It happens or it doesn't, and that's all you need to know." He started to reach for the door and Alex knew he wouldn't say any more.

Without being prompted.

"But what does it mean when it does happen?"

Donovan paused; then he pivoted, giving her lots of time to back away. There was something about the glitter of her eyes that seemed portentous, as if he might change shape right in front of her, as if it would be smart to run first and ask questions later.

Alex stayed put, even though her heart was racing.

"The firestorm is a mating sign for our kind," Donovan said. "In practical terms, it means that you and I can feel each other's presence. It means that sparks fly between us."

He held up his hand and Alex raised hers more tentatively. When their palms were several inches apart, sparks did jump between their two hands, electrifying and heating the air between them.

Spontaneous combustion. But how? Why? "How does it do that?"

"I don't know." Donovan's eyes gleamed as he looked down at her. Alex swallowed and couldn't look away. "I do know that I can hear your heart beating from thirty feet away. I can hear you breathing. I can hear whether you are afraid or happy." He paused and arched one brow. "Or aroused."

Alex sizzled. *He knew.* She stared into the glorious green shimmer of his eyes and couldn't move.

Donovan's voice dropped to a murmur, a very sexy murmur. "The firestorm means that my body tries to put itself in tune with yours." He caught her hand in his, locking his fingers around hers. Alex liked his firm grip.

She caught her breath as she felt an inferno launch from their entangled hands. It sizzled over her flesh and awakened such desire deep inside that her knees went weak. She leaned her other hand on his chest and felt his heat beneath her hand. He put his free hand on her waist, almost drawing her into his embrace, and Alex didn't want to be anywhere else.

"Listen," Donovan commanded softly.

She heard the beat of his heart, felt it through both palms, heard it match its pace to hers. She could smell his skin, and the scent made her yearn. She was fascinated by the way his eyes shone, the way his mouth was shaped, the way his hair curled past his ears. She noticed the stubble on his chin, the earring in his left ear, the dragon tattoo on his left arm.

She felt as if her skin were on fire, as if she should tear off her clothes right then and there. She wanted to ease the blood from his cheek, push back the thick wave of his hair from his brow, reach up and kiss him. She wanted to feel Donovan and to know him, to taste him and to caress him.

He leaned closer, his words a dark whisper, his breath fanning her cheek. "The firestorm means that we lust for each other. It means that we burn for each other." He arched a brow. "It probably means that the sex would be stupendous."

"You don't know?" Alex whispered, her gaze falling to his lips.

"I've never had a firestorm before." His thumb moved against her waist, easing beneath the top of her sweatpants. *His* sweatpants. Alex took a step closer. She couldn't have done otherwise. It was natural and intuitive, like a lodestone finding magnetic north. Her breasts were against his chest, which was the perfect place for them to be. Heat emanated from every point of contact between them, melting her reservations with lightning speed.

"The firestorm means that we'll drive each other wild," he whispered. "And there's nothing we can do about it."

"I can think of one thing we can do about it," Alex said,

leaning her lips against his throat. He tasted like salt and sweat. She wanted to run her tongue over him, peel off his T-shirt, have her way with him right in the parking garage. She felt alive, relieved, and had the urge to celebrate as much.

In a primal way.

He chuckled, then slid his nose through her hair, as if he found her scent equally seductive. His hands bracketed her waist and he pulled her fully against him. Alex liked how muscled and resolute he was, how he was both strong and gentle. There was blood on his T-shirt, where he had been injured in dragon form, but the wound had already closed.

He was a powerful, sexy man and she wanted him. She knew it intuitively, even though it made no sense. It certainly wasn't sensible.

But it was right.

Alex ran her teeth across his chest, grazing his nipple through his T-shirt, and heard him catch his breath. His lips touched her ear, electrifying her with a caress. His lips slid along her jawline, leaving a burning trail of kisses. Alex's heart leapt when he captured her lips with his.

Donovan's kiss was hard and quick, fiery and in-escapable. It was consuming and seductive, and Alex's body responded with such heat that she was dizzy.

She wound her arms around his neck and hung on.

It could have been Alex's first kiss ever. Donovan's kiss—and her response—was that different from every other kiss she'd ever shared. His kiss was electric, nuclear fission on the lips, launching forest fires throughout her body from that one point of contact. She burned and yearned and wanted more.

Immediately.

Alex had her fingers locked into his hair before she knew what she was about. She opened her mouth to his tongue and arched against him, liking that his hand slid under her shirt to pull her closer. His hand was strong on her bare back; the way his fingers urged her closer was proof that he was as affected as she was.

Donovan broke their kiss abruptly, his breathing as ragged as hers, and almost shoved her away. His voice was a low rumble when he spoke, one Alex could feel as well as hear.

"That's the firestorm, or the first taste of it, and that heat is what it means." Donovan paused, then framed her face and compelled her to meet his gaze. His eyes were cat-bright, as if he could read her thoughts. Alex couldn't look away.

"What happens next?" she whispered.

"We aren't going to find out," he said, then released her and turned away.

He might as well have slapped her.

Alex felt cold outside of Donovan's embrace but refused to shiver. She told herself that his attitude was for the best, even though it annoyed her.

When had a man ever rejected her before?

When had a man ever kissed her like that and rejected her? Who did Donovan Shea think he was?

On the other hand, when had she witnessed dragon fights before?

And when, um, had she nearly done it in a parking garage? If Donovan hadn't stopped their embrace, Alex knew she wouldn't have.

It was a night for unwelcome firsts, that was for sure. Donovan held the door for her and Alex tried to look indifferent as she hurried past him. It was tough to do when she was simmering.

Worse, she knew that he knew how aroused she was.

"What happened at Gilchrist Enterprises two weeks ago?" he asked softly as they stared at the elevator doors and waited.

Alex was surprised into looking at him. "How do you
know about that?"

"It was a *Slayer* attack. It doesn't matter how I know—I
do." Donovan pushed the button for the elevator again. "Did
they kill your partner?"

The memory unfolded in Alex's mind with frightening
clarity. She folded her arms across her chest, fought the urge
to shudder, and watched the floors count down on the display as the elevator drew closer. Donovan's question had
managed to remind her that getting involved with a dragon
shape shifter had to be a bad idea.

It was *good* that he was rejecting her.

Even if it felt like a disappointment.

"Not going to share?" he asked softly.

"I don't want to talk about it."

Donovan watched her, then nodded once as the elevator
doors opened. "Have it that way, then." He indicated for her
to precede him and must have noticed that Alex hesitated a
beat before the small space of the elevator. "I don't take
what I want," he said with such force that she knew he was
insulted.

"How do you get it, then?"

"I wait for it to be offered."

"And then you decline." Alex sniffed. "Don't hold your
breath for a second offer." She stepped past him. He pushed
the button for the eighth floor with force, his expression
dark.

Alex watched his fingers flex as he toyed with the keys
to the bike. He didn't turn when he spoke. "You should
know that I decided a long time ago that firestorms weren't
for me."

He flicked a hot glance over his shoulder, one that made
Alex straighten. She licked her lips without intending to do
so and he caught his breath, his gaze brightening as he
watched the tip of her tongue. The air in the elevator began
to get warm.

Donovan turned his back on her abruptly. "Nothing personal."

"I see," Alex said, trying not to sound insulted.

He threw her a smile and her heart did a somersault. "I ride solo. That's all."

"Why?"

Alex thought he wouldn't answer her but she was wrong. "It's what I know best," he said in an undertone. He gave her a look then, a look so cold that she shivered, one that reminded her of what he could be. "Remember that peridot and silver dragon?"

"The incinerated one?"

He nodded once. "That was my father."

Alex felt her eyes widen in shock.

"Riding solo is what comes naturally to me." He dropped his voice then, looking both hard and unreachable. "Blood of his blood, shard of his talon."

He'd just killed his own father.

Was that the truth? Or was he just trying to frighten her?

The elevator filled with an awkward silence. Donovan watched the display with apparent fascination. Alex pretended to do so as well, but instead she checked him out. There was something about knowing that he had no intention of seducing her that made her feel safe. It made her feel provocative. Contrary, even.

It made her wonder whether she could change his mind.

The man looked every bit as good in jeans as was humanly possible. But then, he wasn't human, was he?

She thought about the spark between their hands, the seductive heat that slipped over her skin when he touched her, the fiery power of his kiss. She reviewed what he'd said about the firestorm and recalled him shifting shape before her very eyes.

She thought about the spark.

Scientific certainty was based upon repeatable results.

Alex reached out, just to check the hypothesis, and touched his elbow.

Donovan jumped when the spark lit. "Don't do that," he muttered, brushing at his arm.

"The firestorm doesn't seem to care that you're not interested," Alex said, watching his response.

He was irritated, so obviously irritated that Alex was intrigued. "It'll pass," he said, but Alex didn't believe it.

She wasn't sure he did, either.

The elevator doors opened on the eighth floor and he gestured for her to go ahead of him. Alex stepped past him into the quiet, carpeted corridor, then turned right as he indicated. It looked as if they were going back to the same hotel suite.

Alex was sure this time she'd be sleeping alone.

As she matched her steps to Donovan's, she acknowledged that a night between the sheets with Donovan and his great butt would have been fun. It would have been the perfect stress buster and an ideal way to focus her thoughts.

Trust Donovan to be not only a distraction, but a principled distraction. If ever there was a man worth a one-nighter, he was it. He said he wasn't interested.

His body was interested.

Just the way hers was.

It was a bit scary to consider how many things they had in common. The fact was that Alex didn't have the time to be distracted right now, not when she had to get her backup prototype running—without Mark's help—for the meeting with Mr. Sinclair. She didn't have time to be obsessing about the way one man kissed, much less to wonder how his skin would feel against hers. She didn't have the luxury of daydreams and fantasies.

Which meant she had to forget Donovan Shea.

There were other men in the main room of the suite they entered. They looked up and several of them stood, as if they'd been waiting on Donovan's arrival. Quinn was there, leaning against one wall with his arms folded across his chest. The hearse driver was there, too. Alex didn't recognize the others, but she didn't want to socialize.

She needed to think.

"You must be exhausted," a woman said from the doorway to the adjoining bedroom. She had hair the color of honey and it was tied up in a ponytail. She was smaller than Alex, petite and pretty, and her smile was warm.

She must be the accountant bookstore owner. Alex wanted to hug her just for being normal.

"I'm Sara. Come and sleep." Sara's smile broadened. "I promise to keep the dragons at bay."

"Ha ha," said a fair-haired man.

Were they all dragon shape shifters? Alex couldn't even think about that. "Thanks. That's a great idea." Alex trusted Sara.

What's more, she trusted Donovan to keep his pledge. She was as safe here as anywhere else, maybe safer.

For the moment.

Donovan didn't even glance Alex's way when she left his side, but she wasn't fooled. The man was aware of her every move.

It might not be smart to get involved with a dragon shape shifter, or even to have sex with him once, but Alex had to wonder whether she'd regret her choice if she didn't. A firestorm couldn't be something that happened every day.

And Donovan didn't look like a man she'd easily forget.

Donovan paced the main room of the suite for the second time that day. He wasn't any less agitated than he had been the first time, even though Alex was safe. The other *Pyr* breathed smoke in unison, surrounding the suite with a barrier impenetrable to *Slayers*. Donovan couldn't calm himself enough to help.

He'd kissed Alex to make a point, to prove to himself that he could resist the firestorm, that he wasn't answerable to fate. His plan had nearly backfired. Alex's kiss sent a yearning through him that undermined everything. The press of her against him dismissed all thoughts that weren't related to lovemaking.

His senses were saturated with her presence: the sweet taste of her, the silken brush of her hair in his hands, the smell of soap and toothpaste, and a faint lingering of antiseptic. Her eyes had shone with a thousand variations of gold and amber and brown, like kaleidoscopes designed to bewitch him. Her voice was low and velvety, a little raspy— as if she sang skat and smoked French cigarettes in the middle of the night.

Donovan had barely been able to step away once the firestorm had had him in its grasp. Its power astonished him.

And frightened him. He'd been aware of nothing but his mate while kissing her. Nothing. Anyone could have attacked him. Anyone could have injured or killed them both. He could have taken her in the parking garage without another thought.

In a *parking garage*.

The firestorm was a liability Donovan needed even less than a partner, mate, and child. He knew that and believed it, but he still paced the room, replaying Alex's kiss.

He felt Rafferty watching him, but couldn't even glance his way. He didn't want to talk about the experience. Not yet.

Maybe not ever.

February and the next eclipse seemed a very long time away.

Erik worked on his laptop over by the window, frowning as he sought some elusive piece of data. Quinn leaned against one wall and watched, probably not missing any nuance. Niall and Sloane had arrived and both looked sleepy. Quinn had been scheduled to work on their armor at his studio in Michigan.

"Cut out the pacing and let me see," Sloane said with rare impatience when Donovan walked past him for the umpteenth time. Sloane had ancient apothecary skills. "I can't tend your wounds if you don't slow down, and I'm not in the mood to chase you."

Donovan stopped and let Sloane study the cuts on his shoulder and chest. The wounds were superficial and he had already forgotten them. He wished he could forget his mate as easily. He tapped his toe while Sloane gently cleaned the wounds.

"Bad?" Erik asked.

"No," Sloane declared. "They're pretty clean." He went to his backpack and returned with a salve. He opened the jar and Donovan recognized the scent.

"That stuff stings," he said when Sloane offered it to him.

The younger *Pyr* was unsympathetic. "Infection stings more. I hear blood poisoning is a treat, as well." He offered the jar again and this time Donovan took some on his fingertips. He grimaced as he eased it over his cuts. It did sting, but then it tingled. He could almost feel the skin knitting together again.

Sloane offered the jar again. "You don't have enough salve on the last one."

Donovan knew better than to argue. He added more salve, then changed to a clean T-shirt under Sloane's instruction.

"Let me guess: he'll be ready to fight tomorrow," Rafferty said.

Sloane nodded. "It won't even take him that long. This guy heals faster than any *Pyr* I've ever known."

"Born to fight," Quinn observed.

Donovan grinned. "I try to stick to what I know." He tapped his chest with a fingertip and spoke to Quinn. "Now that you've patched my missing scale, I'm stronger than. ever."

"How well did it hold up?" Quinn asked, his eyes narrowed.

"It's a thing of beauty."

The patch that Quinn had forged for him should be beautiful: it contained the richest treasure of Donovan's hoard. The Dragon's Tooth was a massive pearl that Quinn had framed in wrought iron and embedded in Donovan's chest. The process had hurt like hell, but had been worth it—his natural armor was flawless again. In human form, it looked as if he had a mole where the pearl was located.

Donovan noticed Quinn's change of mood. "Why? Did you expect otherwise? What's wrong?"

Quinn indicated Sloane and Niall. "I couldn't repair their armor."

"The patches kept separating from our scales," Niall said.

"It wasn't for lack of trying," Sloane said, and shrugged.

"Or lack of skill," Erik contributed. "Quinn is the most skillful Smith in eons."

Quinn inclined his head in acknowledgement of that, but still looked frustrated. "I can't understand what went wrong."

"Maybe they need a firestorm to have their armor healed," Rafferty mused. "You fixed Donovan's after the last eclipse."

"Which heralded his firestorm." Quinn looked thoughtful.

This was the last reminder Donovan needed of Alex's proximity. He was sure he could hear her getting undressed in the next room, the sound of her sweats—*his* sweats—dropping to the carpet. He could imagine her naked, tall and lean with those splendid breasts. Her skin would be tanned to gold and as smooth as satin. She would walk like a queen.

And those dark, dark eyes would be lit from within, promising the surrender of a thousand mysteries in exchange for a kiss. He heard the shower begin and his imagination provided a vision of her under the running water, one that made him ache to join her.

He heard her throaty laugh in response to something Sara said, and his gut clenched. He glanced toward the closed door, trying to muster his resolve, and caught the bemused gaze of Quinn.

"You can't resist it," Quinn said in old-speak. *"Some forces are greater than our will."*

Donovan wasn't interested in anyone's advice.

Erik nodded. "It would make sense that a *Pyr* could be healed only during his firestorm. That which creates vulnerability can also make you strong."

"I would have liked to have healed their weaknesses *before* their firestorms," Quinn said with a flash of irritation.

"Ditto." Sloane was grim. "That's when you need the power."

"And you never know when yours will come," Rafferty said. Donovan felt the heat of his mentor's gaze upon him again. He didn't look up. "Or what secrets it will awaken from your past."

"True enough." Donovan knew that what he would tell the others would surprise them all. "After all, I killed my father tonight."

A ripple of shock passed through the room.

"What?" Rafferty demanded first, roused from his characteristic tranquility. "How can that be?"

"Keir attacked me and I killed him. Quinn saw it." Donovan shook his head. "I haven't seen the old bastard in centuries, but Tyson sent him after me. They must have thought I wouldn't strike my own father."

Rafferty pushed himself to his feet. "But you can't have killed him. That's impossible."

Donovan heard bitterness in his own tone. "You don't think I could kill him? I owed Keir nothing. I owed him less than nothing. It was easier than killing a stranger."

"No, no. It's impossible because Keir died centuries ago."

Donovan was shocked. "What?"

"He hasn't been alive since shortly after you met him, Donovan," Rafferty insisted. "He was killed in a bar fight in Tortuga."

"You never told me this before," Donovan said, unable to hide his skepticism.

"It wasn't for lack of trying," Rafferty retorted, his eyes

flashing. "I tried to tell you, but you refused to discuss Keir. You didn't want to talk about him."

Donovan looked at the carpet, knowing it was true.

Rafferty raised a finger. "It has persistently been your inclination to refuse the assistance and advice of others—"

"Perhaps you might tell us about Keir," Erik interrupted smoothly.

Rafferty heaved a sigh as he halted his lecture. He still looked annoyed. "I was in Tortuga. I saw Keir die. I don't know whom you killed tonight, but Keir Shea is long dead."

Donovan was remembering that Keir hadn't bled and wondered again what his father had become. He met Quinn's gaze across the room as dread slid down his spine.

What had the *Slayers* learned to do?

Chapter 5

Sara stood guard outside the bathroom while Alex showered. Sara thought about the first time she and Quinn had shared a shower, during their own firestorm, and smiled.

She knew the *Pyr* had very keen hearing and wondered whether Quinn could hear the water, whether he was remembering the same night. That made her smile even more.

Alex took her time and Sara couldn't blame her. Steam eased beneath the door, carrying the scent of floral shower gel. Maybe Alex was trying to come to terms with the firestorm. Even Sara was aware of the heat between Alex and Donovan. She knew from experience that it was a much more potent sensation for a participant than an observer.

Donovan had to be sizzling.

Alex probably thought she was coming down with a fever.

Sara remembered the thousands of questions she'd had during her firestorm with Quinn. Quinn had welcomed the chance to explain matters of the *Pyr* to Sara.

Donovan, Sara sensed, had no intention of doing the same.

It wasn't fair. Sara decided that she'd aid the firestorm in her own way. As the wife of a *Pyr* and the mother of a *Pyr*-to-be, Sara knew she was a part of the *Pyr* team, for now and forever. And she liked Donovan. She didn't want him to mess up his own firestorm. She'd answer questions, no matter how many of them Alex had.

Alex finally emerged. She had a towel wrapped around her and a new Band-Aid on her left hand. "That felt so good," she said, and her smile almost lit the room. "Thanks for watching the door."

"I think you can trust Donovan," Sara said. "But I don't mind staying with you tonight if it makes you feel better."

"It would. Thanks." Alex still carried that Ziploc and put it now on the nightstand. She pulled on the T-shirt again, which hung to the top of her thighs, and grimaced.

"I really need to get something decent to wear," she muttered, then took the wet towel back to the bathroom. She hung it up, then combed out her hair, as if she had no questions to ask.

Sara didn't believe it. Alex just didn't want to sound insane by asking about dragons.

Sara leaned in the doorway. "I know that the firestorm can be really confusing, so if you have any questions, feel free to ask."

Alex looked at her, her gaze clear. "You have one?"

"*Had* one. Last summer." Sara smiled. "It was pretty amazing."

"It does end, then?"

"Oh, yes. It's a short-term thing."

Alex straightened the towel, apparently with full concentration, but Sara knew that she was paying more attention than that.

"Ask me anything you want," Sara said, and went back into the bedroom. She sat down in one of the easy chairs.

Alex followed, then crawled into the bed and sighed. She took the plastic bag and put it under her pillow. Sara wondered what was in it. Alex plumped the pillows against the headboard, then eyed Sara. "So, the firestorm is why I got attacked by dragons?"

"Yes. The firestorm happens when a *Pyr* meets his destined mate. *Pyr* and *Slayers* can all sense the firestorm. *Slayers* try to stop *Pyr* from breeding, usually by trying to kill the human mate."

"Nice." Alex grimaced. "How long do *Pyr* live?"

"Long. Hundreds of years."

"And how many firestorms do they get?"

"One in a lifetime, I think, if they're lucky."

Alex grinned impishly. "That's no-hassle birth control."

Sara laughed and her hand fell to her stomach.

Alex watched Sara's gesture. "When was your firestorm?"

"July. The blood test came back positive in August."

"You look happy."

"I am." Sara ran out of words, so she smiled and shrugged. Alex smiled in turn and Sara felt a connection with the other woman.

Alex sobered and wrapped her arms around her bent knees. "How does the firestorm end?"

"When you have sex the first time, the firestorm is over."

"Why?"

"Because the woman conceives."

"The first time?" Alex was skeptical. "The women always conceive the first time they do it with their *Pyr* partner?"

"Yes." Sara patted her belly. "It happened for us."

Alex was clearly unpersuaded. "That's really against the odds. Unless the firestorm synchronizes with the woman's cycle . . ."

"I don't know the biology. I only know what happened to me."

Alex thought about that for a moment. "But you and Quinn are still together, even though the firestorm is over?"

Sara nodded and felt she should warn the other woman. "There are two schools of thought about the firestorm. Some *Pyr*, like Quinn, think that it indicates that the *Pyr* has found his life partner, that he's more with his mate than he is alone. It's like our idea of a one true love."

Alex nodded, her eyelids drooping. She shook herself and straightened. "But others?"

"Think it's just a chance to breed, or maybe an obligation to make more *Pyr*. They have their firestorm, then carry on, leaving the woman to raise the child."

"But isn't the child a *Pyr*? Isn't that the point? If the *Pyr* father left the woman to raise the *Pyr* child alone, how would she teach it what it needed to know?"

"The *Pyr* don't come into their shape shifting abilities until puberty. I guess in those cases when the father leaves early, the other *Pyr* intervene to instruct the boy when he has his change."

"He?" Alex asked, doing a bad job of trying to disguise a yawn. She looked as if she wanted to stay awake and talk, but her body had other ideas. "Aren't there any female *Pyr*?"

"Just one at a time. She's called the Wyvern and is a prophetess." Sara shrugged. "She's lovely, but mysterious."

Alex forced her eyes open. "You met her?"

"We saved her from the *Slayers*." Sara smiled. "But I think that's a story I should save for another night. Get some sleep, Alex. We'll go shopping for clothes in the morning. I promise."

"Shower, sleep, and clean underwear." Alex nestled down into the bed and yawned again. "Forget dragons and *Slayers* and Wyverns: I've found myself a fairy godmother."

Sara laughed, but Alex was already asleep.

"I went looking for Keir right after Donovan found him," Rafferty continued. "I thought I might be able to reconcile the two of them. It must have been three hundred and fifty years ago now."

Donovan sat down heavily. "Three hundred and sixty-five." He believed Rafferty but he knew what he'd seen, as well.

"What happened?" Sloane asked.

"Keir was in Tortuga, where the buccaneers took haven. The tavern was full of drunks when I arrived. The brawl started shortly after that, when I was still figuring out who Keir was." Rafferty spared a glance at Donovan. "There's a resemblance, but it's only skin-deep. You *were* right about him."

"Thank you." Donovan couldn't help but bristle. He didn't like talking about his father, didn't like to remember how that man had abandoned him, didn't like to recall how he'd had to fend for himself for most of his life. The past was over and done.

"The fight broke out and it spread like a disease." Rafferty's words slowed as he remembered the scene. "There were dozens of them, brawling and shouting. It was chaos. I finally saw Keir but I couldn't get to him."

"He was fighting, too?" Niall guessed. "Giving as good as he got?"

Rafferty shook his head.

"He was in dragon form?" Quinn asked. "Meeting fire with fire?"

Donovan was impatient with his friends' attempts to paint his father in any noble light. "Keir told me he refused to shift anymore," he said. "He was determined to be human, because he'd decided the *Pyr* side of him was evil."

Rafferty snorted. "It was the human side of him that was stealing a keg of rum. The owner shot at him with a musket from behind the bar. The shot missed, but Keir tripped when he was ducking it. He broke his neck, either in the fall or in the trampling of the fight."

"He might not have died," Donovan felt obliged to note.

"They buried him the next day," Rafferty insisted. "I went to the funeral, such as it was, to be sure. I asked the earth a month later if he'd stayed put and he had."

"But he was here tonight," Quinn said with a frown. "I saw him. He was peridot and silver, and resembled Donovan in human form."

"It was Keir." Donovan had no doubt.

"But how can that be?" Niall asked. "He was buried a month and the earth doesn't lie. That eliminates all doubt."

"I'm not sure he was alive tonight," Donovan mused, and began his pacing again. "He didn't bleed. He couldn't feel dragonfire, even when it scorched him, and he couldn't tell when he was injured. He just kept on fighting, even when he lost limbs."

"It was as if he didn't notice," Quinn said, and the *Pyr* shuddered as one.

"Then how did you stop him?" Sloane asked.

"We dismembered him," Quinn added softly. "Then burned him to ash. It was the only way."

Rafferty sat down. "I'll ask the earth if he's still in that Caribbean grave."

"He's not," Donovan said. "Somebody roused him and turned him into whatever he was tonight." He turned to Sloane. "What if he wasn't exposed to all four elements when he died? What could happen to him?"

Sloane shrugged. "I don't know."

"The *Slayers* know," Quinn pointed out. "They revived Ambrose when his fallen body wasn't exposed to water."

"Or Ambrose revived himself." Donovan focused on Sloane. "How would you heal one of us, if we seemed dead but hadn't been exposed to all four elements?"

"Theoretically speaking," Rafferty added gently.

Sloane frowned, seeming more intense than usual. "I've been trying to find the secret since we learned about Ambrose last summer. I think I've identified the right manuscript. It's old, though, and it's written in a cipher I can't decode."

"You will," Niall said. "You have the patience for it."

Sloane shuddered. "It's more than an intellectual exercise. I dislike the manuscript. It has a bad feel to it. I had to copy it out to even be able to work on it."

"Maybe there's a protective spell on it," Rafferty said.

"There's no such thing as magic." Quinn's tone was dismissive.

"But there are mysteries we have yet to understand," Rafferty replied. "It could be charged with a protection that looks like magic to us."

Erik cleared his throat. He'd been following the conversation, his eyes gleaming. "Or it might be a new development. The Wyvern said that things were possible during the period of these three eclipses that had never been possible before. She said doors that had never been open before were open to the past."

"Why doesn't that sound good?" Niall murmured.

Donovan decided to tell them the rest. "There's more, too."

"You mean it gets worse?" Niall asked.

"There's another *Slayer*," Donovan said. "He says he's Tyson and intends to avenge Everett's death. I thought that was why he attacked Alex and me, but he didn't challenge me to a blood duel."

"Why not?" Sloane asked.

"Maybe he doesn't know who killed Everett," Rafferty guessed. "He doesn't know that we three did it together."

"We should all challenge him," Quinn said.

"No!" Erik protested. "No blood duels now. It's a distraction from our greater purpose."

"But if he's bent on revenge—" Niall began to argue.

"Let him go without it," Erik snapped. "We don't have the luxury of indulging in blood duels now. Tell him that he has to challenge all three of you simultaneously, if he insists."

Donovan kept quiet, knowing that Tyson would never play according to any rules imposed by the *Pyr*. Nor would he abandon his quest for vengeance. He thought about Rafferty, who was moving more slowly than once he had, and about Quinn's commitment to Sara, and knew that, if it came down to it, he would answer Tyson's challenge alone to protect his fellows.

He might ride solo, but he played for the team.

"How did he find Alex?" Sloane asked.

"He must have been attracted to the firestorm," Quinn said.

Donovan frowned. "How did they know to attack the lab, then? It was before she and I met, before the firestorm sparked."

"It's forbidden for the Wyvern to share the name of the human who will experience the firestorm," Erik said quietly.

"She told you," Donovan reminded his leader.

"She wouldn't have told Boris." Erik was adamant.

"She told Boris Sara's name," Quinn observed.

"She was tortured for that," Erik reminded them, but the truth was that no one knew what Sophie would do.

"I'm thinking that the fire at Gilchrist Enterprises wasn't an accident," Donovan said. "I'm thinking someone is stalking my mate, and was doing so even before I knew she was my mate."

Erik pivoted and turned back to his laptop, his move looking a lot like guilt to Donovan.

"What do you know about it?"

"It was *Slayer*s," Erik said tersely. "Sophie showed me when she told me Alex's name."

Donovan's heart clenched. "In advance? You knew *in advance* that the fire would happen?"

Erik looked irritated. "You know how portents are. I knew pieces of it, but not the whole thing—"

"We could have prevented the fire!" Donovan roared, interrupting his leader. "We could have ensured that Alex was safe, instead of keeping our distance!"

Erik gave him a cool glance. "I thought you didn't want a mate."

"Alex could have been killed in that fire!" The *Pyr*

smothered smiles, as if he'd fulfilled some expectation. Donovan glared at them. "Humans are part of the treasure we are charged to protect."

"You're not talking about protecting humans in general," Sloane commented.

Niall held up a finger. "Just one specific human."

"A pretty one," Sloane noted.

"Who happens to be your destined mate," Rafferty added.

"Who happens to be the one human who has made an invention that could turn the tide against the *Slayers*," Erik said. "Sophie told me that humans have to help themselves to correct the injustices done to the earth. Alex's Green Machine is a big part of that, which is why the *Slayers* tried to destroy it. Sophie also told me that we couldn't prevent the fire."

"Sophie talks a lot of garbage," Donovan said.

"Which is why I tried to stop the fire, anyway," Erik replied. "The lab was hidden, disguised under false names. I only just identified it on the day of the fire."

Donovan wasn't interested in excuses. "Funny. *Slayers* found it easily enough."

Erik met Donovan's glare with one of his own. "Maybe they had more time." He shook his head. "Besides, I don't think they intended to kill her that night."

"She has burns on her hands . . . ," Donovan protested.

"She was outnumbered," Erik interrupted crisply. "And confronted by at least one *Slayer*. They could have easily killed her, as I suspect they killed her partner. I think they wanted to scare her and to destroy the prototype. That done, they let her go."

"But why?" Niall asked.

Erik turned to face him. "Because if you want to destroy an invention, you have to eliminate every crumb of information that would allow it to be rebuilt again. When all of that is destroyed, then you eliminate the last person who remembers how to do it."

Donovan stared out the window at the night. He was thinking of the Ziploc that Alex had retrieved from the lab. *Slayers* had let her go and she was doing exactly what they expected of her. "They're following her. They're going to let her collect all of the backup data, and then they'll kill her."

Erik nodded once and looked at the carpet. "And that's what we have to keep from happening."

No one argued with that.

The smoke was obscuring her vision but Alex knew the way. She eased down the hall to the lab and the Green Machine, hearing the sounds of struggle ahead of her.

He screamed again—Mark, who never raised his voice—and the hair stood up on the back of her neck. She was terrified, her breath coming in anxious gasps, but she had to help Mark.

She froze in the doorway to the lab, her eyes wide. There were two dragons in the bay beside the wreckage of the Green Machine, two dragons so massive that they filled the industrial space. Fire burned all around them, casting the scene in black and orange tones. The prototype vehicle had been smashed beyond recognition.

The large amber dragon held Mark captive. He clutched Alex's partner in massive talons that shone like the weapons they were. His amber scales gleamed like jewels in the firelight as he held Mark off the ground.

Mark was incoherent in his fear. His glasses had broken on one side and his clothing was torn. He was struggling, but it made no difference.

He was bleeding.

The dragons were laughing.

The second dragon, the red one, leaned toward Mark, and Mark flinched at his approach. This one's scales could have been made of rubies edged in gold. He glittered as well, his savage beauty matched with malicious intent. He lifted a claw and held up Mark's broken glasses so he could see his opponent. Mark shook as he was forced to look into the face of his tormentor.

"Tell me," whispered the dragon. His voice was low and horrible. It rasped and resonated, making the walls shake. "Tell me all about the Green Machine."

"No!" Mark shouted, and the amber dragon ripped one talon down the length of Mark's chest. His shirt was shredded and one dark line was opened down the length of his torso. Blood flowed from the open wound and Mark screamed. . . .

Alex awakened, her breath coming in anxious spurts once again. Two nightmares in one night. That had to be a new record.

But then, facing dragons could be expected to have that effect.

She kept still, listening before she opened her eyes. She could hear Sara's slow breathing. It was dark and the hotel was quiet.

Alex opened her eyes and let her vision adjust. A slice of night came through the drapes. The clock radio read three fifteen.

It was early Monday. She didn't have a lot of time left.

Sara was sleeping on the couch on the far side of the room and lamplight spilled through the crack of the door that opened into the main room. In the light that shone at the bottom of the door to the hall, Alex could see two shadows, two shadows the size of a man's two feet.

The *Pyr* were standing guard over her.

Alex didn't know whether that was a good thing or not. On the one hand, Donovan had protected her from that attacking *Slayer*. On the other, he had killed his father, apparently without regrets.

Alex recalled the sight of Donovan in his dragon form and her mouth went dry. He was both splendid and terrifying. And in human form, he certainly made her tingle. She'd never had such mixed feelings in anyone's presence before.

The man was trouble, no matter how she looked at it.

And he was distracting. Even if the *Pyr* had been on her side, Donovan's presence was precisely what could keep Alex from rebuilding her prototype in time. Thinking obsessively about sex was not conducive to analysis and problem solving.

But there were dragons hunting her. Alex's breath hitched. Did she dare to be on her own?

The prospect was terrifying, but how could she do anything else? Alex had a lifetime policy of refusing to let fear govern her choices and she wasn't going to let it govern this one. There was too much at stake. She routinely challenged her own ideas of what she could do. She was afraid of *Slayers*, sure, but she needed to rebuild her prototype.

Away from Donovan.

And really, if she was away from Donovan, then there'd be no heat of the firestorm to attract *Slayers* to her precise location. They'd found her and Mark at the lab before, but that was an obvious place to look for her. After a couple of data collections, Alex intended to retreat to a refuge.

The only one who knew there was a backup prototype was Mark. The only one who knew where that backup prototype was stashed was Mark.

And Mark was dead.

To save her invention, Alex had to escape the *Pyr*'s protective custody. She got out of bed, filled with resolve and terror, and pulled on Donovan's sweats again.

Those two shadows stopped her from taking the obvious exit.

Maybe she'd have better luck with another door.

Alex eased toward the connecting door, then peered into the central room of the suite. The *Pyr* who had driven the hearse was sleeping on one couch. The drapes were open in this room, admitting the glow of streetlights. Alex could see a balcony outside the sliding glass door and sky beyond it.

She took a step into the room; the sleeping *Pyr* didn't stir.

His breathing was steady and deep, too steady and deep for him to be pretending. There was a door on the far side of the room and she assumed there was another bedroom. That door was closed. How many *Pyr* had there been when she arrived? She thought there'd been six altogether, but wouldn't have bet on her count.

The same shadow pattern appeared below the door to the corridor. Another *Pyr* was standing guard there. That made three.

And it left the far bedroom as an escape option.

Or the balcony.

Where was Donovan? Alex wondered whether he was sleeping in the far room or doing sentry duty. She wondered how he looked asleep. She wondered whether the spark would light between them when he was unconscious. She told herself she'd never know and that that was a good thing.

Part of her didn't believe it.

With a glance at the sleeping *Pyr*, Alex took another cautious step into the room. She stopped cold when the hair prickled on the back of her neck—someone was watching her. She surveyed the room, her heart leaping when she saw him.

Donovan lounged in one of the easy chairs on the far side of the room. He'd pushed it back into the corner, as if he were guarding the sliding door to the balcony, and he was wreathed in shadows.

But he was watching her. His eyes were gleaming slits, narrow and unblinking and fixed upon her. He was so still that she couldn't see him breathing. Donovan had changed, because his T-shirt was white now. It made him look even more like James Dean than he had before, more tanned and more sexy.

More dangerous.

When their gazes locked and held, Alex forgot about leaving. The glittering green of Donovan's eyes held her motionless. Captive. The air in the room seemed to shimmer, the way it did over pavement in the middle of summer. The hotel room was sweltering.

She felt the perspiration sliding down the center of her back, felt the dampness gather between her thighs. Her heartbeat accelerated. Her breath came more quickly and her temples were damp. Sweat moistened her palms and gathered on her upper lip.

All Alex could think of was Donovan. Donovan naked; Donovan tanned and strong; Donovan touching her with those fabulous hands; Donovan easing a fingertip over her nipple; Donovan fanning the flames of her desire.

Donovan shifted on his seat and the shadow in his jeans revealed they were thinking exactly the same thing.

"That's far enough." Donovan's low words reminded Alex of what he was and what he could do, and a part of her was afraid. He was dangerous, a relentless killing machine. He was a dragon, a whole lot like the dragons who had killed Mark so viciously.

The other part of her lusted for him with a frightening intensity, to the exclusion of everything else. Had he been a normal man, she would have indulged in a one-nighter, then forgotten him.

But Donovan wasn't a normal man.

He pointed back to the bedroom she'd left. Alex hesitated. It wasn't like her to back down, but she wasn't going to get past him to the other bedroom. She certainly wasn't going to manage to run, not with his attention so firmly fixed on her.

She tore her gaze away from Donovan's with an effort and immediately felt that she'd surrendered something precious. She fled back into the bedroom, pulling the door behind herself so it closed with a resolute click.

Alex leaned back against the door, still simmering, and stared at the ceiling. She knew when she'd reached an impasse—it happened all the time in her research. A dead end meant retracking, formulating a new hypothesis, and seeking a new solution. Escaping Donovan tonight wasn't going to happen.

Her moment would come—she just had to be vigilant.

Time for Plan B.

She frowned in the darkness and knew she couldn't just run. No, she'd have to disguise herself. She recalled her earlier thought of releasing her inner biker chick and liked it.

When Sara took her shopping in the morning, Alex would buy things she'd never usually buy. No one who knew Alex Madison would be looking for her in spiked boots and leather. It wouldn't be a disguise that would work for long, but it might work long enough.

All she had to do was retrieve two different sets of backups and get to her refuge without being caught.

By dragons.

Deep in the forest, the Wyvern stretched her body across the snow. She laid her ear to the earth and listened to anguish.

She understood that Gaia fought for her own survival with the four elements at her disposal. Earthquakes gathered force deep underground, their fissures working toward the surface. Tsunamis roiled in the midst of the oceans, mustering toward coastlines. Tropical storms swirled into the intensity of hurricanes, then headed for islands. Fires raged over hillsides and rolled down toward sleeping towns.

The Wyvern knew that she had waited too long to intervene in human affairs. She could have ensured that the *Pyr* bred with greater haste, that they had made better choices. She tasted failure, a failure more imminent due to her own choices, and knew that the time for standing aside was past.

She put herself in tune with the earth, listening to the planet's moans, then tried to influence events. She eased the landfall of a tsunami farther along the shore, so that it missed a large town. She blew a fire back into the mountains, away from the homes of humans. She eased the

tension along a fault line, diminishing the force of an earth-
quake in a populous region. She coaxed a tropical storm
back out over the water, so that its might fell upon the
breadth of the sea instead of on shore.

It was exhausting work and a losing battle. Each disaster
she averted was replaced by half a dozen new potential dis-
asters. Gaia would find her balance again, regardless of the
human cost.

Unless the *Pyr* helped.

Sophie felt the bedrock of Donovan's resistance to his
own firestorm and feared the worst. Her optimism faltered,
then took a fatal hit when she sensed again the black void of
the *Slayers'* secret academy.

It drew her thoughts closer, as if it would suck her into its
vortex. It snared her, summoning her thoughts like a dark
magnet. Sophie knew it had found her because she had in-
tervened. Those in the dark academy also tried to use Gaia's
power for their own ends and they resented any interference.

They would destroy humans. They were *Slayers*.

What was the nature of their academy? Sophie was
tempted to explore, but she knew the temptation was treachery. They would snare her own power and turn it to their
dark purpose. They would destroy her forever, Sophie knew.

She wrenched her thoughts away from the dark vortex
with an effort. There was one who could probe its secrets
and emerge unscathed—but she didn't know who it was.

She knew only who it *wasn't*.

Sophie closed her eyes against the obstacles before her.
She felt the anguish of the humans she hadn't been able to
help on this night. She was burdened by the knowledge she
possessed and terrified of the extent of her ignorance.

The *Pyr* were losing this last battle, unaware of the evils
against them. Along with the *Pyr*, humans would be lost.
The mission of the Wyvern and her kind would fail, and fail
beyond redemption.

And she was partly to blame.

Futility cast a shadow on her heart. In the quiet of the forest, the Wyvern wept.

Much later, Sophie rolled to her back and opened her eyes. Countless stars glistened overhead, their beauty a reminder of the power and compassion of the Great Wyvern. She tasted the spark of human optimism and felt hope.

All was not lost. It could not be. It was said that no one was granted a burden she could not carry. Sophie stared at the starry sky and reviewed what tools she had at her disposal. She wondered how best she could muster her own forces.

Then she knew.

It was against tradition to interfere directly with the *Pyr*, but the rules were being shattered by the *Slayers*. Sophie saw no reason not to break a few of her own.

The price of failure was too great to do otherwise.

Sophie closed her eyes and prayed for the Great Wyvern's aid. She didn't wait for an approval that might not come. It was time to act. Instead, she conjured a fistful of dreams and cast them into the night, directing them to those who had need of them.

First, the Seer.

Sara dreamed of furrows in the earth.

She was buried in the soil, one of a long line of seeds. The seeds looked like pearls against the rich loam, or like drops of moonlight. As Sara watched, the seeds on each side of her sprouted, but they didn't grow roots and leaves and shoots.

They grew arms and legs, fingers and toes. They turned into men as she watched, men as strong and fierce as Quinn. They sprang from the soil, fully formed and ready to fight.

Sara's hand curved protectively over her belly. She knew that she dreamed of Quinn's seed taking root in her womb.

She knew there were lots of seeds in her dream because she'd have many sons with Quinn.

But Sara was wrong about her dream's meaning.

In the darkness of a Minneapolis hotel room, Erik entered a meditative state, close to sleep but not quite the same. He dispatched his thoughts in the direction of the shadow he had sensed time and again. It was a place he could locate only by feel, a place he did not want to find.

He found its aura of evil and guided his thoughts stealthily to the portal. It was open, but filled with a brooding darkness. He was both drawn to it and repelled by it. He feared his own fate if he entered, but feared more for the *Pyr* if he did not enter.

It was his role to lead, after all, and lead without regard to his own survival. Ignorance did them no service.

Erik drew ever closer, eased to the threshold, and braced himself to enter its foul darkness. . . .

The portal suddenly disappeared, as surely as if a door had been slammed and barred against him.

"Not you," the Wyvern whispered in old-speak, and Erik was honest enough to acknowledge his relief.

Not him. His eyes flew open in the darkness.

Then who?

Sloane bent over his book in Erik's bedroom. Despite having solved similar riddles dozens of times, the key to this ancient script eluded him. He was tired and impatient but couldn't let down his fellow *Pyr*. He had to solve this.

Sloane felt Erik stir, and cast a glance at the leader of the *Pyr*. Erik was awake but lost in thought, frowning at the ceiling.

Sloane turned back to his work, unwilling to disturb Erik with his doubts. The letters of the transcription shimmered before his eyes, as if a magnifying glass had been passed across them. He blinked, fearing that he was too tired to work, then stared.

He could read the text. It had transformed itself. Sloane read greedily, devouring the information presented in the first two sentences; then that glimmer passed over the work again.

The text had returned to its original state.

But Sloane had had a glimpse of its deciphered truth.

He quickly wrote down what he had seen. With the first two sentences decoded, he could find the key. He set to work with new enthusiasm, knowing that he'd learn the hidden truth soon.

Quinn dreamed of his forge.

He was back in his studio, hammering the scales that should have repaired the armor of Sloane and Niall. He watched the flames leap, felt their healing power. He welcomed the weight of the hammer in his hand, knew the grip of the tongs on each scale in turn was sure. He felt the power of the Smith surge through him as he hammered each scale into its true shape.

He tasted the bitterness of failure when each refused to adhere. He was the Smith. His role was to heal his kind. How could that be impossible?

"Not impossible," whispered a woman in old-speak, and Quinn knew he was not alone. He turned to face the Wyvern, who had silently entered both his dream and his shop.

He stared into the magnificent turquoise of her eyes and felt a communion with something older and wiser than himself. Quinn's heart skipped when he saw his father in the Wyvern's eyes, the clear blue of his father's eyes so much like Quinn's own.

His father, the father Quinn had known for only five short years, smiled; then he shared his knowledge. Quinn could hear his father's wisdom, echoing in his thoughts like old-speak, as long as he held the Wyvern's unblinking gaze.

She let him look. She opened a portal to the past for Quinn.

His father's knowledge flowed to him, like heat moving along a length of steel, illuminating the metal as it progressed. Quinn *could* heal his fellows. Rafferty was right: it had to happen during the firestorm. But the key to success was the willingness of the human mate to participate.

Quinn had to learn to wait. He had to learn to identify the best moment.

But he could do it.

The lost knowledge of Thierry de Béziers that Quinn found in Sophie's eyes told him how.

Rafferty dreamed of the past. He dreamed in the rich hues of medieval manuscripts; he dreamed of blood and glory and triumph. He dreamed of old stories of valor.

He found himself at a familiar hearth, smelling the peat fire he had known as a child. He saw his grandfather, sitting by the fire with his long legs crossed at the ankle. Rafferty's grandfather had never been old and feeble. His eyes had flashed with frequent fire and even when he slept, there had been a glimmer of watchfulness between his lids.

He had taught Rafferty everything Rafferty knew.

Rafferty was back at that fireside, rapt at his grandfather's feet as the flames leapt high on the hearth. His grandfather leaned down, eyes gleaming with ancient fire, and confided a prophecy Rafferty had never heard before.

It made perfect sense, as prophecies seldom do.

Rafferty awakened abruptly, startled to find himself in the chill of a hotel room instead of beside that fire. His grandfather's words resonated in his thoughts.

Rafferty studied Donovan, who dozed opposite him. He knew that any change in Donovan was Alex's to make.

Rafferty would wait for his moment.

Donovan dreamed of his own past. He was on the streets of Dublin, begging for pennies and scrounging food, as he had done for years. He was lean and young and hungry. He turned a corner and almost collided with a younger version of himself.

He stared in shock at Delaney, and Delaney stared in shock at him. There was an instant connection between them, some recognition of their similarity. It was beyond a physical resemblance, and he remembered the compelling force of that recognition.

They were both *Pyr*, although neither of them knew the name of their nature at the time. It would be weeks before they confided their secret in each other, but from that moment of meeting, they were inseparable. They were a team.

Donovan called them cousins as a joke. Neither had had any family, but they had each other. Why not be cousins?

In his dream, he raised a hand to Delaney as he had on that long-ago day, and Delaney lifted his hand, too.

But in the dream, as Delaney's fingertips approached Donovan's own, a clear barrier descended between them. The wall of glass turned all beyond it to darkness. The light in Delaney's eyes died when contact was obstructed, and recognition disappeared.

Shard of my talon. Keir's last taunt echoed in Donovan's thoughts and carried the resonance of truth. Donovan had promised to protect Delaney. He'd promised to take care of him.

He'd failed. Delaney had been killed by *Slayers*, and worse, his body had been claimed by them. Donovan stirred in his sleep, not liking the reminder of his failure.

Then the barrier was abruptly lit, turning from glass to a mirror. Donovan saw Keir's reflection beside him. He might have turned to fight his father, but Keir's image was superimposed on Delaney's face. Donovan's own reflection—and his shock—was alongside. The similarities were striking.

"Not cousins," whispered the Wyvern in old-speak.

No.

Brothers.

Shards of Keir's talon, both cast out by their mother when their *Pyr* nature made itself known. His father had come back, unbeknownst to Donovan, and slept with his mother again.

It must have been before she knew what Donovan was, before she had called him devil's spawn. Or maybe the realization had been concurrent with her discovery that she was pregnant again.

Donovan's eyes flew open and he stared unseeingly at the hotel room as his heart pounded. Delaney was about a dozen years younger than he was. Donovan had been cast out of his mother's home at twelve, at puberty. They had different surnames, but Donovan's mother had been capable of telling a lie.

Brothers.

Donovan had let Delaney down when it mattered most. Was he truly his father's son? Was he as selfish as Keir?

Or could he choose to be different?

Chapter 6

The next morning, Donovan and Quinn loitered outside a women's clothing store, standing guard over a pile of packages while Sara and Alex shopped. It didn't fit Donovan's idea of hoard, but no one was asking for his input. Quinn stared into the store, keeping a vigilant eye on his mate.

"You're going to spook someone," Donovan advised. "Some woman will decide you're a creep and set the mall cops on us."

Quinn folded his arms across his chest but otherwise didn't move. "Sara will defend me."

"Being one woman's personal peeper isn't much better."

Quinn didn't move.

"And you can sense her fear without watching her, anyway."

"She might not see the threat first." Quinn gave Donovan a stern look. "*Slayers* are hunting your mate. I'm not going to let Sara get caught in the cross fire."

"Thanks for the reminder." Donovan scowled. "I hate malls."

"Don't tell me it makes you long for the old days." Quinn moved a step closer to the store and narrowed his eyes. "They've gone into the fitting rooms."

"There's no way a *Slayer* could sneak in there."

"Don't be so sure."

Silence stretched between them. There were a lot of women in the mall, most of them pushing fancy strollers and sipping fancy coffees. Seniors in the midst of their power walks ducked around the women, relentless in their pursuit of a quicker speed. A group of half a dozen young children with their mothers passed by, noisily negotiating their visit to the aquarium.

Donovan was impatient with all of it. "What if it does make me think of the old days?" He pushed himself to his feet. "You have to remember how stupendous a woman could look. Brocade shoes and lace collars, velvet doublets and corsets."

"Fuss," Quinn said.

"Yes, *fuss*. I love fuss." Donovan pushed the image of Olivia out of his thoughts. "Stockings and garters and acres of petticoats. Undressing a woman was an adventure and a half. It could take all night." His voice dropped low. "There'd be lace everywhere. Great Wyvern, but I love the look of white lace against a woman's skin."

He scowled at the floor, convinced that Alex would make practical purchases. She'd reappear in Dockers and a polo shirt, with a sensible sports bra underneath it all. She'd wear walking shoes and would dress in taupe and olive, or navy and white. While he could appreciate a cleanly athletic look, there were times when a little feminine flourish was welcome.

Maybe her practical clothing choices were a kind of gift, a chance for him to keep from consummating his firestorm.

Was Erik misleading him about the *Pyr* needing to complete these three firestorms to survive? Erik always wanted the *Pyr* to breed—if nothing else, Erik knew exactly how to get to him. He knew that Donovan would play for the team.

Donovan wasn't going to imagine Alex in lace. The sight of her breasts beneath his own T-shirt was branded on his brain. He didn't want to even begin to envision her tanned curves accented with lace, but his imagination did it anyway.

The firestorm didn't fight fair.

Meanwhile, Quinn smiled at his comments. "You can take the dragon out of the Renaissance," he drawled, and Donovan laughed.

"Pretty much."

"There are things about the past that you don't miss." Quinn mused. "I don't miss medieval sanitary facilities, for example."

Donovan tried to play along with the conversational diversion. "Rats. There's a species I'm happy to live without."

"Not many Ducatis in the Renaissance," Quinn teased.

Donovan laughed. "Although a beautiful horse is almost as good. There was one stallion I had, just as black as coal. There was something a bit wild about him. I remember Delaney riding him—" He stopped, unable to continue because of the lump in his throat.

The past was showing an annoying tendency not to stay put.

"Dental care is better," Quinn said, offering a way past a painful memory.

Donovan felt obliged to reply in kind. "Wine is better."

"Central heating."

"Air-conditioning." Donovan nodded. "Spa bathrooms. Hotels."

"Towels."

This time Donovan didn't reply. He was too busy staring. Sara and Alex were at the cash desk at the front of the store and Alex had changed clothes in the fitting room.

She was stunning. She wore black leather pants that clung like a second skin, emphasizing the length of her legs. They and the black boots with stiletto heels made her look as fast and wild as the racehorse he'd been remembering.

She'd bought a white poet's blouse that was full, cut low, sheer, and edged with miles of lace. White lace. She was poetry in motion, her choices edgy yet elegant. Donovan's eyes nearly fell out of his head.

"Fuss," Quinn commented under his breath.

"Got it in one," Donovan muttered in shock. His objection to the firestorm, which he'd been sure was so logical, now seemed as substantial as a house of cards.

He wanted Alex with a force that stunned him.

Alex turned to glance his way and even at a distance, the sight of her stopped his heart. Her dark eyes were outlined and her lashes darkened, making her eyes look more exotic and mysterious. She wore red lipstick and had a candy red leather jacket slung over her shoulder. Gold hoop earrings brushed against her cheek.

She smiled slowly, maybe sensing his appreciation, and the firestorm kicked it up a notch.

What was he going to do?

Before he could decide, he and Quinn had company.

"How nice," drawled a familiar voice.

Donovan and Quinn spun. Boris Vassily stood a dozen feet away in his human form, his hands shoved into his pockets. He was as pale and predatory as always and Donovan didn't trust him one bit. The stocky man behind him was the *Slayer* Donovan had fought the previous night.

"Tyson," he muttered in old-speak to Quinn.

"Caught his scent," Quinn agreed.

"Shopping with the ladies," sneered Tyson. "How bourgeois."

"Unmanly," Boris agreed, and smiled coldly.

"When did you last have some, Boris?" Donovan taunted.

Boris's eyes flashed as he glanced toward the store where Alex and Sara were. His smile became colder. "I like the women of the *Pyr* well enough not to need one of my own. I can't decide, though, whether I prefer a pregnant mate to a mate in firestorm." He turned to Tyson. "You?"

"Tough call," Tyson said, frowning. "Maybe we should do a blind taste test. There's one of each available, after all."

The two *Slayers* took a step forward. Donovan could feel that Quinn was within a hair of shifting shape in defense of his mate.

In a crowded mall. There was no amount of beguiling that could fix that sight.

He had to do something, Erik's edict be damned.

Donovan tossed his challenge coin at Tyson.

The credit card faked in the name of Meredith Maloney was approved time and again without a quibble, which meant that no one was on to her yet. Alex smiled at the clerk as she took the pen to sign, acting as if she'd expected nothing different.

Sara picked up her purchases from the cash desk, then halted beside Alex. "*Slayers*," she hissed, catching her breath.

Alex glanced at the smaller woman with confusion. Sara was staring into the mall, watching Donovan and Quinn talk to two other men. Alex could feel the hostility of the exchange even from this distance.

"How do you know?" she asked.

"The fair one is Boris Vassily, leader of the *Slayers*." Sara spoke quickly, betraying her own nervousness. "I don't know the other one, but they're together."

"You know Boris?"

Sara shivered and swallowed. "He beguiled and kidnapped me last summer." She watched the exchange intently. "Quinn will rip him apart, given half a chance. I hope that's not what they're counting on." She scanned the mall, probably seeking other dragon men of her acquaintance.

Alex felt Plan B coming on. Two *Slayers* were confronted by Donovan and Quinn. A third *Slayer* was burned to cinders. This could be all of the bad dragons, present and/or accounted for.

Even better, the effect of the firestorm was diminished

with distance. She was aware of Donovan waiting in the
mall, but his presence wasn't as distracting as it had been.
More distance might diminish the effect even more.

Enough that she could work.

Enough that *Slayers* couldn't find her.

This might be her only chance.

"Should we stay here, then?" she asked, pretending to be
less decisive than she was.

Sara scanned the store, as if she expected *Slayers* to leap
out of the racks of jeans and sweaters. "Let's just keep shopping for a minute or two," she suggested. "And watch."

"We should separate," Alex suggested, "so it's less obvious that we're together."

"Good idea," Sara said, and Alex felt a twinge of guilt for
tricking someone who had only been nice to her.

But the Green Machine was more important than a tiny
bit of deception. Alex headed for the back of the store as if
browsing, making steady progress toward the employees'
entrance she'd seen beyond the fitting rooms.

She could get a taxi and get to her apartment while the
Pyr kept the *Slayers* busy. That would be one more predictable stop behind her. She'd be one step closer to refuge.

Sara was looking out the front of the store. Alex seized
her moment and lunged toward the employees' entrance.
She was through the door and on the sidewalk in a heartbeat,
looking for a cab.

On the way, Alex pulled the new cell phone out of her
Ziploc and called Mr. Sinclair. He wasn't in, so she left a
message, confirming that she'd pick him up Thursday.

Alex and the Green Machine would be ready.

Tyson caught Donovan's coin instinctively.

Then he opened his hand, as if surprised by what he had
done. The four shape shifters stared at the silver dollar on
his palm. They all knew that the blood duel of Donovan's
challenge had been accepted.

And that only one dragon would survive the fight.

"Fool," Quinn chided in old-speak.

Donovan said nothing. He was right and he knew it. He had no doubt that he'd win.

"Idiot," Boris said to Tyson. "You should have let it fall."

Tyson's gaze rose slowly to meet Donovan's.

"I killed Everett," Donovan lied, feeling Quinn's disapproval of this claim. Quinn, like Rafferty, preferred full truths. Donovan found use in partial stories—especially when he was protecting Quinn, Sara, and Rafferty from a fight none of them needed. "We have unfinished business, you and I."

Tyson smiled and closed his hand over the coin before he pocketed it. "You're right." He glanced around, smiling at the milling shoppers. "But not here. Not now."

"When?" Donovan tried to sound casual, even though he wanted to fight immediately. "Where?"

"I'll let you know." Tyson smiled, then nudged Boris.

"That's not how it's done," Quinn protested.

"Rules are for fools," Boris said, his cold smile proving that he had overheard Quinn's old-speak.

The two *Slayers* turned and sauntered away. They disappeared into the crowd, two men with their hands shoved in their pockets. They looked for all the world as if they were killing time while waiting on their wives.

"That was stupid," Quinn told Donovan. "Now he can call you out anytime. He can surprise you, or wait for you to be alone."

"Would you rather he challenged you?"

Quinn got a stubborn look. "He could take Alex, the way he took Sara. She could be hurt."

"You have obligations now, Quinn."

"So do you!"

"You have more. What about Sara? You can't just undertake a blood duel whenever it suits you."

"What *about* Sara?" Quinn would have lunged for the

clothing store, but Sara was only a dozen feet away and closing fast. His relief was tangible.

"Are they gone?" she asked in an undertone.

"For now," Quinn said grimly. He took her parcels, still
shimmering on the cusp of change. Donovan averted his
gaze, knowing very well how Quinn would prefer to reassure himself of his mate's safety.

There was no sign of a leggy brunette in a red leather
jacket. Donovan suddenly had a bad feeling. "Where's
Alex?"

Sara glanced back. "I called to her. She suggested we
separate and she headed for the back of the store. . . ."

Donovan didn't listen to any more. He raced into the
store, not really surprised to find no sign of his mate. He understood now why she'd gotten up in the middle of the
night—she'd been planning to run again and his presence
had stopped her.

He barged into the fitting-room area, startling the clerk.

"Sir! You *cannot* be here." The older woman stood up
and tried to block his path. "It's not allowed—"

"A woman, dark hair, red jacket, leather pants." Donovan
interrupted her impatiently. "Did she come through here?"

The woman pinched her lips together as if she'd lie and
Donovan let his fury slide into his eyes.

The clerk took a step back as she paled. She swallowed.
"She left by the back door." She pointed and Donovan didn't
wait for more information.

Donovan ran toward the back door, ignoring the chatter
of women behind him. He flung it open, finding himself at
a delivery dock. The fire door swung closed behind him just
as he spied Alex. She was far down the sidewalk, just stepping into a cab.

She was alone.

Slayers hadn't gotten her.

Yet.

Alex glanced back as she got into the cab as if she sensed

his presence. She hesitated for a moment when she saw Donovan.

Then she swung into the cab, pulling the door behind her. She leaned forward to talk to the driver and the cab made a U-turn.

Where was she going?

Donovan knew it would be logical. He liked that she wasn't afraid, but he didn't want her to pay for it.

He knew she would be in danger.

He had to follow her.

It had to be some cruel trick of fate that Alex had left the mall at the farthest possible point from where he had parked his bike. He pivoted to retrieve it and ran into Quinn.

"She's made for you," his friend muttered as he saw what had happened.

"Don't even go there," Donovan said. He had to get to his bike.

Now.

A cab appeared on the road and Donovan hailed it. He was in the front passenger seat, urging the driver to hit the gas before the door was closed. Sara and Quinn leapt into the backseat.

"You aren't going after her alone," Quinn said.

"Watch me."

"But where did she go?" Sara asked.

"There," he told the cab driver, directing him to the parked Ducati. "Down that lane, almost at the end. Hurry!"

Donovan thought of Erik's theory. Where would Alex have stored backups? At the lab, at her home . . .

He tugged out his cell phone and called directory assistance. He asked for the listing for A. Madison, then slapped the phone shut after the voice-automated system replied.

"She's going to her home," Sara guessed.

"For her backup files," Quinn agreed.

Sara's lips tightened. "And whatever happened at the lab can happen at her apartment, too."

Donovan didn't wait for their answer. He chucked a twenty at Quinn as he leapt out of the cab. He got on his bike and peeled out of the parking lot before the cab driver even pulled away.

He just hoped he could get to Alex before the *Slayers* did.

Sigmund Guthrie ordered another beer. He was sitting at the end of the bar that was across the street from Alex Madison's apartment building. He'd been a regular in that bar for the past three weeks. He'd had every lunch special three times. He'd tried every beer they had on tap and knew all the staff by name.

He didn't even like beer.

He preferred tea, but he liked being alive. When Boris Vassily gave you a job, you did that job or died trying. If not, Boris would make sure you had enough time to regret your failure before he finished you off. Given that Sigmund had supplied Boris with all the ways to make a dragon suffer, Sigmund respected what Boris could do.

Or could have done, as it were. Boris tended to keep his talons clean and let his accomplices do the nasty jobs.

So, Sigmund sat in the pub and sipped another glass of Coors. The excuse of a meal they called pasta primavera sat in his gut like a rock, but Sigmund didn't complain.

He watched the building across the street.

To his surprise, Alex did what Boris had said she would do.

She came home, alone.

If he'd had only his vision to rely upon, Sigmund wouldn't have recognized her. She was dressed in a different—more provocative—style than when he'd seen her last. But he had caught her scent, and any scent once caught is never forgotten by *Pyr* or *Slayer*.

Her disguise was worthless.

Which meant she had no idea whom she was up against.

Sigmund made a show of checking his watch, then settled his bill as if he were late for an appointment.

"Finally gotta go somewhere other than the john, huh?" the bartender teased.

Sigmund gave him a look instead of an answer and neglected to tip. Alex had gone into the apartment building by the time he got to the sidewalk, but he knew she'd be back.

Boris had said she would retrieve her backup copies and her notes, in order to replicate her research. Boris had said that there might be a second prototype for the Green Machine and that Alex would lead them straight to it. Boris had said to follow her until Sigmund was sure, then to destroy everything so that the research could never be replicated.

But Alex wasn't coming back. The intensity of her scent revealed that she hadn't left. What was she doing?

Sigmund moved toward the apartment building to check.

Alex was getting used to a life of derring-do.

It was frightening, but exciting, too. This was completely different from the humdrum routine that her working life had taken on in the past few years. She'd become accustomed to having every adrenaline rush associated with progress on the Green Machine.

Getting a charge from real life was a sensation she'd forgotten.

If Donovan and the *Pyr* could be considered real life.

Now, she was going to become a criminal. Sort of. Alex had pulled on her new red gloves in the cab and plopped a pair of big sunglasses on her nose. She was pretty sure no one would recognize sensible Alex Madison as she was dressed now.

Dressing flamboyantly was the best disguise of all. People looked at her pants or her breasts and never glanced at her face. Even if they remembered her clothes, they wouldn't be able to describe her features.

She was incognito. She could do anything. Maybe she should have released her inner biker chick years ago.

But this was no game—the *Slayers* played for keeps.

How quickly could they come after her? Alex didn't know, but she had to anticipate challenges and danger. Her heart skipped a beat and she was keenly aware of Donovan's absence.

He hadn't been happy to see her getting into the cab, that was for sure. Alex hadn't needed mind-reading abilities to pick that up. But it was better this way.

Even if she found that hard to believe herself.

She paid for the cab, then, heart pounding, strode to the entrance of her own building.

Would she have to use her key to get through the security door?

No. There was a guy entering just in front of her—the movie fiend from the fourth floor. Alex always saw him in the rental store and had thought about starting a conversation once or twice. He held the security door open for her like a gentleman.

Or an idiot. The point of a security door was that each person who entered was supposed to unlock it with his or her own key.

Normally, Alex would have told him off but on this day, she thanked him. He ogled her pants as they waited for the elevator. She was glad she'd never bothered to talk to him before.

On the other hand, the movie guy had never even noticed her in the past. Donovan—it was impossible to avoid the comparison—had been attracted to her, even when she was wearing a backless hospital gown. He was a man who could look past the surface. That kind of man was rare.

As rare as dragon dudes?

When the elevator came and the movie guy let her precede him—probably so he could check the view—Alex pushed the button for the sixth floor. The doors closed behind them and she saw that he was carrying a copy of *The Saint*.

Val Kilmer. She could respect the choice.

When the movie guy got off at the fourth floor, he paused in the corridor as if he would ask Alex something but wasn't sure of the words. Alex pushed the button for the doors to close. It was surprisingly easy to be rude while in disguise.

Then she pushed the button for the eleventh floor. That wasn't her floor, either, but she wasn't sure whether the elevator had any kind of recording mechanism for when it went where.

She doubted it, given the age of the building, but she was going to be extra careful. Just like a spy.

Matt Damon in *The Bourne Conspiracy*. Uh-huh.

The corridor on eleven was quiet. A television could be heard faintly in an apartment to the left. Not wanting to take a chance of being spotted through a peephole, Alex strode to the right.

There was a stairwell at each end of the corridor. Alex ran down one floor carefully, keeping her heels from clicking on the steps, slipping into the corridor on ten. Everyone on her floor had a day job, so the coast should be clear.

Alex paused at the end of the hall and listened.

Silence. For the first time, she appreciated that the doors to individual apartments were staggered: there wasn't one directly opposite hers. Anyone who was home would get a distorted view of her through the fish eye in the peephole.

Still, she moved quickly.

She pulled out the credit card that Peter's bank had foolishly issued to Meredith Maloney and found a new use for it. The building was old and the locks were a far cry from the latest and greatest. Alex leaned her weight against the door and it moved inward a fraction of an inch. That was enough. She picked the lock with the card, just like they did in the movies.

It was easier than she'd expected. She wanted to hoot with glee when the lock opened. She'd be the next James Bond—008.

Alex moved into her own foyer, closed the door behind

her, and froze in shock. The lights were out and the curtains were drawn, just the way she'd left them. Even in the dim light, though, Alex could see that her apartment had been trashed.

She stared.

Her home had been turned upside down. Every drawer was dumped; every table was tipped; every cupboard had been emptied. There was stuff everywhere, tangled and scattered and smashed. Cutlery was mixed with shattered bowls, CDs, and socks. Alex hadn't thought she was a minimalist, but it sure looked like a lot of stuff, cast all over the floor like worthless junk.

The sliding glass door to the balcony was open, and she knew she hadn't left it that way. A breeze wafted into the apartment, ruffling the magazines that had been chucked on the floor.

It didn't dissipate the smell of smoke.

Dragons. Alex shivered.

Good thing she hadn't been home.

She could hear that the apartment was empty. There was no sense of a malicious presence, no sound of anyone breathing or waiting. She could hear the tap of the bathtub dripping, as it had dripped since she had moved in.

She eased through the chaos that had been her living room and peeked out the sliding glass door. Her bicycle was still locked there and everything looked as it should. No one lurked on the balcony and she was careful not to let herself be seen.

They were gone, but they could come back.

They might, in fact, have left some dragon means of notifying themselves if she came back.

Alex headed for the bedroom, her heart pounding.

To think that Mark had teased her about her need to safeguard her files. Alex was starting to feel as if her so-called neurotic tendency to protect her data in complicated ways wasn't so neurotic at all.

She was starting to feel smart.

The smartest thing, though, would be surviving this ordeal intact. Thursday seemed to be a thousand years away.

Her heart skipped when she entered her bedroom. It was a mess like the living room, but it was more upsetting, maybe because of the intimacy of the space. Her underwear had been thrown around and the mirror on the wall over the dresser was shattered.

Surely she couldn't be up for seven whole years of bad luck?

Someone had urinated in the room, from the smell. Nice touch.

The bedding had been tossed on the floor and the mattress had been tipped. No! Alex raced to the bed. Her hands shook as she shoved the mattress aside. She peeled back the corner of the box spring lining, where she'd made a resealable hiding place.

It was still sealed. Alex wouldn't believe anything until she pulled it open and looked. The Velcro fastening seemed to make too loud a noise when she tore it open.

Alex winced, then shoved a hand into the dark nook inside the box spring. Her fingers closed on a CD jewel box and her knees nearly collapsed with relief. She pulled it out and checked that it was the same box, the same label, the same CD inside. Then she held it over her pounding heart and took a deep breath of relief.

They hadn't found it.

The safety deposit box key was still there, too, taped to the inside of the box spring with packing tape. Alex worked it loose, feeling like she'd won the lottery. She slid the box and the key into the inside pocket of her jacket, and knew there was one more thing she had to retrieve.

She didn't like guns. She didn't like owning one. She didn't like that Peter had insisted on buying her one for Christmas a few years back, after his fancy house in the fancy suburbs had been burgled and his fancy toys had been stolen. She didn't know if a bullet could stop a dragon, but it was worth a shot.

Alex grimaced at her unintentional pun as she returned to the galley kitchen. Sugar and spices were strewn on the floor and dishes broken all over the counter. She reached around the corner, not wanting to leave her boot print in the sugar, and reached into the bottom cabinet closest to her.

All the way at the back was a tin of crackers.

It didn't have crackers in it anymore. Alex had removed the crackers and put the gun and the ammo in the tin, then sealed it all up as if it were new.

The gun was there, just as shiny as ever. Her hands shook a bit as she loaded it, put the safety on, and put it in the inside pocket of her jacket. It felt heavy, like trouble waiting to happen, but Alex knew she needed all the help she could get.

Dragons were trying to kill her and no one was going to believe that enough to help her.

No one except a good dragon, like Donovan.

With dragons, though, *good* seemed to be comparative. Donovan was still dangerous.

He'd killed his own father.

Alex almost left the apartment, then remembered the one thing she couldn't abandon. She darted into the bathroom, rummaged under the sink, and removed what looked like a tin of talcum powder. She ripped off the lid and dumped the tissue-wrapped treasure into her hand. The way her grandmother had always hidden her treasured brooch had worked for Alex, too. She stuffed it into her pocket.

What if she was being followed?

She had to anticipate the worst-case scenario. She snatched up a dozen boxed CDs that were held together with a pair of rubber bands. They were filled with games and movies, a loan from Mark. Dropped into her purse, the pile made a bulge.

If anyone was following her and stole her purse, they'd

have lots of bits and bytes to sort through before they realized they had nothing at all.

Alex removed Meredith's fake identification and fake credit card from the purse and put them in her jacket, too. Good thing it had a chunky design and didn't look as if she'd jammed it full of her worldly possessions.

She refused to dwell on the wreckage of her apartment. She doubted that she'd ever be back and that made her a little bit sad. She'd had some good times in that apartment, but it was impossible that she'd ever feel safe there again.

She returned to the door and listened.

Silence.

Alex eased out of her apartment and left the door slightly ajar. That way, her neighbors would notify the police that her apartment had been robbed.

"Got everything?" a man whispered, his voice winding its way into her ears.

Alex spun around to find a sandy-haired man standing at the end of the hall. His eyes glittered. He smiled and it made him look hungry.

Alex ran. She bolted down the opposite stairs all the way to the lobby, hearing his measured steps following her. He was moving faster than she was, but didn't catch up to her. She didn't dare look back, didn't want to see a dragon following her.

She flung herself out the back door, the one that led to the trash cans, and ran down the lane to the end of the building. She heard the door slam behind her but didn't look back.

Instead she emerged on the street and strolled toward the bank as if she hadn't a care in the world.

Got everything?

Alex shuddered. He was following her.

Unfortunately, she had one last retrieval to make. After she got the schematics from the safety deposit box, anyone trying to anticipate what Alex would do or where she would go would have more of a challenge on his or her hands. Even

Peter didn't know that the prototype car was stashed in his boathouse.

Of course, after she got the schematics from the safety deposit box, her new friend might attack. Leaving Donovan behind suddenly seemed like a very bad idea.

Would she have a chance for a Plan C?

Alex glanced over her shoulder, as if checking for traffic, and noticed the sandy-haired guy on the opposite side of the street. He was watching her, but his gaze flicked away when he saw her notice. He took interest in a window display, biding his time.

Alex was scared. She was pretty sure he was a *Slayer*.

Just then, Alex heard the throaty hum of an approaching motorcycle and felt relief at its familiarity. It was being driven aggressively and she had a pretty good idea whose Ducati it was. Alex was smart enough to know when she was out of her league and humble enough to ask for help when she needed it.

When the Ducati came peeling around the corner, Alex stepped out to the curb and stuck out her thumb like a hitchhiker.

She just hoped Donovan stopped for her.

She figured it was even money.

Chapter 7

Alex was more trouble than anyone Donovan had ever known. Given that he had a tendency to find trouble himself and that he was almost five centuries old, that was saying something.

Alex's home address was in an apartment building on a busy street. Donovan turned down the street, saw the building, and was immediately struck by the scent of another *Pyr*.

Except that this *Pyr* had turned *Slayer*. His dark scent reminded Donovan of old horror-film laboratories where experiments of dubious merit were performed on unwilling victims. Dr. Frankenstein's place, maybe. Donovan's hackles rose and he scanned the street. He had a vague sense of familiarity from that smell. They'd met, but not often.

He looked again and didn't see anyone he knew—

Except a woman in black leather pants, stiletto heels, and a red leather jacket. She waved to him from about a block away, then stuck out her thumb as if she were hitchhiking.

So confident, she might have known he'd follow her. Donovan's anger rose another notch. *He* was supposed to be the confident one.

He drove toward her, squealing his tires to stop. Alex smiled and the curve of those red lips reminded him all too well of the taste and the feel of her. The firestorm began to sizzle through his veins, distracting him from what he should be saying to her.

It only got worse. Curiosity was his downfall. As he stopped the idling bike beside her, his gaze followed the length of her neck to the lavish lace edging her white bra.

Lace.

Lace.

Donovan stared as his brain stalled. Alex's tanned skin gleamed gold through the edging on the bra. He tried to look away from the ripe curve of her breast, from the rosy bit of nipple that was visible through the lace; he tried to fight the firestorm.

He lost.

"Hey, gorgeous," she said, her eyes dancing. "Going my way?"

"I should kill you now," he growled, and her smile broadened. It was a bit galling that she wasn't afraid of him, and even more disturbing that she was as unrepentant and charming as he strove to be. "If you had any idea how stupid it was to take off—"

"I think I do now," she said, interrupting his tirade, her serious mood and her confession surprising him to silence. "Do you know that guy? Seven o'clock, sandy hair, short." Her gaze flicked across the street; then she ran a possessive hand over his shoulder. She acted as if they were lovers meeting, which was probably a good choice. Donovan had a hard time appreciating its strategic merit with the firestorm striking his blood like lightning.

He glanced over his shoulder, trying to look casual. There was a man studying the baked goods displayed in a store window across the street. Donovan inhaled slowly, letting his eyes narrow as he took the man's scent.

Slayer.

"You do know him," Alex said. She had guessed his thoughts. That should have worried Donovan more than it did.

It certainly shouldn't have sent a thrill through him.

"I know his scent, but not his shape."

"What does that mean?"

"I must have met him in his other form."

Alex nodded. "So, he is *Pyr*."

"No. He's *Slayer*. He's probably stalking you."

Alarm flickered in her eyes. "So, are you going to help me or leave me to deal with my own mistake?" Donovan liked how she asked for the truth and didn't hide from the answer.

"That depends," he said, although there was no doubt in his mind. "Are we a team, or are you going to bolt again?"

"I thought you rode alone."

"I've been known to fight for the team."

Her lips set. "I have to rebuild my prototype by Thursday."

"I'll assume you have a plan."

Her smile flashed unexpectedly, sending a blaze over his skin. "I had Plan B. The one without you."

Fear shot through Donovan and he heard urgency in his own voice. "Without me? The risk is too high, Alex. You need me to protect you. You can't fight these guys alone."

She licked her lips and he knew she understood. She was thinking, reformulating her scheme. "How many *Slayers* are there?"

"In total? I don't know. Three are on the scene so far."

"But there could be more?"

Donovan wasn't going to lie to her. He nodded and watched her pale. "What happened at the lab, Alex?"

Her gaze flicked to the guy across the street. "Let's go with Plan C—you give me a ride and I'll tell you about it."

Donovan liked her decisiveness. He knew he hadn't imagined the flash of fear in the dark depths of her eyes. She had witnessed whatever had happened to Mark Sullivan and that was the root of her fear of dragons. He really didn't need to know more to guess the truth—*Slayers* had killed her partner while she watched. They'd wanted to scare her and it had worked.

As frightened as she was, though, she wasn't surrendering. He respected that.

Donovan wondered what Alex and Mark's relationship had been. What kind of partners had they been? He didn't want to ask. It would imply that his own interest was greater than it was.

"There's an offer I can't refuse." Donovan offered her the helmet, but she shook her head.

"You need it."

"But we only have one, at least for the moment, and it's my duty to protect you."

She took it then, her eyes narrowing in assessment. "Does that make me part of your team?"

"I don't want to talk about that," Donovan muttered, and shoved the helmet at her. He revved the bike. "Let's go."

Alex climbed onto the seat behind him and he closed his eyes at the sweet press of her thighs wrapped around him. Sparks danced over his skin and he almost groaned when she slid her arms around his waist. He felt her breasts against his back, smelled her perfume, and felt her breath against his ear. He felt as if he were burning up in his own skin, his desire for her at such a fever pitch that it nearly shorted his circuits.

"Phew!" Alex said, making it clear that she felt the same thing. "You're really hot stuff, you know?" He glanced back in time to see her lick her fingertip. She made a hissing sound as she touched it to his shoulder and he liked how her eyes sparkled.

Donovan grinned. He felt better, just having her close, as dangerous as it might be. She *was* part of his team, at least for the duration of the firestorm.

"Speak for yourself." He pulled away from the curb, sparing a glance back for oncoming traffic. The *Slayer* stood on the opposite sidewalk, gaping at them. Donovan had no doubt that he could feel the firestorm and was shocked by its power. "Where to?"

"The bank three blocks down," Alex said. "I need to get something from my safety deposit box."

"Something like what?"

"That's for me to know," she said, her tone stubborn.

Donovan guessed that it was more backup files. "Anywhere else?"

She paused for a moment and he thought she wouldn't say anything. "A drugstore," she said finally. "We need condoms and spermicidal jelly."

Donovan almost missed a gear. "What?"

She leaned against him, distracting him with her touch as only she could do. Her breasts were crushed against his back and Donovan thought about the white lace that edged her bra. The memory of that glimpse lit a bonfire inside him.

"This firestorm is too distracting," she said, echoing his thoughts perfectly. "We're going to make a mistake because of it. I could die and I have too much work to do for that."

"A little bit of a workaholic?" Donovan murmured, wondering where she was going with this.

"It's vital that I have a running prototype for the meeting on Thursday," she said with a determination he was beginning to associate with her. "To do that, I need to concentrate, and if you're going to be around—"

"I will be," Donovan said with some determination of his own.

"Then we have to extinguish the firestorm. I don't believe for a minute that every woman gets pregnant the first time she does it with a *Pyr*, but let's not take chances. If you think you're going to leave me with a dragon baby, you can think again."

Donovan was so shocked that he didn't know what to say.

Alex settled against him, but her resolve was inescapable. "We eliminate the firestorm by doing the horizontal tango, get the Green Machine running again by Thursday, and on Friday, the *Slayers* can kill me." Her tone lightened. "That's Plan C. How do you like it so far?"

"They're not going to kill you Friday if I have anything to say about it." Donovan was surprised by the vehemence of his own response. He wanted Alex to survive and prosper.

It should have worried him how much he wanted to ensure that.

"But the rest?" she prompted.

Donovan couldn't even think straight about the rest of her plan. He'd never heard of anyone thwarting the firestorm. It seemed as if it shouldn't work.

But he couldn't think of a reason why.

He parked in front of the bank and Alex hopped off, handing him his helmet. A spark danced between their fingertips and they both caught their breath at the same time. Their gazes met then, locking and holding, and Donovan felt tight.

And hard.

"See what I mean?" Alex said softly. "We can't afford it."

"We can't stop it. And it won't pass until the next eclipse."

"Which is when?"

Donovan grimaced. "February."

Alex shook her head. "Then we have to diffuse it. There's too much at stake."

She made perfect sense.

"But . . ."

She looked at him, her eyes sparkling with mischief. "Don't tell me you're shy?"

"No."

She arched a brow. "A virgin?"

He laughed, surprised into it.

"Me neither," she admitted, her smile broadening. "Spoiler alert."

"Doesn't spoil anything for me." He liked how she smiled at that, but shook his head. "I'm just not sure it can be done."

Alex grinned. "Can't hurt to try, can it?"

Donovan stared into her eyes and felt his body respond in a predictable way. In her presence, it wasn't easy to think of anything other than seducing her and protecting her.

"Think about it," she urged, and there was no doubt in Donovan's mind that he would.

Alex walked away and he watched, losing himself in the rhythm of her movement before he caught himself.

"Wait," he said. "You're not going alone."

He got off the bike and turned off the ignition, carrying the helmet under one arm. He snagged her fingers with his free hand and gave her hand a squeeze.

"You look happier," she said.

"I'm liking the way you think." He spared her a grin, easily imagining that they could spend hours cheating the firestorm.

His thoughts were cut short by the scent of the *Slayer*. He glanced back to find the sandy-haired man approaching his bike, and a primal fury joined the heat of the firestorm.

"What is it?" she asked, then followed his gaze. "What's he doing?"

"Nothing good. Go, quickly."

"But—"

"I'll know if you're in danger," he said. "I've caught your scent and the firestorm has been awakened." He smiled for her. "You can believe that I'll come to you."

"Okay." It was obvious that she still felt some trepidation.

"Trust me, gorgeous." He winked and Alex blushed a little. She smiled; then she did as he suggested.

Which meant that she trusted him a bit.

Donovan was too busy to think much about that. He hid in the shadows beside the automatic tellers at the entrance to the bank and summoned smoke from the deepest depths of his belly. It was cold, thick smoke and he exhaled it with force.

Donovan didn't breathe smoke often, because he didn't

tend to stay in any place for long, but he was good at it. Rafferty had taught him well. Donovan watched with pride as his smoke rolled across the pavement, watched it seethe toward his bike with frightening speed, and kept breathing more.

The *Slayer* was as yet unaware of the smoke, so bent was he on damaging Donovan's bike. He probably wanted to make sure that they had to walk, to make it easier for him to catch them.

He could think again.

Donovan pushed the smoke harder, urging it toward the *Slayer*. His smoke swirled around the bike and closed into a circle. The ring snapped shut like a trap. The smoke circle emitted a crystal clear ring when it did so, one that was audible only to the sharp hearing of *Pyr* and *Slayers*.

In this case, it was hard to hear the ring of the perfect smoke circle, because the *Slayer* shouted in pain. Donovan had closed the loop so that the *Slayer*'s foot was trapped inside the ring. Donovan smiled, knowing that his smoke was burning the *Slayer*.

Served him right.

The *Slayer* pulled his foot free of the smoke with a bellow. A few tendrils followed him, the eddies of smoke trying to slide into his shoe and under the hem of his jeans.

The *Slayer* stamped his foot on the ground, trying to stop the smoke from searing his flesh. His impromptu dance attracted looks from a number of passersby. That would teach this *Slayer* not to mess with anything—or anyone—belonging to Donovan.

There was a flicker of the *Slayer*'s dragon guise, as the *Slayer* almost changed shape unwillingly in his anguish. It was a flicker that happened so quickly that no human would have noticed it. But with that glimpse of the *Slayer*'s malachite green and silver form, Donovan sobered. He recognized Alex's stalker.

It was Sigmund Guthrie.

Sigmund was Erik's son, who had turned to the *Slayer* side and compiled the only book about killing dragons.

Sigmund glared directly at Donovan, then turned and fled down the street. There was viciousness in that stare and Donovan knew better than to let Alex be anywhere in the *Slayer's* proximity.

Now, Sigmund would take his vengeance for the smoke upon Alex.

Donovan felt a bit sick. He'd inadvertently ensured that his mate would be tortured if the *Slayers* captured her. That was far worse than her simply being killed, and it guaranteed that he couldn't leave her alone.

Period.

Alex returned then, her gaze darting over him in concern. "Everything all right?" she asked quietly.

Donovan nodded. "You done?" At her nod, he indicated the bike. "Forget the drugstore. We need to get out of here now."

Alex scanned the street. "Where did he go?"

"Away," Donovan said grimly. "For now, but not for long." He didn't have to look to feel her fear.

"Where are you going?"

"Back to Erik's place," he said, knowing she'd be safe surrounded by other *Pyr*.

"No," she said to his surprise. "We need to do something unpredictable, and I need space to work. Get another helmet and let's get out of town."

"You have a destination in mind?"

"I know just the place." She spoke with such confidence that Donovan nodded agreement. He thought her instincts were right. Being predictable made it too easy to be targeted.

And he was certain that he could defend her alone. He was the greatest fighter of the *Pyr*, after all. Alex had a location in mind and once they were there, Donovan could breathe smoke to protect her in that place.

He could ask for details but she'd trusted him; it was time

to show some trust in return. He wasn't going to even think about her plan to thwart the firestorm.

That was too distracting an idea.

Plan C it would be. Alex couldn't defend herself against the dragons who were tracking her, and Donovan was determined to protect her.

There was no denying that he was good at it.

That must have been why she was so glad to see him again.

Donovan stopped and bought another helmet, insisting that she come into the store with him. It was a quick purchase and they were back on the bike in record time.

"Are we being followed?" she asked.

"Not so far as I can tell." Donovan was grim.

"Why doesn't that sound as reassuring as I think it should?"

He shrugged, and Alex realized she wasn't the only one with secrets. "We can all sense the presence of other *Pyr*. The problem is that some old *Slayers* are good at disguising their presence."

"Only the bad guys can do it?"

"They're not sharing the secret, oddly enough." Donovan paused. "That Russian guy at the mall is Boris Vassily, the leader of the *Slayers*. He's really good at hiding his presence."

"And he's in the area." Alex spared a worried glance to the road behind them. "So, they could be anywhere?"

"Pretty much."

"Tell me, then, what's the best solution?"

Donovan answered without hesitation. "A temporary lair. If we settle in one place, I can protect the perimeter with smoke."

"Smoke?"

"Dragonsmoke. It's a boundary mark that no other *Pyr* or *Slayer* can cross without the permission of the one who breathed it."

"Erik did that in his hotel room."

"We all did it in Erik's hotel room. The place was a fortress."

"Then how did I leave so easily?"

"Humans are unaffected by dragonsmoke. You might feel a chill when you pass through it, but that's it and that will only happen if you're particularly sensitive." He glanced at her. "Do you have a spot in mind to work, or should we just find a hotel room?"

"I can't work in a hotel. I need a computer. . . ."

"We could stop and buy one. . . ."

"No. I know just the place." Alex's decision was made. "Get on the highway up here and head west."

"How far is it?" Donovan looked quickly at the gas gauge.

"Maybe a hundred miles."

They roared out of the parking lot, both of them pulling down their visors. Alex hung on as Donovan turned onto the highway and eased the bike up to speed. She felt like she was running away from everything that had haunted her, racing toward the future. She was excited about getting back to work, but that wasn't the only thing that made her heart skip.

She was on the run with Donovan and she was honest enough to admit she liked that; she liked it a lot.

It wasn't just because she knew he would protect her, either.

She was thinking about thwarting the firestorm.

Donovan stopped about an hour later at a diner and gas station at the side of the highway. He would have preferred to keep going, but the bike wasn't the only one in need of fuel. He filled the bike's tank, watching the road for signs of pursuit. Alex stood beside him, right where he wanted her to be.

"Your senses are sharper than mine, aren't they?" she asked in an undertone, and he nodded. "Then you can be sentry."

Donovan smiled briefly, pleased that she was so observant. The road was empty in both directions and only two other cars were parked at the diner. He couldn't sense any *Pyr*. He still didn't like it and he didn't trust Boris, but they needed to eat.

"I think we're good," he murmured, then paid cash for the gas. "Let's get something to eat, while we have the chance."

The diner was quiet, and he assumed it was in between the breakfast and lunch traffic. He chose a booth in the back and sat in the corner, where he could watch the door and his bike.

"Strategic," Alex said as she slid into the bench opposite him.

"Alive," he corrected. They ordered coffee and the all-day breakfast special from a bored waitress.

Not a single car pulled in as they waited for their meals. Donovan was edgy all the same. It couldn't have been that easy to lose the *Slayers*. He didn't want to frighten Alex, but the hum of electricity between them would draw *Slayers* like moths to a flame.

He drummed his fingers and scanned the road outside, watching and waiting.

"If you could put that restless energy in a bottle, we could eliminate our dependence on fossil fuels," Alex said.

He glanced up to find her smiling.

"Never mind that spark," she added with a frown. "I'd love to know how that works."

"Destiny?" he suggested playfully, and Alex shook her head.

"No. It's energy of some kind. Energy is never destroyed or created—it just changes form." She watched his restless fingers and he could see that she was thinking about it. She reached out and tentatively touched a fingertip to his hands.

The spark lit but she didn't pull her hand away.

"I thought you were afraid," Donovan said quietly, watching her.

"I am." Alex met his gaze with a smile, then studied their fingers again. "But fear doesn't solve anything. It's just energy pointed in the wrong direction."

"I don't understand."

"Like anger, or jealousy." Alex focused on their hands. He watched as she experimented to determine how close their hands had to be for the sparks to light. "Negative emotions carry a charge or a power. It's a force you can turn around and put to work. You can harness it to solve the problem, whatever it is, instead of dwelling on the issue and achieving nothing."

"How do you do that?"

"Well, I can fuel courage with fear—I can investigate what terrifies me, learn something about its nature, and maybe move past my fear with that new information."

The waitress brought their meals then and Alex pulled her hand away. The waitress slid the plates of eggs, bacon, and hash browns onto the table, plunked down plates of toast, and refilled their coffees. She rummaged in her apron pocket for packs of jam and creamer, then left them to it.

Donovan was surprised by how hungry he was. The food smelled good to him, and he dug in quickly. He supposed that Alex's comment was the best intro he was going to get.

"Can you tell me about Gilchrist Enterprises?"

Alex flicked him a glance. "What about it?"

"Tell me about the Green Machine. It's an environmentally friendly vehicle, right?"

Alex nodded. "The Green Machine developed from the issue of fossil fuels. What are we going to do without them? There are less and less all the time." She pushed her plate aside, her meal only half eaten, and leaned forward. He loved her intensity and passion for her work. "Imagine if we didn't need so much oil on a daily basis. We could be self-sufficient in energy. . . ."

"But we love our cars too much to ditch them." Donovan played devil's advocate. "People can't walk everywhere or always take public transit. And electric cars aren't always practical, because there's not always a place to charge them."

"I'm talking about a more radical solution. I'm talking about changing the fuel we burn." Alex took a bite of toast, but Donovan could tell she wasn't really interested in it. "The problem is that with the tooling required to build car engines, there's an enormous vested interest in continuing to use gasoline to propel cars. Never mind the investments in building refineries."

"Which means there's a resistance to change, even though supplies of oil are running out."

Alex smiled. "People dislike change. We need to find a way to allow people to continue to drive the way they do, but make it more sustainable."

"By changing the fuel." Donovan nodded. "But to what?"

"The Green Machine is a car with an engine that runs on"—Alex glanced to either side, then leaned over the table to whisper—"*water*." Her eyes were shining with sincerity.

Donovan dropped his fork. "Be serious."

"I am. Salt water can be made to burn. You need a radio frequency generator, which splits the molecule so that the hydrogen can burn."

"Really?"

"Really."

Donovan was astounded. "But there's salt water everywhere. We've got oceans of it."

"And we can make more," Alex said. "It's completely renewable as a resource. Burns clean, too."

"What about the engine?"

"Modifications are required. The radio frequency needs to be sustained for the burn to continue. So, you need to factor the energy needed to create the radio frequency into the equation, and you want to come out with a net gain in power in order to propel a vehicle. It makes a lot of energy and you need to control the volume at an even level."

"So?"

"We had a prototype car at the lab, which we reworked and tested. Mark was the best mechanic you ever saw. It was one hot machine." She caught her breath and looked away.

"What happened to him?" Donovan asked softly.

"I don't want to talk about it yet." Alex's throat worked and her voice was more husky than usual. She stabbed her fork into her cold hash browns.

"You saw?"

She nodded and frowned, but didn't say anything. The power of her reaction made Donovan wonder again what her relationship with Mark had been.

It was *not* his business.

He drained his coffee cup, irritated by the direction of his thoughts. "You were close to revealing your invention?"

She leaned forward, her manner intent, as she held her finger and thumb slightly apart. "We're this close. We've had an angel—"

"Angels are involved in this, too?" Donovan teased, wanting to see her smile.

She did, briefly. "That's what they call early investors, the venture capitalists who fund projects well before there's anything to see. I have an appointment with ours on Thursday. He's got the facilities lined up for production and a whole team of experts in place to make this happen. There's a big car show in two weeks where he wants to unveil the Green Machine. *If* it works. I need a working prototype for that meeting to make everything come together. All the other work is done."

"I can't blame him for wanting to see it work."

"No. It'll take a lot of money to begin production."

"But there's a lot more money to be made."

"And the planet to be saved," Alex said. She shoved a hand through her hair with some frustration. "There are other people working on similar schemes, but the Green Machine is the cleanest and the best. If we miss this opportunity, some hybrid will be introduced instead. We heard about three, which still rely partly on fossil fuels, that are going to be introduced at that show."

"Compromise is easier than change."

"Exactly." Alex's manner turned urgent and her conviction made Donovan's heart skip a beat. "There's a window of opportunity here to really make a difference—"

"To save the world."

"Don't make fun of me!"

"I'm perfectly serious."

She spoke with quiet force. "I don't want to miss this chance. I don't think we can mess around with compromise anymore. We need to make a big technological change and we need to make it now." She met his gaze warily. "It sounds flaky but there was a convergence that pulled the Green Machine together more quickly than either of us expected. The universe was moving in support of the idea. I feel like I was given a responsibility and that it's my job to make it happen."

"That doesn't sound flaky to me at all."

Alex rolled her eyes and took another bite of toast. "Consider the source," she said, her eyes dancing.

Donovan grinned that she could joke about his nature. "So, where do we go from here?"

"Mark and I had planned to pick Mr. Sinclair up at the airport in the Green Machine on Thursday, but the better prototype was destroyed in the fire." She fell silent suddenly and looked at her coffee, as if she regretted having said so much.

Better meant that there were at least two prototypes.

The other one was still stashed somewhere. She had the disks and the backup data, so she needed to get to the prototype. He could work with that.

So long as they worked together.

Donovan sat back as the waitress came to refill their coffees. She offered pie, which they both declined.

When she was gone, Donovan leaned across the table and caught Alex's wary gaze. "I know you've got to protect your invention and that maybe you're worried you've told me too much. But I need to go with you to wherever you have the prototype stashed, to ensure your survival. Only a *Pyr* can defend you from *Slayers*."

A light glimmered in her eyes. "And you're volunteering?"

"We've seen what they'll do." Donovan tried to convince her to trust him, knowing that she didn't have all of the facts. "If we establish a lair wherever your prototype is, I can breathe smoke to defend its perimeter. I can summon other *Pyr* to help protect the space and you can get to work, knowing you're safe."

Alex sat back to consider him. "There's that team thing again." She took a sip of coffee. "From Mr. Lone Rider."

"Some things are important." Donovan felt like it was an excuse as soon as he said the words.

"Like this? Or like me?"

"Does it matter?"

Alex studied him and Donovan feared he had made a mistake.

Then she offered her hand across the table. "Okay. Deal. It'll be good to have a partner again."

Donovan shook her hand, catching his breath at the tide of heat that rolled through him from the point of contact. He wouldn't think about how close a partnership they might have.

Not yet. He couldn't even think about her proposal to cheat the firestorm until they were both secured in a temporary lair.

Then the idea would have his full attention.

Alex was staring at the spark between their hands. The flame startled Donovan with its intensity. Was it burning hotter?

"Put that in a jar and save the world," she murmured. "Look at it. It's spontaneous combustion, clean burning. If we could figure it out, we could put that energy to work."

Her touch was more than distracting. Donovan tried to

pull his hand from hers, but Alex tightened her grip. "Don't do that."

"Why? Because it makes you blow your cool?" Alex's smile was teasing, which was even more distracting.

"It attracts the others." When she looked puzzled, Donovan elaborated. "We can all feel the heat of the firestorm. It attracts us, like a magnetic force."

She nodded. "Sara said that. Like moths to the flame maybe?"

"Those who play with fire are going to get burned, more likely."

Alex watched him for a moment and he wondered what she saw. "Or do you really mean once burned, twice shy?" she asked quietly.

"What do you mean?"

"I'm wondering what worries you so much about me. You've got firewalls in place like nobody's business."

"Ha ha."

"I'm not joking. What do dragons have to be afraid of?"

"It's a question of safety—" Donovan tried to divert her interest, although he doubted it could be done.

"I don't think so." Alex interrupted him. "It's the firestorm that has you spooked. Maybe that's what burned you the last time you played with fire."

"No. I've never had a firestorm before—"

"Okay, you can't be afraid of that." Alex moved on to the next possibility with a logical precision that Donovan could have respected more if it was applied elsewhere. "Maybe it's just the emotional connection that spooks you."

"I don't think this is important—"

"Did you love somebody before?" Alex was undeterred. She studied him. "Maybe somebody who didn't love you back?"

Donovan glared at her, not appreciating that she was trying to read his thoughts—never mind that she was doing so well at it. "Time to go," he said.

"Avoiding the discussion doesn't change anything," Alex said as she got to her feet. "You think you're the only one who's ever gotten burned?" Donovan met her gaze in surprise and found an unexpected understanding there. "Ha ha?"

She had cared for Mark.

Donovan didn't need to know how much he had in common with Alex. He didn't need to get emotionally involved.

He tore his gaze away from hers and found trouble.

A stocky man who looked familiar was standing at the cash register, where he had bought a pack of cigarettes. He turned and glanced over his shoulder, casting a sly smile in Donovan's direction.

Tyson.

There was a gold SUV at the pumps, a second man in the passenger's seat. He unrolled the window and exhaled a smoke ring, one that floated toward Donovan's bike. He had pale eyes, a cold manner, and Donovan knew he had a Russian accent.

Donovan saw the silhouette of another man in the backseat of the car. It had to be Sigmund.

Once again, the firestorm had made him forget his surroundings.

"We're so out of here," he said, throwing cash on the table.

"What's wrong?" Alex asked.

"Guess." He shoved her helmet at her, then had an idea. "You'd better drive."

Her gaze danced to the man walking back to the SUV and he knew she recognized Boris. She nodded understanding, her eyes wide.

"Just, please, take it easy when you change gears."

"Three words," she said grimly as she pulled on her helmet.

"Archibald Forrester's Buick," they said in unison, and shared a smile that made Donovan even more determined to win. He pulled on the gloves that Quinn had made for him before getting on the bike behind Alex, knowing that the retractable steel blades might provide just the advantage he needed.

They pulled out of the gas station and Alex kicked the bike up to speed. She changed gears so smoothly that Donovan was proud. She was driving with more verve now, becoming accustomed to the bike in a way he could understand.

Donovan glanced back in time to see the SUV, its gold bush bar gleaming in the sun. The *Slayers* stayed a steady distance behind, and Donovan knew they were waiting for their moment. It would be three against one, but he was good enough to thump them all.

The stakes were all or nothing.

Chapter 8

Alex kept an eye on the SUV in the side mirrors. The *Slayers* remained exactly the same distance behind the bike for the better part of an hour. Alex wasn't fooled—with every passing mile, the traffic became lighter. She knew they were waiting to catch Donovan alone.

It was cooling off and the sky was clear. The trees were finishing their fall display out here and many branches were bare. Clusters of orange and yellow leaves caught the late-afternoon sunlight. They looked like flames against the vivid blue sky.

Alex would not think about fire.

As the shadows drew longer, Alex wondered whether the *Slayers* would wait until night fell, or until she and Donovan reached their destination. They'd have to wait a while for that, given that she'd told Donovan to head in the wrong direction. The only thing out this way, as far as she knew, was Iowa.

Alex decided not to mention that just yet. The road took a big turn to the right, pine trees marching right up to the ditch. She and Donovan leaned into the curve together and she liked the feel of his thighs around hers. He had his hands on her waist and his chest touched her back at intervals. The firestorm made Alex feel languid and sexy, just generally good all over.

They came out of the curve and there was no SUV behind them.

"They're gone," Alex had time to say before two dragons appeared over the crest of the trees.

"Just go," Donovan said. Alex slowed down. He hauled off his helmet as he leapt off the bike, then hooked the strap to the back of the seat. He looked her straight in the eye. "Don't stop and don't look back."

"But . . ."

"I'll find you." He grinned and winked. "Don't worry, gorgeous. We're a team now. It's Plan C all the way." Before Alex could reply, he leapt into the air and changed shape. It happened so quickly that she couldn't see the moment when he ceased to be human. She heard the clash of dragons colliding overhead, but she had other problems.

A ruby red and brass dragon landed on the road, ten feet in front of her, and smiled. "We meet again, Alex."

He was the one who had been in Mark's office, the one who had . . .

Alex revved the bike, ducked her head, and rode straight at him. He took flight and his tail thumped the handlebars when she passed beneath him. The bike skidded into the gravel of the shoulder and he laughed, thinking he had her beaten.

He could think again. Alex righted the bike with an effort, got her balance, then accelerated. The road was straight and empty, and she was going to follow Donovan's advice.

The *Slayer* flew immediately behind her, breathing fire and smoke. Alex didn't look back, just went faster and faster. He wasn't going to do the same thing to her that he'd done to Mark, not if Alex had anything to say about it. He kept up easily, his throaty chuckle echoing in her ears.

"Roast mate," he said, and licked his lips. Alex yelped as her back was singed.

She realized that she was quickly leaving Donovan far behind.

The farther she was from Donovan, the less able he would be to defend her against bad dragons.

Like this one.

Her heart was thundering in fear and her hands were sweating on the handles. She reminded herself that anything that didn't kill her would make her stronger and knew she'd be a powerhouse by the time this adventure was done.

Fear solves nothing. Alex needed an evasive tactic.

And there it was—the side road appeared as if by magic.

Alex took the right turn so abruptly that she nearly skidded out. This road was narrow and quiet, like a shared driveway. It was lined with massive old maples that arched over the road. The *Slayer* swore as he ascended. He had to fly over the trees, which didn't give him many chances to blast Alex.

Alex bent over the bike, calculating how far she had come in order to choose her turn. The road wound in a way that would have been more fun to drive if she hadn't been so panicked. She heard a roar and a bellow and knew she was getting closer to Donovan's dragon fight.

She needed to turn right again, but the road wound to the left, running alongside a river. The *Slayer* seized the opportunity to descend and fly alongside Alex. He loosed a torrent of fire at her and Alex turned instinctively away.

She was over the ditch and into the woods before she could stop herself. The bike leapt over the rough terrain and the engine stuttered. Was this his plan? Was he driving her toward some pitfall? Alex wasn't going to be manipulated like that.

She took advantage of a residential driveway, one that undoubtedly wound back to a secluded retreat in the woods, made a tight turn, and raced back toward the road. The

Slayer hovered above the branches of the trees, tracking her progress.

She bent low right before she emerged into a clearing, knowing he'd take a shot at her.

He did.

The tips of the tree branches around the clearing caught fire and Alex knew her shiny red leather jacket wasn't so shiny anymore. She had to survive, though—and to do that, she had to get back to Donovan.

If you had to fight fire with fire, then only dragons could fight dragons.

She turned onto the main road, retracing her earlier course. The river ran alongside the road only for another couple of hundred yards, and Alex was sure she could make it. She bent low, preparing to accelerate, but the *Slayer* landed square in the middle of the pavement in front of her. His eyes narrowed; then he loosed a torrent of flames.

The scrub on the one side of the road began to burn. The bulrushes alongside the river lit like torches. He kept breathing fire and Alex saw the pavement start to melt.

She was going too fast to do a one-eighty and there was nowhere to turn. She braked hard and the bike tires squealed as the bike fishtailed to a stop. She was sideways on the road, not a dozen feet from the inferno the *Slayer* had lit.

Not a dozen feet from the *Slayer* himself. The bike stalled and she flooded the engine in her fear.

His smile broadened and Alex's heart stopped cold.

Donovan barely got into the sky before Tyson was on him. The *Slayer* latched on to his back, his talons digging into Donovan's shoulders.

"I take your challenge," Tyson whispered.

"But you had to cheat to have a chance of winning." Donovan sprung his metal talons, twisted and slashed at the *Slayer*.

Tyson recoiled in pain, hovering as he eyed Donovan

with suspicion. The pair circled each other warily, talons up, tails lashing. "Those aren't natural."

Donovan flicked his metal talons. "A little addition to my natural charm."

"Yet you're the one who accuses us of fighting unfairly."

"Ask the other *Slayers* about Lucien. These babies were his idea. I'm just keeping up with the Joneses."

"Not for much longer," Tyson growled. "Only one of us will fly away from here."

"And I know who it's going to be," Donovan said. "You must know, too, otherwise you wouldn't be avoiding the fight." He grinned. "Are you scared to die, Tyson? What do they do to the corpses at Boris's secret academy?"

The *Slayer* roared and dove for Donovan, talons extended. They locked claws and grappled for dominance, tumbling end over end through the sky. Donovan dug his claws in deep and drove Tyson toward the pavement, keeping all four claws locked. Tyson thrashed and swung his tail, but Donovan expected his move. He wound his own tail around the length of the *Slayer*'s and held it down.

"Funny," he mused. "I thought you'd put up more of a fight." Tyson inhaled deeply to breathe fire, and Donovan braced himself to remember his lesson from Quinn. He ignored Tyson's inhalation and made the most of his opportunity. He scanned the *Slayer*'s chest and found a damaged scale.

Tyson loosed dragonfire on Donovan. Donovan felt it burn and fought to turn the power of the flame to his advantage. He had some success but couldn't take the fire as well as Quinn.

Yet.

When Tyson stopped for breath, Donovan bent quickly. He tore open a wound with his teeth at Tyson's vulnerable spot. Black blood spurted from Tyson's chest and the *Slayer* shrieked in pain.

Tyson filled his lungs and Donovan knew he couldn't

take another hit of dragonfire. He picked up the *Slayer* and flung him into the woods, ascending like a hawk after he released Tyson.

The plume of Tyson's dragonfire followed Donovan, nipping at the tip of his tail. Tyson crashed into the forest and the tree branches began to burn. Donovan scanned the sky. There was only a smaller *Slayer* hovering out of range.

Where was Boris?

Where was Sigmund?

Or was this other *Slayer* the one he had seen silhouetted in the backseat of the SUV?

Donovan could hear the faint thrum of his bike's engine and was afraid that he knew where the others were. He steadied himself and felt the racing beat of Alex's heart. She was frightened but not immediately in danger.

Tyson extricated himself from the trees and glared at Donovan. Donovan hovered, letting Tyson come to him. He ignored the smaller *Slayer*, who was obviously going to hang back and wait for Donovan to be softened up a bit.

As if that would happen.

Tyson lunged at Donovan with sudden speed, but Donovan was ready for him. He exhaled a tendril of smoke, one that wound its way directly toward Tyson's new chest wound. The *Slayer* screamed as the smoke eased beneath his scales. It would burn, Donovan knew, burn and itch and destroy all the flesh it touched.

Tyson writhed in pain, then moved out of range. "This isn't over yet," he muttered.

"No, it's not," Donovan said. "Let's finish what we've started. Unless you're afraid to do so."

"I'm not afraid of you," Tyson sneered. "But I'm not going to give you an easy victory, either." He flew farther away.

Donovan was incensed. "You're not supposed to fight a challenge in increments. It's supposed to be once and to the death. Come on, let's go!"

"Rules are for humans and their defenders," Tyson sneered. "Let's level the field first, shall we?"

"What are you talking about?" Donovan was aware that he could no longer hear his bike's engine.

Where was Alex?

"You've killed one of mine. I want you to pay first with one of yours," Tyson said as he paused beside the smaller *Slayer*. He gave the smaller dragon a push. "Go on, kid. Say hello to an old friend." With that, Tyson flew away, his flight more erratic than it had been originally.

An old friend? Donovan fought to make sense of the taunt even as he worried about Alex.

The smaller *Slayer* flew closer. He was young, but moved oddly. It was as if he were in a trance or sedated. He jerked, like a windup toy, or a puppet being manipulated by someone else. His coloring was familiar, but Donovan was sure he didn't know him.

His scent was deeply wrong. As he inhaled it, Donovan felt a cold shadow. He quickly scanned the sky but there were no other dragons in sight.

That didn't mean Boris had left the scene. In fact, Donovan was pretty sure Boris was wherever Alex was.

Donovan didn't like that he couldn't sense Alex's presence, although he tried to catch her scent again. She could be dead. Unconscious. Beguiled and captured, the way Sara had been. The prospect terrified him. Donovan had no obligation to fight this smaller *Slayer* and he turned to seek his mate instead.

Shots rang out just then, shots that made Donovan scan the forest in terror.

Alex?

While he was distracted, the smaller *Slayer* attacked.

"I thought the flames might change your mind," the *Slayer* said to Alex. His great leathery wings spread wide and he flapped them leisurely. He took flight as if in defiance of gravity. He was far more massive than Alex had realized. He smiled and his teeth seemed to number in the thousands.

Each and every one was sharp and yellow.

His talons were downright evil.

Alex's mouth went dry.

The *Slayer* rose slowly, appearing to her in increments over the wall of flames, as if letting her appreciate his power. The firelight danced off his ruby red scales and made the brass along their edges sparkle. His talons gleamed in vicious splendor. There were red feathers on his tail and down the center of his back, feathers that waved in updraft from the fire like streamers. His eyes shone with hunger or malice—Alex wasn't sure which and didn't much care—and she was terrified by his size and strength.

"Impressive, aren't I?" he mused. His voice was low, like a rumble from the earth. "I'm Boris Vassily, leader of the *Slayers*."

"I'm not impressed," Alex lied.

He smiled, showing more sharp teeth. "Tell me everything you know, right now."

Alex was skeptical. "And you'd let me go, then?"

He laughed. "Humans have such a ridiculous optimism." He sobered then, his eyes glinting. Alex had the sense that he was deciding just how much of a meal she'd make. "You will die. Don't imagine otherwise."

"Then why would I tell you anything?"

"Because that will make the pain stop. The only thing we're negotiating is the amount you will suffer before you die." That smile was even meaner this time. "And I know so many ways to make humans suffer. You might be surprised."

"The firestorm isn't my fault. . . ."

"Stopping this firestorm is an interesting prospect, a bonus offer for me, shall we say, but it's not my main objective."

"Why me, then?"

"I want the Green Machine to disappear, of course."

"You've destroyed my prototype. You've stopped the project."

"Don't lie to me!" Boris blasted the ground in front of the bike with fire and Alex winced at the burning heat. "You'll only stop working on your project when you're dead. And other humans will abandon the project only if all records of it are destroyed. I must ensure that no one else can use your knowledge. If the Green Machine is eliminated now, the moment that it could have made its greatest impact will pass."

"It's too late for that," Alex lied. "I passed my notes along—"

"Liar!" Boris extended his talons and flew closer, seeming to compose his anger as he did so. "I wonder whether lying changes the taste of human flesh," he mused. "Let's find out, shall we?"

Alex didn't share his curiosity about the taste of human flesh, particularly of *her* flesh. He closed his eyes, reared back to bare his teeth, and Alex pulled the gun from inside her jacket.

She locked both hands on the .45 to steady it, just the way she'd been taught, and fired straight where his heart should be.

Assuming that Boris Vassily had one.

The *Slayer* fell upon Donovan, taking advantage of his surprise, and sank strong teeth into Donovan's chest.

Donovan fought the *Slayer* and flung off his weight. He tried to put distance between them, but the *Slayer* came after him again immediately.

The attacking *Slayer* did look familiar to Donovan. He was green, as green as emeralds, his scales touched with copper in a way that made Donovan's breath catch in memory of a lost fellow.

A lost brother.

But he moved so oddly.

"Delaney?" Donovan demanded, certain he was wrong. Had they found a *Slayer* who looked like Delaney to surprise him? Delaney's body had been taken away by the *Slayers* so that they could ensure he remained dead. Had they changed another *Slayer* to resemble him?

Donovan thought of Keir again.

What if Delaney wasn't dead?

The *Slayer* attacked again and Donovan saw that his eyes weren't like Delaney's. Instead of sparkling brown eyes, this dragon's eyes were black and cold.

Flat. Empty. Donovan shuddered at the evidence that no one was home, then understood.

His brother's body had been stolen.

His soul had been evicted, and this thing had been created. Neither alive nor dead, a conversion made against Delaney's will. Donovan was pretty sure his opponent wouldn't bleed.

It was a horrible notion, deeply wrong and offensive.

But the proof was clawing at Donovan's chest, seemingly fascinated by the new scale that Quinn had lodged in Donovan's chest. Maybe he sensed it had been a point of weakness. Maybe he knew it was Donovan's prize. Maybe some shred of Delaney remembered. His talon slashed at it as he tried to rip it loose.

No one was taking the Dragon's Tooth from Donovan.

Donovan breathed dragonfire on the smaller dragon and struck him aside. Delaney had never been a fighter and he was sure he could defeat him easily.

Donovan was wrong.

He clawed the *Slayer* and struck him repeatedly, pummeled him and it made no difference. The *Slayer* was like a wild animal, snapping and biting and grappling, returning to the fray over and over again. He didn't seem to tire. He didn't seem to feel his wounds. His scales burned and blackened under the dragonfire, but he did not even notice. He did not bleed.

He was just like Keir.

Donovan felt dread again. He couldn't accept that the Delaney he had known was completely gone. Keir had still been resident in the abomination he had become. If Donovan could make contact with his brother again, maybe Delaney could be saved.

He had to try.

Donovan had to prove that he was different from Keir.

"Delaney!" he shouted as the pair locked claws again. He felt the *Slayer*'s vicious strength as they grappled for supremacy. "Delaney! Remember when we met? When we touched fingertips and recognized each other? Remember when we first shifted shape together?"

The *Slayer* hauled his claw free and took another swipe at Donovan's chest. He left a gaping wound that trailed blood.

Donovan was desperate to find an incident that triggered Delaney's memory. "Remember how seasick you were on the ship to England? Remember when we met Rafferty in Magnus's cave? Remember when I took Olivia the pearl she so desired?"

The sharp green talon hesitated for a moment over the Dragon's Tooth and there was a flicker deep in those dark eyes.

Delaney was still in there. He'd always hated Olivia.

Was that why he wanted the Dragon's Tooth?

Donovan caught the *Slayer*'s claws in his and held him spread-eagled as they hovered together. The *Slayer* struggled desperately. Donovan spoke with urgency, not knowing how long he could restrain him. "Remember Olivia's maid, the blonde who liked you so well? Remember how we planned for you to be alone? Remember the night of that party, the last party?"

Delaney snarled and screamed, as if a battle raged deep within him. He tipped back his head and roared in anguish, the sound of his pain making Donovan ache in sympathy.

"Remember . . . ," Donovan began, but got no further.

The darkness flashed in his eyes as Delaney ripped his

claw free and snatched at the embedded pearl. His sudden move tore the Dragon's Tooth free of its setting.

The pearl fell, glimmering as it turned in the air.

"No!" Donovan bellowed. He pivoted instinctively to dive after the gem, to snatch it from the air before it was lost.

His move, or maybe his inattention, gave the *Slayer* who had once been Delaney a clear shot.

Donovan felt movement behind him but thought he had time. His grip closed around the pearl, he glanced back, and the *Slayer*'s tail caught him across the side of the head. It was a fierce blow, harder and meaner than anything Delaney could have done.

Donovan lost consciousness and fell.

Alex would have reloaded and shot Boris again, but he screamed and flew away. Black blood dripped from him as he ascended, the drops sizzling as they hit the pavement.

Alex must have hit him—she wasn't sure because she'd kept her eyes closed—but she had no idea how many hits he'd taken. He was hurt, though, and she was glad. As he flew away, he just barely cleared the tops of the trees.

Too bad she hadn't managed to kill him.

What did it take to kill a dragon? Alex really wanted to know.

The flames Boris had lit on the pavement extinguished themselves, as if they had lost interest in burning in his absence.

Alex took a shuddering breath, reloaded the gun and put the safety back on. Her hands were shaking and so was she. There were no other dragons in sight. She was careful and started the engine successfully this time. She drove the bike back down the road to the turn she'd initially taken.

Where was Donovan? If he hadn't come to defend her, then something was wrong. Alex couldn't hear any sounds of dragons fighting and there didn't seem to be any flames in the forest ahead of her. She heard a car engine start and wondered whether it was that gold SUV.

She accelerated in her concern. She turned back onto the secondary highway in time to see Donovan dive from the sky, stretching after something that shone in the sunlight. A smaller copper and green dragon leapt after her dragon.

The vicious blow caught Donovan hard and fast from behind. Even from a distance, Alex heard the horrible thump of the *Slayer*'s tail connecting with the side of Donovan's head.

No! Alex let the bike rip. She raced down the road, not having the first clue what she'd do when she got to Donovan.

She winced as Donovan fell heavily to the ground. The impact made the pavement jump. His blue scales were singed from the other dragon's fire and his wings hung limply. His chest was ripped open and there was a lot of red blood. He didn't look powerful and invincible anymore.

He looked broken.

Alex squealed the tires as she stopped and got off the bike in a heartbeat. She knelt beside Donovan, terrified by his size and strength, even when he was injured.

She had a moment to stare at him in his dragon form, all jeweled and splendid, lapis lazuli and gold. His chest had been ripped open, and there was something clutched in his right claw.

Then he shimmered and changed shape.

In a heartbeat, Donovan was a man again. A tall, sexy man with auburn hair sprawled on the ground in front of Alex, unconscious and injured. He didn't look as if he'd be winking anytime soon.

That bothered Alex.

A lot more than would have been sensible.

The car engine she'd heard had been the gold SUV: Alex saw the vehicle farther down the road as the driver made a U-turn. The truck sped back toward Minneapolis.

She heard the beat of wings and glanced up to see the

green and copper dragon glance after the SUV. He looked wounded, too, but seemed untroubled by his injuries. Alex thought about Donovan's father the previous night and how he didn't seem to feel pain.

Why did good dragons bleed, and bad dragons didn't?

But Boris had bled black blood. This dragon and Donovan's father were somehow different from the others.

He hesitated as she stared, hovering overhead and looking down at Donovan. Alex watched him in terror. What if he descended to finish off Donovan? Could she shoot a dragon who didn't bleed?

He abruptly turned and flew in the opposite direction of the SUV. Alex watched until he was out of sight, then released a breath. She didn't care where he went. The *Slayers* were gone.

That was good enough for her.

Alex dropped to one knee beside Donovan, uncertain what she could do to help him. He was breathing at least.

He had bleeding wounds on his shoulder, and his face and chest were burned. The gouge in his chest was deep and nasty. She recalled that he had had a pearl embedded there in dragon form. She opened his fingers and found the large pearl in his right hand. It was oddly shaped, jagged like a mountain peak, and set in iron. Alex put it into her pocket to keep it safe for him.

She tried to stop the bleeding with a strip off the bottom of his T-shirt and couldn't tell if she was helping him or not. Too bad she didn't know anything about first aid. Applying Band-Aids was the extent of her expertise and Donovan looked as if he needed more care than that.

Taking him to the hospital had to be a bad idea. His physiology might be entirely different from that of a human, and a battery of tests could lead to more questions than answers. Any cure might kill him. Would he change shape again as he healed? If he died? Alex didn't know.

She had no idea how to contact the other *Pyr*, so that they could help him. She took his cell phone from his pocket and checked the address book: he had no numbers saved. Although she knew the advantages of keeping all important information in one's head, there certainly were disadvantages.

She pulled out Donovan's wallet and checked his driver's license. His home address was in Chicago. Other than a pair of credit cards in his name and a couple of hundred dollars in cash, there was nothing else in the wallet.

He was a better spy than she was.

But then, being a dragon shape shifter had to require a certain amount of subterfuge.

Alex looked from Donovan to the bike and back again, wondering how she would move him. With a car, she could have managed. With the Green Machine, she could have managed. The Ducati posed a challenge.

Just her rotten luck: a woman was walking down the road toward them. She had long fair hair that was blowing in the wind. It was so blond that it looked almost white. She was dressed in jeans and a quilted purple jacket, a woman out for a walk. She turned her steps directly toward Alex and approached with purpose.

Uh-oh.

Alex stood up and waited for the woman. There was nowhere she could go, nowhere to hide, and she wasn't leaving Donovan. She was going to need a plausible story to ask for help.

Too bad Alex had no idea what that story might be.

Sophie heard the chorus of the *Pyr* throughout her days and nights. It was a constant hum in her thoughts. It was both her gift and her curse as the Wyvern. She was the first to hear a sour note or a voice cut short.

She heard Donovan fall. Once she would have trusted in the wisdom of the Great Wyvern and left the matter be, but those days were gone. She had learned that it was not possible for her to remain beyond the daily concerns of her kind.

The *Slayers* had taught her that.

It seemed that they had also taught Donovan that he wasn't omnipotent. She didn't imagine that he would take easily to that lesson.

Sophie was torn between the tradition and a world in transition. It was her role to aid the *Pyr*, but traditionally, the Wyvern had remained aloof from worldly affairs. A part of her believed that her gift of prophecy relied upon her avoidance of active participation in worldly events.

Another part of her insisted that the time for remote observation and indifference was past.

The *Pyr* needed her.

Donovan needed her.

Sophie didn't know what price she would pay for involving herself in the mundane, but she couldn't stand aside and watch the *Pyr* lose the fight for their own existence. She couldn't let Donovan sacrifice his chance to become the foretold Warrior.

There was too much at stake.

She had to help.

She manifested close to him. As she walked down the road in human guise, Sophie tasted the terror of Donovan's mate. This was the Wizard of the prophecy, the one who could transform Donovan into the Warrior. Together, these two could do a big part of pulling the planet from the brink of disaster.

Alex Madison wasn't what Sophie had expected. Her black leather pants and spike-heeled boots were not what one would expect a Wizard to wear. Sophie had expected practical clothing, a focus on the intellectual and not the sensual.

Interesting.

Perhaps Donovan had also found his mate's choices interesting.

Perhaps the Great Wyvern had a number of tricks up Her sleeve.

Sophie smelled blood and violence, *Slayer* blood and *Pyr* blood in nauseating combination. There was something else, too, a scent of cinders and ash, of death and dark shadows. She didn't know what it was but she had an instinctive dislike of that smell.

It was wicked.

Like the academy.

Perhaps from the academy.

Sophie focused on the human's fear and noted her resolve. She felt the power of this firestorm, even with Donovan fallen and unconscious. There was heat even at a distance. She observed all of this as she walked a hundred paces toward the Wizard.

"Oh!" she exclaimed, as if she hadn't known she'd find a wounded man at the side of the road in this precise place. "You must have had an accident. Can I help?"

Alex was wary. "Thank you, but I'm not sure what to do."

Sophie sampled the Wizard's scent as she stood beside her, recognizing intelligence and caution mingled with that fear. Donovan, she was glad to note, was not fatally wounded. He was injured and he was shocked. She pushed another dream into his thoughts, then spoke. "Surely he needs assistance."

Alex looked away. "He likes to be self-reliant. I'm not sure he'd be happy to wake up in a hospital."

Sophie understood. Alex knew what Donovan was and she had made her peace with it. They were together. It was more than she had hoped for.

"He won't change shape while he's injured," she said softly.

Alex stepped back in shock. "I don't understand what you mean," she lied, trying to hide what she knew.

It wasn't that easy to fool the Wyvern.

"On the contrary, you know exactly what I mean." Sophie recounted an old verse:

Elements four disguise weapons three,
Revealed if love harnesses fury.
The Wizard can work her alchemy
Only with the Warrior's lost key.
Transformation in the firestorm's might,
Will forge a foretold force for right.
Warrior, Wizard and Pyr army
Shall lead the world to victory.

"I beg your pardon?" Alex said.

"You will remember my words when you have need of their counsel. My arrival here is not a coincidence, for all its timeliness."

"Who are you?" Alex demanded.

Sophie smiled with her characteristic serenity. "You know who I am. Or, perhaps more accurately, what I am."

"I don't think so—"

"Where do you intend to take him?" Sophie asked, interrupting her quietly. "Tell me and I will ensure his safe arrival. After that, the task of healing him is yours."

"I'm not letting you take him anywhere. . . ."

Sophie met Alex's gaze and held it. Something in her own silenced the woman's protest as she stared. Alex was afraid, but she refused to be cornered by that fear. She faced it. The Wyvern respected that. Alex feared dragons but she aided Donovan, even though she knew his truth and it terrified her.

Sophie could help.

"You are the Wizard long foretold," she said. "Look upon that which you fear." She heard Alex take a quick breath, but she didn't step away. The intelligence in her gaze told Sophie that Alex knew what to expect.

Sophie summoned the change and felt the shift shimmer within herself. As always, she reveled in the power that made her what she was. She felt the vibration of change and let her body do what it did best.

She shifted shape, in broad daylight, in the middle of a Minnesota country road. She did it slowly, as slowly as she could possibly do it, the better to let the Wizard see the truth of transformation. The slow transition was a sight that could drive a human to madness—as Donovan well knew—but Sophie had faith in her instincts. She knew Donovan would never to do this to Alex, just as she knew it had to be done.

The Wizard must be as stalwart as the Warrior, yet have the ability to consider known matters in a new way. The Wizard must be able to make sense of what seemed to be madness. Or magic. The Wizard must be able to witness this transformation and survive to make use of what she had seen.

Sophie unfurled her dragon form, praying to the Great Wyvern that this Wizard had all of that and more.

The *Pyr* who could become the Warrior was going to need it.

Chapter 9

Alex's mouth fell open as the woman changed shape right before her eyes. Her eyes glittered when she looked up that last time, a jewellike light appearing from their turquoise depths. Alex thought she knew what that glitter meant.

The woman then began to shimmer, the edges of her body taking on a strange brilliance. It reminded Alex of a chemical reaction, an element on the cusp of transformation. It was hard to tell where the woman ended and where the air around her began.

That was when Alex knew exactly what was going to happen.

That was when she knew exactly who the woman was. She remembered what Sara had told her and realized that she was in the presence of the Wyvern, the only female *Pyr*.

The beautiful but mysterious prophetess.

The Wyvern became larger and larger. She stretched out her arms with languid grace, moving more like a bird than a human. Her nails grew into talons; her skin turned to scales. She threw back her head, apparently glorying in the change, and bared her teeth. They became long and sharp; her jawbone extended, as her tail coiled across the pavement. She was white, as white as milk or a bucket of pearls, as pale and ethereal as a dragon made of glass.

She was magnificent, terrifying, and beautiful.

Alex trembled right to her toes, but she looked.

The Wyvern's hair flowed into long pearlescent feathers, plumage that reminded Alex of a swan. Wings sprouted from her back and stretched wide overhead, adorned with those same feathers. She glistened in the sunlight, looking otherworldly and unreal. There seemed to be a translucence about her, and her presence was more serene than that of the *Pyr* Alex had met.

Those talons and teeth, that piercing gaze, told Alex that she was still a formidable foe.

"You're the Wyvern," Alex said, and the Wyvern inclined her head in agreement. She moved with easy grace to shelter Donovan, a great tenderness in her manner. She arched her wings over him to shade him from the sun and bent to run the gloss of her pearly claw across his cheek. There was sadness in the gesture, a sadness that made Alex fear for Donovan's survival.

"Can he be healed?" Alex asked.

The Wyvern lifted her head slowly to look at Alex. Her eyes were the same bright turquoise. "That depends upon you, Wizard."

"Why can't you heal your own kind?"

"It is the Wizard whose alchemy can heal the Warrior."

Alex felt as if the Wyvern's answers only provided more questions, but she was determined to learn what she could. "What's the matter with him? He doesn't seem to be that badly hurt."

The Wyvern hesitated, her gaze lingering on Donovan. Her words were lower and more thoughtful than they had been. "It is in trial that a warrior learns his true strength, not in triumph. We all shall learn the measure of this fighter in this test."

"That doesn't sound very encouraging."

The Wyvern raised her gaze. "It can be. He can become the foretold Warrior."

"How?"

"The alchemy is yours."

Alex flung out her hands. "I don't know what I'm supposed to do. I don't know much about first aid and I don't know anything about healing dragons. How can you leave something important up to me?"

The Wyvern seemed to smile. "The union of the firestorm is more than seed meeting womb; it is a cohesion of all four elements. The Warrior brings the fire of passion to the union. The Wizard brings the intellectual power of air. Their firestorm will not be a complete union until they add earth and water."

Alex folded her arms across her chest. Mating again. Didn't these *Pyr* understand that she had work to do? "What if they don't want a complete union?"

The Wyvern chuckled. She lifted Donovan with her front claws, as effortlessly as if she cradled a child. She fired a glance at Alex, one that made her take a step back. "Where?"

"I can't heal him. I don't know how."

"You are the Wizard." The Wyvern reared up to her full height, holding Donovan high above the ground. "Where?"

"I think you're making a mistake in expecting me to do this. If Donovan is so important and you can't heal him, then you need to get a *Pyr* doctor to fix him up."

The Wyvern's wings began to beat and her feet lifted slightly off the ground. Alex panicked, not certain where the Wyvern was going, not at all certain she was ready to have Donovan leave her life forever.

The Wyvern was three feet above the pavement. The beat of her wings stirred the grasses and made Alex's hair blow.

"Where?" she demanded once again, her tone sharper.

Alex knew the answer, even though she didn't like it. She and Donovan had agreed to work on her project together, after all. Maybe she could somehow heal him at Peter's cottage. She was skeptical, despite the Wyvern's faith, but it didn't seem as if there were any other options.

"I can't explain easily how to get there, especially from the air—," she began, but got no further.

"Think of it," the Wyvern commanded. "Fill your thoughts with the place and I will find it."

"You're joking."

"I am the Wyvern and not without my gifts." Alex knew she didn't imagine the haughtiness that tinged the white dragon's tone.

Alex did what she was told. She closed her eyes and imagined her brother's cottage, nestled in its hundred acres of perfection. She envisioned the winding road that led to it from the main road, the way the ancient lilac hedge obscured any sight of the building itself until you came around the last curve. She remembered going there in the spring, the smell of lilacs like a slice of heaven, their purple blooms tossing in the wind.

She recalled how the house had been a farmhouse, how its foundation was made with stones that had been hand-fitted by some forgotten mason. She thought about the square-headed nails that held the big old beams together, the dirt floor in the basement.

In her mind's eye, she saw how the one long wall gave a stupendous view of hills and lakes over Itasca State Park. She remembered the day that hole had been opened by the contractor and how they had all stood and marveled at the view.

She remembered arguing with Peter about making his executive retreat more ecologically friendly. She remembered having to help the contractor install the solar panels on the roof and helping Mark make the whole system work. She remembered Peter being impressed at how little he'd had to sacrifice.

She remembered how she had run down to the edge of the lake with Peter's kids in the early morning just this past summer, the grass wet and cold on their bare feet, the water sparkling in invitation. She saw Mark doing cannonballs off the dock, after installing those solar panels, after hiding the first Green Machine before everyone else arrived. She saw Mark lose his glasses in the lake and smiled.

She thought about the crisp edge of the air there in the autumn, the colors of the leaves, the scent of distant wood smoke. She remembered how the fire crackled on the big stone hearth, how the hand-hooked rug in front of that fireplace seemed to glow in the firelight, how hot chocolate tasted better there than anywhere else in the whole world. She thought about snow against the porch, the Christmas tree glittering in the main room and duvets pulled up to her chin as snowflakes fell fast and thick outside.

She recalled how she felt free and alive at Peter's cottage, in a way that she never experienced in the city. She thought about blue herons fishing in the shallows and the silhouettes of fish in deep water, the gleam of dragonflies, the call of the pair of loons who took up residence on the lake each summer. She remembered guiding a canoe across the lake as the first rosy light of dawn touched the water and tasted that tranquility again.

When Alex opened her eyes, she stood alone on the road. She thought she could see a speck high above that might have been the Wyvern, but she couldn't be sure. It was heading north, though, the very direction she needed to go.

Alex started Donovan's bike, pulled on her helmet, and turned in the direction of Peter's cottage. She believed that the Wyvern would be there before her, waiting, with Donovan.

With any luck, the first Green Machine was still there, too.

Lost in shadows, Donovan dreamed of his past.
He dreamed of betrayal.
He dreamed of deceit and he dreamed of greed.
He dreamed, inevitably, of Olivia.

*   *   *

The pair descend to the cellar, her skirts rustling. He will follow her anywhere, and he suspects she knows as much. He is unsated by their lovemaking and prepared to do anything to join her abed again.

Olivia has asked a favor.

Donovan will do it.

He will do anything for her.

When she leads him to a dark corner of her cellar, one filled with cobwebs, he thinks she has planned an amorous game. Instead, at her command, he turns a great lock and opens a hidden door.

Her eyes gleam with satisfaction that she has surprised him and she holds a finger to her lips when he might have commented upon it. He holds the lantern high and looks.

There are stairs that descend from the cellar to points unknown. They are rough-hewn from rock but fairly even. He leans into the space but can see only stairs descending endlessly. He can smell the dampness and hear the drip of water far below.

She leans against him, her high lace collar prickling against his throat, her perfume tempting him to take her again. The light from the lantern plays lovingly with the white curve of her breast and he yearns to cup it, kiss it, run his tongue across its ruby nipple. She whispers, her voice so soft that he has to strain for her words, even though her lips are against his ear.

"It is said that at the base of the stairs, there is a grotto."

He nods, unsurprised. He hears the water dripping, after all.

"And in that grotto is a lake," she continues, her hand rising to caress the necklace of pearls that he has given to her. "And in that lake is a pearl beyond price."

She smiles and he knows what she wants of him. She has a weakness for pearls, after all. It was with a pearl-encrusted doublet that he first gained her attention, without any intent of doing so; a pearl pendant that saw him invited

*first to her home; this very pearl necklace that gained him
entry to her bedchamber. His blood quickens with the
prospect of what she will surrender if he fetches this pearl
for her.*

*"The Dragon's Tooth," she says, and he fears that she
has glimpsed his secret.*

But no. It is simply the name of the pearl.

"And you desire it?" he asks, no question in his voice.

*She nods, her eyes glowing with anticipation. "I will do
anything for it."*

*He considers the stairs for only a moment. He is a cham-
pion, a duelist who takes every challenge and triumphs
every time. He is invincible. Unassailable. Without peer. He
is a Pyr disguised in human society, a man who wins his
every desire.*

He wants this lady for his wife.

She wants the pearl.

Her challenge is a barter he cannot refuse.

*He smiles agreement, senses her relief, then bends to kiss
her. She turns her face in the last moment so his lips brush
against her cheek, a tease typical of her flirtatious games.
He has no doubt that her reward will be worth its cost.*

*He lifts the lantern higher and steps into the hidden space.
The flame wavers in a cold draft from the darkness below.*

*The door slams behind him. He raises a hand to it in time
to hear the key turn in the lock. He runs his hands over it but
there is no latch on this side.*

*"Farewell," whispers the lady whom he had believed to
be his love. There is poison in her voice. "I shall miss the
pleasure you offered, if nothing else."*

"What of the Dragon's Tooth?"

*She laughs low. "No man returns alive with it. I have sold
you to its keeper in exchange for the prize."*

"But—"

*"If you are the first to defeat him, this portal will be the
least of your obstacles."*

As her footsteps retreat, his heart takes on the chill of the hewn-stone walls. A thousand tiny incidents take on new importance; a hundred overheard rumors align themselves with her most recent deed. He has been tricked by one he mistakenly trusted. He has been only another pawn to her, another means of achieving her desire.

He will not be so foolish as to trust a woman again.

In fact, he will teach Olivia a lesson. He will win the pearl, but his terms will not be easily met. She will pay a price for her treachery.

He draws his sword, tightens his grip on the light, and begins his descent into darkness.

It was twilight when Alex reached the cottage. The sky was thick with stars overhead, but she didn't take the time to stop and look. The Ducati's engine sounded loud on the winding drive to the house, and the shadows felt ominous. Alex wondered whether her decision to come here was really that unpredictable.

It was good to know that the Wyvern would be on the porch, waiting for her.

At least, Alex hoped she would be. What if the imaginary navigation system was a failure? What if there were a thousand other cottages that were more or less like Peter's cottage?

Alex turned the last curve, catching her breath the way she always did when she first saw the house. Peter's country retreat shouldn't really have been called a cottage. It was massive, an architectural marvel outfitted with every luxury known to modern man. There were seven bedrooms with en suite baths, a stainless steel chef's kitchen, a viewing room for movies, and a security system that was cutting-edge technology.

Locked up until Peter's family's arrival for Christmas, the place was a fortress.

That was part of what Alex liked about it.

Every window was dark, although Alex knew this was

because of the metal blinds that locked down over the wide
expanses of glass. There was only one point of entry when
the house was secured: the front-porch door alongside the
triple garage. There was always a light on there—the house
had an enormous generator for backup power in the case of
a power failure or battery exhaustion.

And there was Oscar. Oscar was the voice-activated heart
and soul of Peter's smart house.

Alex was disappointed to see that the porch was empty.
Her doubts grew—and so did her trepidation—as she parked
the bike. She turned it around, in case she needed to make a
quick departure, and hid it against the far side of the garage
where there was a path to the back side of the house. The
lilacs were tall there, and the shadows deep enough to disguise the bike.

She stepped into the night, well aware of the rustlings in
the darkness. Were there *Slayers* lying in wait for her here?
Even if there were, Alex knew she'd feel better in the house.
It'd be like sleeping in Fort Knox. Oscar would watch the
gates.

She trotted up the steps, noting that there was no sign of
anyone having been there. There was a scuttle of fallen
leaves on the porch, undisturbed by any footsteps.

Maybe the Wyvern had reconsidered and taken Donovan
to some dragon rehab center. Alex frowned as she punched
in the string of access codes. Oscar scanned her iris and reviewed her thumbprint. After a beat, a green light flashed
that her access was approved.

"Good evening, Ms. Madison," Oscar said in his usual
dulcet tones. "I trust you had a good journey."

"No, actually. It was hell, but I'm glad to be here, Oscar."

"Welcome, then." Alex wondered whether Oscar would
notify Peter that she had entered his retreat. She'd never
thought of that, but it wouldn't have surprised her.

"You are not alone tonight, Ms. Madison," Oscar said
quietly. "There is one unidentified guest in the house."

Alex pivoted and peered at the speaker, her mouth opening in shock. How could there be anyone in the house? How could someone have gotten into the house without providing identification? It made absolutely no sense.

Oscar had to have a glitch.

"Are you sure, Oscar? Or are you joking?"

"It is not in my programming to err or to make jokes, Ms. Madison."

It had to be a mistake. That didn't stop Alex's heart from hammering. She half thought any intruder would hear her coming, just from the thunder of her heart.

Better safe than sorry. Before she entered the house, Alex pulled her gun. She checked that it was loaded, then took a deep breath. Years of watching cop movies gave her some ideas.

The *Mission Impossible* theme song echoed in her thoughts.

Alex flicked the door open with her wrist, then leaned back against the outside wall. She let the door swing all the way open before she moved.

There wasn't a sound from inside.

She strained her ears, but was unable to hear any sound of life. Mosquitoes were gathering, doubtless intending to take advantage of the buffet she offered, and Alex wasn't going to stay outside.

She slid through the door, trying to be one with the shadows. Alex let her eyes adjust to the dim light as she held the gun high and the door closed. She could smell the chlorine in the lap pool and hear the low thrum of the filtering pump. The lights were on a low setting that she might have called romantic at another time.

Between the front door and the great room was the conservatory, a space that housed the sauna and lap pool. There was a long planter of ferns that was suspended from the ceiling and ran the length of the conservatory. With the shutters closed, there was no external light. Alex could see the gas fireplace in the main room, a long way ahead, because it was on. Low flames flicked on the simulated coals.

She paused to consider this. She knew that Peter would never have left it on. Could Oscar have turned it on for her? Or had the smart house put the fire on for the guest who wasn't here?

Or was there really a second guest here?

Had somebody turned the fire on, to beckon her forward? Alex couldn't see many other choices. There was in or out, forward or back. She took a deep breath and started to walk down the length of the conservatory, one careful step at a time.

All she could hear was the low hum of the house around her, the familiar sound of it managing and monitoring itself.

Beyond the conservatory, there was one enormous room. Once over that threshold, the walls to Alex's left and straight ahead would be made of glass, the left one providing that view and the one ahead facing the lake. Again, they were shuttered down and dark.

To her right would be the original farmhouse, which now was a three-story tower containing the bedrooms. The stone fireplace was in the common wall between old and new, and Peter had had that huge hearth built on this side. The open-concept kitchen was to Alex's immediate right. She knew the layout perfectly.

Her mouth was dry and her heart was racing when she got to the end of the conservatory. The fire flickered as if to welcome her. Alex surveyed the familiar shadows for a long time before she was sufficiently confident to take a step farther into the room.

That was when she heard the faint whisper of someone breathing.

There *was* someone in the house! She hit one light switch abruptly with her left hand, aiming the gun in the direction of the sound.

Alex saw the man lying in front of the fireplace and nearly had heart failure.

Donovan.
And he was alone.

Alex turned away and took a shaking breath. She ran a hand over her forehead and sat down before her knees gave out. Her heart skipped, then lodged right in her throat. She checked the room to be sure that it wasn't a trap, but there was only Donovan.

He was still out cold. His face was pale and the blood had dried on his wounds. Did he look better? Alex couldn't say.

She lit a smaller light, then went through the entire house like a cop looking for a felon, leading with her gun. She knew what she'd find and she was right. All doors and windows were still locked and the house was undisturbed.

Except for Donovan. Apparently high-tech security systems didn't stop the Wyvern. Oscar had been outfoxed, but not by human intruders.

What did that mean about *Slayers*? Alex didn't want to think about that, but she knew she had to. She put her gun on the coffee table, not wanting it to be too far away, and took off her jacket. She went to Donovan's side and knelt beside him, uncertain what to do to help him.

At least he was still breathing. She could see the slow and steady flicker of his pulse at his throat. The burn on his face might have been a little less angry, or it could have been the lack of light. That gouge in his chest was still ugly. His breathing was deep and she wondered whether he was dreaming. The firelight played over his features, casting them in golden light, making him look like a romantic hero.

Alex thought about checking Donovan's pulse. She reached out a hand, remembered what he could become and how he had killed his father, then pulled her hand back.

She could *see* his pulse, moving the tanned skin of his throat in a regular rhythm.

Alex didn't like that she was rationalizing out of fear. She reached to touch Donovan again, then noticed that something was wrong with the glass front on the fireplace. A pattern was forming there and she leaned closer, wondering what had happened to it. The pattern shaped suddenly into letters, as if someone had written on the glass in flame.

"You know in your heart what to do."

The letters burned brightly just long enough for Alex to read them, then disappeared as if they had never been.

If only Alex shared the Wyvern's confidence. A little more instruction would have been welcome. Did the *Pyr* self-heal? Did Donovan just need some sleep? Alex didn't know and it annoyed her. She unzipped her boots and kicked them off, stretching her toes and flexing her feet. That made her feel better, unaccustomed as she was to foxy boots, but she was still irritated.

Alex liked to fix things. She liked to accomplish things. She liked to be part of the solution, not just a passive by-stander.

But she had a wounded dragon on her hands, one who had been attacked because he had been defending her. She was responsible for Donovan and his condition, whether she liked it or not. And somehow, she had to help him.

Too bad she didn't know how.

She wasn't going to do anything to make his condition worse, that was for sure.

To Alex's surprise, the big flat-screen television on the opposite wall suddenly flickered to life. She eyed it warily. There was an outside chance that Oscar had been pro-grammed to play a movie when someone arrived at night.

"There are other justifications than that."

Alex spun at the sound of the Wyvern's voice, coming from everywhere and nowhere simultaneously. She ran to check Oscar's control panel but no one had entered the house.

Of course not. It had been the Wyvern's voice and she was claiming responsibility for the television coming on. Alex was smart enough to know when to pay attention, even if a movie was the lesson.

Especially if a movie was the lesson.

The image on the wide screen was vivid in the darkness of the house. Alex could have walked right into the movie. She didn't recognize the movie or any of the cast and that was pretty strange, given how many movies she watched. It looked like a period piece.

The opening scene was a crowded party. Music lilted and a fire blazed on a huge hearth. The actors' clothing was lavish: richly embroidered, embellished with jewels, cut of velvet and brocade; it gleamed in the golden light. They all wore high, lace-edged white collars.

They looked like actors in a Shakespearean play. Alex didn't know the lines, though, and it wasn't iambic pentameter. The camera moved through the crowd like a person crossing the room, capturing furtive expressions, smiles and winks and flirtatious glances. The audio was overheard snippets, gossip about a famous duelist and scandalous affairs.

The camera paused to focus on a beautiful woman who stood at one side of the room. Her hair was dark and she wore a long necklace of pearls. Her collar was higher than most, and the white of it framed her lovely face. Her lips were red and her eyes were blue.

The woman turned to look steadily into the camera as it drew nearer. She smiled as if she and the camera were on intimate terms. Alex had never seen this actress before, which surprised her. With a face like that, she should have gotten a ton of roles.

"It is done," she murmured as the camera sidled up to her. She took a sip of her wine and glanced across the room, failing to disguise her satisfaction. "He is determined to get the Dragon's Tooth." There was greed in the depths of her eyes and a hard line to her lips. "You have your prey—now bring me my prize."

"Do you not care that he will die?" a man's voice asked brusquely. Alex realized that his was the view the camera shared.

She was looking through his eyes.

The woman sneered. "Men are all useful, but in the end I have only myself to rely upon." She made to sip from her pewter cup, but a man's hand seized it and cast the wine against the wall. His sleeve was red velvet.

"A foolish admission, Olivia," he said, his voice filled with menace. "For now I have proof of the truth of your heart."

The woman was afraid. "I spoke of him!"

"You spoke of men, and I did not miss the detail." He wisibly tightened his grip on her wrist and she whimpered. "You had best hope that your champion wins this duel, for I shall demand much more for the prize you would claim as your own."

"You promised!"

His voice dropped low. "I lied."

Rage contorted her features, but before she spoke the scene cut to darkness. The contrast was startling. Alex sat down on the edge of the couch, transfixed. She could see rock gleaming wetly in the darkness, as if the camera had entered a cave.

There was a light coming from far below. Water dripped, and as the camera wound its way down a roughly hewn staircase, the drips and pillars of calcium became clear.

The camera closed in on the silhouette of a man, as if coming up behind him. He carried the lantern that was the source of light. Alex saw the gleam of a knife in the hand of the man whose view she shared. He followed the first man in silence.

This wasn't good.

The lead man moved warily. He was dressed in a green velvet doublet with lace collar and cuffs. His boots were high and his tights showed that he had great legs.

He didn't look in the least bit effeminate, but then, with a build like his, Alex couldn't imagine that any outfit could make him look less than all man. She was also pretty sure his tights weren't padded. That was real muscle.

She wondered who the actor was and yearned for a glimpse of his face. He moved with easy grace, like a dancer or a runner. He held a sword high in his right hand and a lantern in his left. His hair was russet, the same deep auburn shade as Donovan's.

She glanced down at Donovan, who was still out cold, then back at the screen.

"What do you seek in my lair, intruder?" demanded that deep male voice Alex had heard before.

The man with the russet hair spun. He swung his blade immediately to defend himself and the two blades clashed. Alex would have recognized him anywhere.

Donovan!

Chapter 10

How could a cameraman fight a battle with Donovan while juggling the weight of a camera? Then Alex knew. She really was looking through the eyes of Donovan's opponent.

The Wyvern had conjured this display from Donovan's past as a lesson for Alex.

Alex sat down, ignoring the voice in her mind that insisted things were getting too weird. She watched as the two men battled each other, their swords clashing mightily. She wished she could have seen the attacker: all she saw of him was the bloodred velvet of his sleeve, the wrist edged with pearls and lace. He had a hand like a ham hock—again, there was no question of the frills making him look feminine.

He backed Donovan down the stairs, into the grotto below. Donovan flung his lantern on a rock shelf and it cast a feeble light into the considerable dimensions of the cavern.

The scene was otherworldly. Stalactites and stalagmites clustered like ungainly teeth. Some were encrusted with white residue from the dripping water, yet others were stained rich ocher. The roof of the cave arched high overhead.

There was a lake, one as dark as a mirror and with nary a ripple. A pile gleamed near it, a pile of precious objects.

As the attacker forced Donovan away from the lantern, Donovan abruptly pulled out a shorter blade. He fought with both hands, stabbing at his assailant with a flurry of blows. He was fast and unpredictable, faster and more agile than his opponent.

The attacker cried out in pain as a blade found its mark, and Alex wanted to cheer.

His perspective suddenly changed. He got taller, because suddenly she was looking down on Donovan. Alex guessed that the attacker had changed shape. She looked for his shadow and saw it stretched across the floor of the cave. He had wings and talons and a long tail.

More dragons. If this was in the past, then this dragon could do to Donovan what Boris and Tyson had done to Mark.

And the Wyvern expected Alex to watch.

She looked for the remote. Then she realized that Donovan was here, whole and sleeping. He'd survived this battle.

Sometimes it was good to know the ending of the story.

The attacker's vision had become crisper, far more detailed than his vision in human guise. When he focused on something, his sight seemed to spiral in, increasing the level of detail so quickly that it made Alex dizzy. Alex was awed by the resolution.

Was this how the world looked to Donovan in dragon form? He had said that his senses were more keen, but this was amazing.

Meanwhile, Donovan bellowed and changed shape as well, taking much less time for the transition. His scales glimmered in the lantern's light, as rich an ornament as his Elizabethan garb. He was all muscle and sinew, all power, and Alex wanted to applaud. He looked like a champion.

Donovan didn't have that embedded pearl on his chest, the one that was now in her pocket. Was the difference important?

The pair locked claws and grappled for supremacy. Donovan was younger, Alex could see, more slender and quick. Lighter, too—his opponent flung Donovan across the cavern so that he fell hard against the floor.

Donovan didn't immediately move. Alex stood up.

Donovan's opponent turned his gaze on the lantern. Alex saw his vision fixate on the flame to the exclusion of all else. The lantern flame became larger and larger.

He was controlling the fire with his will. The flame leapt high, higher, higher, then was abruptly extinguished.

The cavern was plunged into darkness. Alex watched the vision of Donovan's opponent adjust to the change with remarkable speed. Shadows redefined themselves into walls and floor and lake and hoard. He almost had night vision, seeing the world in so many shades of black and red and gold. He seemed to have become taller.

Then she guessed what he'd done. He'd stolen the energy of the flame and turned it to his own uses. He'd coaxed it to its maximum power, then taken the energy for his own.

He turned to consider Donovan with such deliberation that Alex had a bad feeling.

The ground rumbled. Donovan's opponent looked around in confusion. The floor of the cavern was jumping and ripples crossed the lake's surface. The golden hoard was disturbed, several items falling into the lake with splashes. The cave floor vibrated with force and Donovan's assailant lost his balance.

He took flight just as several large stalactites fell and shattered on the floor of the cave. He pivoted in midair and his vision locked again on the fallen blue dragon. He obviously intended to finish what he had started, ASAP.

Donovan stirred, raised his head, and shook it. He looked straight at his assailant, eyes flashing as he exhaled smoke.

But before Donovan could rise to his feet, a massive dragon of opal and gold erupted from the earth right in front of him. He made an impressive barrier between Donovan and his attacker, rock crumbling from his shoulders and back.

The assailant took a step back. "You," he breathed, his hatred audible.

Donovan looked surprised, too.

"Ah, Magnus," the new arrival said, shaking his head slowly. His voice was deep and ancient and Alex recognized it right away—he was the *Pyr* who had driven the hearse. "I am disappointed in you."

The assailant—Magnus—snorted. "Why should I care?"

"Once you cared for my friendship and respect." The new arrival's eyes gleamed.

Magnus laughed. "Once I did not know the old secrets of power."

"Once," Rafferty said quietly, "you were among the true *Pyr*."

"What stirs you, Rafferty, after all these years?" demanded Magnus. "We know already that you cannot defeat me."

Rafferty apparently didn't accept this as a given. His eyes glittered. "Perhaps I have learned something in two centuries."

"Perhaps your ability to snore will not affect the outcome."

Magnus breathed a stream of fire that lit the cave with brilliant orange. Rafferty reared back and the pair lunged for each other.

If he was on Donovan's side, then Rafferty was a good dragon. Alex cheered for all good dragons. It was her new policy.

Rafferty struck Magnus with his tail. Magnus ripped Rafferty's wings with his claws and the red blood of the *Pyr* dripped into the lake below. Rafferty rammed Magnus into the wall of the cave, causing it to shake. Several chunks of rock loosed themselves and shattered below, one splashing in the lake.

Magnus had forgotten Donovan, but Alex hadn't. Where was he?

Magnus roared and bit, his teeth digging deep into the *Pyr*'s throat. Alex saw Rafferty's eyes dim and feared he was lost. He fought on, but more weakly than before. His breathing was labored and Magnus locked his talons around the *Pyr*'s neck.

"A strange treasure for my hoard," Magnus muttered. "A trophy of the most uncommon kind. You fought well, Rafferty, but you never were a match for me."

There was only the barest glimmer in Rafferty's eyes to warn Alex before Magnus was struck suddenly from behind. The view jolted as Magnus's head was snapped suddenly to the left; then he tumbled through the air.

Magnus fell, crashing into the pile of his hoard. The coins spilled like so many loose stones, sparkling as they slid toward the lake.

A resplendent Donovan hovered overhead, then dove to attack again. Alex's bones vibrated with Magnus's bellow of rage and her heart leapt as he jumped into the air. He attacked Donovan, but Rafferty assailed him from behind. The pair of good dragons fought from either side, slashing at the *Slayer* with their claws and pummeling him with their tails.

Magnus seethed against them, striking and clawing and thrashing, slowing steadily all the while. As Magnus weakened, Rafferty began to hum. His was a low chant, unfamiliar yet curiously stirring. It was like a military march, insistent and rousing.

The rock of the cavern floor began to move, undulating in response to Rafferty's chant. Stone and earth danced to his tune. His voice became louder, his song working an ancient magic.

Meanwhile, Donovan breathed a fearsome stream of fire upon Magnus, backing him into the stone walls of the cavern. Magnus screamed and writhed in pain; then Donovan exhaled smoke to add to his torment. Magnus landed so heavily that the walls shook even more.

Rafferty sang more loudly and the high stone ceiling of the cave began to fall in chunks. The rock floor rippled and split, and Alex could hear the rumble of an angry earth.

"Mercy!" Magnus screamed. "I beg you for mercy."

Donovan paused and looked to the older *Pyr* for guidance.

Rafferty halted his song, his expression amused. "Would you have spared either of us such mercy?" he asked quietly. "Would you have given either of us a chance to live?"

"Take my hoard!"

"It is not enough," Rafferty said. "Mere wealth is not enough. Even the Dragon's Tooth will not suffice now. You must die, Magnus."

"No!" Magnus roared.

Rafferty's song became more strident. Rock and stone and soil responded; the cave began to collapse. Rock continued to fall in a ceaseless torrent, and the view across the cavern was obscured. The stairs that Donovan had descended groaned, then slid into the cavern in a jumble of stone.

Alex knew that Magnus wasn't dead, for she could see the view through the slits of his eyes. She bit her lip, fearing the *Slayer*'s intent. She heard Donovan's heavy breathing, heard Rafferty cease his song.

"He has cared for another," Rafferty counseled, his breath labored, "though her name is not important now. There will be a damaged scale that shows the truth, and there is his weakness. Hurry! I cannot halt what I have begun."

With that, Alex knew what dragons were afraid of: love made them vulnerable, because caring for someone meant the dragon in question gained a flaw in his armor.

Donovan landed beside the fallen *Slayer* and quickly surveyed him. Magnus meanwhile studied Donovan. From such close proximity, Alex was amazed again by the brilliant shine of Donovan's scales. They didn't look as metallic as they did now, but their lapis lazuli color was vivid. Magnus's gaze locked upon a broken scale on Donovan's chest.

Alex understood that Donovan had cared for someone. *Who?*

The *Slayer* struck as suddenly as a cobra.

He sank his teeth into Donovan's vulnerable spot, using the last of his strength to injure his opponent. Donovan roared and ripped Magnus away, casting him aside. He dug his own claws into Magnus's chest, ripping the flesh where one scale had fallen away. He ravaged and tore the *Slayer*, leaving nothing to chance. Magnus's dark blood steadily stained the gold of his hoard.

"How badly do you desire the Dragon's Tooth?" Magnus whispered, his words low and angry. Donovan froze. "How much do you think she will surrender in exchange?"

Magnus plunged one claw into the gleaming abundance of his hoard, whispering a chant under his breath. When he pulled out his claw, a magnificent, jagged pearl was hooked on one talon. It was so luminescent that it could have been made of moonlight. Its shape was more like a small mountain range than a typical pearl.

Alex reached into her pocket and pulled out the pearl that had been embedded in Donovan's chest. It was the same gem; she was sure of it.

It had been mounted to cover the space where he'd been missing a scale. She eyed him, wondering.

She glanced up at the screen in time to see Donovan's eyes light with desire. Magnus chuckled as the younger *Pyr* snatched at the gem. "Still Olivia's pawn, are you?" Magnus rasped. Donovan jolted at the sound of the woman's name and Alex knew who had caused him to lose the scale.

"Fetch her prize then," Magnus snarled, and flung the pearl.

The Dragon's Tooth glittered as it sailed through the darkness, then splashed into the lake. It glimmered, then disappeared.

Only when Donovan dove into the lake did Magnus's vision dim.

"It will not save you, even if you retrieve it," Magnus muttered, and no one heard but Alex. "Only I know the truth of the Dragon's Tooth, and that secret dies with me."

Magnus chuckled one last time as Rafferty shouted a warning. Rocks fell with increasing speed, the cavern turning to chaos and darkness. Donovan was still in the lake.

And the screen faded to black.

Obviously Donovan had lived, but Alex wanted to know how he and Rafferty had survived. Alex waited for the lesson to continue. The television might as well have been turned off.

Nothing happened.

Donovan continued to sleep. He could have been in a coma.

Alex realized this was the part where she was supposed to know what to do. Except she didn't. She pushed herself to her feet and paced, not liking that she had only half the story.

Did they ever figure out what Magnus had known about the Dragon's Tooth? Donovan's fascination with it had something to do with this Olivia, the woman responsible for his losing a scale. Did Donovan not want the firestorm because he still loved Olivia? And what was Alex supposed to do about any of this?

The excerpt had created more questions than it had answered. Alex remembered that Sara had made a similar comment about the Wyvern, and that didn't improve her mood.

Alex paced. She knew she wouldn't sleep anytime soon. It was after midnight, but she was wide-awake.

She should work.

She was not going down to the boathouse alone in the dark to check her prototype.

She could have loaded up Peter's computer with the programs and data on her backup disks, but she felt too twitchy to concentrate. She could make saltwater solution, but she wasn't inclined. She looked down at Donovan, watching the firelight caress his features.

What kind of a man could kill his father with no regrets? Was Donovan just hiding his emotional response? Alex didn't think so. He was the kind of person who wore his heart on his sleeve, even if he did talk a good show.

She remembered how he had spat on his father's ashes. She recalled Donovan's bitterness when he had referred to himself as his father's son. There was no love lost there.

From what Alex had seen, Donovan was strong, principled, and loyal to his friends. His team, as he called it.

His father clearly wasn't in that company and never had been.

Maybe it was smarter to wonder what kind of father didn't deserve the respect of a man like Donovan.

The kind of father whose legacy persuaded a man that he shouldn't become a father himself. The answer came to Alex with such perfect clarity that she recognized the truth in it.

That was part of the reason why Donovan didn't want a firestorm and why he didn't want to father a child. He was afraid that he was too much like his father. He wasn't going to risk the well-being of a child on that chance.

Alex could respect that.

In fact, she admired the nobility of the impulse. The scary truth was that she liked Donovan, despite his ability to become a dragon. She thought he was incredibly sexy. She admired him and she wanted him.

The other part of the puzzle was obviously this mysterious Olivia, a woman he'd cared for centuries ago and whose affection had left him vulnerable. Dragons were afraid of loving, because it put holes in their armor.

Alex could understand that, too. She watched Donovan sleep and tried to figure out what she was supposed to do.

Maybe he *was* in a coma.

Maybe if all this fairy-tale stuff was really true, there was an obvious way to wake him up. He wasn't exactly a princess in a glass coffin—why didn't princes ever fall into an endless slumber?—but there was something unnatural about his state.

Maybe he was enchanted.

Maybe the spark of the firestorm could give him a jump start, much like starting a stalled car. Like redirecting the energy.

Maybe it couldn't hurt to find out.

Alex dropped to her knees. Donovan was so still that he barely seemed to be breathing. When she watched carefully, Alex could see the rise and fall of his chest.

He hadn't aged very much since that scene she'd witnessed. She wondered when it had happened. The lace collars had looked Elizabethan, which would have been around 1600. Four hundred years or so, then, give or take. She had a sense that he was bigger and stronger, more muscled and a more skillful fighter. So he'd learned something—that was good. But other than the lack of a beard, he looked just the same.

How long did the *Pyr* live?

Did they often check out like this, and sleep off a few decades? Or centuries? Did the firestorm work when the dragon was asleep?

Alex put her fingertips against Donovan's throat. A spark lit between them but it was small, a flicker of its former self. It was like starting a fire with wet kindling. She instinctively put her whole hand against Donovan's throat.

The spark flickered, lighting and then dying, but as Alex kept her hand in place, it gained power. It became brighter and brighter, until it surpassed the brilliance she had already seen. The flame was so bright that Alex couldn't look straight at the point of contact. She was lighting an inferno and she didn't care.

She could feel the heat of the firestorm melting her reservations, kindling her desire, becoming force enough to illuminate the room. Donovan's pulse beat with increasing power beneath her palm and Alex felt their heartbeats synchronize.

She caught her breath at the surge of strength that rolled through her when their pulses matched pace. Their breathing was in rhythm, she noted then, the room hot enough to make her sweat. The fire even burned brighter on the hearth, the flames leaping higher in sympathy even though she hadn't changed the setting.

There was only one thing Alex wanted.

And he was right in front of her.

She leaned forward and liked the press of her breasts against Donovan's chest. She studied him from close range, noting the sweep of his russet lashes, the firm shape of his lips, the stubble on his chin. The firelight glinted on his gold ear stud, and he looked both disreputable and breathtakingly sexy.

Her own pirate rogue.

It was time to taste the firestorm.

Alex touched her lips to Donovan's mouth. The jolt of electricity between them startled her and made her shiver, but it didn't stop her.

If she was going to awaken Donovan with a kiss, she would make sure it was a kiss worth waking up for.

In the darkness of the night, a lost dragon felt the heat of his brother's firestorm. The flame that kindled between Alex and Donovan sent a pang of yearning through him. The light shone within him, sang to the last shard of his own spark, lit the corners of forgotten memory.

He remembered Donovan.

He remembered companionship.

He remembered loyalty and affection.

He remembered the warmth that had once burned within

his heart. The firestorm found the tiny spark that Donovan had awakened and urged it to burn higher and brighter.

Until the lost dragon could see his way through the darkness that surrounded him.

He changed course, ignoring the call of the shadows, flying directly to Peter's rural retreat. Denying the summons of the dark powers left him weak; defying the command of those who had twisted him took more strength than he had.

The firestorm gave him strength. When he thought only of it, his determination grew, his strength multiplied. He was still weak, still less than once he had been. The shadow had eaten at him and devoured much of his will.

It took so long to draw near to the firestorm.

Finally, he fell exhausted against the exterior of the house in relief and shifted shape. He was slick with sweat, trembling and weak, but he was close.

Maybe close enough.

Delaney flattened his palms against the shutters, leaned his cheek against the steel, closed his eyes and savored the heat of Donovan's firestorm.

The firestorm reminded him of who he really was.

Delaney understood instinctively that Donovan—and the affection the two *Pyr* shared—could summon him back to the land of the living. The *Slayers*, in their dark academy, had failed to destroy Delaney completely.

He had the will to heal and the firestorm had the power. Would it be enough? Delaney could only hope.

Needing to get closer to the healing fire, he began to dig.

Donovan's dark dreams were suddenly pierced with radiant light. The glow was golden and warm, welcoming and invigorating. It sent a sizzle through his veins, an invitation that was impossible to refuse. The firestorm summoned him back from his nightmares.

He felt a woman's hand against his throat, felt her breasts

against his chest, tasted her lips upon his, and knew it was
Alex.

Alex. The woman stirred him as no one else ever had. Her
disregard for the rules when there was a greater good to defend, her intellect, and her humor combined with her physical attributes to make her irresistible. Firestorm or not, she
was a feast he wanted to sample.

Donovan reached for Alex and surrendered to sensation.
He wasn't interested in the mission of the *Pyr* or the future
of Alex's invention or the location of *Slayers*.

Pleasure was the only item on his agenda.

Lots of it.

Now.

Donovan pushed his fingers into Alex's hair, curving his
hand around the back of her neck and pulling her closer. Her
kiss lit an inferno within him, fueling his desire to a fever
pitch. He didn't have to open his eyes to remember the silky
dark swing of her hair, the mischief in her eyes, the curve of
her lips right before she laughed.

He loved her audacity. He loved her zest for life, her conviction that all obstacles could be overcome. He loved how
her lips set when she wasn't taking no for an answer.

He wanted her. The firestorm destroyed every other
thought he might have had, leaving him burning for Alex
and only Alex. He groaned and pulled her closer. He felt her
smile briefly; then she slid her tongue between his teeth. Her
hands were in his hair, then framing his face as if she feared
he might squirm away.

There was no chance of that.

He caught her around the waist and pulled her on top of
him. Her butt was firm and round, still encased in those
leather pants. She rolled her hips against him and he thought
he would explode.

"You wake up as if you mean business," she teased, her
words a tickle against his ear. He felt her lips slide across his
earlobe and shivered when she exhaled.

"I do." Donovan opened his eyes to find Alex smiling down at him. He remembered her idea about cheating the firestorm and liked it even more than he had before. Her cheeks were flushed and the light from the fireplace beside them touched her skin with gold.

He rolled her beneath him and caught her mouth beneath his own, claiming her with a kiss.

Then Alex's fingers were in his hair and his hands were unfastening her shirt. He broke their kiss to glance down at her bra and nearly lost control at the sight of the lace edging against her tanned skin.

"You do like it," she said with satisfaction. He liked that she had thought about his reaction. "I was thinking that maybe a biker chick should go with black. . . ."

"If you're a biker chick, you're one that challenges expectation," he growled, and slid his fingers into the cup. Alex arched and gasped as he toyed with her nipple. She was beautifully disheveled, writhing on the carpet beneath his caress. He liked that she didn't play games, that she wasn't afraid to show her pleasure or tell him what she wanted.

He watched her, his own need building to a fever pitch, then flicked the front bra clasp open with his thumb. He swallowed as he gazed at her breasts, then bent his head.

He flicked his tongue across her nipples, teasing them to taut peaks. His hand, meanwhile, slid down, his palm easing over the smooth heat of her belly. He unfastened her pants and slipped his hand down the front of them. Something trembled deep inside him as he fingered the lace edging of her panties.

"Lace," he whispered with reverence, breaking his kiss to steal a glance at temptation. She was every bit as gorgeous as he'd anticipated; the way those white whorls contrasted with her dark pubic hair was enough to send him to the moon.

Alex shoved her leather pants down, making her desire clear. She kicked them off and the firelight danced over her long legs as she cast off her bra. She was naked except for her panties, the firelight making her look like a siren.

The welcome in her eyes was the only invitation he needed. He caught her close and kissed her again, loving how she wound her legs around his thighs as they rolled across the sheepskin rug.

This place was almost, but not quite, as good as his own lair.

"You, too," she urged, tugging at the hem of his T-shirt. He pulled it over his head and threw it aside. He caught his breath when her skin touched his, the point of contact sending waves of fire through him.

"Wow," Alex whispered when they broke their kiss. She fanned herself with one hand.

"Wow," Donovan agreed. He bracketed her waist with his hands, holding them slightly apart. He glanced around, needing a moment to catch his breath. Whose lair was it? "Where are we?"

"My brother's cottage."

It didn't look much like a cottage to Donovan. "Cottage?"

"High-tech palace in the woods, more like." Alex wrinkled her nose. "It's over the top. I find it a bit frightening how easily I get used to its many comforts."

Donovan frowned. "But how did we get here?"

"The Wyvern brought you." His astonishment must have showed, because Alex smiled. "Blond chick, enigmatic, turquoise eyes. She looks more like a glass swan than a dragon when she shifts."

"That would be Sophie. Did she tell you anything useful?"

Alex sobered. "She let me watch her shift. She did it really slowly so I could see."

Donovan watched her carefully. "And?"

Alex exhaled. "It was incredible, but fascinating. If she'd done it fast, right in front of me, I might have had heart failure."

"But slowly?"

"I could witness it. Think about it. Try to figure out how it was done." Her eyes narrowed and Donovan didn't want her to start thinking about anything else just yet.

"Did she say anything about me?" he teased, and Alex laughed.

"Men!" She leaned forward, touching the tip of her nose to his. When the spark lit, her eyes widened and he was intrigued by how brilliantly they sparkled. There were amber lights in those chocolate depths. Her voice dropped to a throaty purr that had a predictable effect on him. "She said I'd know what to do."

"Do you?"

Alex's eyes closed slightly and she smiled a little, the combination making her look provocative and sexy as all hell. The firelight was loving her, caressing her features and making her look so beautiful that Donovan ached for her. Those eyes danced with mischief. "You know, I think I do." She leaned forward and dropped another sizzler of a kiss on his mouth. "Let's thwart the firestorm," she whispered against his mouth.

Donovan wasn't going to argue with that. "We didn't stop at a drugstore," he reminded her.

"Diane is a hostess who thinks of everything."

He inhaled sharply as Alex's hand eased between them, launching a zillion forest fires on the way. She unfastened his jeans slowly, punctuating each inch of opening with a kiss. Her hair slid over his skin like silk. Her tongue was in his navel, sliding over his skin. Her teeth grazed his belly and he was the one writhing on the rug. She slid her hand into his jeans to caress him and Donovan couldn't stand the restraint anymore.

He kicked off his jeans and boots then, joining her before the hearth in nothing but his Jockeys.

"Good choice," she said with a smile. "Nice view." Donovan kissed her again. His kiss was rougher and more demanding; if he'd thought about it, he might have realized that it was possessive, but Donovan was well past thinking.

He was feeling. He was seducing and being seduced. He was exploring and being explored—he wouldn't be ready to stop any time soon. Alex's touch was magical and powerful. The way his body tingled, his acute sensitivity while in the clutch of the firestorm, the way he was attuned to her combined to make this the best lovemaking ever. They were truly in union, each intent only on pleasing the other, and it was astounding.

He never wanted it to end.

At the same time, he wasn't sure how long he could last.

Alex was no shy virgin and he liked that a lot. She met him touch for touch, reciprocating with every bit as much heat as he. She knew how to drive him wild, just as well as he knew how to arouse her. They paid attention to each other, learning what the other liked best. Their kisses were endless, one fusing into the next, a chorus of tongues and teeth and need. Their caresses alternated between feather-light touches and powerful demands. She offered all he had ever wanted from a woman and more.

Donovan rolled Alex to her back again, then slipped his fingers along the lace of her panties. She smiled at him, arching with anticipation. His fingers slid under the lace and into her own slick heat. He watched her eyes widen and her breath catch.

"I'll bet you a bottle of champagne that you can't hold out long," he teased, and she laughed.

"I'll bet that same bottle that I can hold out longer than you," she challenged, her eyes dancing.

Donovan grinned. It was his kind of bet. He bent to run his teeth across her tight nipple. "So long as we agree that the winner shares the spoils."

Alex laughed again. "I like how you think."

"I like more than that about you." Donovan moved his fingers and, when she gasped, he eased those lace panties down to her knees. He slid quickly down her length, catching her hips in his hands as his tongue darted between her thighs.

"Ditto," Alex gasped, then moaned from the depths of her soul. He watched her grasp fistfuls of the rug and arch her back, spreading her legs for his questing tongue. He was just settling in when he heard a scratching overhead.

It wasn't a good sound.

It was, in fact, a sound that made his hackles rise and his body shimmer on the verge of change. There was a threat to his mate in close proximity.

Slayer alert.

Chapter 11

Donovan glanced up. The ceiling of the room was dark, although it had a gleam like glass. "What's that?" he whispered, almost as softly as old-speak.

Alex pulled up her underwear and reached for the gun that Donovan now saw on an end table. She checked the chamber with shaking hands, then spared him a glance.

"Talons on steel," she said. "Steel shutters roll down over the windows."

Donovan heard the faint sniffing of one of his kind checking a scent, then caught the scent himself of a familiar *Slayer*.

Too late he realized that their indulgence in his firestorm had been a mistake. Its growing heat had drawn Tyson to the precise location of his mate.

Had the other *Slayers* come as well?

"Tyson," Donovan muttered. "The amber one. He's come to finish the challenge."

"What challenge?"

"He wanted to avenge the death of a *Slayer* we killed during Quinn's firestorm last summer. I challenged him to a blood duel."

Alex's eyes narrowed, as if she didn't like what she was hearing. "What does that mean?"

He gave her a steady look. "It means we fight until there's one survivor. Winner take all."

"When did this happen?"

"At the mall. When you were running away."

Alex put her hands on her hips, her disgust clear. "You challenged a *Slayer* to a blood duel in the middle of your firestorm? How are you going to protect me if you lose?"

Donovan fired a grim glance her way. "I'm not going to lose."

Those talons scratched overhead and Alex glanced up. "Explain to me why a blood duel right here and right now is a good idea."

"You can stop sounding like Erik anytime."

"You're the only *Pyr* between me and at least one hungry *Slayer*!"

"I did what I had to do." Donovan rummaged in his discarded jacket, avoiding Alex's perceptive gaze, and pulled on the gloves Quinn had made for him. "Otherwise Tyson would have challenged Quinn, and Quinn needs to ensure Sara's safety."

He looked up to find Alex watching him, her expression thoughtful. "Doesn't sound like you're riding solo to me."

The scratching got louder. "Do we need to talk about this now?"

"It might be our only chance," Alex retorted, unafraid of his anger. "Unless you win."

"Thank you very much for the vote of confidence."

They glared at each other for a moment; then the scratching moved across the roof. Donovan felt his body ease toward the shift with sudden vehemence. He thought of Olivia.

Could he keep himself from changing before Alex's eyes?

Could he prevent his past from repeating itself?

*   *   *

Alex took a shaking breath, telling herself to keep her cool. She should be getting used to dragons by now.

"Tell me about the entrances and exits." Donovan looked lethal, even though he was almost naked. Alex could have sworn he had gotten bigger and more pumped since they'd heard those talons. His eyes were glittering, and the edges of his body shimmered.

Alex sensed that he was close to changing shape. Did she really want to watch?

How could she *not* watch?

She just hoped he did it fast. Really fast.

"There's only the main entrance when the place is locked down like it is now." Alex found her shirt and pulled it on while she answered. Then she pulled on her pants. "All the windows are covered with steel shutters and so are the other doors. The main door has a keypad security system."

"Which will short out in dragonfire."

"There's a backup system, but yes, any fire will eventually cook it all." Alex looked around the shadowed house. "Then none of the locked windows and doors can be opened, because the computer won't be accessible through the security system. It has to be overriden manually with another set of passwords, either from inside the house or from a remote location."

"What else?"

"There's a steel door in the foyer that automatically descends when the security system is overridden. Any attempt to breach it sends a message to Peter and contacts the police."

Donovan arched a brow. "Is your brother a drug runner?"

Alex shook her head and grimaced. "Just completely risk-averse. Consulting for banks on security issues suits him pretty well."

Donovan nodded understanding. "He's doing all right with it, though. The front door?"

"Right there. Beyond the lap pool. The steel door that drops is in the ceiling just before the lap pool."

"Got it." Flames erupted at the far end of the corridor that led to the front door, orange tongues licking beneath the front door. The steel door began to glow on the side adjacent to the lock.

"Company calling," Donovan said as he raced for the door.

Alex knew the exact moment that the security system failed because a number of things happened in rapid succession.

There was a flash and small explosion from the door lock.

The front door swung open.

A large amber dragon stepped over the threshold.

Donovan shifted on the run into his full splendor, a dazzling display of lapis lazuli and gold.

And the steel door rumbled as it began to plummet.

Donovan obviously assumed that Alex was going to stay safely behind, but he had that wrong. Alex ran as the door dropped with frightening speed. She fell and rolled beneath the guillotine of the door, staring straight up at it for one heart-stopping moment.

She was barely out of the way when it fell home with a thud behind her. She felt the vibration of its impact and thought the edge grazed her shoulders.

In front of her, the dragons locked claws and roared.

The alarm started to beep and a red light flashed beside the front door. "Unauthorized access," said Oscar, his mild tone echoing through the in-house speaker system. "Location secured. Intruders confined."

To Alex's shock and dismay, a second stainless steel door slid down on the far side of the conservatory. The front door was inaccessible to them now and they were surrounded by steel.

With the exception of the saltillo floor tiles that Diane had had imported for the conservatory.

Uh-oh. The only thing that would burn in this space was flesh.

The *Slayer* seemed to follow Alex's thoughts.

"Nothing like an after-battle snack," Tyson hissed to

Donovan, licking his lips with pleasure. He cast a spurt of dragonfire in Alex's direction, so that Donovan couldn't miss his reference. Alex danced back, lifted her gun, and pinched off a shot.

She missed. The bullet bounced off the stainless steel door, then ricocheted to the opposite end of the conservatory. Alex ducked and thought she heard it whizz past her head. The *Slayer* shouted as it caught him in the leg on the rebound.

Then he raged fire and fury, fire hot enough to make the grout spark between the floor tiles. Alex backed into a corner, holding her gun before herself in terror.

Donovan swore with more force than she thought the situation deserved. "Do not do that again," he ordered, his eyes blazing.

Alex lifted her chin, irritated with him for assuming she hadn't observed the results of her action. She wasn't a helpless fainting female.

Even if she *had* fainted after Tyson attacked the Buick.

Tyson laughed. "Good thing I like my treats well done."

"This treat is all mine," Donovan snarled, and the dragons locked claws again.

Being trapped in the conservatory with a pair of dragons who were fighting to the death no longer seemed like a great choice. The *Slayer*'s dark blood dripped onto the floor and hissed on impact. It left black holes in the tiles. Meanwhile, the dragons battled ferociously overhead, slamming each other into the walls and breathing fire. It was awesome to see their power.

But they had a vulnerability. Alex remembered Rafferty's advice and looked. All she had to do was find Tyson's missing scale.

Then shoot him right in that spot.

In the dark.

While Tyson and Donovan twined around each other and fought.

Alex swallowed. Shooting at paper silhouettes in target practice no longer seemed very relevant training for her use of a firearm.

Donovan didn't know whether to be more angry with Tyson or with his mate. Alex should have remained secure in the house, but instead she'd followed him right into the heart of danger.

He could have admired her courage if he hadn't been so afraid she would die for it.

They might both die for it. Her presence distracted him almost as much as her vulnerability. His instinct to protect his mate was so primal that its power was frightening. He didn't feel entirely in control of his dragon self with the stakes so high.

He was ready to pillage and destroy.

Fortunately, the perfect candidate to take the brunt of his hostility was present and accounted for.

Tyson.

The *Slayer* ducked away from Donovan's enhanced claws. He dodged and feinted, as slippery as a python, and not a predator that Donovan wanted close to Alex.

Tyson's wounds from earlier in the day had healed remarkably well: in fact, Donovan could not see any sign of the slash he'd give the *Slayer*. Donovan was aware of his own wounds, the gouge on his chest from Delaney and the missing patch in his armor.

Tyson ducked around the long cylindrical planter, playing hide-and-seek. Donovan blasted the *Slayer* with dragonfire, and the plants took it badly.

An alarm began to beep insistently. "Fire detected," declared that same mild-mannered male voice.

The sprinkler system came on.

"What the hell?" Tyson paused to look around. Making every surface in the conservatory glisten, the water sparkled through the air and tinkled into the lap pool.

"The house is smarter than you," Donovan declared. He dove across the surface of the pool while Tyson was distracted by the sprinklers. The long planter and the darkness disguised his choice. He came up abruptly at the other end where Tyson lurked, blasting the *Slayer* with dragonfire again. "See?"

The dragonfire reflected off the steel security wall, burning Tyson across the back as well, and Tyson bellowed in pain at the double burn. He raged at Donovan, snatching for him with talons outstretched. Donovan led him on, then leapt over the planter at the last minute. Tyson landed heavily across it. The cylinder of steel broke away from the ceiling at one end from the impact of his weight.

It fell slowly, one end splashing into the lap pool. The potting soil spilled down the incline to make a pile of dirt.

"More room to fight," Tyson snarled, and deliberately broke the other end with a swing of his tail. The planter fell with a crash and a clatter.

Alex jumped when the length of it tumbled noisily onto the floor. The first end was tipped out of the pool when the rest fell, plants and soil scattering across the entire room. The steady sprinkle of water combined with the wet dirt to make the room smell like a rain forest.

Except for the scent of charred ferns.

And the taste of human terror.

The sprinkling water made Tyson hard to grasp, more snakelike. The pair ducked and evaded each other, until Donovan pivoted, surprising his opponent, and decked Tyson instead.

The *Slayer* fell into a barricaded window. The glass cracked and splintered, but the steel shutter on the outside took only a dint. Another alarm began to beep when the glass broke, but the dragons fought on. There wasn't a lot of room to maneuver in the space, especially as Donovan was trying to keep Tyson away from Alex.

The pair locked claws, biting and snatching as they tumbled the length of the conservatory. Donovan dug his steel talons into the backs of Tyson's claws and the *Slayer* howled. He slammed Donovan into the wall, stunning him with the force of his blow. Then he dunked Donovan into the pool, holding his head under the water.

Donovan choked. He struggled. He fought, but was unable to free himself from Tyson's lethal grip. He felt the lack of air in his lungs and tasted his own fear.

"This one is for Everett," Tyson murmured in old-speak. The bitter words echoed in Donovan's thoughts even as he felt his body weaken. He became aware of Alex's consternation.

She would be faced with a dragon determined to incinerate her if he died. The possibility infuriated Donovan, filling him with an anger he could barely contain.

But to change the course of events, he had to overcome Tyson somehow. He remembered Alex's assertion that energy was never destroyed, that it was just redirected.

Could his passion for Alex be used to give him new strength?

Boris Vassily was irritated.

Boris was always irritated, it seemed, on one level or another. He was tired of incompetence, of *Slayers* who surrendered to their blood lust and raged into situations that could have been avoided with an increment of foresight. He was fed up with the audacity of this particular human mate and insulted that she had shot him.

Shot him! The woman didn't know her place.

He circled the roof of the luxury retreat—thinking that it would make a sweet lair—and noted the security features in place. He liked the steel shutters that locked over the windows and nodded with approval when he heard the steel doors descend.

Tyson was trapped in the conservatory because he had stupidly triggered the alarm system. Boris landed silently on the roof, hoping the battle wasn't lost before it was begun.

He was surrounded by morons.

"He's in!" Sigmund gloated in old-speak as he landed beside the leader of the *Slayers*.

Boris noted the arrival of another incompetent. Sigmund was the scholar who should have brought him triumph, the son of the leader of the *Pyr* who should have been the *Slayers'* greatest asset.

Yet somehow wasn't. Was Sigmund too much his father's son?

Or was he a spy?

Boris pondered that possibility. He heard the banter between the two dragons inside the house and was slightly appeased. At least Donovan was trapped in the conservatory with Tyson. At least Tyson had cornered his opponent: Donovan was equally unable to summon assistance. They would battle to the death in the old style.

Too bad Boris wasn't certain that Tyson could win.

It was critical that Donovan, a formidable fighter, never transform himself into the Warrior. Just a day ago, Boris had been sure that the *Slayers'* triumph was secured, that having Alex be the human for this second firestorm was fortuitous beyond belief. He'd encouraged Tyson to go after Donovan, thinking it a good opportunity to hinder Donovan's chances of victory.

But his confidence had proven to be premature.

Boris sighed. It was unfortunate that Tyson had so much in common with Everett, his dead and thickheaded student.

There was a crash and a hiss from inside the house, as well as the muted beep of another alarm being activated. Sigmund rubbed his claws together with glee, and only Boris's lethal look kept the younger *Slayer* from commenting.

Doubtless he'd say something clever, maybe how he'd like to watch the fight. Boris had no interest in watching the fight. He had no interest in revealing his presence here too early. He simply wanted to know that Donovan Shea and Alex Madison were both dead. The unlikelihood of that and

Tyson's responsibility for stacking the odds against himself made Boris even more irritable.

Then he caught a whiff of something that put a sparkle in his eye. *Terrified human.* He sniffed again and smiled. Absolutely.

And even better, terrified human *mate*.

He spread his claw flat against the steel shutter, his smile broadening as he felt the heat of the firestorm. Alex was in the conservatory, as well, which tilted the odds in Tyson's favor. On the other hand, Donovan would fight even more valiantly, given the presence of his mate. They could finish it all this very night.

"I should like to have witnessed this fight," Boris murmured, and Sigmund nodded with enthusiasm.

"Tyson will kill him, for sure. And then Donovan's mate will be undefended. What do you plan to do with her?"

Boris thought immediately of a dozen equally horrible prospects. She had, after all, shot him. "Ensure the failure of her Green Machine, first and foremost. Then, we'll see."

"We could fry her when she leaves the house. . . ," Sigmund began.

"I prefer to use human nature against her. It makes for a more elegant and satisfying solution."

"What do you mean?"

"I mean hope defeated adds spice." When Sigmund would have asked more questions, Boris held up a talon for silence. *Hope.* He scanned the property thoughtfully. He had already checked and knew this was the only access to the house.

Why had Alex chosen to come here? The place was obviously familiar to her, because she had ridden directly to it from the other side of the state, and ridden without hesitation.

Clearly, the house was a sanctuary. He wouldn't have put it past a human to have come due to an emotional attachment to the place—and a false sense of security—but he wondered if there was more.

This human was more logical than most. She'd retrieved

materials steadily all day. He had no doubt that she intended to continue her research, so she must be planning to do so here.

His gaze fell on the boathouse. Anything of value would surely be secured in the house. Still, it couldn't hurt to check.

The lock to the boathouse door was easily picked, as none of the same electronics were in place. Boris immediately saw why. The boathouse was empty, with the exception of a canoe, several oars, and half a dozen life jackets. The life jackets and oars were hung on the wall, and the canoe hung from the roof. It swayed slightly overhead as they shifted and stood on the dock that lined three sides of the interior. There was water in the middle of the boathouse, a finger from the lake beyond, and it radiated cold.

"They must have a boat," Sigmund said.

"It's probably in storage for the winter," Boris mused. "The lake must freeze, at least on the surface." He had a sense that he was missing something obvious, the still water drawing his gaze. Something might be submerged there. He looked and began to smile.

The undercarriage of a car was reflected perfectly on the surface.

Boris tipped back his head and considered the automobile tucked into the rafters of the boathouse. There could be only one reason why it was there. He focused upon it and inhaled, his smile broadening when he detected the faint scent of the human he had killed at Gilchrist Enterprises.

"A backup prototype," he said, with no small satisfaction.

"We could burn it," Sigmund suggested, but Boris scoffed.

"I shall teach you something about subtlety, if it's the last thing I do," he said. "The critical meeting is Thursday. We shall ensure that there is no way this prototype can be made to work in that amount of time."

"But why not just destroy it?"

Boris sighed with forbearance. "A fire would set off alarms, I expect, even here. And the destruction would alert them immediately to our presence. They might intervene. They might respond. They might have an alternate plan. Better that we delay the discovery of our deed for as long as possible." He smiled. "Better to let the human feel the full burden of her failure when it's too late to repair anything."

"So, what's the plan?"

"You will remove the engine, but leave the prototype undisturbed. You will destroy the engine in your lair. And before you leave, you will disguise all signs of our presence here."

Sigmund frowned. "And what are you going to do?"

Boris snarled at the younger dragon. "I do not sully my claws with physical labor. There are better uses for my talents."

"Such as?"

Boris chose to forgive Sigmund's audacity, for the moment. "I intend to meet Mr. Sinclair, the potential investor and key contact. According to the Day-Timer of the first human, he arrives Thursday in Minneapolis from Chicago. It is entirely possible that he can be dissuaded from the folly of making this investment."

Sigmund looked impressed. "That's devious."

"Of course." Boris knew he sounded bored. "My ideas are always both devious and brilliant; it's their execution that's the persistent problem."

Sigmund bristled, predictably. "What are you talking about?"

"The *Pyr* thrive as much because of their own abilities as the incompetence of my minions."

"You can't say that to me after all I've done."

"Can I not?" Boris turned on Sigmund, and the other dragon backed away in surprise. Boris bared his teeth and Sigmund took another step back. He didn't move fast enough. Boris seized him by the throat and enjoyed how Sigmund's eyes widened when he felt the sharp edge of Boris's talon against his windpipe.

"You shouldn't be able to do that," Sigmund whispered, eying the dragon talon on Boris's human hand.

Boris ignored that and spoke in a hiss of old-speak. *"Explain to me again how Donovan survived that battle that was supposed to eliminate him. Explain to me again your flawless plan to make Delaney a* Slayer *against his will, the one that would make him our helpless pawn. Explain to me how your pet has eluded recapture."*

"It was an experiment. . . ," Sigmund squeaked aloud.

"It was a failure." Boris bared his teeth in a cold smile. *"I do not like failure, Sigmund. I think it shows a lack of foresight on the part of the planner."* He let his gaze brighten as Sigmund's throat worked in fear, then spoke aloud. "That would be you."

Boris exhaled dragonfire in a long, slow stream, mingling it with smoke in the way he had perfected. Sigmund winced and twitched as the combination touched his skin.

"And finally, explain to me why I do not hold the Dragon's Tooth right now, despite all of your pretty promises to that effect."

Sigmund squirmed. "Everyone makes mistakes—"

"I do not make mistakes." Boris cast Sigmund aside. "I tire of being surrounded by incompetence."

Before Sigmund could try to excuse his failures again, a shot echoed from the house. Boris winced. He knew who had fired that gun and he could guess who had taken the hit.

Alex Madison was going to pay.

Boris scowled at the car overhead. "If only I could clone myself a dozen times, we would be rid of the *Pyr* and their pesky humans."

There was a pause, one that caught Boris's attention. He turned to find Sigmund looking thoughtful, even as he rubbed the red mark on his throat.

"Maybe I can do something about that," Sigmund said. "Would that count as competence?"

Boris snorted, even though the possibility made his pulse leap. Dozens of himself! Encouragement didn't motivate as well as fear.

"It's all so much idle speculation," he said, using his bored tone. "Let me know if you can manage it." He pointed at the car overhead. "Now, get to work before I really get annoyed."

The claw on the back of his neck, the darkness of the water, and the lack of air reminded Donovan of another struggle.

Another battle he had nearly lost.

Another betrayal.

He had fought Magnus because Olivia had betrayed him.

He seethed with rage at the memory. Donovan let his anger build. He wasn't ready to die just yet. He wasn't ready to let down anyone else. He wasn't ready to see Alex injured.

This time, he would not fail.

His anger burned hotter and hotter, even as he let his body fall limp. He stoked his rage to epic proportions; he let the energy of his fury build. He heard Tyson chuckling to himself and knew he'd stop the *Slayer*'s laughter.

For good.

Donovan held his breath so that there were no more bubbles floating to the surface. He sensed Alex's terror, but ignored it. He allowed Tyson to enjoy his moment.

It wouldn't last.

Donovan felt the moment when the *Slayer* eased his grip, the instant when he was confident he had won.

Then Donovan turned the power of his anger to his own use. He converted it to strength; he used it to fuel his own escape. It shot through him, invigorating him and doubling his power.

He stretched his back claw out of the water and seized

Tyson's genitals. He sank his steel talons in deep, locked them into the tender flesh, and squeezed.

Tyson screamed.

Donovan held tight. Tyson released Donovan, and his claws scrabbled against Donovan's grip.

Donovan raged skyward, leaping out of the lap pool. He hauled the *Slayer* to the ceiling by his balls. Tyson was incoherent in his anguish, but Donovan didn't care.

He flung the *Slayer* into the shuttered windows, keeping his grip all the while. Three more windows broke. Tyson wept and went limp.

Donovan wasn't fooled. He pulled back to thrash the *Slayer* again. Two more windows paid the price.

"There!" Alex shouted as Tyson moaned.

Donovan saw it, too. The *Slayer* was missing a single scale, low on his belly. The white skin showed through the gap in his golden scales. He glanced toward Alex and saw her lifting her gun, aiming to shoot, and knew he had to give her a better shot.

"No," he commanded, and she blinked in surprise. She stopped though, maybe guessing what he was going to do.

Or maybe she trusted him.

Tyson began to rouse himself, but Donovan gave him no chance. He hauled the *Slayer* into the air, biting his neck from behind. He sank his teeth in deep, tasting the foul blackness of *Slayer* blood. He locked his claws around each of Tyson's, then entwined their tails. He flapped to keep them both airborne, then pulled the *Slayer* out spread-eagled in front of him.

"Don't miss," he muttered as Alex raised her gun.

When Donovan pulled Tyson back against him, holding the *Slayer* captive and airborne, Alex was stunned by his power. The *Slayer* thrashed and twisted, roused by his terror of what might happen next. He tried desperately to cast off Donovan's grip.

He didn't succeed.

The *Slayer* breathed fire, but could only scorch Donovan's knuckles. Alex heard a rumble like thunder but ignored it.

She focused on her shot.

Just before Alex fired, Tyson twisted and sank his teeth into Donovan's front claw. Donovan swore. He slammed the *Slayer* into the stainless steel barrier and the steel clanged with the impact.

There was a dint in it when Donovan flew backward, the *Slayer* still in his grip. He repeated his move, driving the *Slayer* into the cold steel. Tyson sagged in Donovan's grip as he pulled the *Slayer* out again. Blood was dripping in profusion, black blood mingled with red on the tile floor.

"Now!" Donovan roared.

But Tyson twisted and locked gazes with Alex. "You don't want to kill me," he said in a low, melodic voice. His words were more persuasive than they should have been.

There were little flames flickering in the depths of his gaze, flames that Alex instinctively distrusted. The *Slayer*'s smile turned malicious. He was fighting for his life.

But then, so was she.

"Don't I?" she asked, narrowing her eyes.

"Of course you don't," Tyson said with that same smooth assurance. "And what if you injured Donovan? Think of the risk. . . ." The words wound into her thoughts, tempting her to agree with the villain.

The light *could* have been better. She didn't want to hit Donovan. Doubt assailed Alex, doubt in her own abilities.

"Alex!" Donovan shouted, and she knew she was being warned of something. The shadows were so distorted by the falling water that she wasn't sure she could hit her target. "He's beguiling you."

Alex didn't know what that meant, but she understood that Tyson was feeding her doubts.

"I'm not interested in whatever you're selling," she said. Then she fired twice in rapid succession.

Alex thought that she must have missed. The *Slayer* breathed fire in enormous quantities before she could shoot again. A brilliant orange wall of flame came toward Alex with frightening speed.

She darted backward until she was trapped against steel.

And the flames kept coming.

Then she remembered what Magnus had done.

"You can turn the flames," she shouted at Donovan. "Harness the energy and use it."

She saw the glitter of Donovan's eyes through the fire. She saw him concentrate, then closed her eyes against the approaching fire. She raised a hand and winced as the heat grew hotter.

But the flames never reached her.

She peeked to discover that they were receding. The fire stopped in the middle of the conservatory, burning like a campfire with no fuel whatsoever. Donovan was brilliant, his eyes shining, coiled with new power.

Tyson hung limp in Donovan's grip, and there were two smoking holes in his chest. One, right where the missing scale had been, was bleeding profusely.

Alex took a shaking breath. She'd killed her first dragon.

Donovan wasn't taking any chances. He had released one of Tyson's claws and as Alex watched, Donovan ripped his metal front claws across the *Slayer*'s stomach. They cut like the knives they were. Black blood and innards spilled all over Diane's beloved imported tiles; then Donovan dropped the *Slayer* into the last of the flames. He glared at the blaze and it leapt higher, gobbling the *Slayer*'s scales.

The fire went out as he sucked the last of its energy.

He glittered so brightly that she couldn't look straight at him. Then Donovan chucked Tyson's burned body into the lap pool. The water boiled, simmered, and steam filled the conservatory.

When the steam cleared, Alex leaned forward to look.

Lying in the pool was the swarthy man from the diner, not a dragon at all.

"*Slayers* and *Pyr* have to be exposed to all four elements to truly die," Donovan said from close behind her.

Alex ticked them off on her fingers. "Fire, water, air." She glanced at Donovan.

He picked up the end of the planter in his powerful claws. Alex was impressed, given the size and weight of it. He dumped the last of the potting soil and ferns into the lap pool.

"And earth," he said with satisfaction.

Alex exhaled shakily. Tyson was dead and would stay that way. Her knees were shaking.

"Nice shot," Donovan said, and she thought she could see his amusement even in his dragon form. He was wet from the water of the sprinklers, the water glistening on his scales and reflecting their brilliant blue. There might have been a thousand crystal beads rolling across him and she was awed again by his splendor.

"You just keep getting bigger and scarier," she said, her words husky. "Are you trying to drive me crazy?"

Donovan gave her a sharp look. "Anything but that."

Alex took a deep breath. "Then let's get over this. Let me touch you." She beckoned to him. Her heart was in her throat, but she had to do it.

Donovan hesitated. "Aren't you going to faint if I come closer?"

"I don't know. Come closer and let's see what happens."

He landed beside her. She was surprised that he was so graceful, given his size and musculature. She'd thought that his feet would thud, but he landed with the elegance of a bird. When she didn't pass out cold, he extended his arm, inviting her touch.

Alex's guts shook. She reached out all the same. This was part of what Donovan was. Maybe it was even the essence of what he was.

His blue scales were firm and warm. She'd thought they'd be slippery or cold, either like a fish or a suit of armor. In reality, they were somewhere in between. Each one appeared to be edged in gold, which was what made him glitter so when he moved. The scales overlapped by a good third, covering his body in an impressive protective shield.

The blue gave way to gold on his chest, as splendid as an ornamental suit of armor. That wound was still open on his chest, the one where the pearl had been. It wasn't infected or bleeding, though, so he must be healing.

She met his eyes, thought about how Magnus saw the world, and figured that Donovan could probably read her thoughts. There was compassion in those glittering depths and a bit of unexpected trepidation.

"Okay," she said, hearing how her voice shook. "Now change."

"You want to look away?"

"No. I'm going to watch." Alex swallowed and put her hand back on his claw. "I'm going to stay right here while you do it. Change shape really slowly so I can see exactly what you are."

Chapter 12

Donovan was shocked.

He'd expected Alex to faint when she touched him, but she was made of sterner stuff that that. He was impressed by her resilience, but that didn't mean he was going to fulfill her request. He couldn't help thinking of Olivia.

Again.

He hadn't cared about Olivia's response when he'd taken the Dragon's Tooth to her, but still it had been disturbing to watch her mind unhinge.

He always changed shape quickly, as quickly as he could manage the deed. There was something about a slow and deliberate change, of hovering between forms, that was almost impossible for the human mind to accept. Olivia's reaction, Donovan had learned since, was perfectly typical.

He would not repeat his past with Alex.

For any price.

"No," Donovan said flatly.

"Yes," Alex insisted. "I need to see this."

"You're wrong. You don't need to see anything." He

caught her by the shoulders and spun her around, changing shape with lightning speed while her back was turned to him.

"Cheat," Alex said when she saw what he had done. Her lips tightened with anger, but she wasn't insane.

That worked for Donovan in a big way.

He forced himself to recall that they'd just worked together to finish a *Slayer* and that was a good thing. He felt his usual postfight euphoria. He was more than ready to celebrate in the time-honored tradition.

Wine.

Women.

Sex.

Lots of sex.

He didn't imagine that Alex had any doubt what was on his mind, given that he was standing in front of her in his underwear. It was easy to remember what they'd been doing when Tyson arrived.

He was more than ready to find out whether the firestorm could be thwarted.

All he had to do was get them both out of the conservatory.

That and disperse Alex's annoyance with him.

She folded her arms across her chest and glared at him. "You did that on purpose, so I couldn't see you change. Don't tell me you're shy."

Donovan felt a flash of irritation. "I'm not going to show you the change, and that's all there is to it."

"Why not?"

"You don't know what you're asking of me."

"I do." Alex nodded. "The Wyvern showed me her change."

"Then you've seen it already." He looked around the conservatory, ready for a change of subject. "How are we going to get out of here, anyway?"

Alex pulled something out of her pocket, her lips drawn in a tight line. She stretched out her hand and Donovan was shocked to see the Dragon's Tooth on her palm.

"How'd you get that?" he demanded.

"I took it, so it wouldn't fall out of your hand. The point is that I have it and that you want it back. Guess what my terms are?"

Donovan was infuriated by the idea. "I am not going to shift in front of you, no matter what you say."

Alex looked as if she were summoning an argument, but there was a sound of a car engine outside. They froze as one.

Was it the police?

Or was it Alex's brother? There were no sirens, so Donovan knew what he'd put his money on. He was suddenly very aware of their situation and how it might be compromising for Alex.

Having a visible erection wasn't going to improve matters. Donovan would have sold his soul for his jeans at that moment.

She seemed to be thinking the same thing. "You could be hard to explain," she said with a glance to his underwear. She shoved the pearl back into her pocket.

"I'm thinking the corpse in the lap pool is going to be even tougher." Donovan surveyed the damage. "Never mind the demolition plan. This place looks like a wreck."

"It looks like it survived a dragon attack," Alex corrected.

Footsteps sounded on the veranda.

Donovan was going to have to beguile Peter, but he hoped he wouldn't have to beguile Alex as well. It was a bad precedent to set, and he liked the honesty between the two of them.

Even if they did disagree on some things. He didn't doubt that she'd agree with him if he explained himself, but that would mean telling her about Olivia, and Donovan wasn't going to go there.

"What are we going to do?" Alex asked in a whisper.

"Alex?" A man shouted before Donovan could figure out how to summarize his plan. "Is that really you in there?"

"Peter," Alex muttered, confirming that it was her brother. Then she raised her voice. "Hi, Peter. Sorry!"

There was a sequence of beeps as the security system was accessed from outside by Peter's own code. Then both steel doors slid skyward in unison. Donovan watched them disappear into the ceiling, secreting themselves perfectly, and was impressed. He knew what kind of upgrade he was going to install in his lair.

Then he focused on the problem at hand.

Peter looked just like the risk-averse bank security adviser Alex had said he was. And he didn't look happy.

This could go very badly.

Peter was on his cell phone, obviously talking to the police. Alex hoped he kept his cool. If nothing else, her brother had a good poker face.

"False alarm, Lieutenant," he said with his easy charm. "I'm very sorry for the disturbance. I guess my sister forgot the access codes. Yes, better safe than sorry." His gaze flicked over Donovan and his eyebrows rose as he met Alex's gaze. She felt herself blush. "In future, I hope my sister tells me that she intends to use the house, but maybe this was an impulse visit."

That was an accurate summary of the situation. Peter listened, apologized again, then ended the call. He snapped his phone shut, the click seeming very loud, then put it away. His gaze darted from Donovan in his underwear, to the burned saltillo tiles, then to Tyson's body bobbing in his lap pool.

Alex knew she didn't imagine that Peter paled.

"I don't suppose you'd care to tell me what's going on here?"

Alex cleared her throat and pushed a hand through her hair. She needed to distract her brother and get rid of him. It wasn't going to be easy, but she knew one thing that would get his attention. "It's kind of a long story." She smiled. "Do you want a drink, Peter? It's a bit of a drive from the city. . . ."

Peter's gaze fell to Tyson's body again. "We should call the police," he said, and pulled out his cell phone.

Donovan stepped forward then, his voice dropping to the same low tone that Tyson had used. She watched as he leaned toward Peter.

Alex was transfixed by the change in Donovan. His voice dropped to a melodic murmur and his eyes took on a curious radiance. She saw a flame flicker in their depths, even from her oblique angle. She wanted to move around, stand beside Peter, and stare directly into those flames. Donovan raised his left hand toward her. Even though she didn't understand, she stayed put.

He was doing to Peter exactly what Tyson had tried to do to her.

But what was it, exactly?

"What a strange evening," Donovan said to Peter, his voice a musical variant of his usual tone. He always had a faint Irish accent, but it was a full rolling brogue as he spoke to Peter. It was so enchanting that Alex could have listened to him all night.

Even if he'd been reading the phone book to her.

"A strange evening," Peter agreed. His voice was so lacking in inflection that Alex looked at him. He was staring fixedly at Donovan, as if he couldn't turn away.

Alex glanced Donovan's way again, and those intriguing flames in his eyes drew her closer. What were they? It must be an illusion of some kind, and she desperately wanted to know more about them.

It was odd how much she wanted to know.

Donovan made a quick dismissive gesture with his hand. Alex understood that he didn't want her to look and wondered why.

"So much fuss for so little reason," Donovan said in that same low tone.

"So much fuss for so little reason," Peter agreed.

Alex opened her mouth to argue this conclusion. There

was a dead man in the lap pool, after all, and the security system was roasted. The plants were dead, the planter was a wreck, and Diane's tiles would have to be replaced. Never mind the broken windows.

Donovan tore his gaze away from Peter and glared at Alex. There were no flames in his eyes at all, but they were snapping with anger. "Why don't you get Peter a drink?" he hissed, and Alex knew her presence was unwelcome.

Peter, seemingly back to normal, cleared his throat, frowning as he glanced toward the lap pool. "That *is* a dead man, isn't it?"

Donovan leaned toward Peter once more, his manner intent again. "There is no corpse."

"No corpse," Peter echoed with obvious relief.

"There is no trouble," Donovan said. "It was a false alarm."

"It was a false alarm." Peter sighed, reassured.

Alex retreated, but didn't go far. She understood that Donovan didn't want her interference, but what he was doing was really interesting.

She'd never seen Peter agree so easily with anyone before. It was bizarre, given what he'd seen with his own eyes. But he looked ready to be persuaded that there was nothing wrong.

Donovan was doing the persuading with the ease of an expert.

"Alex forgot the codes," Donovan said in that reassuring tone.

"Alex forgot the codes," Peter agreed.

Alex bristled that she was being blamed for this, but then, it was an easier situation to explain than the dead *Slayer* in the pool. She wondered how Donovan was going to get Peter past that.

"The security system overreacted," Donovan said. "Perhaps it has a flaw."

"Perhaps the security system has a flaw."

"A review should be booked. In two weeks."

"A review should be booked in two weeks."

"It's time to go home."

"Time to go home," Peter said, reaching into his pocket for his keys.

"There's no need to worry your wife." Donovan spared Alex a quick glance, a question in his eyes. Obviously he did need her for something, and she was tempted to deny him. Peter was wavering though, now that Donovan's attention wasn't fixed upon him.

"Worry," Peter murmured, and looked around the conservatory with a frown. He seemed to be trying to remember the root of his concern, and his gaze flicked to the lap pool.

The last thing they needed was Peter calling the police back.

Alex wasn't ready to go to jail for killing a man. She doubted that admitting he was a *Slayer* would help. She'd just end up in a different psych ward, one with bars on the windows.

"Diane," she supplied in a whisper. "His wife is Diane. Kids are Jared and Kirsten." Peter was pulling out his cell phone, opening it, punching in a number.

Donovan intercepted him, laying a hand on his arm, leaning close. "There's no need to worry Diane," he murmured. He reached to clear the number that Peter had punched in. "You need to call Diane," he urged. "You need to tell her that everything is fine."

"Everything is fine," Peter echoed, staring into Donovan's eyes.

"It was a false alarm."

"It was a false alarm."

"Alex forgot the codes."

Peter repeated this with more assurance than he had the last time. Donovan led him to the conservatory. Peter continued to stare into Donovan's eyes. "I need to call Diane," he said in that same flat tone. "Everything is fine."

"Except the plants," Donovan said as they walked through the conservatory. He directed Peter's gaze to the long planter of ferns that hung over the lap pool. They were all cooked to cinders. "Diane's plants have died."

"Diane's plants have died."

"The security system malfunctioned."

"The security system malfunctioned." Peter shook his head as he said this.

"A review should be booked in two weeks."

"A review should be booked in two weeks."

Donovan sighed. "Money doesn't buy everything."

Peter sighed in his turn. "Money doesn't buy everything."

Alex wished she had a recording of her materialistic brother uttering those words. The pair reached the exterior door and Donovan opened it. He seemed to take a scent of the wind and then he nodded slightly.

"And it's time to go home, Peter."

"And it's time to go home."

"Go home to Diane."

"Home to Diane."

"You're going home, Peter."

"I'm going home."

No matter how hypnotized he might be, there were some things Peter couldn't be programmed to forget. He offered his hand to Donovan, who shook it with solemnity.

Then Peter left.

Alex joined Donovan at the door, astonished by what he had done. She watched her brother walk to his big Mercedes sedan.

"What did you do to him?"

"I beguiled him," Donovan said, sounding as if he'd rather not talk about it.

Alex didn't really care much what he wanted. She wanted to know more. "You put a spell on him."

"No. It's a kind of hypnosis."

"You made him do what you wanted him to do."

"Correction: what *we* wanted him to do."

"Don't blame this on me. It wasn't my idea to trick my brother."

"I didn't trick him!"

"Oh, right. He just decided to ignore the dead body in his summer retreat and went home of his own volition to tuck in the kids. I don't think so!"

Donovan fidgeted. "There wasn't time to talk to you about it. I had to act."

"You chose to lie to him."

"It wasn't a lie." Donovan winced and Alex knew he didn't like what he had done any more than she did. "Not really."

"You got those flames in your eyes. Tyson did it, too."

"Humans stare at flames. You have a primal attraction to fire. And as humans stare at the beguiling flames, they become susceptible to entertaining ideas that are not necessarily their own." Donovan spared Alex a look. "It's a useful way of disguising our presence among your kind."

"It's a lie."

Donovan didn't say anything to that. Peter started the engine and the big Benz's headlights sliced through the darkness as he drove down the driveway.

Alex couldn't leave it alone. "Anyone who knows me even a little bit knows I never forget security codes."

"And what was the alternative?" Donovan flung out his hands in frustration. "To let Peter call the police? To let a coroner do an autopsy on a dead *Slayer*? To let the forensics people find you guilty of shooting the gun that killed a man?"

"There's always a better solution than lying. . . ." Alex heard the lack of conviction in her own tone.

"Are you saying your brother would have looked the other way for the greater good?"

Now Alex fidgeted. "Well, no, but—"

"There's no *but*!" Donovan said with irritation. "We had a problem. I solved it." He shook a finger at her. "Say 'Thank you very much, Donovan.'"

Alex gestured to the body in the pool. "I'll thank you when you really fix it, not when you make one person believe it's not a problem. We're not out of the proverbial woods yet."

"One step at a time," Donovan growled.

"Why didn't you just beguile the entire police force?"

He spoke through gritted teeth. "It's not that easy to do. I did this for you, you know, to make your life simpler. I think you could show a little gratitude."

"I could, if I were sure that you'd never beguiled me."

Donovan looked so genuinely upset by the idea that Alex knew he hadn't. "I'd never do that. . . ."

"Why not?"

"The firestorm is a sacred trust, whether we consummate it or not." He glared at her. "I'd never do that to you, Alex."

"Promise," she said. She liked the way her name rolled off his tongue. She smiled. "Or I'll always wonder why it is that women always give you what you want."

The back of Donovan's neck turned red and his eyes became a vivid hue of green. He was utterly serious as he held her gaze and there were no flames in his eyes at all. "I swear to you that I have never done that to you and never will. I don't like beguiling." He grimaced. "In fact, I'm not very good at it."

"Why not?"

"Practice makes perfect." His expression was rueful.

Alex believed him.

She still couldn't believe what Peter had done. She looked after his departing car and saw a familiar shadow descending from the sky. She grabbed Donovan's arm, unable to voice her terror.

A dragon was following Peter's car.

Donovan spoke with assurance. "Don't worry. It's Niall."

"Who's Niall?"

"One of the *Pyr*. You might have seen him at the hotel. He's blond, shorter than me."

"How do you know for sure?"

"I know the scent of every *Pyr* and *Slayer* I've ever met."

"And you remember them all?"

"Yes." There was no doubt in Donovan's tone.

"Accurately?"

Donovan flicked a look at her. "Yes. He must have been assigned to stand sentry over Peter and his family until this is done."

"You don't mean that the *Slayers* will target them?" Her family couldn't suffer because of her invention. It wasn't right.

But then, Mark shouldn't have died, either.

"I don't know what the *Slayers* will do." Donovan was grim. "Erik obviously has his suspicions."

"I have to warn Peter," Alex said, heading back into the house to call him on his cell. "He has to know the risk."

"Does he?" Donovan put a hand on her arm to stop her.

Alex turned to meet his gaze, his question feeding her doubts.

"What will he think if you tell him to watch out for dragons?"

Alex halted. Peter would think she was nuts.

Donovan was firm. "It's better if Niall takes care of any trouble. It's better if Peter doesn't even know."

There were no flames in Donovan's eyes. "But what if there are lots of them? What if Niall is overwhelmed?"

"He'll call for help. Niall sings the song of the wind and it does him favors. He can send a message anywhere, instantly." Donovan's gaze was steady and normal, locked on hers. "Trust me."

"Can you beguile without the flame?"

"No." His tone left no doubt. "I promised you, Alex. Those weren't just empty words."

They stared at each other for a long moment; then she nodded. She trusted him. "Why won't you show me your shift?"

He met her gaze again. "It's my task to protect you."

Before Alex could make sense of that, Donovan glanced up, as if he had heard something. He stepped out onto the porch and scanned the sky, then started to smile. "We're going to have company," he said. "Maybe Erik can answer your questions better than I can."

A beat later, his fellow *Pyr* landed in the driveway and shifted to human form. One second there were four dragons descending from the sky and in the next, four men were walking toward the front door with purpose.

It said something about the kind of night they'd had that Alex was glad to see dragons arrive unannounced. There was a rumble like thunder; then Donovan headed for the living room to get dressed. Alex remained on the porch to welcome the arrivals.

Best of all, Sara had come, too.

Sara came directly to her. Alex had an urge to hug her, even though she wasn't a huggy kind of person. The last twenty-four hours had been a test of her ability to deal with change.

"I know." Sara nodded. "It gets easier."

"It would be hard to believe that it got worse." Alex felt better when Sara laughed.

Alex remembered the four men from the hotel room—although she knew only Quinn's name. The fair one was gone, so he must be Niall. Donovan returned and Alex heard that faint rumble, like thunder gathering. She looked but the sky was clear.

"Old-speak," Sara said, seeing her confusion. "It's how they talk to each other without us hearing what's said."

"It's a lower frequency," Alex guessed. "One that only they can discern. Like dog whistles, but at the other end of the scale."

"Exactly." Sara watched the men. The sound of thunder had stopped and they seemed to be shimmering together. Their silhouettes sparkled against the night's darkness.

They exhaled in unison. Their breathing was so slow and deliberate, and they were otherwise so motionless that they could have been rocks in the driveway.

Hunk-shaped rocks.

"Good," Sara said. "They're breathing smoke."

"Their territory mark." Alex nodded, remembering what Donovan had told her. She couldn't help watching him, couldn't help thinking he was the best-looking one of the bunch. He did seem to glimmer more brightly than the others.

"Right. When they breathe it together, it's even stronger. We'll be safe in the house once they're done." Sara looked at the house and her amazement was clear. "Is this your place?"

"My brother's cottage," Alex said, relieved to have a fairly normal conversation. "He likes all the toys. Come on in. There's some wine I can open."

"If there's fruit juice it would be better for me," Sara said, and patted her stomach. "I have a hitchhiker to consider."

"I'm sure there's some. We'll ask Oscar for the inventory."

"Oscar?"

"It's a smart house," Alex explained. "I named it Oscar when I customized the software."

Only because Peter hadn't let her call it Meredith.

The two women went into the house, leaving the *Pyr* in the driveway. Alex heard Sara catch her breath as they entered the wreckage that had been the conservatory. It smelled of soot and burned plants and wet potting soil. Alex was aware of the broken glass and the various blinking red alarm lights.

How was she was going to get all of this fixed, without Peter noticing?

Sara went straight to the lap pool and looked at the fallen

Slayer. "Isn't he the one whom Donovan challenged at the mall?"

"Yes. Tyson. He's also one of the dragons who came to Gilchrist Enterprises two weeks ago," Alex admitted. She skipped past her memory of that night. "He's the one who attacked me last night when I went back there, too. Can we go into the house?"

"Sure. Sorry to linger; I was just curious." Sara matched steps with Alex, and caught her breath when they entered the house itself. "It's beautiful!"

"This is nothing. You should see it when all the windows are open in the daytime. They have shutters over them now."

"Don't open them just yet."

Alex laughed under her breath. "I wasn't going to. I'm never going to forget the sound of that *Slayer*'s talons overhead." She took a shaking breath. "If the shutters had been open, he would have dropped right into the room."

Sara watched her carefully, but didn't say anything. Alex opened some wine, occupying herself with hospitality. She knew that Sara was taking careful note of her attitude, but she couldn't fully hide her fear.

Peter's house was going to be full of dragons. The bad dragons knew where she was and only one of them was dead. And Alex was a bit too much of a skeptic to believe that invisible smoke was going to keep the *Slayers* at bay.

Never mind that Donovan's friends might not all be good dragons.

With a tight smile Alex handed Sara a glass of juice.

"What's your plan for the Green Machine, Alex?" Sara asked softly.

Alex's heart leapt. "I don't want to talk about it."

"But you're a target of the *Slayers*. It's important that we know everything so that we can help you."

Alex figured there was no point in beating around the proverbial bush. "How do I know I can trust all of you? Why would the *Pyr* want to help me?" She jumped when a man answered from behind her.

"Because the Green Machine can help to save the planet," he said, his British accent faint.

Alex turned to find on the threshold a tall man with dark hair, a touch of silver at his temples. Donovan, Quinn, and the other two *Pyr* stood behind him.

"That's our mission: to save the earth before it's too late," he continued. "It's imperative that humans make an effort to change their ways themselves—the Green Machine is a big step in that direction."

It was one thing to confide a bit in Donovan over an all-day breakfast platter in a diner after he'd saved her life a couple of times. It was quite another to have a bunch of strangers turn up and act as if they had a right to know her secrets.

Never mind that they already knew a bunch of them.

Alex immediately changed to her defensive mode. She would confirm what these *Pyr* knew, and their intentions, before she told them anything.

She wasn't going to make a travesty of Mark's death by spilling everything to dragons now. He hadn't told the *Slayers* anything, despite what they had done to him. No one was hurting her, so she should be able to be just as tough.

She owed him that much.

"You can't know anything about my invention."

"It's a car," the same *Pyr* said, and Alex's heart fell to her toes. "A car called the Green Machine because it runs on an alternative, eco-friendly fuel."

Had Donovan told this dragon her secret in their so-called old-speak? Her gaze flew to his, but he shook his head minutely.

"Erik knew about this before," he said, and Alex believed him.

But how? What powers did dragons have? She took a step back.

The other *Pyr*—Erik—continued. "More accurately, it's a car engine, one that runs on an alternative fuel. That fuel is plentiful and cheap: it has no waste products and creates no pollution. Your invention will revolutionize the automobile industry." The speaker shook his head. "I don't know what kind of fuel it is, Alex, but its credentials are impressive."

"*Slayers* destroyed the prototype at the lab," Donovan continued. "They let you live so you could retrieve all of your data."

"You've been doing that," Erik agreed. "And now you have a plan to continue. Is there a second prototype? Is it hidden here?"

Alex felt the big stainless steel fridge against her back. "Who are you and how do you know all of this?"

"I'm Erik Sorensson, leader of the *Pyr*." He smiled as if to reassure her and offered his hand. "We've been looking for you, Alex. We knew your name, and we knew about Gilchrist Enterprises, but I couldn't find the secret location of the lab in time."

"We hid it," Alex admitted.

"You hid it well," Erik agreed. "I wish I could have found you sooner."

"Why?"

His expression turned grim. "Because I would have ensured that Mark Sullivan didn't die." His voice softened. "He is dead, isn't he, Alex?"

Alex nodded and looked away. She was tempted to trust Erik, but wasn't sure she should. At least there were no beguiling flames in his eyes. "What do you want from me?"

"We want to protect you so that you can finish your work. We want to ensure that your invention gets into production."

"In exchange for what?"

"In exchange for seeing a change for the better in our world."

"That's all?" Alex was skeptical that anyone had such altruistic intentions as she and Mark.

"That's all. It's a matter of principle, for us, of doing what we were born to do." Erik smiled. "We are all ancient and inclined to hoard our riches. We don't need financial compensation."

"Although stray coins are always welcome," Donovan joked, and the other *Pyr* chuckled. The mood in the room lightened slightly.

"So, what's your plan?" Alex asked Erik.

"We'll protect you and help in any way we can to get the Green Machine running."

"We'll stand guard until you have your investor meeting," Donovan interjected. "Until the Green Machine's debut is secured."

Alex looked between them all, admitting to herself that she couldn't have picked a better-looking team of body-guards. "And then all dragons will disappear from my life forever?"

Erik spared a pointed glance at Donovan, who looked at the floor. Alex wondered at his change of mood.

Erik turned back to Alex and nodded, his manner thoughtful. "Yes. It's likely that even the *Slayers* will leave you alone then. Your existence will no longer be important to them."

Alex liked the sound of that.

"What about the firestorm?" Sara asked.

"I'll protect Alex until the next eclipse," Donovan said grimly. "I know my obligations."

"Even though you ride solo?" Alex couldn't resist re-minding him.

His lips tightened. "I play for the team."

"Do you?" Erik's sidelong look at Donovan could have cut glass. "Then you should breed."

"No," Donovan said flatly, his gaze locking with Alex's. "I'm not going to debate this with all of you." His voice rose slightly. "There will be no child."

Alex's heart fluttered at his intensity. Did he still want to cheat the firestorm? She was surprised to realize how much she did.

Despite everything.

Donovan folded his arms across his chest and glared at Alex. He must have guessed her question because he certainly answered it. "Once the firestorm passes, Alex will be safe."

Message received: in February, Donovan would leave her life for good. Why didn't losing this particular dragon sound like a good thing?

Alex wondered what had changed. Donovan had been pretty willing to do the deed before Tyson arrived. They'd worked together to kill Tyson, which should have brought them closer.

But Donovan had a stubborn look, one that Alex recognized. Peter got that look sometimes and Mark had had it once in a while, too. It invariably turned up when anything emotional needed to be discussed. Men usually then found an excuse to go for a beer, work on something mechanical, or otherwise disappear.

She knew the change was because she'd asked him to shift in front of her, but she didn't know why.

"Where did you say you put my bike?" Donovan asked then, as male a question as there could be.

Alex sighed, much to the amusement of the others. "I hid it on the other side of the garage." He looked unpersuaded. "If I'd traded it for a cup of coffee, I would have had a long walk—the Wyvern didn't offer me a lift. Go see for yourself."

Donovan pivoted immediately and strode out the door. The hearse driver, the *Pyr* who looked older, went with him.

"Donovan's one true love is his Ducati," Sara said. The young, dark-haired *Pyr* grinned and Quinn shook his head.

It wasn't exactly news to Alex. She didn't expect a long-term relationship with Donovan, although she had hoped for some great sex. If that wasn't in the cards, she had work to do. Donovan and his firestorm had already cost her precious time.

Alex had to admit there were benefits to having met Donovan. He'd supplied protection, pleasure, humor, and eye candy as well. That wasn't bad for one day.

But if he didn't want to find out what else was in store for them, she certainly wasn't going to beg.

She wasn't going to let Peter's wine go to waste, either.

Chapter 13

Donovan was more upset than he'd been in a long time. He remembered that last exchange with Olivia and again felt the responsibility that came with his power. He hadn't known then what he was doing—then he'd acted out of spite and anger.

He was terrified that it could happen again. There was a new force growing within him, one that he'd used to defeat Tyson but one that he was uncertain he could fully control. The dragon stirred and grew stronger.

Donovan didn't want Alex to pay the price.

His growing affection and admiration for Alex had to be a bad thing. Human women didn't deal well with the reality of his nature. He'd vowed long ago that he'd never trust a woman with his truth again, much less commit to one woman for more than a night. He'd certainly never reveal himself fully to a woman.

But Alex was undermining his determination. He had to put distance between them, bank the firestorm into embers, so that he could think straight. He felt Rafferty following him, knew his mentor would have something to say, and wasn't interested in listening just yet.

His bike was fine, a bit dusty but otherwise undamaged. He had the urge to sit down and polish it, no matter how long it took. He checked the air, but there was no scent of *Slayer*.

Alex must have hit the security codes for the garage, because one door opened as he stood there. Well aware of Rafferty's watchful presence, Donovan moved the Ducati into the garage.

"What a firestorm." Rafferty exhaled slowly and closed his eyes. "I could feel it from five miles away, resonating like a beacon."

Donovan didn't need to be reminded. The firestorm seemed to have gotten more intense.

More insistent.

Harder to ignore.

Rafferty lowered his voice, his eyes gleaming. "It would be easier to defend Alex, you know, if you *did* consummate the firestorm. The *Slayers* wouldn't have such an easy time targeting the two of you."

"They already know where we are."

"You could move. They won't be sure. The heat is extinguished immediately."

Donovan straightened at this morsel of news. "Immediately? Isn't that just a myth?"

Rafferty shook his head. "Quinn and Sara's stopped as soon as they slept together." He smiled. "Although, obviously, they weren't *sleeping*."

Donovan wondered whether the rest was a myth as well. Alex's doubts about instant conception made sense to him. "Is it true that the woman always conceives the first time?"

Rafferty shrugged. "That's the official story. We don't exactly have exhaustive statistical records, though, do we?"

Was it the sex that stopped the firestorm, or the conception of an heir? Could Alex's scheme to cheat the firestorm actually work? Everything quickened within him, then was silenced when he remembered her terms.

He couldn't risk doing that to Alex.

Donovan spared a glance at Rafferty. "You just can't stand the idea that someone would pass on the firestorm."

"Your resistance to Alex isn't really about the ongoing responsibility of a child. It's not about running free and un-encumbered, or riding solo." Rafferty paused, but Donovan didn't answer him. "Is it?" Acting as if he knew everything was probably Rafferty's most annoying trait.

Especially as he was usually right.

"Then, what is it about?" Donovan asked, then met the older *Pyr*'s gaze. "I'll bet you're going to tell me, aren't you?"

Even Rafferty didn't know this story.

"I know you, and I know that the real issue here is trust."

"Trust?" Donovan scoffed in his relief. "I don't have any problems with trust. I trust all of you guys, don't I?"

Rafferty shook his head, his gaze knowing. "You don't trust women. You haven't trusted women since Olivia—"

"Don't even say her name!"

"Or maybe since your mother threw you out for being what you are." Rafferty put a hand on Donovan's shoulder. "Not all women are selfish vipers like Olivia."

And not all women deserved Olivia's fate.

Donovan strode toward the house with impatience. "I don't distrust women. I have sex all the time and—"

"And you always leave before the morning, don't you?" Rafferty interrupted, following close behind him. "Once the pleasure is over, you're gone. You never return twice to the same bed."

That was a bit too close to Keir's last taunt for Donovan's comfort. He pivoted and jabbed a finger at Rafferty. "Don't say that the spark never falls far from the blaze."

Rafferty was dismissive. "You aren't like Keir. Anyone can see that." His eyes narrowed. "But what if your choices lead to the same results?"

Donovan stuck to his cover story. "You're making too much of this. I like variety. I'm not interested in commitment. So what?"

Rafferty folded his arms across his chest. "So, maybe this firestorm is the means of learning what you really need to know."

"I learn new stuff all the time."

"Maybe you're down to what you really need to know," Rafferty insisted. "Maybe trusting women, trusting a mate, and making a long-term commitment is your last frontier."

Donovan met his friend's gaze. "You're serious."

"Maybe it's what you need to know to become the Warrior."

Donovan's heart skipped a beat; then he shook his head. "The Warrior's powers are legendary. His role is foretold. There's never been a Warrior—"

"And why wouldn't there be one now, when we face a challenge to our very survival? A destined challenge?"

Donovan met Rafferty's knowing gaze. Could there be a purpose to all he was experiencing? Could loving Alex and surrendering to the firestorm be the best thing he could do for the *Pyr*?

But how would he protect her from himself?

Rafferty cocked a finger at the younger *Pyr*. "But you're afraid. You're afraid that if you surrender to the firestorm and it's the best you ever had, that you'll go back to Alex. You're afraid that you'll go back over and over again, that you'll get hooked, that you'll trust her and maybe even fall in love. You're afraid of making that commitment, that personal commitment to a much more intimate team."

Donovan's heart started to pound, but he couldn't walk away from Rafferty and his intensity.

"And you're terrified that she'll do just what Olivia did." Rafferty nodded. "You're afraid that she'll wait until you're committed and vulnerable, and then she'll betray you. You're afraid that another one of us, or maybe even all of us, will pay the price for your misplaced trust."

The bottom fell out of Donovan's gut.

Rafferty leaned in close again. "Isn't it funny how Alex has the same coloring as Olivia? They're not doppelgangers, but there's a resemblance. . . ."

"No!" Donovan shouted, and flung himself away from the words he didn't want to hear.

Rafferty strode right behind him and didn't let it go. "What if you *knew*, all those years ago? What if you had a vision of your destined mate, and when you saw Olivia, you thought she was Alex?"

"That's crazy talk."

"I don't think so. You don't remember, but I do. Olivia was always conniving, always *obviously* conniving. I could never understand what you saw in her." Rafferty dropped his voice to a whisper. "You always said the truth was in the way her eyes sparkled before she laughed, in the pure mischief of her expression. I saw only malice. You saw her once and were smitten. Were you seeing the truth, or just what you wanted to see?"

Donovan felt a lump rise in his throat. "That was a long time ago, Rafferty."

"It all makes perfect sense. Alex is different from Olivia, Donovan," Rafferty insisted. "Hers is a different soul. She's genuine and honest, and she would never take up with a *Slayer* like Magnus, no matter what prize he offered."

"You've only just met her."

"I know that you can trust the firestorm. It takes a long time, because it's not easy to find a perfect match for a dragon. Don't be afraid to trust, Donovan. . . ."

That was enough. Donovan faced his old friend.

"No, I'm not afraid to trust," he said, his tone harsh in his honesty. "I'm afraid that I'll destroy Alex, exactly the way I destroyed Olivia." Donovan paused as Rafferty stared at him, then admitted the rest. "Or maybe I'll let her down exactly the way I let down Delaney. Is the difference really important? Maybe I am the shard of Keir's talon, no matter what I do or say. Maybe my choices don't really change the result."

"No." Rafferty shook his head. "You're blaming yourself too much for the loss of Delaney."

"He's not lost, Rafferty." Donovan knew that the rest of what he had witnessed had to be shared with the others. "I need to tell this to Erik." Rafferty's brow wrinkled in concern as they headed back into the house together.

Donovan was on the threshold when he saw Alex and that predictable fire surged through his body. He wanted her as he'd never wanted another woman before. Rafferty was right—he'd always been tempted by tall women, women with athletic builds, intelligence, and raven-dark hair.

Had he been seeking Alex all these years without knowing it?

He jumped when Rafferty's hand landed heavily on his shoulder. "You're lucky," the older *Pyr* murmured, yearning in his voice as he observed the firestorm's effects. "So very lucky."

Donovan glanced back and met Rafferty's gaze. "It should have been your firestorm. You've waited a long time."

Rafferty's smile was rueful. "Patience is a virtue I have in abundance." He heaved a sigh. "You're too smart to piss into the wind, Donovan. Think twice before you throw this opportunity away." With that, Rafferty stepped past Donovan and accepted a glass of red wine from Alex.

There was irritation in her expression and she didn't look at Donovan directly. Her decision to ignore him had the opposite effect upon Donovan: she was the only light in the room for him. He was aware of the softness of her skin and the way the low light played over her cheeks. He remembered the soft heat of her lips and the feel of her curves beneath his hands. He respected her grace under fire, her ability to process and use new information, her determination to face her fears and annihilate them.

It made him think that if he had to pick a mate for himself, she'd be a whole lot like Alex Madison.

Not that it mattered. He'd protect her until February, then they'd go their separate ways.

Would he regret his choice?

Or would he be glad that he'd avoided temptation?

Assuming that he *could* avoid temptation for four entire months. It wasn't Donovan's best trick, that was for sure.

"Donovan has some news for us," Rafferty said, and every face turned at the urgency in his tone.

"Delaney isn't dead," Donovan said. "He's *Slayer*."

After Donovan's announcement, Alex watched the ripple pass through the group of *Pyr*. They clearly had believed that Delaney was dead, whoever he was.

Alex knew Quinn and Sara already, and Erik had introduced Sloane. The hearse-driving *Pyr* had introduced himself as Rafferty when he accepted a glass of wine.

"Are you opal and gold in dragon form?" she asked, and he nodded, clearly surprised.

He studied her for a moment, then stepped away after Donovan's announcement, maybe because of it. Rafferty moved quietly, his presence like a low thrum in the room, and his gaze kept flicking back to Alex. It was easy to believe that he could make the earth quake, and that he knew its songs.

"Delaney can't be alive," Sloane protested. "He died in Quinn's firestorm, when he and Erik were defending Sara."

"He can't be a *Slayer*," Erik said. "He would never make such a choice."

"Keir did, and Keir was Delaney's father," Donovan said. "Our father," he corrected. "The Wyvern sent me a dream."

"But Keir's heart was always dark," Erik insisted. "Delaney's was not. A *Pyr* cannot be made *Slayer* against his will."

"What would it take to change your mind?" Sloane murmured, and the *Pyr* seemed to shudder as one.

Alex thought of Mark's final moments.

"Delaney hadn't been exposed to all four elements," Sara noted. "Maybe they didn't take his body to ensure that he stayed dead."

"Well, what else would they do?" Quinn demanded with impatience. "Keep him alive as a slave?"

Sloane looked grim. "It's not out of the question." Another ripple of alarm passed through the group. "When Niall and I took down Xavier at the cabin last summer, he taunted us with the prospect of being turned *Slayer*. He said if we were injured, then Boris would have us on his side."

"Is that possible?" Rafferty asked. "Isn't the true heart of a *Pyr* enough to protect him from such evil?"

"It is taught that *Pyr* are born and *Slayers* are made," Quinn said thoughtfully. "The lesson doesn't say how *Slayers* are made."

"Delaney fights like an animal," Donovan said, and Alex saw how much the truth troubled him. "He never could fight well, but now he's fearless and ferocious. He's oblivious to his own pain, just keeps coming back for more."

"Did he know you?" Erik asked quietly.

Donovan shook his head. "I couldn't tell."

The only sound in the room was the crackle of the fire.

"The thing is that he's not really *Slayer*." Donovan threw back half a glass of wine. "He doesn't bleed."

"Neither did Keir," Quinn observed.

"What's darker than *Slayer*?" Sara asked.

Sloane cleared his throat. "I think I know. That manuscript I was translating, the old one—"

"The one that felt bad to you," Rafferty said.

Sloane nodded. "I found the key to the cipher. It's a mystical treatise, about the divine spark of the Great Wyvern. That spark is what gives us life; it's what animates our bodies."

"The spark never falls far from the blaze," Donovan said grimly. "And the Great Wyvern is the biggest blaze of all."

"Yes." Sloane nodded. "And there's a spark of Her divinity in each of us. The firestorm, according to this document, is a mark of Her favor. It burns because She's more emphatically present. She's indicating Her choice."

"What about free will?" Donovan asked, and Alex didn't miss his implication. She filled up her wineglass.

"There's a debate for another day," Erik said, then beckoned to Sloane. "What else does the document say?"

"That to become *Slayer* is to choose the darkness over the light, to choose the cold rather than the heat. It is to step away from the fire of divinity, so to speak, and to deny the eternal spark within each of us. To become *Slayer* is to deny the will of the Great Wyvern, to extinguish Her spark and become self-motivated instead of concerned with the fate of the collective."

"One instead of all," Erik mused. "Selfish."

"And it says that the truth of any individual's choice lies in his heart. That with free will, any of us can choose the shadows, but that the manifestation of that choice can't be stopped."

"It's a one-way street," Rafferty said with a nod.

Sloane heaved a sigh. "It also says that the Great Wyvern rescinds Her sign from those who deny Her, that their blood reflects the truth of their choice."

"It's black because they've chosen darkness," Quinn said with a nod of approval. "Instead of red for the fire."

"But what if they don't have any blood?" Sara asked.

"Then they have no souls," Alex guessed, following the logic. "They're not alive." The *Pyr* all stared at her in shock.

"Great Wyvern, what did I do?" Donovan whispered, and drank. He was pale and she knew he blamed himself for the fate of Delaney.

"It wasn't your fault," Erik said sharply. "I made the choice. If any carry the burden of Delaney's loss, it's me."

Donovan didn't look reassured. "He was my brother."

"I thought you were cousins," Rafferty said.

"I always said that, because we looked similar. And we were both cast out because we were *Pyr*. It was a kind of a joke." Donovan shoved a hand through his hair. "But the Wyvern sent me a dream, showing me that we were both Keir's sons."

"But not shards of his talon," Rafferty said quietly.

Alex could see that Donovan wasn't sure of that.

"Then how did Delaney become *Slayer*?" Donovan demanded.

"You see, that's just it," Sloane said. "This treatise lists the way to steal a soul. Obviously, it can be done only when the *Pyr* in question is unable to defend himself."

"Exposed to only three elements, but not quite dead," Sara said.

Donovan sat down and drained his glass.

"What happens to the soul?" Rafferty asked.

"The spark is released and it returns to the Great Wyvern, just as it does when we die," Sloane said. "But there's a complex process of implanting a shadow in its stead, of embedding darkness where the light should be, and thus turning the *Pyr* into a *Slayer*." He swallowed and looked around the room. "Into a slave who does not bleed."

"Impossible," Erik said, but his tone hinted at his doubt.

"It's risky, but not impossible," Sloane corrected. "Because the personality of the *Pyr* in question is still resident. A noble or good character will balk at the intrusion and fight it. The manuscript warns about madness and about uncontrollable results. The problem is that a slave with a heart of darkness is hard to kill. It suggests imprisonment for the duration of the process."

"How do you kill them?" Quinn asked.

Sloane frowned. "It recommends dismemberment and incineration for the ones who go insane."

"At least we got that right," Quinn said heavily.

"But Keir was dead and buried," Sara said.

"For a month," Rafferty agreed.

Erik began to pace the room. "Imagine if they can harvest all dead *Pyr* from the duration of our history." The notion made everyone in the room shudder. "Imagine if they can find all of those corpses and revive the ones who had not been exposed to all four elements immediately after their death."

"They'd have an army of ghouls," Sloane said. "Fighters who didn't bleed and were hard to kill."

Even Alex was shocked by this notion.

"That's what they do at that dark academy," Donovan guessed.

"And someone has to stop them," Erik said with resolve.

"None of you," the Wyvern agreed.

They all jumped, Alex included, and Sophie waved her fingertips from the doorway to the conservatory. "Surprise." She walked into the room then. "I can't see who will throw open the doors of the academy and release the *Pyr* trapped there. I can see though that it's none of you."

"There are other younger *Pyr* whom I watch and mentor—," Erik began, but Sophie interrupted him.

"No. It will be an older *Pyr*. Older than any of you. Someone who was born before the notion of *Pyr* and *Slayer* was so well articulated, someone whose heart holds both shadow and light."

"But who?" Sloane asked.

"I don't know."

"But Rafferty is the oldest of our kind," Erik argued.

"Is he," Sophie replied, no question in her tone.

"What do you know that we do not?" Erik demanded.

Sophie smiled. She waved her fingertips and, right before the eyes of all of them, disappeared.

"I hate when she does that," Rafferty muttered.

Alex had had enough. She had to think about her invention. She had to sleep. She had to rid herself of the distraction of dragons and Donovan and the promise of great sex.

Which meant she had to leave.

If the firestorm was going to last through February, then she could deal with it—and him—next week, after her investor meeting was over.

Alex took her bottle and her glass and headed for the door. "Feel free to make yourselves comfortable. I just ask that you don't burn the place down. I'm in enough trouble with Peter as it is, and Diane is going to lose it over those tiles."

"But where are you going?" Sara asked with alarm.

"Down to the boathouse. I've got some work to do."

"But it's two in the morning!" Sara called as Alex marched through the conservatory. Alex didn't stop and she certainly didn't look at Tyson's body. The memory of his malice was enough to make her walk quickly past him.

"I do my best work in the middle of the night," Alex lied. The truth was that she didn't want to have a dragon nightmare in the company of dragons.

It seemed rude.

She opened the front door and took a deep breath of the crisp autumn air. The stars were out by the thousands overhead and there was no sign of any dragons on the horizon.

It could have been a normal night.

Alex turned her steps toward the boathouse, and heard Erik's voice just before the door closed behind her.

"Your firestorm, I believe," he said, and Alex knew whom he had addressed.

Alex was glad she couldn't hear Donovan's response. She could guess that it wasn't polite. He wasn't happy with her, that much was clear, but she wasn't ready to establish his fan club, either.

Asking to see him change hadn't been wrong.

And coming so close to having great sex but not having it, over and over again, was making her cranky. She marched down to the boathouse, trying to remember the last time that having her own orgasm hadn't been good enough.

She couldn't remember that ever happening.

That realization just made her more cranky.

Alex heard the door open and close behind her but didn't look back. She didn't have to. She felt a shimmer of heat on her back and knew precisely who had followed her.

If Donovan had something to say, he could come after her and say it.

Was it possible for a woman to be more stubborn than Alex Madison? Donovan doubted it.

On the other hand, most women would have backed down from a dragon's challenge, or been unable to shoot one dead. Few who had seen whatever she had witnessed at Gilchrist Enterprises could have remained in the same room with dragons. No woman could have stirred his blood with such ease.

The firestorm really didn't fight fair. Donovan watched the way Alex walked, the sweet sway of her hips, and the way she held her head high. He liked that she was tall and took long strides. He liked her easy athleticism. He liked her honesty.

He liked her.

He was falling for her.

That was the trouble. He wanted to protect her from himself.

Alex had had a bit of wine. Donovan noticed it in her stride. It didn't matter: there was little trouble she could find with him right behind her. He was keenly aware of their surroundings, and alert after the battle with Tyson. His body was still ready to celebrate, but more easily controlled now that time had passed.

There was a faint scent of *Slayer* in the vicinity, so faint that he decided it must be residue from Tyson's arrival. Had other *Slayers* come with Tyson? Donovan thought he detected Sigmund's scent, but it had diminished almost to nothing.

He would have preferred to have found the air clean, but

he knew what he had to do to protect Alex from any hidden threat.

She did go into the boathouse. She locked the door against him. He wasn't surprised. He doubted that either of them believed that a door lock would keep him out if she found trouble inside.

The boathouse was made of wood and had an A-frame roof. There was a regular door on one side, the one Alex had used, and a larger opening on the lake side for the boat. The modified garage door securing access from the lake side was locked. On the roof was a cupola with a copper roof and a weather vane. The cupola was shuttered on all four sides and acted as a vent.

Donovan had no idea what she was going to do in there—probably finish that bottle of wine and sleep in some deluxe boat of her brother's, complete with all the amenities—and he didn't care. He shifted and flew to the roof of the boathouse, knowing she'd hear the sound of him landing.

Then he changed back to human form and sat straddling the ridgepole, his back against the cupola. He could see the house fitted into the slope of the hill before him, and it was an impressive building. The stainless steel shutters gleamed in the moonlight. Behind him, the lake spread like ink.

There were trees on either side of the house, running all the way down to the shore, and Peter's house might have been the only one on the lake. Donovan could smell wood fires and see the flicker of lights through the trees. There were other homes tucked into the woods, each ensured some privacy by the trees.

It was tranquil here, almost romantic. Donovan could have used a glass of that wine Alex had brought down here. He could have used some of her company, but he knew better than to ask. The woman could tempt a saint, and he was no saint.

"I'm breathing smoke," he said. "I'm making a boundary mark around the boathouse so you can work in peace."

"I don't believe in the invisible," she shouted from inside.

"What about motion detectors?" he replied. "Or magnetic fields? Sonic waves? Radio waves? Electrons?"

"You have a tendency to be irritating, you know."

Donovan grinned. "Well, there's something else we have in common." He heard her laugh in surprise, a throaty sound that made his pulse leap. "You don't have to talk to me, Alex. I just have to protect you, and I will."

There was a long pause and he didn't think she would answer him. He composed his thoughts and began to breathe smoke. Alex's sudden words startled him into snapping the first tendril.

"So, how exactly is it that you figure you aren't responsible?"

Donovan stopped breathing the smoke. He blinked and stared down at the roof. Her words made him think.

"You don't fool me, you know," she said, her conviction winding its way through his emotional barriers. "You would have died defending me in the conservatory. You would have done anything to beat Tyson, and it wasn't just about winning. It was about doing right by me and don't try to pretend otherwise."

Donovan couldn't think of a word to say.

"Good," Alex whispered. "At least you're not trying to tell me stories anymore." He heard her yawn. "If you ever want to talk about why you think you can't be counted on, I'm listening."

Donovan was intrigued. "I thought you were worried about being beguiled."

"If you ever tried to beguile me, I'd make you regret it," she said, and he smiled. "I saw what you were doing to Peter. I just wanted to understand it."

"That's the idea. It's supposed to be interesting, then fascinating, then hypnotic."

"There are people who are lousy hypnosis candidates and I'm one of them." He heard her take a shaking breath.

"Look, I owe you one. More than one, actually. I could have been destroyed by *Slayers* several times over in the past day, but you keep charging into the rescue." Her voice softened. "So, thanks, Donovan. And if you want to talk about anything, I'm listening."

It was a generous offer and one he knew he should accept. He looked across the lake, thinking. "You said they tortured Mark."

"Let's talk about that some other time," Alex said, her breath catching slightly. "When it's bright and sunny and there are no dragons to be seen. Maybe *after* Thursday."

"Deal," he said, smiling slightly. "But you don't fool me, either, Alex."

"What do you mean?"

"I don't believe you're afraid of anything or anyone."

She laughed. "Wrong. I'm afraid of a lot of things."

"Let me put that another way, then." Donovan tapped the roof. "Your fear doesn't stop you. You might be afraid, but you don't let it keep you from doing what you need or want to do."

"The Green Machine is important."

"It's not just with regard to the car. I've never seen anyone face their fears with such determination."

Alex sighed. "I refuse to live in terror," she said quietly. "I refuse to let anything or anyone restrict me, even myself."

"That's a tough code."

"Sometimes it is. I just don't think anyone gains anything by hiding away or playing it safe."

Donovan thought about that.

Alex half laughed. "On the other hand, a little security is welcome sometimes. If you felt inclined to be my guardian tonight, maybe breathe a little of that magic smoke, well, I'd be grateful."

Donovan's heart skipped at the prospect of how she might show her gratitude. "It's not magic, Alex."

"No. It's using dragons to defend against dragons. Or

fighting fire with fire. Something like that." He heard her
yawn. "I really need to get some sleep. I'm not making sense
anymore."

Donovan thought she was making perfect sense, but he
let it be. He heard Alex settling somewhere below him and
refused to consider whether she was planning to sleep
naked. Little sparks were dancing from his body to the
rooftop all around him.

It was as if the firestorm were upping the ante, burning
hotter the longer they denied it.

Donovan sat on the roof of Peter's boathouse and began
to breathe a continuous stream of smoke. He heard Alex's
breathing become more rhythmic and her pulse slow. His
own matched pace and his smoke flowed more thickly.

He wove his smoke around and around the small building, securing the windows and the doors, the access from the
lake and the roof. He exhaled circuit after circuit, lulled to a
meditative state by the sound of Alex sleeping in the boathouse below him, meshing it all into a coherent web to protect her.

The smoke shimmered as it flowed from him. It shone as
it spilled over the roof and it glimmered as he wove each
tendril into the others. The perimeter mark began to resonate
as it grew more and more solid, and Donovan could feel the
strength of it.

He kept weaving, kept breathing, kept thinking about
Alex's words. He leaned against the cupola and breathed.

Donovan opened his eyes and his field of view was filled
with stars. He listened to the clear crystalline ping of his
smoke mark and knew that it was the best barrier he'd ever
woven.

But then, he'd never had such motivation.

He listened to the vibration of his fellows inside Peter's
cottage and had no desire to join them. The sky overhead
was utterly cloud free, and so deep an indigo that he wanted
to caress it. He leaned back against the cupola and forced

himself to relax. For the moment, Alex was safe, secure within the smoke he had breathed. There was no scent of *Slayer* and no sign of trouble. He should take the opportunity to rest.

That was when the impossible happened.

Alex screamed.

Erik awakened suddenly.

He lay in the darkness and listened, but heard nothing out of the ordinary. He tried to recall whether he had had a dream or nightmare, but there had been only his old familiar one.

He shivered and shoved its reminder aside.

Then he knew what had roused him. He felt a tingle, a sense of something about to happen.

Erik sat up. He listened, straining his ears, and he knew that the *Slayers* were making trouble again. Niall didn't even realize as much yet, but Erik sent him a message on the wind.

Then he summoned Sloane to be his second.

He met the younger *Pyr* in the hall and they moved as one in the shadows. They slipped silently down the stairs, not even pausing for Erik's brief exchange of old-speak with Rafferty.

All would be well here, with Rafferty standing sentry.

Erik stopped to ask the house a question, one to which Oscar responded discreetly. With a nod at Sloane, the two leapt into the night sky, shifted shape, and set course for Minneapolis.

Erik only hoped they could arrive in time.

Rafferty dozed, watchful but conserving his energy. He listened to the song of the earth and thought about the dream the Wyvern had sent him. He knew it was best to let a student find his own path. Only if Donovan strayed or if time ran out would Rafferty prompt him with the prophecy he had dreamed.

Until then, Rafferty would bide his time. It had been only a day, and Donovan made more progress than he knew.

The earth was restless, her song more agitated than had long been the case. Rafferty had become used to the discord in her rhythms. He didn't like it, but he couldn't change it. Rafferty listened, trying to see her course, trying to learn how to better anticipate her angry mood.

This motion was different, though.

Closer.

More violent.

Not of the earth herself but within her soil.

Rafferty heard the disruption of soil, but mostly he heard the earth's displeasure with the intrusion. No, with the intruder. She recoiled from it, whatever it was. Her indignation caught Rafferty's ear and he listened more closely.

It was digging under the house.

It was not an animal.

It was not a human.

Only when he listened very closely could Rafferty detect that it was something neither *Pyr* nor *Slayer*. It carried a vestige of both. Rafferty thought of Sloane's manuscript and the back of his neck prickled.

He would have bet that whatever was digging did not bleed.

But why was it digging under the house?

What was its plan?

Rafferty didn't care to find out. He wouldn't risk his fellows, never mind Donovan and Alex's firestorm. He'd stop the intruder in a prison of soil. He began to hum a low chant, a melody dispatched to the earth and attuned to her rhythms. She responded slowly, as troubled as she was, but gradually she warmed to Rafferty's call. He was, in many ways, an old friend and ally. Once she recognized him, she responded to his melody.

Rafferty knew the moment that she blocked the digger's path, trapping him in a cavern of its own making. Rafferty heard the earth close the tunnel behind the intruder.

He heard the digger bellow in rage and thrash in its confines.

As the intruder battled in futility, Rafferty thought about the strange mingling of *Slayer* and *Pyr* in its vibration. He could not understand it. It had been *Pyr*, or it was becoming *Pyr*. Rafferty wasn't certain but he wouldn't kill it. He could not destroy anyone or anything charged with the spark of the Great Wyvern.

It was not Rafferty's place to make such decisions.

But whatever it was, it would die, buried in the earth as he was now. Its breathing was already labored. Rafferty murmured to the soil and opened an air passage from the surface to the intruder's dungeon. It wasn't much, but it was enough. He heard the captive gulp at the air.

The decision could wait until Erik returned.

Chapter 14

*D**ragons.**

    Alex awakened in terror. For a moment she didn't realize where she was; then she recognized the interior of Peter's boathouse.

"Alex?" Donovan said from the door. He knocked on it hard. "Are you all right? What's going on?"

His concern reassured Alex as nothing else could have done.

"Just a nightmare," she said, then climbed out of the canoe where she'd been sleeping. She loved sleeping there—it was like a hammock when hung from the roof. It rocked gently and with all the life jackets piled in it, it was reasonably comfortable.

"Are you sure?" he demanded. He jiggled the door and Alex smiled at his impatience.

Then she realized he hadn't shifted shape to defend her. That would have been his instinctive choice and it must have been hard for him to stop it. He was determined to shelter her from the sight of him changing. Even though she didn't understand why he thought it so important, Alex's heart warmed.

"Seulement un cauchemar," she said, remembering an old movie.

"That's from a movie, *Murder on the Orient Express*."

"Right." Alex smiled as she moved closer to the door. She liked that he'd understood her reference. The boathouse was chilly but she felt warmer with each step she took closer to Donovan, as if she were drawing close to a bonfire.

The firestorm was becoming a reassuring constant in her life.

Or maybe it was Donovan.

Donovan laughed. "How is that supposed to make me feel better? It was the murderer who said it, pretending to be the victim."

"Who didn't speak French," Alex agreed. "He couldn't fool Hercule Poirot."

"Maybe you should open the door and prove you're okay."

Alex laid her hands against the bolted wooden door and watched the sparks leap toward her hands. The firestorm was burning hotter, shooting sparks even when there was a barrier between them.

It wasn't going to be ignored.

"I'll make you a deal," Alex said impulsively. "I'll let you see that I'm okay if you let me watch you shift."

"No." Donovan's tone allowed no room for negotiation.

Alex opened the door at the force of his reply. He glared at her but she didn't back down. "It's because of Olivia, isn't it?"

His shock was obvious. "What?"

"You lost a scale because you loved her, and now the patch has come off and you don't want to risk losing another scale, too."

Donovan took a step back. "That's not it."

"Sure it is. The Dragon's Tooth is the only souvenir you have of her, so that's why you were upset that it fell off. You dove after it because you didn't want to lose the memento. It makes perfect sense. She must have died hundreds of years ago. . . ."

Donovan was obviously shocked. "How do you know about Olivia and the Dragon's Tooth?"

"The Wyvern showed me your past." At his obvious astonishment, Alex continued. "On the television. She must have been warning me that you were emotionally unavailable, but you have to know, Donovan, that sex doesn't have to be about forever."

"That's not it," Donovan snapped.

"Liar." Alex held his gaze, feeling his irritation. Why was he so angry?

Because she knew about his past, without him telling her? That would have annoyed Alex, too, but she knew that Donovan wasn't the kind of man to confide the details of his history, either.

He leaned closer and dropped his voice low. She couldn't look away from the vivid green of his eyes. "It is because of Olivia, but not for the reason you suggest. I didn't love her. I thought I did, but I was wrong."

Alex frowned. "But you lost a scale. Isn't that what that means?"

"Yes."

Alex waited, but he wasn't going to help. "So, you loved somebody else?" she prompted.

Donovan shrugged and looked over the lake. "Romantic love isn't the only kind, Alex."

She watched him. "You said you had a cousin who was like a brother to you," she said, and knew by the tightening of Donovan's lips that she'd guessed right.

"We were inseparable," he admitted, his voice husky.

"A team," Alex guessed, understanding something more of him.

Donovan met her gaze steadily. "Exactly. Except Delaney wasn't my cousin. He was my brother. The Wyvern showed me that."

"Delaney?" Alex recognized the name. "He's the one

who's dead but not. The green and copper dragon who attacked you yesterday."

"Right." He averted his gaze again and swallowed. Then he changed the subject, as Alex might have anticipated. She'd seen how upset he was about Delaney's fate, and his own sense of responsibility for it. "Olivia was a different problem."

Alex was encouraged that he kept talking. "What then?"

Donovan looked at her, something of the cold predator in his expression. "She betrayed me."

"She sent you after the Dragon's Tooth, knowing that Magnus would attack you."

"You saw all that?"

Alex nodded.

Donovan shoved a hand through his hair in frustration. "The firestorm doesn't fight fair," he muttered.

"Neither does the Wyvern."

"Right. Okay. Olivia betrayed me, but I survived, with Rafferty's help."

"But Magnus threw the Dragon's Tooth in the lake. You must have gotten it before everything fell in."

"Of course. It was what I had come for." His lips set in a grim line. "So, I took the prize to Olivia."

His attitude gave Alex a bad feeling. "It was the pearl she wanted, at any price."

His smile was cold. "It was."

"So, what happened?"

"The price was higher than she expected."

"What?"

Donovan turned his glittering gaze upon Alex and spoke with quiet force. "I showed her what I am."

Alex's heart stopped, then leapt. Donovan had shifted in front of Olivia and that was why he wouldn't do it for her. Something really bad had happened. "Tell me."

"I told her she could have the gem if she took me to her bed one last time."

Alex swallowed, not sure she really wanted to hear this. "And?"

"She did. Of course." He inhaled and turned to look across the lake. "She even locked the bedroom door. It was a small room, nearly filled with the curtained bed. I took the key, which troubled her. I could tell by the pitch of her laughter. Then I offered her the pearl, and she forgot her worries in her lust."

"For you or the pearl?"

"Guess."

Alex understood his bitterness. "But?"

"But when she reached for it, I let my hand change. Just the thumbnail first, just two talons."

"The two holding the gem."

"Yes. She hesitated and I continued to shift, very slowly. I made sure that she knew what she was seeing, that she understood that she had locked herself into a room with a dragon and that the dragon had the key. I made sure she knew just whom she had betrayed." He swallowed and looked at the ground.

"If the room was small, you must have filled it," Alex prompted softly.

Donovan shot her a look. "She had nowhere to go, no place to run. She tried, but I was furious. I cornered her. She begged, but I was in no mood to negotiate." He frowned. "I'm not proud of what I did that night, Alex. I'm not proud that I acted in anger and took vengeance—even though she believed she was sending me to my death." He glanced at her, his gaze bright. "I didn't love her. Trust me on that."

"What happened to her?"

"She went insane. By the time I left, she was writhing on the floor, incoherent, unable to accept what she had witnessed." He shrugged, but didn't manage to hide his sense of responsibility for what he had done. Nor could he hide his regret.

But he didn't love Olivia.

"I heard she lost everything and died on the streets," he said heavily. "I kept the Dragon's Tooth to remind myself of what I could do, as a talisman to never repeat that crime."

Alex watched him and felt his guilt.

He faced her again. "So now you know what you're asking."

What Alex knew was that they both had demons to conquer. She believed they could make those conquests together.

As a team.

"Show me." She spoke with force and knew she surprised him.

She also knew he understood exactly what she meant.

Donovan flicked her a hot glance. "I won't."

"You have to show me, Donovan. You can conquer your fear of the past only by facing it."

"Alex—"

"You have to know that a woman can look at all of what you are and not lose her jelly beans."

He got that stubborn look. "It's my duty to protect you, not drive you nuts."

Alex could be stubborn herself. "Quit arguing with me. You know I'm right."

He smiled then in his surprise. "Do I?"

"Just do it. Do it now." She smiled back at him, hoping she looked more confident than she felt. "Prove to me that not all dragons are scary. Maybe I'll get over my nightmares, too."

He studied her for a long moment, his gaze so searching that Alex was sure he could read her thoughts. She wondered what he found, because he nodded abruptly and turned to face her. He glanced around, apparently assured himself that they were alone, then took a deep breath.

"Slowly," Alex said. "Do it really slowly."

Donovan's grin flashed. "Slowly is always better," he murmured, a knowing glint in his eyes.

Alex tingled right to her toes, the firestorm burning bright within her.

Then she took his hand in hers and lit an inferno.

It was the prospect of ending Alex's nightmares that convinced Donovan to do as she asked. Donovan watched the sparks dance, felt his body respond with enthusiasm, and wondered how the hell he'd resist Alex until February.

Four months was an eternity.

He was in trouble.

The firestorm steadily became more insistent. It was as if destiny wanted to ensure that it couldn't be ignored or denied.

Or as if everything and everyone were allied against him. All of Donovan's secrets had been laid bare to Alex, thanks to the Wyvern's interference. Alex knew his age—or enough of it to know that he wasn't a normal man—his past, his nature. She knew about Olivia and the Dragon's Tooth. Given the choice, he would never have told her so much, but the choice had been taken from him.

On the other hand, she was still standing in front of him, asking for more.

Did he dare to believe that the firestorm had chosen the perfect mate for him? Did he dare to wonder whether there could be a woman who truly accepted all of him?

He'd soon know. Donovan watched Alex carefully as he began to shimmer on the cusp of change, ready to stop if she showed any signs of agitation. He was glad she was holding his hand; it was even easier to feel her pulse and read her uncertainty. She was trembling slightly, but stared straight at him.

Fearless.

Invincible.

Willing to reconsider everything she knew.

Donovan admired that—and so much more—about Alex. The night's shadows tangled in her hair, deepened the mys-

teries in her eyes, made her face look fair and her lips dark.
The flames danced between their fingertips, casting a circle
of light around them like a sparkler.

"Do it," Alex urged with a nod.

Donovan let his thumbnail change. It slowly grew into a
talon, a long sharp claw, that rested against Alex's hand. She
watched it, eyes wide, then ran her fingertips over it.

She was learning his shape.

His truth.

She swallowed and smiled at him. Donovan took a deep
breath and mustered every vestige of his control. The change
had a force of its own, a tendency to happen quickly. It was
hard to control it, to linger between forms. Donovan let the
rest of his hand change, which left Alex's hand looking frag-
ile within his. He held her fingers gently, not wanting to
frighten her with his strength.

"Where'd your watch go?"

"Garments are folded away, jewelry too, and hidden beneath the scales."

Alex arched a dark brow, looking impish. "Because you
might need them again."

"Something like that. Okay?"

She smiled at him. "It's easier when you talk to me a bit.
It reminds me of whom I'm dealing with here."

"You want to put some distance between us?"

"No. I've got to get used to this."

Donovan liked the sound of that. "Okay. Up to the shoulder now; then I'm not sure how well I can control it."

Alex nodded and tightened her grip on his hand. "Do it."

Donovan savored the ripple of strength that rolled
through him as his body did what it did best. He enjoyed the
power of his dragon form, its near invincibility, its percep-
tiveness. He'd never shifted so slowly and enjoyed the
chance to leisurely observe the change in his body.

Even if it was killing him to control it so carefully.

Alex was nearly hyperventilating, but she held on to his

talon. He watched her throat work and heard the hammer of her heart.

"So far so good?"

Her breath was coming a bit quicker and she'd bit her lip. She nodded though, as tough as he'd hoped. "The teeth are going to be the difficult bit," she said with a rueful grimace.

"It comes fast now," he warned as the tide of change grew within him. Alex had time to nod; then the shift took ascendancy. Its force rolled through Donovan like a tidal wave.

He tried to slow it down, but his body was in the full grip of the change. In the presence of his mate, who had been threatened, his body was ready to fight. He tipped back his head and roared as the heat surged through him, as the firestorm kindled to the heat of a forest fire, as his body responded to her presence.

When it was done, he looked down at his mate.

Alex was paler, but she smiled bravely for him. And she hadn't let go of his claw. Donovan felt triumphant that she had survived the sight of him.

"I will never get used to that," she said with a shake of her head. "But it's impressive. I'll give you that."

"You know I won't hurt you."

"I know. I trust you." She nodded. "You're a good dragon."

Before he could reply, she took a deep breath and reached for him. Her fingertips danced over him, sparks flying as she familiarized herself with his dragon form. A line of sparks lit behind her caress.

Donovan was awed. Alex was confronting her fear, turning it into courage, and he loved her for it.

Alex ran her hand over his foreleg, her touch arousing him even in dragon form. She swallowed, then examined the plumes that streamed from his back. She touched his wings, fingering their leathery texture. She stared into his eyes, then stretched to run an exploratory finger over his teeth.

"Fighting machine," she murmured, and he grinned.

"That's me. Lean and mean." He watched her become aware of his smile, watched her anxiety ease an increment. Donovan stood and let her explore. She walked around him, touching him with increasing bravery, and he tasted his relief.

She hadn't gone mad.

Before he could consider the differences between Olivia and Alex, never mind the rest of Rafferty's comments, Alex reached up and touched the wound on his chest. The spot where the Dragon's Tooth had been torn away was still a bit sore, but it had scabbed over. He caught his breath—it was that sensitive that the light brush of her fingers sent a stab of pain through him.

Worse, the scale beside it fell into Alex's hand.

Donovan gaped at it. His vulnerability had just doubled.

And he knew why.

Sloane and Erik landed on the roof of a executive house in a luxury suburb. The lots were generous; the streetlights were broadly spaced; the security systems quietly hummed. Each house was large, and rich with amenities—swimming pools, hot tubs, and triple garages. Sloane spied Niall on the peaked roof of one that was a slightly downscaled version of a French château from the Loire Valley.

The roof was all jagged peaks, with a small balcony hidden on the back side of the house. It looked to Sloane as if it led from the master suite and would give a view over the backyard and trees beyond.

It would also be an excellent place for a *Slayer* to break into the house. There was no ladder and the roof was steep, so humans might not be worried about securing the door. A *Slayer*, though, could simply land on the balcony.

It wasn't a surprise to Sloane that Niall perched near this balcony and that his smoke was thickest outside its glass door.

"No sign," Niall said in old-speak as they landed beside him on the cedar-shingled roof.

The three remained in dragon form. They settled with their backs to one another, each watching in a different direction, without discussion. Sloane looked down at the small balcony, where he noticed a bistro table and chairs.

"I don't like it." Erik sounded irritated.

There was a lot that Sloane didn't like. He'd been reading more of that manuscript when Erik summoned him and was glad to put it aside. It gave instruction for deeds he found abhorrent, ones he had previously found unthinkable.

Now he was thinking about them all the time and he didn't like it. He was wondering which trick the *Slayers* intended to use next. He was worried about almost dying and being made into something else. He was glad to stretch his wings, protect some humans, and potentially face a good old-fashioned dragon attack.

"Boris can disguise his scent and presence, remember," Erik advised. "He may have taught the others."

"Your smoke is good," Sloane acknowledged, admiring the protective ring that Niall had breathed.

"I want it thicker and deeper," Erik said. "We need to cocoon the whole house."

"It's big. I need help," Niall said.

"We'll breathe it together and interweave it," Sloane said.

"We'll make Peter's house a fortress," Erik agreed. They all inhaled as one, synchronizing their breathing and exhaling in unison. The smoke flowed thick and entangled.

And Sloane saw movement at the sliding glass door.

He bent to look closer and found a little boy staring back at him, his eyes wide with wonder. He was towheaded and blond, maybe four years old, and dressed in pajamas. He stared at Sloane in awe and his eyes were as dark a brown as chocolate.

Before Sloane could think to beguile him, the child pivoted and ran into the depths of the house. There was no way to catch him without revealing himself further.

"Shit!" Sloane said, leaning toward the balcony. He peered into the house but the little boy was gone.

Erik caught at his claw. "Children are hard to beguile," he said quietly. "It's better not to try."

"But he could tell his parents that we're here!" Sloane said.

Erik smiled. "And who will believe him when he says there are dragons on the roof?"

Niall chuckled and the three of them settled back to breathe smoke. Erik might have been right, but Sloane kept thinking about that little boy.

As Donovan fought to control his shock, Alex stared at the scale in her hand. She looked up at him; then her dismay was obvious. "What did I do?" she whispered.

Donovan wasn't going to talk about it. He shifted back to human form fast. He scooped the scale from her hand and pushed it into his pocket, feeling it nudge up against the Dragon's Tooth on its makeshift scale.

"Nothing," he said, and it was true.

The issue wasn't what she had done.

It was what he had done.

He was falling in love and his body knew the truth better than he did. It also made him more vulnerable, just when he needed to be strongest. Donovan wasn't sure what to do with that, how he was supposed to defend his mate when his weakness was growing.

He changed the subject, rather than give Alex any clues. She'd probably figure out the truth, and he was feeling too exposed already.

"You're really okay?" he asked, and didn't have to pretend to be concerned.

Alex watched him carefully for a moment. "I'm fine."

"Even watching me shift slowly like that?"

"Absolutely." She spread her hands. "Not even a little bit incoherent."

"Good."

Alex smiled at him. "Maybe Olivia was a wimp. Maybe

she would have lost her jelly beans whether you shifted or not."

"Maybe," Donovan agreed. He was thinking that Alex was the one who was unique, the one with special gifts, but that only made him admire her more.

Just how many scales could he lose over one woman? The question was terrifying.

Alex smiled, then stifled a yawn. "I could use a bit more sleep before I get to work, but I can sleep Friday."

Donovan halted his agreement before it was voiced. He realized her implication—she planned to work here.

Which meant she had everything she needed to do so.

Which meant the *Slayers* might return at any time.

To kill Alex and eliminate the Green Machine forever. Donovan felt his body on the cusp of change once more.

There was urgency in his tone, an urgency he couldn't stifle. "Where's the prototype for the Green Machine, Alex? It's here, right?"

Alex's smile was mischievous. "Guess."

Donovan's gaze trailed back to the garage but before he could speak, she tapped him on the arm. "Too obvious!" she chided. "Guess again."

"Tell me instead."

His seriousness must have gotten through to her, because her smile faded. She took his hand and drew him through the boathouse door. "Here."

"Where?" Donovan blinked at the empty expanse of water surrounded on three sides by a dock. "Did you sink it?"

Alex pointed up to the rafters. "There."

Donovan hit the light switch and saw the undercarriage of a car suspended from the rafters of the boathouse.

Relief rolled through him. It was here.

"Last place I'd look."

"That's the point," Alex scoffed. "You don't hide something where people will find it."

"But how did you get it up there?" Donovan walked on

the docks around the perimeter of the boathouse, staring upward in amazement. Even in the darkness, he could see there was a system of pulleys and ropes holding the car up.

"It was Mark's project for the weekend. It wasn't easy." Alex grinned. "I think it was more of a challenge than he expected."

"Who knows it's here?"

"Just me, now." Her smile faded and she stared up at the car. Donovan knew he'd caught another glimpse of her feelings for Mark.

He didn't like the view any more than he had before.

He focused on the problem at hand.

"I'll need the help of the others to get it down," he said. "We should move it to the garage to get it running. How did you plan to get it down?"

"We never thought we'd need it," Alex admitted. "It was Mr. Sinclair's requirement that we store a prototype off-site. We thought he was too cautious." She frowned. "It has a steel chassis, like the other prototype, but the parts that would typically be made of plastic are made instead of plant material. It's lighter than a typical car."

"It still can't be that light."

"But it's here." Alex spoke with resolve. "Some tinkering and a batch of salt water and we'll be ready to go." She held up her hand, her finger and thumb barely apart. "I'm *this* close."

"Good thing you have a team of dragons around to do the dirty work for you," Donovan teased, wanting to make her smile.

She did. "So maybe it's a good thing to have dragons on your side. The good ones, anyway."

"Present company included?"

Alex smiled and a flush lit her cheeks. "Absolutely."

Donovan stared back at her. She'd seen the full truth of him and hadn't flinched. Were he and Alex a new team? They certainly worked well together, so well that Donovan dared to think of the future. They'd killed Tyson together. His need to keep her safe had given him extra strength right when he had needed it.

Could she help to heal his missing scale, the way Sara had helped Quinn heal? Was that the benefit of surrendering to the firestorm?

It certainly wouldn't be the only one.

And it wasn't the only reason that satisfying the firestorm sounded like such a good idea.

Heat rose in Donovan as they eyed each other, the firestorm redoubling once again. He felt a trickle of sweat run down the center of his back and he saw Alex lick her lips. Her nipples were beaded and he could smell her skin.

He caught Alex's hand in his, giving her time to step away if that was what she wanted. He watched the point of contact, awed by the sparks that danced between their hands. Alex squeezed his fingers, then glanced up at him, her eyes dancing with relief and anticipation. She smiled, totally unafraid of him.

This was as good as it got. Donovan bent his head and kissed Alex. His was a slow and thorough kiss, a leisurely kiss that left his blood simmering and his heart leaping.

It was a kiss that coaxed the firestorm to new heat, a kiss that tasted of acceptance and transformation. Alex was changing Donovan's ideas about his own future, and he only hoped he could protect her to ensure that future had a chance.

When Alex turned and twined her arms around Donovan's neck, he was sure they'd start a conflagration.

And he didn't care. He just deepened his kiss.

Donovan was going to melt every one of Alex's reservations. He slid his tongue between her teeth, pleasure shot through her veins, and Alex tried to remember why she should care about having reservations.

Donovan was a dragon.

Surrendering to the firestorm led to the conception of dragon babies—if she chose to believe the *Pyr*'s publicity.

Indulging in the pleasure of the firestorm could attract other dragons, *Pyr* and *Slayer* alike.

But the man was irresistible.

Alex leaned into his kiss, enjoying every spark that it kindled. She'd never had much use for reservations, anyway.

When Donovan lifted his head, Alex was dizzy. She leaned against him, pressing her lips to the pulse at his throat.

"It's too early to wake the others," she murmured, and heard Donovan chuckle.

"Too early to go shopping," he agreed, grazing her ear with his lips. His hands were moving across her back in a ceaseless caress. Alex wished there weren't so much fabric between them.

"We could pick up where we left off," she said as he touched his lips to hers.

"You mean where we were interrupted."

"Not exactly there. Somewhere more private."

She saw his smile flash. "I like a woman who knows what she wants," he murmured, his voice low and seductive.

Alex was already seduced. "Good thing you've found one, then," she said, curling her hand around the back of his neck and pulling his head down for another kiss. "And I want you," she said, just before their lips touched.

Donovan ducked her kiss, bending down to cast her over his shoulder. Alex squealed and he laughed, but he still headed directly for the house. "We need to be inside a smoke boundary mark," he said.

"Doing it in the canoe isn't good enough for you?" she teased, and he chuckled again.

"No. And I'll show you why."

"Promise?"

He chuckled as he carried her up the sloping hill to the house, setting her on her feet on the front porch. He kissed her soundly again, leaving her hungry for more; then Alex verified her identity to Oscar for admission.

Alex kept her gaze fixed straight ahead as she and Donovan hurried through the conservatory. She didn't want to see the wreckage from the fight with Tyson, and really didn't want to see Tyson himself, floating in the lap pool. It was pretty dark in there because of the shutters and the early hour, but she fixed her gaze on the door to the living room just in case.

She thought about the promise of what was ahead.

The low flames from the fireplace showed an unfamiliar silhouette in the living room. It took Alex a minute to realize that Rafferty was sitting on one of the leather couches in the living room, his back to them and his breathing slow. She assumed he was keeping watch. She heard that low rumble ever so briefly and knew that he and Donovan had acknowledged each other.

Old-speak, Sara had called it.

Rafferty was so still, though, that he might have been hewn from stone. Alex was interested that he could be so quiet and so observant at the same time.

Then Donovan tugged her up the stairs and she didn't think about Rafferty anymore.

To Alex's delight, the room she usually used hadn't been claimed by any of the *Pyr*. They probably had been able to detect her scent in the room and had selected others as a result. In fact, from Donovan's signals, Alex realized the *Pyr* had chosen the guest rooms that were least frequently used and had left the master bedroom undisturbed.

How strange to think of dragons as good houseguests.

Donovan closed the door behind them and they were alone in the shadows of Alex's usual room. The darkness was complete, given that the shutters were still locked over the windows, and Alex felt her senses heighten.

She could hear Donovan breathing beside her, could smell his scent. This moment was special, something she knew she would always remember. Donovan would be hard to forget.

It wasn't just the fact that he was a dragon. There was a powerful attraction between them, one that she thought would have been between them even if he hadn't been *Pyr*. She liked his integrity and his power. She liked his sense of humor, his forthright attitude, his ability to surrender to pleasure. She liked that he was both strong and tender. She liked his loyalty to whomever he defined as being on his team.

But having a dragon baby still wasn't on Alex's agenda. Diane was the hostess who thought of everything; Alex knew there were condoms in every bedroom, just in case.

Donovan waited for her to make the first move. Alex reached out to touch him, marveling at the bright orange flames that flickered between them. She could see by the light of the sparks, as if an army of candles were lit between them.

Alex moved closer, into the circle of his arms, and slid her palms over his chest. She could feel his heartbeat beneath her hand, and see his muscles in the radiance that spread from the point of contact. The golden light was magical and awesome.

She wanted to make love, lit only by the fire between them.

"Let's not turn on the lights," she whispered, stretching to press her lips to Donovan's throat. He caught his breath as heat flared between them. Her breasts brushed against his chest and her skin tingled at the immediate flush of heat there.

"I don't think we're going to need more illumination than this," Donovan whispered. His features were gilded, his expression seeming all the more warm and welcoming. Alex reached up and traced the firm outline of his lips, liking how his eyes glinted in the light of the firestorm.

Had there been only one spark when they met?

"Is it getting hotter and brighter?" she whispered.

"I think so." Donovan angled his head and kissed her fingertip. Alex watched the sweep of his lashes, the way the light danced over his jaw. She saw the stubble on his chin, and his sudden wicked smile made her heart jump.

"You don't know?"

"I've never had a firestorm before." He arched a brow, glancing down at her as he pressed a sizzling kiss into her palm. "No one much talks about theirs."

Alex half laughed. "Of course not. Men wouldn't."

"Ask Sara," Donovan advised in a murmur, then dipped his head toward her. His mouth closed over hers in quiet demand and Alex surrendered to the heat of the moment.

After all, the time for conversation was past.

Sara dreamed of a dragon fight. It was a vicious battle, between a man in ancient armor and an enormous dragon with eyes of fire. She was uncertain whom to cheer for—the warrior of her own kind, or the one of Quinn's—and was frightened by the feral strength of the dragon.

He looked old.

Primitive.

Savage.

He nearly shredded the warrior. In the last moment, Sara heard a woman singing, her song low and melodic. The dragon was entranced by the song. He turned, the flames in his eyes dying to glowing coals as he succumbed to the woman's spell.

She looked, come to think of it, a lot like Sophie.

And she sang the dragon to sleep. The warrior slaughtered the dragon while he was beguiled, then cut away the dragon's massive teeth on the woman's instruction.

The woman then disappeared, as surely as if she had never been. That was like Sophie, too. The warrior looked down at the bloody harvest of teeth piled at his feet. He bent to pick them up, gathering them into a sack of some kind.

Sara awakened as he was planting them in furrows.

Like rows of pearls.

Sara nestled closer to Quinn in the darkness, her thoughts flying as she recalled her earlier dream. Were these the seeds she had seen planted? How could teeth grow?

Cadmus. The woman had called the warrior Cadmus.

Sara knew a citation when she heard one. She reached for the light, then remembered the pile of teeth. Each one possessed a number of jagged peaks, like a back tooth of a dog or wolf.

She'd seen something like that before.

She looked across the room at Quinn as he slept. As usual, his lids were open the barest bit and she could see the shimmer of the blue of his eyes. He was sleeping, but alert. If anything happened or if she moved suddenly, he'd be instantly awake. It had taken Sara a while to get used to that, but now she liked it a lot.

She felt safe with Quinn.

Then she knew when she'd seen a shape like those teeth. The pearl Donovan had brought to Quinn last summer for his replacement scale had been that shape.

Hadn't he called the pearl the Dragon's Tooth?

Was that really what it was?

Cadmus. Sara stared at what she had written, then went looking for an Internet connection.

This house, of all houses, had to have one.

Chapter 15

The firestorm was like lovemaking in the dark, but better. Much better. The velvety darkness of the room was lit by the sparks between them.

The heat of Alex's touch swept across Donovan's skin and resonated in his blood. Alex stoked his fire with each caress, and every kiss kindled the blaze between them to greater heights. He'd intended a slow seduction, but their embrace turned hot and hungry almost immediately.

Alex locked her mouth on his, her fingers knotted in his hair. She kissed him as if she would eat him alive—and Donovan wasn't going to argue with that. He kissed her back with every bit as much heat. He was raging and was sure she felt the same way.

They backed across the room, kissing all the way. He trusted Alex to lead him wherever she wanted him to be, and smiled into her kiss when his knees collided with a bed.

She tugged him and they fell onto the mattress, their legs entangled. Alex rolled on top of him and held down his wrists as she kissed him. Her tongue was between his teeth, her hair brushing over his face, her breasts against his chest.

The sparks that danced between them electrified Donovan. She raised her head, breathless, and he was enchanted by the mischief in her eyes.

"Give up?" she teased.

"I surrender completely," he said, pretending to be serious.

"As if," she scoffed, and bent to kiss him again. Her hands moved to the fly of his jeans, but Donovan wanted this to last.

He rolled Alex to her back and she hooted with surprise. He reached for the hem of her blouse and tugged it over her head before she could argue with him.

He had to pause to catch his breath.

The white lace of her bra glowed in the flickering golden light, her skin looking exotic and shadowed in contrast. He ran a fingertip over her curves, tracing the edge of the bra cup, savoring the way each pearl of trim nestled against her skin.

He caught her gaze. "Curves in all the right places."

"I try." Alex winked and Donovan grinned as he slid down the length of her. He unfastened the front clasp of her bra and caught her breasts in his hands. He liked their weight, the fullness of their curves. He ran his thumbs across her nipples, enjoying how she closed her eyes in pleasure. She gripped his shoulders but wasn't afraid to show her response.

He liked that a lot.

Donovan took one nipple gently in his mouth. Alex gasped and he flicked his tongue across her. She moaned and arched her back, sliding her hand into his hair. She pulled him closer, as if to ensure that he couldn't stop.

He ran his teeth across the tightened peak, teasing her until she writhed. He turned his attention to the other breast and her hands locked on to either side of his head.

She pulled his face to hers in silent demand. Their kiss was even hotter than it had been before. Donovan thought of volcanoes, his blood like molten lava, and knew he'd soon erupt. Alex caught the hem of his T-shirt and pulled it over his head, her hands returning to stroke his back.

His hands meanwhile slid down over the neat indent of her waist. He unfastened her pants and pushed them down. He felt the lace edge on those panties and she shivered as if his touch tickled. He didn't trust himself to look.

He was too close to exploding as it was. There was only Alex in his world, the scent of her and the heat of her, the insistence of her caress, and his own response to her passion. His hands were full of her, his senses denuded with her. He couldn't remember ever wanting another woman—or imagine that he'd desire another. Alex was his partner and his equal, and making love with her was a union of spirit such as Donovan had never felt before.

Alex launched forest fires everywhere she touched him. Her hands were in his jeans, her fingers sliding around him, and he knew he'd lose it if she touched him any more.

She was irresistible.

The scent of her arousal drew him lower. He locked his hands around her waist and teased her with his tongue, stoking the flames of her desire. She was naked and golden beneath him, a treasure worth any sacrifice, and he caressed her hidden pearl with increasing surety. The heat built between them and he felt a trickle of sweat moving down his own spine.

Alex wriggled but Donovan didn't let her go. Her fingers dug at his shoulders as he held her captive to the pleasure he was determined to give. She was hot and wet. Her hips started to buck, but he didn't stop. He knew that her blood was simmering, that her skin was sizzling, that the heat between them was impossible to ignore. He wanted to give her the most pleasure she'd ever had.

He wanted her to remember this forever.

He knew that he would.

He drove her onward and upward, pausing just short of the threshold three times. Alex moaned each time; then she growled in frustration. She looked as if she were on fire.

He bent to coax her toward orgasm again. The sparks grew in brightness and intensity, spreading from the points of contact into a brilliant halo of radiance. The light pulsed between them, keeping pace with hearts and breath and the quiver of pleasure. Alex climaxed with a roar and the light grew to blinding intensity.

It had barely died down to a glow when she sat up in front of him. Her hair was tousled; her lips were ruddy; her eyes glinted with intent. She crooked one finger at him.

"Come here," she murmured, a husky invitation he had no intention of declining. "Now I get even."

She reached into the nightstand as Donovan stretched out beside her, giving him a sweet view of her bare buttocks. She rolled over and knelt beside him, opening the package with her teeth. She caressed him, then smoothed the condom over him with sure strokes. Donovan thought he would lose it before they really started.

"Oh, I'm going to make you earn it," she threatened in that husky tone that drove him crazy. Donovan's heart skipped a beat. She looked like a tigress in the flickering golden light, a woman who would have her way with him.

Then demand more.

He could hardly wait.

Alex wanted to make sure she gave Donovan as much pleasure as he'd given her. That had been the most powerful orgasm of her life, but then, he'd lived more than four hundred years. He must have had some memorable moments in bed in all that time.

Alex wanted this time to crowd out the other memories.

Donovan was huge and hard, ready to go; just looking at him sprawled on her bed in the golden light made Alex ready for another round, too. The question was how to make him last longer, how to torment him without risking a quick orgasm. She considered Donovan for a moment, then stretched out alongside him.

She picked up her discarded bra on one fingertip and dragged it across his chest. "You like the bra?"

"White lace," he admitted, his teeth gritted.

Alex kissed his ear, sliding her tongue around the perimeter, then whispering so that he shivered. "White lace?"

He nodded and swallowed. "White lace against tanned skin. That drives me wild." His grin flashed. "Quinn says you can take the dragon out of the Renaissance. . . ."

Alex laughed. Donovan ran one hand admiringly over her curves, as if he was prepared to make an exception in this case.

But Alex had an idea. She rolled from the bed and went to the dresser. She didn't keep many things here, mostly clothing that she didn't wear often and didn't miss from her own closet. There was a nightgown here that had been a gift from Diane—it was more of a short slip made of stretchy white lace. It was a garment that had been without purpose in her life.

Until now.

Alex pulled it out of the drawer and tugged it on. It was so short that it barely covered her pubic hair. It fit like a second skin, in white lace. The back was open down to her waist, and the spaghetti straps and elastic weren't sufficient to give her breasts support for more than five minutes.

Alex had a feeling that she might not be wearing it longer than that. Donovan reclined on the bed, watching her with bright eyes.

She had his undivided attention.

He smiled, his teeth white in the shadows, his obvious appreciation making Alex feel very sexy. "You don't have to dress up for me," he said. "Naked works, too."

"But you like the lace?"

He nodded, then swallowed and closed his eyes for a beat. His voice was tight when he spoke, as if overwhelmed. "No doubt about it."

If anything, he was bigger than before, more tense, more

fixed upon her. Alex wasn't used to feeling sexy. She was a tomboy from the get-go, but she liked this new sense of feminine power.

She strolled back toward the bed, feeling her hips sway with a seductive rhythm. The light grew between them, turning from palest yellow to gold and finally to the orange of leaping flames.

Donovan caught her hand in his and kissed her fingertips, his gallantry making her smile. His touch made her catch her breath, a wave of desire nearly taking her to her knees. Donovan's touch was like a new sensation, the way they understood each other seemed intuitive and magical.

Destined.

Alex could have been discovering sex for the first time— but it was better than the first time, because she knew what to do.

"Maybe you knew I would turn up," he breathed, sliding a fingertip across the lace hem. His hand grazed her pubic hair, his finger slipping over her thigh. "Maybe you saved this for me."

Alex smiled. "Isn't the firestorm supposed to be about destiny? Maybe I kept this for you, without even knowing it." She bent and kissed him soundly, letting her hair trail across his face. She heard him catch his breath, saw him close his eyes in surrender, and loved how he savored the moment.

She'd give him plenty to savor.

She ran her hand across his shoulders and onto his chest, watching the sparks light all along the way. She slipped her fingertips through the russet hair on his chest, following the central V to his navel, then down farther.

Donovan caught his breath and Alex met his gaze. His eyes were more green than she remembered them being, glittering like emeralds in the darkness. He seemed to shimmer before her eyes, appeared to be bigger and brighter and more buff.

She understood that this was the power of the firestorm, that it was capable of making each of them more than they would be otherwise. It was a transformative process, but Alex wasn't afraid of what might be ahead. Something that felt this good couldn't be bad for her.

She trusted Donovan.

She trusted the *Pyr*.

She trusted her firestorm and whatever it brought to her. She bent and touched her lips to his. Alex eased down to the bed without breaking their kiss and Donovan pulled her on top of him. She liked the grip of his strong fingers around her waist, the spellbinding magic of his tongue.

This was the only way he could beguile her.

Because she surrendered willingly.

Alex caressed Donovan, wanting to know everything about him. He was powerful, his muscles developed for battle. He moved with the grace of someone comfortable with his body, aware of its strength, confident in its power. He had scars, as befit any warrior, and there was that tattoo. She recalled the sight of him in dragon form, the sheer beauty of him. He was all magnificent power.

Yet he had trusted her. He had believed her and he had displayed his truth to her. She was awed by his trust.

She pulled away to look at the tattoo, keeping her hand close to his bicep to illuminate it. It was a dragon, coiled and breathing fire, a dragon in the thick of battle.

"It's what I am," Donovan murmured, his voice a low thrum that vibrated against her breasts. He was watching her, his eyes glowing green and filled with warmth. Alex smiled, liking that he wasn't one to play games or hide his secrets away.

"When did you get it?"

"About twenty years ago. At a complete hole of a tattoo parlor in Atlantic City." He grinned, looking young and virile and unapologetic. "Rafferty got me drunk."

"You probably lost a bet," Alex guessed.

"Pretty much."

She sealed his admission with a long, slow kiss, one that left them both steaming. "What about the earring?" she breathed, running her tongue over it and into his ear.

Donovan caught his breath. "I was a privateer for a while."

"A pirate, you mean."

"Privateer was the job description. Looting and pillaging were legal, if you raised the right flag." His grin was rakish. "It was a good way to build a hoard, but a lousy way to meet women."

"Didn't pirates get earrings for killing someone?"

"It doesn't matter," he said roughly, and she knew it was true. She didn't doubt that the victim had deserved his fate, like Tyson, and the details beyond that were irrelevant.

"You've done lots of things," she murmured against his skin.

"There's always more to do."

"Do you ever get bored?"

His eyes flashed. "Never."

Then Alex didn't have time for more questions. Donovan caught her nape and pulled her lips down to his. His kiss was urgent and she rolled her hips against his hardness. He gasped and she knelt atop him, taking his strength inside her in increments. She felt Donovan trembling and his desire for her made her feel powerful. He waited, letting her set the pace, and she kept it slow.

Very slow.

"Slower is better," she reminded him, and he groaned.

He reached to caress her breasts through the lace slip. Alex arched her back and stretched her arms over her head, knowing by the way he caught his breath that he liked the view. There was a timeless moment when they stared at each other, both aroused beyond all expectation, both enjoying his heat inside her, both cast in the golden flicker of the firestorm.

Then she moved more quickly. Donovan inhaled sharply and caught her against him, his arm like a steel band around

her waist. Alex claimed his mouth, kissing him with a
hunger that she guessed would never be sated. She already
wanted him again.

And again and again.

She rubbed herself against him and he gripped her buttocks, pulling her even closer. His thumb was suddenly between them and Alex was jolted by the surge of pleasure.
She lost her rhythm and Donovan rolled them over in one
smooth move, his eyes shining as he waited for her to orgasm. Alex was burning from head to toe, burning with a desire that only left her aching for more.

Alex rode the crest of the wave he launched. He grew
bigger and harder, more demanding. His kiss had a furious
power. She gripped his shoulders and held out for as long as
she could. His finger coaxed more and more from her, until
Alex could bear it no longer.

She knew she cried out as the pleasure of the firestorm
claimed her once again. Donovan's mouth locked over hers,
devouring her cry; then she felt him shake with the violence
of his own release.

There was only darkness, and the rich red of shimmering
coals in the bedroom. Alex lay and listened to Donovan's
breathing as he dozed, exhausted. She ran her fingers across
the slickness of perspiration on his back. She could feel his
heart pounding against her own, the two beating in powerful
union.

She kissed his ear and a spark lit between her lips and his
earlobe. She watched it with awe, certain that it was brighter
again than it had been before.

How long did the firestorm last?

Was it ever extinguished? She didn't recall seeing a spark
between Quinn and Sara, but this spark was undimmed.

It seemed redoubled.

As was her yearning for Donovan.

Alex thought about the *Pyr*'s conviction that the firestorm
always created a child. Even though she had just had two

massive orgasms, she still wanted Donovan as vehemently as if she'd never been with him. Maybe more so. One taste definitely hadn't satisfied her desire, or even quenched it temporarily.

She lay under Donovan's weight, thought about condoms, and wondered.

Could a firestorm truly be cheated?

Did she want it to be?

She ran her fingers through the unruly waves of his hair and thought about destiny, Donovan as a father, and all the paths she'd always been sure she'd never follow. She'd never wanted marriage and children before; they seemed like distractions from her work. Alex had been content to leave the demands of biology to other people, maybe people who were more conventional or cared less about their work. Life with Donovan would be far from conventional. And he would encourage her work, even help her.

Was it possible to have it all?

She pressed a kiss to his temple, tasted the spark, and wondered whether he might want the same things.

February suddenly seemed all too soon.

The room Alex used in Peter's retreat faced east and was in the corner on the second floor. Her favorite feature was the light there in the morning and the view over the untouched wilderness of Itasca State Park. Alex loved waking up to have the house to herself, and in this room, she felt as if she owned the world.

The room also had a perfect balance of old and new. The original house had had a peaked roof, which meant the second floor had an angled ceiling. Peter's architect had squared off the room with glass: the fitted stone walls were exposed in Alex's room, then met smooth glass. The bathroom and bedroom were passively solar heated, and there were solar panels on the roof as well.

The house was large and luxurious, but it was also

outfitted with all the latest green features, thanks to Alex's many arguments with her brother. The sun did much of the work of heating the house, the shutters ensuring that the house didn't lose heat when it was empty. Peter had bought into a power cooperative, which supplied electricity from green sources, such as a local wind farm.

Alex slipped from the bed as Donovan dozed and crossed the room. When she left his side, the light of the firestorm dimmed, but she knew the room's layout even in the dark. She hit the controls for the steel shutters. The dark metal panels slid into the roof, revealing the glass corner and a good six feet of glass ceiling.

The sunlight spilled like warm honey into the room. Alex turned to find Donovan watching her, his smile filled with sleepy satisfaction.

"Want a shower?" she said. "It's low-flow volume with solar-heated water."

"It would only be environmentally responsible for us to share." Donovan eased out of bed and Alex caught her breath at the size of him.

"So, are you *Pyr* insatiable, too?" she teased.

He grinned. "Not usually. Maybe it's part of the firestorm." He came to her side and caught her close, giving her a kiss that made her simmer again. The sparks danced between them and although Alex was getting used to them, Donovan watched them with a frown.

"Have they changed?" she asked.

"I thought they'd stop." He slid his fingertips across her shoulders and the sparks crackled over her flesh.

The heat within Alex was greater than before. She could feel herself perspiring, but she knew the room wasn't that warm. She licked her lip and tasted salt, felt dampness under her hair. It could have been summer in the city.

But it was autumn. The heat was from Donovan.

"It's hotter." She let her gaze run over him, so splendidly male, and her pulse accelerated again.

Donovan shook his head. "Maybe humans are the ones who cast spells," he muttered.

"I don't cast spells." Alex turned and headed for the shower, knowing that if she didn't, they'd spend all day in bed.

With any luck, they'd have the Green Machine humming by lunchtime and then could come back to bed.

She started the water, well aware of Donovan's admiring gaze. It was amazing how the man could make her feel so feminine. She'd never been a girlie-girl, but his reaction to white lace lingerie made her want to start a collection.

She wanted to keep Donovan's attention, in bed and out of it.

Alex stepped into the shower and he was right behind her, the sunlight pouring through the ceiling to gild their skins. She turned and slipped her arms around her neck, raising her lips to his kiss. The water bubbled between them, heating in the press of their skin. Steam rose from the shower and fogged the windows. They necked like teenagers, but there was work to do.

Alex broke their kiss with an effort, then reached for the soap. "I've got to get that prototype running."

"So, playtime is over?" Donovan teased, and Alex smiled.

"I'll be happier when this meeting with Mr. Sinclair is over."

"You could find another investor, if it doesn't work out."

Alex shook her head. "No, the fit is perfect. Mark researched his background and nearly stalked him. He's built a partnership with other experts and is ready to move us into a big auto show, if the prototype is satisfactory. I *could* find another investor, but we'd lose a lot of time. This is the meeting to make."

Donovan glanced up through the glass ceiling, his eyes narrowed.

"What do you sense?"

"Nothing." He grimaced. "That's what I'm wondering about."

"How so?"

"The *Slayers* know where we are. Why haven't they attacked again? There's something we don't know."

"Maybe they gave it up."

Donovan scoffed. "*Slayers* never give it up."

"Maybe losing Tyson was too big a blow."

"I doubt it."

Alex was in too good a mood to get worked up about something that was not happening. No *Slayers* in the vicinity was a good thing. She was going to enjoy it. "Maybe they're just tired or healing. Or too injured to fight."

Donovan looked skeptical, so Alex changed the subject. Dwelling on bad things that might happen had a way of making them happen. In her experience, enough bad things happened on their own, completely unanticipated, and she didn't need any extra ones.

"Let's talk about something else," she said lightly. She laughed at Donovan's sidelong glance. "Nothing epic. No more big secrets. I just want to know your favorite movie."

"Why?" To her relief, he seemed content to match her mood.

"Because I'm curious, that's why. You can tell a lot about someone by their favorite movie."

"How so?"

"Well, take Mark, for example." Alex's voice faltered over her partner's name, but she forced herself to think of something fun about him.

More fun than her last sight of him.

That should be easy.

"Did you take Mark?" Donovan's question was low and silky.

Alex met the heat of his gaze. The fact that he had even wondered told her more than Donovan probably wanted her to know.

Men weren't possessive unless they cared.

"I did, for a while," she admitted. "Mark and I were a

couple until I realized we'd make better friends. I had a vague sense of it, but couldn't put my finger on why. I kept breaking up with him, and he kept showing up to plead his case. Because I couldn't make a rational argument, I kept losing the argument."

Donovan folded his arms across his chest and looked possessive. "How did he make his case?"

"With words." Alex held up a hand when his eyes glimmered. "Yes, I know you would have been persuasive with action instead, and maybe that was part of what was going on." Donovan arched a brow. She really liked how he listened, giving her his full attention without interrupting. That was sexy, too. "Anyway, one night he began to explain to me that *Barbarella* is an art flick, perhaps the greatest art movie of all time."

Donovan snorted, his laughter surprised out of him.

"See what I mean?" Alex said. "I knew then that the relationship was doomed and I knew why. We didn't appreciate the same things. We didn't look at the world in the same way." They got out of the shower and she tossed him a towel, wrapping hers around herself before she put her hands on her hips. "So, 'fess up. What's your fave movie? It will tell me all that I need to know."

Donovan looked wicked and unpredictable. He did not knot the towel around his waist, which gave Alex plenty to look at. "It changes, depending on what I've seen."

"Give me your top five, then." Alex expected him to name *Easy Rider* or one of the Mad Max movies, but Donovan surprised her. His choices echoed a lot of her favorites.

"Okay. *I, Robot*."

"Will Smith," Alex said with a nod. "Good choice."

"*The Matrix*."

"Keanu Reeves." Alex smiled. "Another excellent choice."

"*Blade Runner*."

"Harrison Ford." Alex combed out her hair. "Good one."

"*Pirates of the Caribbean.*"

"Johnny Depp." Alex shivered. "Oooh, I like how you think."

Donovan gave her a skeptical look. "Are you telling me that *Barbarella* isn't an art flick just because you don't want to look at Jane Fonda?"

"It's not my fault I'm heterosexual," Alex said, and Donovan looked startled. "We're not talking about my fave movie. We're talking about your top five and that's only four."

"*Babel,*" he admitted, watching her avidly.

"Brad Pitt." Alex caught herself when Donovan gave her a grim look. "And some pretty deep stuff in that plot, too."

"I liked the way the different stories wove together. You couldn't just forget it." Donovan glanced at her and smiled. "Okay, what about you?"

"Easy. *It's a Wonderful Life.*" She laughed when he blinked in astonishment. "And no, it's not Jimmy Stewart. I'm just a sucker for a happy ending."

Would their story have a happy ending? Alex hoped so. They stared at each other for a long moment and she wondered what Donovan was thinking. The sunlight that pierced the room took on an extra sparkle and the bathroom heated an increment more.

"Tell me what happened to Mark," Donovan urged finally.

Alex swallowed and looked away. She fiddled with the comb on the counter, needing something to do with her hands. "They tortured him." She blinked back unexpected tears and was surprised to hear her voice turn husky. Donovan just waited for her to tell the story the way she wanted and she appreciated that.

"They burned his fingers to cinders, one at a time. Then they started on his toes." Alex took an unsteady breath, then looked straight at Donovan, letting him see her horror. "Then they cut him open and ate him, one bite at a time." Her mind nearly stalled on the memory. "He was still alive."

Donovan scowled. "Who was it?"

"Boris and Tyson." Alex squeezed her eyes shut, wishing she could drive the sight, the sound, and the smell of that night out of her thoughts. Her stomach churned at the memory. "I couldn't do anything to help him, not against two fire-breathing dragons. They didn't know I was there—"

Donovan interrupted her flatly. "They knew you were there." Alex glanced up to find his gaze locked upon her. His expression was grim. "The show was for you, Alex."

"You mean it was my fault?"

"No!" He crossed the room with two long strides and caught her into a tight hug. "They would have done it anyway, but they wanted to frighten you. They ensured that you saw it."

"It worked." Alex swallowed.

She couldn't imagine how horrible it would be to be eaten alive.

"He didn't tell them anything," she said, shaking her head in wonder. She'd always thought that Mark was a bit soft, but when it got right down to it, he'd been tough. "He didn't tell them about the extra prototype. He didn't tell them about the backup disks. He didn't tell them about the investor meeting or where I was."

"He protected you," Donovan said gently.

"He protected the Green Machine. He loved it as much as I did."

Donovan smiled down at her. "Maybe he also loved you."

Alex didn't want to think about that. She tried to swallow the lump in her throat and failed. She knew that her decision to end their relationship hadn't been easy for Mark. She knew that he had still been smitten with her, and it had been difficult to continue to work together. She'd hoped that over time, as it became easier, he had gotten over her in the name of the greater good.

But Donovan was right. She leaned into his caress and acknowledged it. She'd still caught Mark looking at her sometimes with that light in his eyes. She'd still felt guilty about her inability to reciprocate his feelings.

And now she felt guilty that she hadn't been able to help him.

Donovan seemed to understand what she couldn't express and Alex was glad. She turned into his embrace and let him hold her close.

Then she cried. Alex cried for Mark as she had never cried for anything or anyone. Donovan just let her weep. He understood that she didn't need to hear platitudes or reassurances.

"I didn't make a sound," she admitted finally. "I was so afraid and he was so brave. I just stood and watched. I heard them laugh, and I watched him die."

Donovan pressed a kiss to her temple. "You couldn't have stopped them. If you'd tried, they would have just killed you, too. Then where would the Green Machine have been?"

Alex pulled back and wiped the tears from her cheeks with shaking fingers. "I have to make it work. I can't let Mark down a third time."

"You won't." Donovan gripped her shoulders in his hands. "You won't, Alex. I'll keep the dragons away and you'll make the prototype work."

"It's not that simple."

His grin widened, making him look like trouble. "I thought you were the one who didn't take no for an answer."

He was right again.

Donovan was good for her, and Alex had a feeling that she was good for him. She knew with sudden clarity then what she wanted most of all.

She wanted to be with Donovan Shea for the duration.

But he said he was determined to ride solo and Alex Madison never begged. She'd take what he offered and enjoy every bit of it, knowing all the while that he'd be leaving in February.

She considered him, hard and huge again, and smiled.

Maybe breakfast could wait a few minutes. There were condoms in the vanity and Alex snagged another one, wagging it at Donovan.

He caught her close and kissed her deeply. Then there was nothing but the firestorm once more.

Chapter 16

Donovan followed Alex downstairs, weighing his options. Rafferty was on the couch in front of the fire. He looked for all the world as if he were asleep, but Donovan knew better.

Did Alex?

On the far side of the room, Sara was working at a computer, her features illuminated by the reflection of the screen. She glanced up and briefly smiled, then returned to her task. Alex crossed the room to her discarded leather jacket.

Donovan was startled by Rafferty's old-speak.

"Erik and Sloane are gone," his mentor murmured. *"Erik had a premonition.* Slayers *at Alex's brother's home."*

Donovan flicked a glance at Alex, knowing she couldn't hear their conversation. She was stacking CDs on an end table with purpose, apparently sorting them as she removed them from the pockets. *"Are they all right?"*

"No word yet. Erik warned Niall in advance. They haven't called for help."

"Didn't Niall breathe smoke?"

"I'd expect so." Rafferty stirred then, opening his eyes and smiling at Alex as if he'd just awakened. *"Don't tell her,"* he concluded as he stretched. Donovan wasn't arguing with that.

Alex had enough on her mind.

"Is it morning?" Rafferty asked aloud. He sounded sleepy and relaxed, the way he always did. "It's hard to tell the time with the shutters drawn."

Alex fingered her disks, counting them, then dug in the pockets once more. She pulled one out of a pocket she'd missed with visible relief and wagged it at Rafferty.

"It's still before dawn," she said. "But I'd like to get the Green Machine running as soon as possible."

"Anything we can do to help?" Rafferty asked.

"We have to get it out of the boathouse," Donovan said.

Alex nodded. "I have the schematics and Mark's notes. There were a lot of modifications made to the newer version and I'd like to integrate as many of them as possible."

"Do you need this computer?" Sara asked. "I'm done."

"Checking your e-mail?" Donovan teased.

"Looking up a reference," Sara replied without smiling, but Donovan had other things on his mind.

"We'll get the Green Machine into the garage first," he said to Alex. He turned to Rafferty, who seemed to be distracted. "Is Quinn awake yet?" When Rafferty didn't answer, he nudged the older *Pyr* as if teasing him. "Hello, Rafferty! Wake up."

Alex smiled. "He fell back asleep, maybe."

Rafferty shook himself and frowned, then straightened. "Sorry to be rude," he said, smiling an apology at Alex. *"I thought I heard something,"* he added in old-speak.

Donovan was immediately concerned. *"Like what?"*

"Something moving in the earth." The two *Pyrs'* gazes met for a charged moment and Donovan was aware of Sara watching the exchange. Alex seemed to be oblivious.

"Things move in the earth all the time," Donovan replied.

"Not like this."

"What was it?"

Rafferty shrugged and averted his gaze. A chill slid down Donovan's spine. What had Rafferty heard?

Rafferty turned to Alex as if forcing himself awake. "I'm good at scavenger hunts and brute labor," he said to her, and she was again reassured by his confidence. "You have one willing volunteer."

"Two," Donovan added.

"Thanks. It'll be easier to get the Green Machine down when there's a bit more light. Let me just load up these docs for reference now, and we can take the laptop out to the garage."

Alex headed for the laptop, pulled up a chair, and set to work. Sara sorted the documents she'd printed. Rafferty went to stand behind Alex, as emphatic a signal as possible that he wasn't going to tell Donovan any more.

It was clear that Rafferty knew what *it* was, and just as clear that he didn't intend to share the information. *It* must be a threat to Alex for Rafferty to be keeping the news from Donovan, and Donovan didn't like that realization one bit.

"Tell me," he urged Rafferty in old-speak.

The older *Pyr* shook his head minutely, his gaze dancing over the notes Alex was making at lightning speed. *"Not yet."*

Impatience surged through Donovan. *Then when?*

Alex was pretty sure she was missing something.

Something important.

Rafferty and Donovan were doing a lot of old-speak. She saw Donovan shove his hands in his pockets. They were arguing, she was sure of it, and she wondered what the argument was about.

She looked up to find Rafferty watching her closely. There were sympathy and understanding in the older *Pyr*'s gaze. On impulse, Alex asked him a question. "Are you the same Rafferty who helped Donovan fight Magnus?"

"Yes. How did you know that?"

"The Wyvern showed me the whole battle. It was on the television while Donovan was passed out." Alex frowned at the computer display, seeking Mark's part list for his last engine upgrade.

"Why would she do that?" Rafferty asked in the tone of someone who knew the answer to his own question.

Alex reasoned it out aloud, feeling Sara's gaze on her, too. "I thought she was telling me that Donovan was emotionally unavailable, because he loved Olivia," she said slowly.

"Excuse me?" Donovan interrupted. "Do we have to talk about this?" Alex knew he wasn't happy having his past be the topic of discussion.

But Rafferty was right—the Wyvern must have had a point.

Alex realized that she wasn't sure what it was.

"Of course we have to talk about it," Sara said with a smile. "The firestorm leaves no stones uncovered."

Donovan spun away to pace the room.

Rafferty smiled, keeping his attention on Alex. "But now you know she wasn't?"

"Right." Alex drummed her fingertips on the desktop, reviewing the movielike vision and thinking. She watched Donovan, aware of the sizzle of heat between them. It was amazing how it waxed and waned, depending on the physical distance between them. It never went away completely, but proximity made it burn hotter.

Or made Alex burn hotter.

Funny how sex hadn't diminished the firestorm's force after all. Did it require a conception to be dimmed?

That it would keep escalating until there was a conception made more sense to Alex than the myth that conception happened the first time, every time.

She still wasn't ready to get pregnant, though.

"It must have been about the *Pyr* being vulnerable where

they lose scales," she mused. "Because that was what I needed to know."

"Alex shot Tyson right in the spot where he was missing a scale," Donovan said with pride as he turned to face them.

"So you defeated him together." Rafferty nodded, his manner watchful and patient.

"Yes," Donovan agreed.

"Like a team," Alex said, and felt the glow of Donovan's approval. She knew from Rafferty's attentiveness that she was missing another point.

"Or it was about the Dragon's Tooth," she said. "And its history."

Sara's eyes lit. "Isn't that the pearl Quinn embedded in your chest, to patch your own missing scale?"

"That's it." Donovan dug in his pocket.

"Delaney tore it free," Alex said. "It's not attached anymore."

"That shouldn't have happened," Sara said with concern. "Quinn's patch hasn't moved at all and you were at his studio in your firestorm."

"Maybe it's more than that. Maybe a *Pyr*'s destined mate needs to be part of his healing for it to be permanent," Rafferty suggested.

Donovan pulled the two scales from his pocket and the other three caught their breath in unison.

The lapis lazuli scale was vivid blue against his hand, almost as broad as his palm. Rimmed in gold, it looked even more like a piece of jewelry. The scale Quinn had made of wrought iron mounted with the Dragon's Tooth leaned against it, the gleam of the big jagged pearl contrasting with the blue scale.

Alex thought they were awed by the pearl, which was impressive, but they seemed to be looking intently at the blue scale.

Donovan's own scale.

Rafferty stretched out a fingertip. Alex thought he was going to touch the pearl, but his finger landed on the blue scale first.

She heard that rumble of old-speak and saw Donovan's impatience.

"Collateral damage," he said with irritation, and Rafferty hid a smile. "Delaney ripped the Dragon's Tooth free. It wouldn't have come off if he hadn't attacked it."

"He wanted it," Alex said.

"Of course," Sara said with a nod. Alex assumed she was referring to the gem's value.

Rafferty caressed it with a single fingertip. "It's no wonder Olivia wanted it at any price. It's beautiful and large."

"It's more than that," Sara said. "I'll bet it's really a dragon's tooth, one from the story of Cadmus."

"Who?" Donovan asked, looking as confused as Alex felt. "What?"

"The oldest extant story about dragons is the Greek story of Cadmus . . . ," Sara began. Then Quinn appeared at the top of the stairs.

"You had another dream, didn't you?" he said to Sara. "I felt you leave."

"It was so vivid," Sara said. "I knew it was important. It was about the Dragon's Tooth, this pearl."

"But wait—a tooth isn't a pearl," Alex argued.

"An oyster will build a pearl out of anything," Sara told her. "I just looked it up. A round pearl is a grain of sand that has many coatings on it. People have put other things into oysters over the centuries to get that finish on them."

"You'd have to keep track of the oyster," Rafferty noted.

"They don't move very fast," Quinn joked. "Did anyone make coffee?"

"What difference does it make whether it's really a dragon tooth or not?" Donovan demanded. "It's a pearl, a pearl named the Dragon's Tooth for its shape. That's all."

Sara put out her hand. "Give it to me."

Donovan took a step back, closing his fingers over the two scales. "It's mine."

"It's the key," Sara said with authority.

"What key?" Donovan asked.

Alex remembered what the Wyvern had told her, as clearly as if she'd just heard it. She repeated the verse carefully, watching Rafferty's smile broaden.

> *Elements four disguise weapons three,*
> *Revealed if passion harnesses fury.*
> *The Wizard can work her alchemy*
> *Only with the Warrior's lost key.*
> *Transformation in the firestorm's might,*
> *Will forge a foretold force for right.*
> *Warrior, Wizard and* Pyr *army*
> *Shall lead the world to victory.*

"Well done," Rafferty said with approval. He gestured to Sara. "Tell us the story."

"Coffee," Alex said. "We need to multitask if we're going to get everything done in time."

"Alex is right," Donovan agreed. "We don't have time to sit and tell stories to each other."

"It's not just a story," Sara said firmly. "It's something we need to know to make a plan."

"Oscar!" Alex addressed the smart house. "What's in the freezer that we can eat quickly?"

Sara made breakfast while Donovan and Rafferty and Quinn accompanied Alex to the boathouse. Donovan was pretty sure they could get the car down and move it by the time the coffee was made. The *Pyr* stepped into the conservatory, and Alex fixed her gaze on the front door as she walked with them.

"Don't want to check out Tyson?" Donovan teased,

knowing what she feared. He also knew she had no cause for concern.

"The only good *Slayer* is a dead *Slayer*," Quinn agreed, a thread of humor in his tone.

"I still don't want to look," Alex insisted.

Donovan clucked and she laughed.

"I am not a chicken!"

"I know. That's why it's funny to see you act like one."

Her eyes flashed. "You can't make me look. He's probably all bloated. . . ." She shuddered.

"No, he isn't," Rafferty said.

"There's nothing to see, anyway," Quinn agreed.

"Right!" Alex was halfway down the conservatory. "Nothing but a corpse in the lap pool that I have no idea how to get rid of. Peter is going to kill me."

"Then he'll have a body to dispose of."

"Two," Alex corrected.

"Just one."

Alex faced Donovan. There was trepidation in her eyes as well as confusion. "You're not making any sense."

"Sure I am. What corpse are you worried about?"

Alex looked between the three of them, then squared her shoulders and looked into the lap pool. Just as Donovan had expected, there was nothing in the water, nothing except his own challenge coin shining from the tiled bottom.

Alex stared, then stepped closer. It was almost comical how she scanned the conservatory, looking for Tyson's hidden body. "Where is he?"

"Gone." At her glare, Donovan smiled. "Once exposed to the four elements, the body of a fallen *Pyr* or *Slayer* returns to those elements."

"You mean he dissolved."

Rafferty nodded. "Pretty much."

"And you knew he would. That's why you weren't worried about getting rid of the body last night."

Donovan nodded.

"You could have told me," Alex complained.

"Would you have believed me?"

"No." She smiled, then frowned at the water. "What's that?" She reached into the pool and retrieved the silver dollar from the bottom. She turned it in her hands, then looked at Donovan.

"My challenge coin." He took it from her fingertips, dried it off, and put it back in his pocket. It tinkled against the Dragon's Tooth and his fallen scale, a reminder of new trouble that he didn't need.

"From the blood duel," Alex said, remembering what he'd told her. "Why a coin?"

"It's tradition," Quinn said.

Rafferty shrugged. "Maybe because it's winner take all, and traditionally, the loser had a hoard."

"What about Tyson's hoard?"

The *Pyr* exchanged a glance. "Erik will know," Rafferty said.

"Won't the *Slayers* contest the transfer of funds, if there are any?"

"They wouldn't dare." Donovan spoke with force. "It's tradition and it's always been upheld. If Boris thinks he's going to rip me off, he can think again."

Alex slanted him a teasing glance. "Hey, I thought we took him down together. Do I get half?"

Donovan grinned. "What do I get for saving you from Tyson?"

"Hmmm. Maybe we'll call it square."

"Hmmm. Maybe we will." Donovan arched a brow, holding her gaze. He smiled slowly, knowing that it made him look wicked and unpredictable. He was feeling wicked and unpredictable. He let his voice drop to a suggestive purr. "And maybe we won't."

He reached for her and the spark of the firestorm arced between them when they were still three feet apart.

Alex caught her breath and her eyes widened.

"I thought you took care of that," Quinn muttered.

Donovan felt the back of his neck heat and he cursed the keen hearing of the *Pyr*. "*So did I,*" he admitted in old-speak. Rafferty's eyes shone, but Donovan didn't want to know his mentor's interpretation of events.

He had a feeling that he already knew what the problem was.

The condom. The firestorm demanded a conception. It accepted no compromise. The firestorm would not be cheated or thwarted. It was pushing him toward a commitment he didn't want to make.

He didn't even know what Alex thought about it. He could guess, given that she'd suggested the condoms. He liked that they were in agreement on another matter, but didn't like the sense that their relationship had a best-before date.

It wasn't like him to consider the long term, but Alex was changing his perspective.

Or was it the heat of the firestorm?

Either way, if the firestorm kept redoubling, how would they survive until February?

The sight of the Green Machine prototype overhead made Alex smile again. It was so good that it was here and safe. She felt better just looking at it.

"Let's see how to get it down," Donovan said, and indicated one of the ladders mounted on the inside of the boathouse.

Alex climbed the ladder ahead of Donovan, her anticipation rising with every rung. The *Pyr* would help her get the Green Machine down, she'd mix up some saltwater solution, and they'd be ready to go for a test-drive before lunch. If the engine wasn't running very smoothly, Donovan could probably tweak it in the afternoon.

There were so few obstacles and so many hands to help remove them that Alex's old optimism was back. If her luck held, they'd be ready a whole day in advance.

She should have recognized by now that her luck was AWOL.

Donovan was right behind her on the ladder. She could feel his presence, that familiar heat at her back.

"Hold on," he said when she got to the beam that ran alongside the car. He offered his outstretched hand and even though Alex wasn't afraid of falling, she took it anyway. The spark was so hot that she had to close her eyes.

Alex wanted to touch the prototype all over, to reassure herself that it was exactly as she had left it. She was being neurotic again and she knew it, but it would feel good to be proven wrong.

The car rocked slightly as Alex leaned through the passenger window. She frowned. The Green Machine seemed lighter. It rocked differently. She had a bad feeling about that.

Alex walked the beam to the front of the car, ignoring Donovan's warning. She popped the hood, looked into the empty chassis, and swore like a sailor.

The car had been gutted.

The engine was gone.

"They wrecked it!" Alex shouted, more angry than she had ever been in her life. It had to have been *Slayers*. It was one thing to attack her, to kill Mark, and to stalk her. It was one thing for them to be bent on the destruction of the human race.

It was quite another for Boris and his team to mess with the Green Machine. Alex could have spit sparks.

"Who? Where's the engine?" Donovan was right beside her. "Did you store it separately?" He was hoping and Alex knew it.

"Ask the *Slayers*. They've really done it this time." Alex ground her teeth. She wanted to sit down and cry. "There's no way I'll have a working prototype by Thursday."

Donovan's expression was rueful. "That was probably the plan."

"What the hell am I going to do?"

He spared her a bright glance. "Don't jump."

"I'm not self-destructive." Alex rubbed her forehead. "Just mad. Frustrated. Deeply unhappy." She turned away from him, afraid that she was going to cry.

She would have thought there would have been more people willing to help get her invention into production. It was a green solution, a way to save the earth. After five years of fighting, Alex suddenly felt very tired.

Donovan meanwhile bent to look where the engine should have been. Alex saw him shimmer around his edges, the usual precursor to his shifting shape. He caught himself with a visible effort, then leaned forward. His expression was intense, his eyes glittering.

"Sigmund," he murmured.

"What?" Rafferty called from below.

"Sigmund took the engine."

"But when?" Quinn demanded.

Alex's thoughts flew. "The fire at the lab was only two weeks ago. Did the *Slayers* come here first or afterward?"

"How would they have known to do so?" Donovan asked. "Did you tell anyone that you'd stored this here?"

"No. Peter didn't know and Mark told them nothing."

Alex watched Donovan. He was working his way slowly around the hood of the car. She knew he was seeing something that she couldn't. "It makes no sense," he said. "The scent is so faint that the mark could be years old."

"This Green Machine didn't exist years ago," Alex said.

"So, it's a new mark, but disguised," Rafferty concluded. "Interesting."

Donovan paused and retraced his course, his expression focused. "Except here." He gestured to the latch for the hood. "It's strong here. It could be hours old."

"How can it be so inconsistent?" Alex asked.

Quinn folded his arms across his chest. "It makes me think of thieves wiping their fingerprints off the getaway car, as though Sigmund missed a spot."

"Can you all remove your scent?" Alex asked.

Donovan shook his head. "No. This is new and it's not good."

Alex wasn't going to think about how bad things must be if Donovan was worried. Instead she was going to let the *Pyr* do what they did best, while she did what she did best. That rumble of thunder began again and she knew they were conferring.

Meanwhile, she was going to make a shopping list to rebuild the engine from scratch. She had the schematics and Mark's notes and Peter's computer. She had a bunch of dragons to help her out.

She had to try her best.

The *Pyr* moved the Green Machine out of the boathouse and into the garage under Alex's supervision. There was new urgency in all of them, knowing as they did now that their task was much greater than they'd believed. In the garage, the smell of fresh coffee teased their nostrils, along with bacon and blueberry pancakes. Alex paused beside the Green Machine.

She looked so lost that Donovan put his arm around her shoulders and gave her a quick hug. She leaned against him for a beat, then straightened to considered the *Pyr*. Donovan was impressed by how quickly she became practical. The woman was a problem-solving marvel. "Were you serious about helping me?" she asked.

"Yes," the *Pyr* said in unison.

"Okay." Alex nodded. "I can print out a list of parts and pull up the schematics from the backup disks." She shrugged. "I don't think we're going to get a lot of sleep, but there's an outside chance we can pull it off."

"We don't need a lot of sleep," Donovan said, proud of her for not giving up the fight. "If all of us work together, we should be able to do it."

"Okay. Eat up while I make a list." Alex's smile flashed. "And no complaining that I'm pushing too hard."

"There's no sacrifice too great when the future of the planet is at stake," Rafferty said.

"I like how you think." Alex nodded, patted the car, and headed into the house. Donovan watched her walk, her confidence restored, and was impressed again by his mate.

Alex was amazing to him. She was undaunted by obstacles, even her own fear. She just created a plan and began to work steadily toward a solution.

"Your mate will be a valuable asset to our team," Rafferty murmured in old-speak. *"Her spirit is great."*

Donovan frowned and confessed something he'd never expected to admit. "I'm afraid, Rafferty. You saw the scale."

Rafferty looked at the ground for a moment, as if it would surrender the answers to him. "And now you are missing two."

"I could paint a target on the spot, it's so big."

"A wise man once told me that love heals all wounds and removes all vulnerabilities."

"That seems unlikely." Donovan tried to control the tone of his voice. "What if I have to fight again . . . ?"

Quinn dropped a heavy hand on Donovan's shoulder, silencing his concerns. "It's not easy to welcome the firestorm, but it will make you more than you are."

"It will make you the Warrior you are destined to be," Rafferty agreed.

Donovan started. "Wait a minute. I'm not destined to be the Warrior. There's never even been a Warrior I can remember."

"I saw the potential in you from the first," Rafferty said. "You have learned a great deal, but this firestorm is your final test."

"The firestorm forges new strength and resilience," Quinn said. "Just as the forge tempers iron into steel, the fire makes the blade more than it could have been otherwise."

"The firestorm transforms us into more than we could be otherwise," Rafferty agreed.

Donovan thought about those two missing scales and worried.

"She can heal you," Quinn said. "But it must be her choice."

"How do you know?" Rafferty asked.

"The Wyvern sent me a dream. My father told me of the power of love in a firestorm." Quinn cleared his throat. "He said that only love healed, and that only enduring love healed for the duration."

"Interesting," Rafferty said. "Then you cannot heal a *Pyr* outside of his firestorm—"

"Not for the duration," Quinn agreed.

"And you cannot even do so then without the mate volunteering to assist," Rafferty continued. Quinn nodded and Rafferty turned to Donovan. "And you cannot use your firestorm to armor yourself out of selfishness, not unless you make an enduring commitment to your mate."

"I don't do long term." Donovan said quietly.

"Do you not?" Rafferty asked, his eyes glowing. "You have fought for many centuries with the *Pyr*."

It was true. Donovan was vulnerable because of his affection for Delaney and now for Alex, but the healing of his wound relied upon Alex. He didn't think she did long term, either, which was maybe what he truly feared.

Donovan saw that his concern was with a lack of control. It wasn't up to him whether he was healed and he was used to solving problems himself. Did he dare to trust her? And be patient?

Neither were tricks Donovan did well.

"Only the truly intrepid dare to face their own weaknesses," Quinn said, as if guessing his thoughts.

"Only the bold dare to ask for the aid they need," Rafferty added.

Like Alex. Donovan couldn't evade the comparison. She never accepted her fear as a limitation. She never was too confident to ask for help. She had a talent he could emulate. She could teach him how to become more than he was.

If he dared to surrender fully to the firestorm.

Donovan realized it wasn't so much a question of whether he would do so, but when.

Sara seemed to understand the need for haste, because she started talking as soon as they were all in the kitchen. Alex had brought the laptop to the counter and ate with one hand while she worked with the other.

It looked to Donovan as if she was used to working like that.

"There's an old Greek myth about a warrior named Cadmus who killed a dragon with the help of Athena," Sara explained as she served out pancakes. "The rest of his story isn't that important—the dragon bit is what interests us now."

"Surprise," murmured Quinn, and Sara flashed him a smile.

"Athena told Cadmus to take the dragon's teeth as his trophy, after he killed the dragon. Then she told him to sow the teeth into the ground. The teeth sprouted an army of fighting men, stronger than any Cadmus had ever seen. They would have attacked him, but he threw stones among them. They blamed each other for that and began to fight among themselves."

"Not the brightest bunch," Quinn commented.

"They were spawned of teeth," Rafferty noted. "What can you expect?" The pair nodded at each other as they filled their mugs with coffee.

Sara shushed them both with a glance. "The warriors killed each other until there were only five of them left. These five made a pact of peace and became the founding fathers of the Spartans, which means *sown men*. The story is about the establishment of Thebes and its warrior rulers."

"Myth," Donovan said.

"Fantasy dressed up as truth," Alex agreed, and they exchanged a look of understanding.

"No," Sara said. "It's the story of the *Pyr*, disguised for human consumption. Maybe it's even the story of the *Pyr*'s origins. I dreamed the story of Cadmus, and Athena in my dream looked a lot like Sophie."

The *Pyr* exchanged a glance.

"I dreamed of those teeth being planted in the earth," Sara insisted. "They looked like pearls in the soil. I dreamed of them sprouting into warriors who joined the *Pyr* army."

"Erik mentioned that there were portals open to the past," Rafferty mused. "That some things were possible that had not been possible for centuries."

"Let's find out." Sara put out her hand again. "Give me the tooth."

Donovan produced the pearl from his pocket. It gleamed on his palm, snaring every gaze. It was his and he thought what was done with it should be up to him.

"What are you going to do with it?" he asked, already sure he knew the answer.

"We're going to plant it, just like the story says."

"I have a better idea," Donovan said. "We'll plant it, but we'll plant it on Peter's property and mark the spot."

"Why?" Sara asked.

"Well, what if you're wrong?"

"I'm not wrong," Sara said with force.

"She *is* the Seer," Quinn noted.

"Anyone can be wrong." Donovan held up a hand when Sara might have argued with him. "We'll do what you suggest, but if nothing comes of it by next spring"—Donovan nodded at Alex—"Alex can dig it up and have a memento of this whole adventure."

Donovan saw Rafferty look down into his coffee and knew that his mentor understood, even if the others didn't.

Donovan had lost a scale over Alex. He cared for her, but *Slayers* were determined to kill her. He'd do anything to defend her, even sacrifice himself.

So, his pearl would be her insurance plan. If things went wrong and Donovan died, Alex would have a bit of his hoard for her own. If they conceived a child—Donovan was no longer convinced that they'd manage to hold out until February against the firestorm's escalating power—Donovan's son would have a memento of his father.

It was the best Donovan could offer under current circumstances. It was a whole lot more than Keir had left him or Delaney. He hoped he was around himself to dig it up with Alex.

He didn't think for a minute that Sara really was right.

"Fair enough," said Quinn, plucking the pearl from Donovan's hand. He handed the gem to Rafferty. "You'd better sing it a lullaby to improve the chances of success."

Rafferty took the pearl, turning it over in his hands while he studied it. His eyes narrowed as if he were listening. "It whispers of bone," he said, his gaze rising to meet Donovan's. "Maybe Sara *is* right. Maybe Magnus knew the worth of the gem and that's why he kept it. And maybe Olivia knew exactly what she asked of you."

But Donovan wasn't interested in the past. They had work to do to ensure the future.

"None of that matters anymore," he said, his tone dismissive. "Let's plant the Dragon's Tooth and get to the important work. Ticktock. Time is wasting."

Rafferty chose a spot in the wide expanse of grass behind the house. He had a feeling that something was going to happen and he would have appreciated Erik's input. The force he had sensed in the earth was still.

But close.

And watchful.

It had been agitated when Donovan and Alex had crept into the bedroom upstairs. The muffled sound of their lovemaking clearly had disturbed it.

And drawn it closer. Rafferty himself had felt singed by the heat of the firestorm and awed by its power.

Had the creature in the earth been drawn to it, too?

Rafferty was prepared to keep his own counsel as the others followed their instinct. He had learned long before that the Great Wyvern worked in mysterious ways and that any effort to direct things often turned back on itself. He would wait and facilitate if necessary but not push.

The sky was turning rosy over the lake and birds were beginning to stir in the shadows. Peter's property was a tranquil place, one sufficiently secluded that no one would be observed. It was too early for them to embark on Alex's shopping mission and Donovan had assured her that this wouldn't take long.

Rafferty sensed that it was important. More important maybe than any of them guessed. Without Erik's advice, he couldn't be sure, so he'd follow his instincts.

Rafferty chose a spot with a lot of space around it. He wasn't entirely sure what to expect, but he was listening. Quinn carried the shovel and began to dig where Rafferty pointed.

Back toward the house, a dozen feet underground, the force began to stir. The others didn't notice, but Rafferty felt the movement. The earth parted for its captive, letting it chart a course toward them.

Rafferty trusted the earth in her wisdom.

Was it Donovan's firestorm that attracted this unknown? Or the Dragon's Tooth itself?

Rafferty believed it was the firestorm, glowing with greater heat again now that Donovan and Alex stood beside each other. They looked radiant, outlined in brilliant orange that turned to bright yellow where they were closest to each other. When Rafferty looked into the glow, he saw a flurry of sparks.

The digger drew nearer.

Rafferty let himself shimmer on the cusp of change, ready for anything. "Deeper," he insisted when Quinn hesitated.

Donovan, who knew Rafferty better than any, glanced up at the tone of Rafferty's voice. His gaze danced over the older *Pyr* and Rafferty knew Donovan had discerned the sign of his pending shift.

The earth rippled as the digger drew steadily closer.

Donovan inhaled slowly and scanned the clearing. He seemed to catch a whiff of something because he eased closer to Alex. Flames danced between them as his eyes began to glitter.

"Deeper," Rafferty intoned.

Quinn looked up, even as he followed the older *Pyr*'s bidding. He sank the spade into the soil, lifting a rich layer of dark earth. Rafferty knew what Quinn saw, because his eyes gleamed and his silhouette glimmered.

They were all ready.

Sara looked at the three of them with rising alarm. "What's wrong? What's happening?" she had time to ask before the earth ruptured beneath their feet.

Chapter 17

The surface of the earth broke open like a dark, jagged maw. Quinn's spade fell aside as the digger erupted from its tunnel. It was in dragon form and Rafferty barely had time to note the emerald and copper hue of its scales. It pivoted and snatched at the Dragon's Tooth on Donovan's palm with bared teeth and claws.

"No!" Alex shouted, and grabbed the gem first.

It lunged for Alex, but Donovan had already shifted shape. He blocked the shadow dragon's passage, sheltering Alex behind him. He was all lapis lazuli and rage, larger and more potent than Rafferty had ever seen him. He exhaled dragonfire with impressive force, the flames such a bright yellow that they were almost white.

The digger fell back and screamed. It fell, twitching, into the hole that Quinn had dug. Rafferty saw then that its scales were blackened from dragonfire, from a previous assault, and their brilliant hue had been dimmed.

He knew only one copper and emerald dragon.

Delaney.

The dragon shifted back to human form, whimpering in

pain. He looked ruined and dark, a shadow of the handsome man he had been. Rafferty was startled by the difference in Delaney.

He stretched out a hand toward Alex and the pearl, his gesture hungry and desperate. Donovan blasted him again with dragonfire, flinging Alex farther behind him, and the digger recoiled.

The man who had been Delaney bowed his head, laid his forehead on the ground, and shook.

"You can feel the dragonfire now," Donovan noted. "Yesterday, you felt nothing." He eased closer to the fallen man, his manner cautious and puzzled.

"Help me," Delaney whispered, his words uneven.

The *Pyr* stood and stared, all three of them in dragon form, all three of them uncertain what to do.

"He's hurt," Sara said crisply. "It's Delaney, but he's been damaged somehow."

At the sound of his old name, Rafferty saw hope spark in the stranger's eyes. There was a light there. It was a very small light, but it wasn't extinguished.

He wasn't lost yet.

"He's been changed into one of those shadow dragons, against his will," Alex said, and there was compassion in her tone. "He tried to get the pearl before. He tore it loose from Donovan's chest."

"I'll kill him if he tries to hurt you," Donovan said with heat. "I couldn't yesterday, but I'll do it now."

"But he couldn't feel pain yesterday," Alex reminded Donovan. "Maybe he's healing."

"The firestorm . . ." Delaney began to shake his head and mutter the two words over and over again. He trembled and it was difficult for Rafferty to be afraid of what he had become.

Then Delaney reached out a hand to Alex.

"Stay back!" Donovan raged, but Alex leaned past him to look.

"You were Delaney." Her voice was soft. "What are you now?"

Delaney, still on his knees, shook his head mutely as if powerless to comprehend what had happened to him. Rafferty didn't think he would speak, but was surprised.

"Lost," Delaney whispered, sounding on the verge of tears. "Lost in darkness." He trembled again and couldn't stop shaking his head. "It goes on forever. Except here." He raised his head and stretched out his hand as Donovan shielded Alex again.

"Let me touch him," she urged, and pushed Donovan's claw aside.

The spark of the firestorm leapt between them.

Delaney gasped in wonder. Rafferty saw the hunger in his expression, a yearning that far exceeded Rafferty's own. Delaney reached for the spark as if he couldn't do otherwise. In the same moment Rafferty saw an answering light leap in Delaney's eyes.

"Your firestorm," Delaney said with awe, and his shoulders shook as he began to weep. He stared at Donovan, the tears tracing tracks on his cheeks as he remained on his knees. "Help me, Donovan. Light my way back."

The old Donovan would have destroyed such a creature, such an abomination of all the *Pyr* knew to be right. Rafferty braced himself to intervene, but he felt the change in the warrior he had tutored.

And he was glad. Rafferty knew the moment that Donovan allowed compassion in his heart, that he let sympathy temper his power to mete justice. He knew the moment that Donovan accepted the threat in order to try to heal his brother.

The transformation was occurring. The Wizard was working her alchemy. Rafferty dared to hope for their collective future.

He swallowed the lump in his throat and watched with pride. Donovan changed shape with his usual haste. He never lingered when his decision was made. He never avoided a dark task if he knew it had to be done. Rafferty had always admired his resolve.

Donovan stepped forward and bent to catch Delaney in an embrace. He lifted his brother to his feet and held him tightly. Delaney could not stand well, but he hung on to Donovan's shoulders.

As if his brother were his lifeline.

Rafferty knew that Donovan was.

The pair stared into each other's eyes for a moment and Rafferty knew that Donovan sought some evidence that the brother he had loved was yet in residence.

Rafferty could feel the conflict within Delaney, the battle for ascendancy between his own goodness and the wickedness that the *Slayers* had implanted within him. Could the firestorm truly destroy the darkness completely? Or would there always remain residue of what Delaney had endured? Could the battle for supremacy within Delaney destroy him?

Rafferty didn't know. This evil was all new to him, and he would have been happier without its addition.

If anyone could pull Delaney back to the light, it was Donovan.

If anyone could complete Delaney's healing, it would be Sloane.

Even with that confidence, Rafferty still dreaded the unknown.

Delaney raised his left hand. "Remember?" he whispered, and Donovan set his right hand against Delaney's. Their fingers locked and interlaced, Delaney clinging to Donovan's strength.

Donovan turned to Alex. "Give me your hand."

She came to his side without hesitation, his bold Wizard and catalyst for change, and locked her fingers over his. Delaney stared with fascination at the flame that sparked between their hands, then closed his eyes as if basking in its warmth. It burned hot and furious, a blaze that Rafferty couldn't even look upon.

"The firestorm," Delaney whispered. The golden light caressed his features, making him look whole and healed even before he was.

Without a word, Alex and Donovan touched their entangled hands to Delaney's chest. Delaney tipped back his head with a moan that could have been pleasure or pain. He looked to be reveling in the heat that surged through him, welcoming it as it scorched the wickedness that had been implanted within him. A halo of light emanated from that point of contact and Rafferty felt the Great Wyvern's spark being coaxed to burn hotter.

Could the darkness be eliminated from Delaney? Rafferty prayed that it could. He had to believe that it could—he didn't imagine that it would be dispatched easily.

As the light brightened, Rafferty felt the presence of divinity.

He certainly knew when he saw the work of the Great Wyvern being done. He caught a flash of white in the surrounding trees and thought he had seen Sophie, but by the time he turned to look, if she had been there, she was gone.

"The spark of the Great Wyvern was yet within him," Rafferty said when the light faded to a glow. "It is said that no conjurer can extinguish the light in a heart that is good, that no *Pyr* can be turned *Slayer* against his will."

Rafferty didn't mention his fear that the shadow might not be easily dispelled. He would leave that to Sloane.

"And it's true," Alex said, leaning her cheek on Donovan's shoulder. He cast her a smile as Delaney leaned against his chest.

It was time for Rafferty to confess some of what he knew. "The Warrior has forged the first weapon of his arsenal," he said.

"But how is that a weapon?" Sara asked.

"A true warrior does not simply mete out death and destruction. He must show compassion. He must also heal—otherwise, he is a monster and a threat to all." Rafferty smiled at Donovan. "You have tried to heal with your firestorm. That's a potent weapon against *Slayer* evil."

"Elements four disguise weapons three," Alex repeated from the verse. "What are the others?"

"We'll know when we see them," Rafferty said, preferring to be enigmatic. "Fire stands accounted for."

Donovan smiled down at his brother, sliding his fingers into his hair with affection. "I'm sorry I wasn't there for you when you were attacked. I'm sorry I didn't defend you."

Delaney shook his head. "There is no debt between us, Donovan. You have been father, mentor, and cousin, more than I would have had otherwise."

"Not cousin," Donovan said quietly.

Delaney lifted his head, a question in his eyes.

"Brother," Donovan said with conviction.

The two smiled at each other, recognizing a truth that both must have suspected on some level. The sun slipped over the horizon. They all turned as one to watch the blaze of rosy light, and Rafferty wondered whether he was the only one to see the Great Wyvern's divine spark even in the sunrise.

"The pearl," he said then, holding out his hand for the gem. "We have not the time to linger here. There is work to be done."

They worked on the Green Machine all day Tuesday and well into the night. The *Pyr* were amazing to Alex. They shopped like fiends, fetching everything on her parts list in record time. They worked tirelessly and worked so well together that she was sure they could read one another's thoughts. No matter what she asked of them, the *Pyr* managed to do it.

She was starting to believe that they *could* save the world.

Even though Alex knew there was one big challenge ahead, she refused to admit defeat. She kept thinking about alternative solutions even as they assembled what they could.

She could never have accomplished so much so quickly

alone. The three men worked on the car, moving parts, joining parts, discarding parts. No one talked about Erik and Sloane's absence—or if they did, they did it in old-speak—and Alex assumed there was other *Pyr* business to be managed in the world.

Under Alex's direction—and with Mark's notes—they modified the engine, installed a new saltwater tank, converted an amplifier into a radio frequency generator. Sara brought food at regular intervals, as well as water and coffee. Alex had no doubt that Oscar was helping her with the menu planning.

As the pieces came together, Alex began to worry about the last obstacle confronting the Green Machine. They still had more than twenty-four hours to conquer it, and she had a feeling the *Pyr* would find a solution. She felt so optimistic that Alex was afraid to think about what else could go wrong.

She would have chosen any other alternative than what did.

Jared Madison kicked at his running shoes.

His mother refused to change his Halloween costume. He didn't want to be Spiderman anymore, even though his costume was all ready to go. He had wanted to be Spiderman more than anything else.

Until last night.

Until he had seen a real live dragon on the roof.

It had been a beautiful dragon, so shiny and powerful and magic, and Jared knew it was still up there. No one else had seen it and no one believed him. No one had seen it today when he had pointed to the roof, but he was sure the dragon hid behind the chimney.

He wanted to be just like it, big and beautiful and strong and magic. But his mother said it was too late to change his costume, that he had wanted to be Spiderman and he was going to be Spiderman this year, and next year he could be a dragon.

Jared wanted to be a dragon *now*.

He'd refused to eat spaghetti for dinner because he was quite sure that dragons didn't eat pasta. He would be a dragon and he would eat . . . roast chicken. With french fries. Jared was sure that was what dragons ate, and even his mother's insistence that Spiderman ate spaghetti hadn't been good enough.

He'd been sent to his room to think about eating his spaghetti.

So, he kicked his running shoes around his bedroom and sulked. He didn't want to color and he didn't want to play computer games and he really didn't want to talk to his stupidhead sister. He didn't want to eat spaghetti, even if he was kind of hungry.

He looked out the window. It was getting dark, exactly the right time to be seeing a dragon. He had seen one at this time the night before. He went to the window and pressed his nose against the glass to look into the backyard.

Sure enough, there was a dragon out there.

A different dragon, but a dragon all the same.

This one was green, swirly green, whereas the other one had been green and purple and gold. Jared thought the first dragon had looked more magic. This one waved and beckoned to him instead of looking surprised like the first one.

Maybe Jared couldn't be a dragon, but he could be with one. That might just be magic enough.

He held up a finger to the dragon, telling him not to leave. The dragon nodded and Jared grabbed his running shoes. He crept down the stairs, hearing his mother and sister in the kitchen, his father in his library on the phone. Jared silently opened the front door. He shut it behind him, pulled on his shoes, then ran around the back of the house to find the dragon.

He didn't have to look far.

The dragon was waiting for him.

It was dark on Tuesday night when the *Pyr* had assembled all that they could, and Alex still didn't know how they'd solve the last big problem. She was so tired that she was afraid she was missing something obvious.

They were all marked with oil and grease, all tired and sweaty, but too stubborn to stop. Alex sat down with a sigh. The others looked to her expectantly, waiting for direction.

"The last bit is tough," she admitted. "And I still can't think of how we can get around it."

"Tell us," Donovan said.

Alex indicated the schematics and the *Pyr* leaned closer. "Mark had new head gaskets machined for both prototypes. The different shape made the engine run more smoothly and more powerfully."

"Like a Hemi," Rafferty said, eying the diagram.

"It's not quite round," Alex said. "It was a custom shape. It took weeks to have it made by the machine shop."

"Maybe the engine will run okay with the head gaskets it has," Sara suggested.

Alex frowned and shook her head. "We needed this change to make the engine feasible. Otherwise, the difference between what it costs to generate the radio frequency and the power the engine creates isn't enough to make it worth manufacturing."

"Quinn?" Donovan asked. Alex didn't understand his meaning, but he looked at the other *Pyr* expectantly.

"Quinn sings the song of metal," Sara supplied.

"Let me try to reshape them," Quinn said. He took the schematics from Alex and studied them, seeming to memorize the shape and dimensions required. He then studied the existing head gaskets and she sensed he was creating a plan.

He started to hum, the muscles in his shoulders flexing. He glimmered before Alex's eyes, and she knew that meant he was on the cusp of change. His eyes became a fierce blue, as bright as a laser, and he locked his gaze upon one of the six head gaskets. He cupped one hand over the metal, his low, wordless chant making Alex's blood thrum, then added the other hand on top.

Alex felt the vibration of his song in her sternum. It was old and strong. Quinn closed his eyes and his fingers clenched as he hummed. She could see that his teeth were gritted and the tendons stood out on his throat. His muscles were pumped, and beads of sweat gathered on his temples.

She didn't know how long he sang. She knew only that she was transfixed by the force of his will. The metal tracks for the garage doors vibrated overhead and even the concrete floor of the garage began to resonate.

"Rebar," Donovan muttered, and Alex nodded understanding. She remembered that the contractors had reinforced the poured concrete with metal because of the slope. All of the metal responded to Quinn's song.

Time seemed to stand still while Quinn sang, even though Alex knew it was ticking away with relentless speed.

He exhaled suddenly and lifted his hands, staggering a bit as he stepped away. Alex gasped in amazement.

It was done.

Quinn had changed the head gasket.

Peter Madison was restless.

It wasn't like him to worry. Diane said he was just working too hard, but it was more than that. He sat in the darkness of his office, his brandy glass empty, and fretted. A pool of light from the streetlight outside poured into the room, but otherwise, Peter sat in the dark.

It was how he did his best thinking.

Someone had obtained a credit card from his bank client with false identification. That someone had spent a thousand dollars at a shop at the mall. Peter's new security system was designed to prevent the issue of fraudulent cards. That the system had failed, immediately after its installation, was a professional failure.

But it was even worse than that. The bogus card had been issued in the name of Meredith Maloney. Peter had known Meredith Maloney and he knew she was dead.

She had been his and Alex's childhood nanny, the one who had taught them—well, Alex had learned the lesson better than Peter had—that fear was unacceptable. *We have nothing to fear but fear itself* had been Meredith's favorite quotation.

And now someone had a credit card from his bank client in her name. Peter had a feeling that he knew who it was. It didn't help that he remembered Alex making fun of his confidence in his new security system. *All systems can be hacked,* she'd said, and he had a bad feeling that she'd decided to prove it.

Plus, Alex was missing from the hospital where she'd been treated for her burns and her nightmares. She'd disappeared without a trace. Was she hiding, or was there foul play at root? There had been that strange fire at the research lab and Alex's partner was dead. Peter knew they had been working on something secret.

Had the fire been set by someone trying to stop them?

Did Alex need the card to ensure her own safety?

Or would she?

Peter didn't know and that was what had him pacing the floor. He didn't know what to do to help his sister. Someone was using the card. Was it Alex?

He also had a bad feeling that he'd forgotten something important. He was sure he'd driven to the cottage the night before—the big sedan had the odometer mileage to prove it—but he couldn't remember what he had found there. He was sure that Oscar should be scheduled for service in two weeks—but why? If there was a flaw in the security system at the country house, shouldn't it be fixed immediately?

And why was he convinced that Alex had something to do with all of it?

Just to add to the mess, he'd had a call from the police about the missing persons report he'd filed on Alex as soon as she disappeared from the hospital. Her apartment had been burglarized, although they weren't sure when.

He'd asked after the gun he'd given her, the one she hid in a cracker tin in the kitchen, and the investigating officer had gone back to the apartment to check. He'd just called to say that the gun was gone.

Where was Alex?

Was she safe?

What could he do to help her?

Had he been wrong to file the missing persons report?

Peter paced as he tried to decide what to do. He hadn't told Diane anything about it—she was focused on getting the kids ready for Halloween and Jared wasn't making it any easier by changing his mind at the last minute. Peter didn't want to worry Diane. He was plenty worried himself. He sat in his office and stewed in the darkness.

And that was why he saw Jared being carried off by a stranger.

Right across the front lawn.

Peter leapt out of his chair. What the hell was going on?

The man started, as if realizing that he was being watched. He pivoted slowly, peering into the windows of the house. Peter didn't know how the man saw him, but he knew he did.

The man froze.

Peter wondered why the security alarm hadn't gone off when Jared was snatched. He wondered why he'd ever thought it was smart not to have a panic button installed in his office. He palmed the letter opener on his desk, the only sharp thing within range, and wished he hadn't been so fastidious about locking his gun away.

By the time he got it from upstairs, the man would be gone.

And so would Jared.

The man was shorter than Peter, stocky, and he had sandy hair. Peter was sure he could take him. He went to the gym, a lot, and was fit for his age. The kidnapper looked perfectly average, except for his eyes.

They began to glitter, like cut stones catching a jeweler's light. Peter had time to think that it was the strangest sight.

And that it reminded him of *something*.

Then everything happened very fast.

With rising excitement, Alex took the callipers and measured the new head gasket. "You did it!"

"At what cost?" Rafferty mused, his narrowed gaze on Quinn.

"I can do it again," Quinn insisted, taking a deep breath.

"Have something to eat first," Sara said, her worry obvious.

"He doesn't need food," Donovan said with resolve. "Do you still have the strength to shift?"

Quinn granted him a poisonous look. "I'm tired, not dead."

Donovan stepped away from Alex. "Then shift and I'll give you all the dragonfire you need."

"The Smith draws strength from dragonfire," Rafferty reminded Alex, as he also stepped away from her. "It is part of his legacy. We'll both breathe fire for you, Quinn. Then you can teach me to aid in your song."

Quinn bristled at that. "It is the legacy of the Smith to sing to metal."

"You need to all share your gifts and knowledge," Sara said briskly. "And there are still five head gaskets to go."

The men nodded agreement; then Peter's garage was filled with dragons and their fire.

Alex was proud that her heart missed only one beat. She was getting used to this.

Peter was out the front door and across the lawn in record time.

"Leave him alone!" he shouted.

Then, against all expectation, the sandy-haired man changed to a dragon.

Peter gaped. He blinked and he stared, but the dragon stared right back at him. The dragon smiled coldly, malice emanating from him. The dragon could have been made of gemstones—his scales were striped green like malachite, each scale edged in silver.

But the flames that erupted from his mouth were no ornamentation. He spewed flame at Peter, and Diane's shrubbery caught fire. He exhaled more fire, setting the cedar shingles alight on the house's roof. Jared screamed and struggled. Peter didn't care what it cost him to save his son.

He lunged at the dragon and stabbed the letter opener into the dragon's chest with all his might. The spike hit a scale and clanged as if it had struck metal. The dragon laughed and snatched at Peter with a talon, holding him in the air.

He tightened his grip and that long talon dug deep. Jared watched his father and began to wail.

"Shut up, brat," the dragon snarled, then tossed Peter onto the lawn.

Peter had the sense that the dragon was playing with him, the way a cat can play with a mouse, but the talon had cut deep all the same. It made no sense to be battling a dragon in his own front yard, but the blood that flowed from Peter's shoulder was all too real.

"Feeble human," the dragon mocked.

Peter would show him feeble. He flung himself at his opponent, gritted his teeth, and flailed at the dragon's chest with all his might again and again and again.

To his astonishment, on the fifth strike, the spike sank home.

The dragon bellowed in surprise and rage.

Even better, he dropped Jared.

"Run!" Peter shouted even as the dragon tore at him in fury. Something was flowing from the wound, something vile and black.

Jared shouted but Peter couldn't hear him.

He was busy, fighting to live.

The dragon buried his claws in Peter's chest so slowly that he must have been enjoying the sensation. Peter bit back a scream. He grabbed at the handle of the letter opener, which was slippery and dark, but couldn't get hold of it. He felt Jared's presence and looked to see his son hesitating at the front door, his hand on the latch.

"Go inside!" Peter shouted, sensing that his son didn't want to leave him.

"No, stay," the dragon said, his voice low and melodic. "Stay with me. Follow me." Jared took a step away from the door, his gaze fixed on the dragon. "I'll show you the magic dragons can make."

"No!" Peter screamed, and Jared looked at him. He leapt for the door again, the dragon's spell broken.

The dragon swore and exhaled a torrent of flames at Peter, setting his clothing afire.

"Dragons!" Jared cried, and Peter feared that things were going to get worse.

But the dragon gasped, and Peter was flung toward the front walkway. He rolled and stumbled to his feet as Jared ran to his side. Peter caught his son close with relief.

Then he turned to look and his eyes nearly fell out of his head. Two dragons battled the kidnapper. One was purple and gold and the other was amethyst. Peter blinked, but there were still three dragons fighting on his lawn.

The new arrivals were winning, but he wasn't sure whether that was good news or not.

Niall descended on Sigmund like a hurricane hitting the shore. He brought the wind with him and it whipped the fire into a frenzy. The orange flames on the roof burned high and hot, beyond Sigmund's control, before the *Slayer* even knew Niall was there.

Niall exhaled his own dragonfire on Sigmund, scorching the *Slayer*'s back.

"*Niall!*" Sigmund muttered in old-speak, then snatched for Peter and his son. He was going to use them as a shield or hostages.

Sloane landed between the two humans and the attacking *Slayer*, adding his own torrent of dragonfire in the humans' defense. Sigmund swore and flinched, but kept on fighting to reach Peter and his son. His scales scorched and blackened, but he kept going.

Niall sang to the wind, summoning it to do his bidding. The maelstrom he had already loosed changed its direction. It wound behind Sigmund, pushing him away from Peter and his son.

The wind blew Sigmund back toward Niall, its force like a gale. Niall breathed dragonfire, the flames singeing Sigmund's scales from behind. The wind pushed the *Slayer* steadily into the inferno, whipping up the fire at the same time. Sloane continued to spew fire, as well, and Sigmund was surrounded by flames.

Sigmund roared in frustration.

Then Niall felt Erik behind him. He sensed that the leader of the *Pyr* breathed smoke, then saw the tendrils winding past his own tail. He was too busy with the wind to help, but he noticed that the smoke moved directly into the wind. Erik was guiding the smoke.

Just the way Boris had.

That meant Erik was going to use it as a weapon, just the way Boris had. The leader of the *Pyr* had been practicing a new trick. Niall was impressed.

Sigmund watched the approaching smoke with horror. He tried to back away, but the wind was against him. He struggled and fought, but the smoke wound unerringly closer to him.

It seemed to rise up, like a cobra about to strike. No, more like a thousand cobras preparing to strike. The smoke ascended into points, a many-headed hydra with teeth of venom. Sigmund regarded it with horror.

"Would you do this to your own son?" he asked Erik.

"When you let the shadow fill your heart, you ceased to be my son," Erik said.

Then the smoke struck Sigmund at a thousand points simultaneously. It slipped beneath his scales, biting and tormenting him, sucking the life from him. He screamed and fought, to no avail. The smoke grew thicker, feeding on his life force, weakening him with every strike. Sloane watched with dismay. Erik was impassive.

When he could look upon the *Slayer*'s suffering no longer, Niall whistled to the wind.

It knew exactly what he desired of it.

The cyclone came out of nowhere and surrounded the writhing dragon. It targeted him with precision, swirling around him and him alone. The smoke wound into it, making a cocoon of wind and smoke that held Sigmund captive. The *Slayer* changed shape rapidly, shifting between human and dragon in his struggles, but the wind only tightened its grasp upon him.

When the cyclone lifted and disappeared high into the sky, there was no sign of Sigmund left.

Although the sky had been clear and filled with stars, rain began to fall with sudden intensity. It drenched them all in its abrupt downpour, extinguishing the fire on the roof.

Then the rain stopped, as unexpectedly as it had begun.

Peter looked up at the clear sky in surprise.

Quinn was visibly exhausted by the time they had changed the shape of four of the head gaskets. The fourth one wasn't quite within the tolerance Alex had hoped for, but she didn't complain. Quinn's hair was wet with sweat and the muscles in his shoulders were twitching. Rafferty, too, looked exhausted, and Donovan shoved a hand through his hair.

"Are we going to screw it up if we do another one?" he asked, and Alex knew he had seen the disappointment she'd tried to hide.

Quinn exhaled heavily and eyed the other two head gaskets. "It's a strong song," he said slowly.

"There's no point in wearing yourself out too much," Sara said. "What if the *Slayers* attack again? You won't be fighting at your best." Her obvious concern told Alex what she had to do.

Especially when Quinn flicked a glance at Sara's belly and his lips tightened. Alex couldn't ask them for more.

Only she could call a halt to their work schedule.

"Look," she said. "There's only two head gaskets left and a whole day until my meeting with Mr. Sinclair." The others glanced her way. "We're all tired and hungry, and none of us will do our best work in this state. We have some time, so let's take a break. Let's have a hot meal and get some sleep, then get back to it in the morning."

Quinn's relief was obvious. "Fair enough," he said, and took Sara's hand. "I'm thinking a shower would be the first order of business."

Sara smiled. "Want company?"

Quinn's slow smile told everyone his thoughts. The pair headed into the house, followed by Rafferty. Donovan caught Alex's hand in his, the firestorm burning bright and hot between them again.

Alex looked at the dancing sparks, then met his gaze. He wasn't surprised. "It's still getting hotter."

Donovan nodded. "Harder to ignore."

"Why do I get the idea that the firestorm isn't going to allow any cheating?"

Donovan smiled, his wicked expression making her heart leap. "We could try again," he suggested, his voice low. "Because, you know, it doesn't make sense to give up on anything too early."

"Try, try again," Alex agreed, desire sizzling inside her.

"Can't hurt," Donovan said, and they headed for the house as one.

On the contrary, there would be only pleasure shared between them. Alex couldn't wait.

The fire engines turned down Peter's street, sirens wailing and lights flashing. Niall and the other *Pyr* shifted shape without a word of discussion. Peter stared at them.

"Dragons!" Jared said with awe.

"Not the child," Erik reminded the other two as he turned his attention upon Peter.

Sloane plucked the boy from Erik's grip. "Go tell your mother and sister about the fire," he said. "And hurry back." Jared pivoted and ran into the house, clearly anxious to return as soon as possible.

Erik meanwhile dropped his voice to the melodic rhythm required to beguile a human, and Niall saw the flames appear in the depths of Erik's eyes. "Your house is damaged," he said softly as Peter held his gaze. "Why not go to the cottage for a few days?"

Niall understood Erik's meaning immediately. He feared that the *Slayers* would be back and had decided that it would be simpler for all of the humans they were protecting to be together. It made sense. All of the *Pyr* would be together then as well.

"Why not go to the cottage for a few days," Peter repeated, his tone flat. He looked as if he would ask a question, but Erik continued smoothly.

"You have no idea how the fire started," Erik said, stepping closer. "But you tried to put it out."

"I tried to put it out," Peter said with a sigh. He looked down at his hand, at the letter opener and *Slayer* blood on his skin, and frowned. Sloane was already examining the burn from Sigmund's black blood. He took an antiseptic cloth from his backpack and cleaned it away, his gaze darting to the approaching paramedics as he applied one of his salves to the burn.

"Maybe it was lightning," Erik said. "Such a violent, sudden downpour."

"Such a violent, sudden downpour," Peter agreed.

"You have a burn," Erik insisted quietly. "But you don't need any medical assistance."

Peter stared back at him, transfixed. "I don't need any medical assistance."

"It's time to go to the cottage."

Peter sighed as the firemen came to a stop at the curb. They began unfurling their hoses as the little boy reappeared in the front doorway. Niall suspected the boy wouldn't forget this night's excitement for a long time. His eyes were as round as saucers.

"Weird weather," one of fireman said, looking at the puddles from the sudden downpour, and another grunted an agreement. The captain strode to the house, his gaze flicking over the roof.

"I have no idea how the fire started," Peter said by way of greeting. "But I tried to put it out. Maybe it was lightning. Such a sudden, violent storm."

"You said it. You couldn't have ordered that rain up at a better time," the fireman said, his gaze flicking over the three *Pyr*. "You can't trust cedar shingles, though. We're going to douse it, just to make sure there are no pockets of flame. It'll make a mess, I'll warn you now, but it's the best move." He considered the little boy. "You and your family have somewhere else to sleep tonight?"

"Of course," Peter said smoothly. "We're going to go to the cottage." He turned to greet his wife as she came out of the house with the little girl. She began to ask questions and Peter replied with Erik's answers. The little boy looked between them, listening, then back to the *Pyr*. The firemen focused on the job at hand and the *Pyr* slid into the shadows as one.

They'd fly above Peter's car, ensuring that the family got to their cottage safely, but would remain out of sight. Niall saw Sloane glance back and realized the little boy was still watching them.

He knew Erik was right about beguiling children, but he had a bad feeling about the child's fascination all the same.

Chapter 18

Donovan would have preferred to have spent the day alone with Alex, but there was too much work to be done.

There was a flurry of old-speak when they walked into the main room of the house together. He was surprised to find that Peter had returned. Erik, Sloane, and Niall were also back, and Peter's wife—Diane, Alex had called her—was nursing a coffee in the kitchen. She looked strained and Donovan couldn't blame her, given the state of the conservatory.

"There was a *Slayer* attack at Peter's house," Donovan murmured to Alex. "Everyone is fine, but Sigmund got away. Erik thought it would be better to have everyone here."

"In the smoke fortress," Alex agreed. As always, she moved quickly from an emotional response to practical solutions. It was another thing Donovan loved about her. "Shouldn't you guys breathe some more of that stuff?"

"Yes, ma'am," Donovan agreed with a smile. "What do you think they've been doing all night?"

Alex smiled. "Maybe I should leave dragon matters to dragons and focus on human issues."

"Maybe."

Donovan followed Alex's gaze to her sister-in-law. Diane was blond, slender, and attractive. He sensed that she was an organizational force and that the wreckage in the conservatory would add a wrinkle to her plans. Peter was in the kitchen, too, but looked so untroubled that he was obviously beguiled.

"I tried to keep our interference to a minimum," Erik said in old-speak, and Donovan nodded minutely.

That plan might need a change.

"Alex!" Diane poured the rest of her coffee down the sink and crossed the kitchen quickly. "Why didn't you tell us that you intended to use the house?" Her gaze flicked over the *Pyr* and her voice rose. "Why didn't you mention that you would be bringing so many guests?"

"I'm sorry, Diane. It happened really quickly." Alex paused as if hoping that would do. Diane kept glaring at her, and Donovan watched as Alex smiled and continued. Her tone radiated reassurance and calm—she was doing a kind of beguiling of her own. "We're working together to finish the project Mark and I had started. We'll be done tomorrow. Then we'll repair all the damage to the house."

"I should hope so," Diane said tightly. "The conservatory is a mess. Do you know how long it took to import those saltillo tiles? I can't begin to imagine how you ruined them—"

"Let me see if I can repair them," Rafferty said, interrupting Diane with smooth assurance.

"What do you know about tiles?" Diane snapped.

"Quite a lot," Rafferty said, speaking with his usual slowness. "The clay used to make ceramics is of the earth."

Diane stared at him. "What does that mean?"

"Give me until the weekend. Let's see what I can do."

Diane muttered something under her breath and returned to the coffeepot. She poured herself another cup and ladled in the sugar with a shaking hand. "I can't believe this," she said in a low voice that betrayed her tension. "First the fire at the house, then the damage here. The kids were supposed to go trick-or-treating with their friends tonight. I've no idea how we'll come up with an alternative plan on such short notice. . . ."

"They could go out here," Peter suggested.

Diane glared at him. "Are you nuts? The neighbors are miles away and we don't even know them yet."

"Perhaps the decaffeinated tea would be a better choice," Oscar said mildly.

"When I want the house to tell me what to drink, I'll ask," Diane snapped. She took a gulp of coffee and it was obviously scalding hot. She grimaced as she swallowed it, then put the cup down and pinched the bridge of her nose.

"You worry too much," Peter said mildly.

She looked at him over her fingers and Donovan knew Diane was going to lose it.

"I think I have good cause to be worried right now." Diane's tone was low and tight, as if she was fighting for control. "Both our homes are damaged, you keep talking like some kind of pothead and insisting that everything is fine, Jared says that he's seen dragons, and Kirsten is crying because I forgot her pink princess dress. Imagine!" Her voice rose an increment. "In the crisis of having the house spontaneously burst into flames and then a rainstorm abruptly extinguish the fire, in the midst of having firemen fill the house with water from the roof down and your bizarre decision to come to the cottage immediately, I forgot the pink princess dress, which apparently was the only thing worth saving in the whole goddamn house!"

Peter started to talk, but Diane interrupted him, her tone vicious. "Do not tell me that everything is fine again. Do not tell me again that this house needs its security system examined in two weeks and do not tell me that you have a burn but don't need medical attention. Do not tell me that Alex forgot the codes, because Alex never forgets the codes, and do not tell me that the security system malfunctioned, when

I can see that the conservatory is completely trashed and that the security system was obviously right on the money." She poured the second cup of coffee down the drain. "How did you come here the other night and not notice all of this? Or did you decide to lie to me?"

"Diane," Alex began, but her sister-in-law pointed at her.

"Don't lie to me. What I want to know is what the hell is really going on here."

There was a beat of silence in the kitchen. Donovan wondered whether it was possible to explain things succinctly and with a measure of truth. Before he could decide, Rafferty began to hum.

The choice was made.

Diane would be beguiled, too. He caught Alex's hand in his and squeezed her fingers. The spark that emanated from their interlocked hands was blinding in its brightness. The *Pyr* collectively caught their breath, and Donovan felt singed to his toes. He was hot, burning up, aching for Alex even though they'd spent the night trying to thwart the firestorm. He felt her pulse accelerate and knew she felt the same way.

Diane stared at the glow, her eyes wide, and Alex briefly tried to pull her hand away. Donovan held fast, knowing that it didn't matter what Diane saw in this moment before she was beguiled. He slid his thumb across the back of Alex's hand and knew the moment she understood.

Rafferty could beguile better than most *Pyr* and his effect upon Diane was almost instantaneous. The tension rolled out of her shoulders even before she met his gaze. Alex stood close beside Donovan and watched, but didn't look into Rafferty's eyes.

Just the way he'd taught her. Donovan was proud.

Diane stared at Rafferty. When he spoke, his voice was low and melodic. "What you really want is to be reassured," he said with confidence. "And that is only reasonable."

"I'm only being reasonable," Diane insisted, but the stridency was gone from her voice.

"You're concerned for those you love," Rafferty said.

"Of course, I'm concerned for those I love."

"What better time to appreciate what you have, to enjoy the love that surrounds you?" Rafferty's smile broadened as Diane stared at him. "What better time to celebrate the fact that only material things were damaged in the fire?"

Diane flushed a little and her gaze slanted to Peter. Then she straightened and looked at Rafferty again. "What better time."

"How romantic to share a master bedroom retreat with the man you love," Rafferty said. "How romantic to forget the world and its troubles. How convenient to have Alex here to watch the children."

"How convenient," Diane repeated, then smiled. She eased closer to Peter.

"How lucky you are," Rafferty said.

"How lucky we are." Diane trailed a fingertip down Peter's arm. He captured her hand and kissed her fingertips.

"Celebrate," Rafferty whispered with heat, and the pair looked at each other. They seemed to get lost in each other's eyes and to forget they had a roomful of guests.

Donovan tugged Alex from the kitchen. "Let's leave him to it," he murmured, then nodded at Quinn. "We've got work to do."

The *Pyr* quietly moved toward the garage to fix those last head gaskets.

Alex paused in the conservatory, only just remembering what she'd intended to do. The firestorm was as distracting as ever. "I've got to make a phone call. Just to make sure nothing else is going wrong." She flicked a smile at Donovan. "Not that I'm paranoid or anything."

"A little paranoia can be a good thing," he agreed.

Alex retrieved her cell phone from her purse in the living

room, trying not to make any noise. Diane and Peter were necking in front of the stainless steel fridge.

"My work here is done," Rafferty said with a grin, and followed Alex back into the conservatory.

"Whom are you calling?" Donovan asked.

"I want to check with Mr. Sinclair that he's still coming tomorrow. The last time I called, I could only leave a message." Alex punched in the number in the conservatory and found Erik right behind her.

"Where is Mr. Sinclair?" His manner was more intense than Alex thought the question deserved.

She shrugged. "Chicago. In his office, probably. That's where he usually is." The line connected and Alex smiled at the secretary's familiar voice. "Hi, Megan. This is Alex Madison. Is Mr. Sinclair available?" The line clicked immediately. It was as if Mr. Sinclair had been waiting for her call.

"Alex! How pleasant to hear from you." His tone was officious, as if she were a telemarketer selling timeshares.

Alex realized that Erik was watching her, so she answered with confidence. "I just wanted to confirm our meeting. I'll pick you up at the airport tomorrow, as we planned."

There was caution in his tone. "I'm not sure we have anything to talk about, Alex."

Alex's heart skipped. "What do you mean? We have a meeting scheduled."

"But after the fire at the lab, you can't possibly have a running prototype of the Green Machine to show me."

Relief flooded through Alex. "Oh, but I do! We had a backup of the Green Machine stored off-site, just as you suggested in the summer."

"And it runs?" He sounded wary.

"Of course! It's just not as flashy as the newer version, but the technology is the same—"

Mr. Sinclair sighed, interrupting Alex. "I must be honest with you, Alex. I have considerable doubts about this project and about working with you in future. I'm concerned about Mark's disappearance and this fire at the lab."

"We knew all along that there could be industrial espionage," Alex said, her voice rising.

"Is that what it was?" Mr. Sinclair mused. "Alex, you should know that the authorities contacted me. They are seeking you in connection with the fire at the lab, which they believe to have been deliberately set. They are concerned that Mark may have been killed, because there was blood in his office at the lab. And they told me you left the hospital without authorization just before a transfer to the psychiatric ward could be completed."

"But—"

Mr. Sinclair cleared his throat. "I am not certain, Alex, that it is wise to invest my money in a firm solely administered by a woman who apparently blames dragons for her situation."

"I can explain everything, Mr. Sinclair. . . ."

"I think it wise that we discontinue our discussions about the Green Machine."

"But—"

Mr. Sinclair was brusque and dismissive. "In future, if there is any need to contact me, you can contact my new assistant instead. His name is Boris Vassily and he is well experienced in matters of alternative fuels. Megan will connect you to him now."

No.

Alex stared at the phone. *It couldn't be.*

"What's wrong?" Erik asked with urgency. Donovan and the others had trailed back into the conservatory to listen, their expressions filled with concern.

Alex had to know the truth before she could answer. There was a click as the call was transferred, a bright comment from Megan, and then a familiar voice slithered out of Alex's phone.

"Hello, Alex," Boris said. "Perhaps we could meet to discuss this matter—over dinner, maybe?" He laughed.

Alex broke the connection, shutting the phone with shaking hands. "It's Boris. He's beguiled Mr. Sinclair."

Erik swore. "I knew there was something we were missing."

"We should go there," Rafferty began, but Erik interrupted him.

"No. The battle with Boris is mine." He turned a cold glance upon Alex. "Please tell me everything you know about Mr. Sinclair: where he lives, where he works, where he eats, how much he has invested in Gilchrist Enterprises and when, the nature of your agreement, whatever else you know."

"That's easy." Alex continued to the garage, where she'd left the laptop. She rummaged through the stacks of CDs and chose one. She offered it to Erik. "I kept track of it all in one place so we wouldn't forget anything. It's all on here."

"And the plane he was to take tomorrow?"

"Northwest from Chicago. It lands just after noon."

"Meet it," Erik said with resolve. "With the Green Machine. Mr. Sinclair will be there, no matter what I have to do to ensure it."

"Don't take any unnecessary risks," Rafferty advised.

"There are no longer any risks that are unnecessary. Everything is on the line, Rafferty," Erik said. "The time for half measures is long past." His expression turned more grim. "I'll rid the earth of Boris Vassily if it's the last thing I do."

"Yes," said a woman. They pivoted to see Sophie lounging in the open doorway of one garage bay.

Alex wasn't the only one surprised to see the Wyvern.

"That's pretty much how it will shake out," Sophie said to Erik, holding his gaze steadily.

"I knew it," Erik said. He took the CD and grabbed his jacket, swinging out of the house without slowing down.

"We should help him," Rafferty said with concern. "Be his seconds."

"Your task is here," Sophie said with authority. "The Wizard has need of you for her battle. The Warrior cannot triumph alone."

They stared at her and Alex doubted she was the only one deciding which question she should ask first of the Wyvern. Sophie surveyed them all; then she arched a brow. She waved her fingertips at them and smiled as she faded to nothing.

She was gone.

"You're not the only one who hates when she does that," Niall said to Rafferty.

Alex had a moment when her determination failed. The car didn't run yet, she had only a day left, *Slayers* were targeting her family, and now Mr. Sinclair was having doubts, thanks to Boris. Her optimism faltered, but Donovan stepped into the void.

"Let's get to it," he urged the others, then gave Alex a nudge. "So close and yet so far. Don't worry—if anyone can take Boris out of the picture, it's Erik. And we already know that Quinn can reshape the head gaskets." He winked and her heart skipped a beat. He turned to Quinn. "Did you have your Wheaties yet?"

Quinn smiled with slow confidence. "Of course."

Donovan caught Alex close. "See? We're closing in on the big finish." He pressed a kiss to her temple and his touch made Alex feel good. The firestorm simmered and surged, sending heat through Alex that weakened her knees. Its force reminded her that many more things were possible than she might have previously believed.

"Don't give up yet, gorgeous," Donovan whispered against her ear.

And she couldn't. Not when they were all pulling so hard for the Green Machine. Donovan understood her so well, and knew just how to boost her spirits. She liked her sense that they were on the same team. Alex would never have believed that she could have fallen for anyone so fast, but here she was, falling hard.

Had Donovan lost the second scale because of her? As much as Alex liked the idea, she refused to be responsible for him being vulnerable.

"Wait," she said. The *Pyr* and Sara turned to look at her. "I have a question. You said that Sigmund attacked Peter and his family."

Sloane nodded. "Sigmund tried to kidnap the boy, probably to use him as a hostage to get you to stop the Green Machine."

Alex was horrified at the thought, but it was more important to find a solution. "Well, won't they try again? They really don't seem to give up."

"That's why we came here," Niall said. "So we could work together to defend all of you."

Donovan spoke with resolve. "You know that we can do it."

"But being without that scale makes you vulnerable," Alex said, her hand rising to his chest.

Donovan nodded, his mood turning solemn. "Quinn said something about the firestorm forging each *Pyr* into something stronger," he began cautiously.

"You mean I can help to heal you somehow?" Alex said. Sara nodded minutely. Alex spoke decisively. "Then we have to do that and we have to do it first, in case we get attacked again."

Quinn smiled so slowly that Alex knew she'd said exactly the right thing. Then he nodded at Donovan. "It's like tempering steel. I can make you a scale that will stay in place, but only with Alex's assistance."

"You need all four elements to heal a *Pyr*, just as you need all four elements to kill a *Pyr*," Sara explained. "The firestorm brings a *Pyr* the elements he lacks, so it's only with the help of his destined mate that he can truly be healed."

"How do you know which elements should be supplied by whom?" Alex asked.

Sara smiled. "There's no *should be*. Some things just are and you know when they're right."

"*You* know when they're right," Quinn corrected.

"It's my job," Sara agreed cheerfully.

"I can work with the broken scale," Quinn said. "But it needs a token to empower it." He looked between the two of them. "The scale needs to be a representation of the four elements in union."

"Quinn used wrought iron for his scale," Sara said, "because it represents his element of earth. He forged it with his dragonfire."

"Fire," Alex said, nodding as she thought. The other *Pyr* lounged around the garage, their casual postures belying their obvious interest in the discussion.

"Then you supplied air and water?" Donovan asked Sara.

She smiled and put her hand in Quinn's. "A tear and a breathy confession." Quinn's hand closed possessively over hers.

Alex was thinking. "You're obviously fire," she said to Donovan. "All passion and fury."

"Thanks a lot," he teased. "I'll guess that you're air, with all those brilliant ideas."

"I'm feeling smarter all of a sudden," Niall joked.

"Earth," Rafferty said, pointing at Alex. "Possibly the most pragmatic and practical person I've ever met."

"And determined." Donovan nodded. "You'd give Rafferty a run for his money on determination." The *Pyr* laughed at that and Sloane nudged Rafferty.

"My grandma taught me that giving up accomplishes nothing," Alex said with pride. "What about water? Is that always about tears?"

"Intuition," Sloane said. "Understanding and emotions."

Sara pointed a finger at Donovan. "That's you and your gut-level trust of people. You also fight well because you respond instinctively."

"So what do we do?" Alex asked.

"We need a talisman of earth and air from you," Quinn said to Alex.

Alex smiled. "I know just the thing." She returned to the living room and retrieved the tissue-wrapped bundle she'd taken from her apartment. The kitchen was empty. She thought she heard the children on the stairs, so hurried back through the conservatory to the garage.

Her grandmother's jet brooch was still wrapped in the tissue that smelled faintly of talcum powder. It was circular, about three inches in diameter, and carved to represent a swan in flight. The swan had a red eye, which was a single cabochon stone.

"It's jet," she said as she showed it to the others. "With a garnet."

"Warrior colors," Sara said softly. "Red and black."

"Jet is a kind of coal." Rafferty touched the pin. "It sings deeply of the earth."

"And the swan is in flight," Niall said.

"Are you sure you want to give me this?" Donovan asked Alex. "It looks like a family piece."

"It was my grandmother's. My grandfather gave it to her." Alex could still see her grandmother, the dark brooch pinned on her jacket. "She always wore it, and insisted on giving it to me at the end. I'm not much for jewelry, but she told me that one day I'd know why it was meant for me." She smiled at Donovan. "I guess I do."

Donovan's gaze brightened as he looked down at her. Alex thought for a moment that he was struck speechless, which would have been a feat. Then he bent and kissed her, the passion of his touch warming her right to her toes.

"Thank you," Donovan said, his voice thick and his gaze bright. "You know I'll protect you with everything I've got."

"And soon you'll have more," Quinn said, taking the pin from Alex. He tossed it into the air and caught it, turning toward the garage. "Let's get to work."

Jared and Kirsten came down to breakfast together. Even though the house was full of people, there was no one in the kitchen. Jared had heard their parents talking in the master bedroom suite, and he'd been reassured to hear their mother laughing.

He and Kirsten faced the fridge together. "No one's here," Kirtsten said. "We could have something good for breakfast."

"Froot Loops!" Jared said.

Kirsten gave him the look that older sisters reserve for younger brothers. "Don't be a stupidhead."

"Good morning," Oscar said smoothly.

Kirsten raised her chin. "Oscar, I'd like two cinnamon buns, please. The kind with icing."

Oooh, that *was* a better idea.

"I want three of them, please!" Jared said. Kirsten made a snorting pig noise and Jared bumped her arm. "I can eat three. I did it before."

"I shall check my inventory," Oscar said, and the children grinned at each other in anticipation.

Their smiles faded when the smart house spoke again.

"I regret that there are only whole-wheat bagels in the freezer," Oscar said in his usual mild tone.

"He's lying," Kirsten hissed.

"He can't lie. He's a machine," Jared replied. "Now who's being the stupidhead?"

"There are always cinnamon buns in the freezer," Kirsten insisted. "Because Dad likes them." She opened the freezer and peered into its depths. There were bagels on the door and a big bag of frozen kernel corn. The other stuff was hard to identify, because it was all in silver packaging, with bar codes for Oscar's reader. Jared didn't know the thirteen-digit number for cinnamon buns and he suspected Kirsten didn't, either.

Jared reached for the bagels. "Must have been the dragons that ate the cinnamon buns."

Kirsten pulled out the toaster. "What dragons?" The bagels were already sliced—she pried the two frozen halves apart with a butter knife, then put them into the toaster.

"Those guys. They're dragons."

Kirsten rolled her eyes. "That's stupidhead talk."

"What do you mean? I *saw*."

"You're making stuff up again. I'm not going to believe you." She slanted him a look he knew meant trouble. "Maybe I should tell Mom that you're making up stories again."

"Not fair!"

"Course it's fair. She'll probably give me a cinnamon bun."

Jared considered his sister angrily. He wanted a cinnamon bun, too. "Not if I'm right, she won't."

Kirsten sighed. "You're not right. There's no such thing as dragons. They're not real."

"These ones are."

"Are not."

"Are so."

"Are not."

The toaster popped as they argued, and Kirsten buttered the bagels. Jared got the peanut butter from the fridge and she spread that on, too, under his close supervision.

"Are so," Jared said emphatically when he'd had a bite of bagel. His sister was chewing, which was the best time to argue a point with her. "Come on, I'll prove it to you."

Donovan was awed that Alex would contribute her grandmother's pin to repair his scales, but glad of it. He was anxious to have his missing scales replaced. He would wear Alex's token with pride and take it as a good sign for their future. Everything felt tentative to him, filled with unexpected promise, yet unpredictable.

Sloane was talking to Delaney in the corner, quietly counseling the injured *Pyr* and planning a course for his full recovery. Niall admired the Green Machine, and Rafferty sat quietly as he watched the others. Quinn surveyed the garage. Donovan knew he would have preferred to have been in his studio with his forge.

"*Dragonfire*," he suggested in old-speak.

Quinn nodded and met his gaze. "*Dragonfire*," he agreed. "*It's the only way to do it here.*"

"*And we have to do it now*," Donovan agreed. He was on the cusp of the greatest test of his life and he wanted everything in his favor. He knew the *Slayers* would be back and he knew they would hurl everything they had at the *Pyr* in order to stop Alex. It would happen in the next twenty-four hours, which didn't leave time to go to Quinn's studio and return.

"What are you talking about?" Sara demanded.

"We have to shift to do this," Donovan told Alex, not wanting to startle her. "All of us." Alex nodded her understanding, swallowed, and held her ground.

He was proud of her again.

Quinn, meanwhile, shimmered around his edges. He inhaled and grew larger, his eyes glittering. In the blink of an eye, Quinn had shifted to a massive sapphire and steel dragon.

Niall followed suit, his amethyst and platinum scales gleaming in the dim light of the garage. Rafferty shifted immediately afterward, his opal and gold scales shining. Donovan felt the power of their collective presence and was glad to have such loyal friends. They would beat the *Slayers* and save the world, together.

Alex swallowed and took a small step back.

Sloane changed shape then, showing the splendor of his tourmaline scales. They shaded from green to gold to purple and were edged with gold. Delaney shifted next, and Donovan was glad to see that his copper and emerald scales were already regaining some of their luster.

Alex seemed to be struggling to keep her breathing even. Donovan offered his hand to her. "None of us will hurt you," he murmured, and she swallowed. She put her hand in his and he could feel her trembling through the heat of the firestorm. "There will be dragonfire, but it'll be directed at me and at Quinn."

"Okay," she said, lifting her chin. "Let's do it."

Holding her hand and her gaze, Donovan shifted shape.

No one heard the small boy taunt his sister in the shadows. "See?" Jared whispered. "Now who's the stupidhead?"

There was no reply. To Jared's disappointment, his sister had gone, leaving him alone.

She probably knew where the cinnamon buns were.

Jared didn't care. He hunkered down and watched.

Quinn put out his claw, inviting Alex to give him the jet brooch. She eyed his massive talons for a moment and Donovan felt her fear rise again.

Then she very deliberately put the pin in Quinn's claw. She forced her hand to linger, letting her thumb graze one of his talons. Once again, she compelled herself to act despite her fear.

Donovan was impressed.

Quinn held the pin with the tips of his talons and exhaled dragonfire at it. Alex jumped, even as Donovan moved to protect her from the flames.

The other *Pyr* turned their attention upon Quinn, all of them breathing dragonfire upon the Smith to give him strength. Quinn began to glitter like a faceted stone, the blue of his scales becoming brighter and more vivid. He arched his back and reared high, filling the garage with his power. His talons were fierce, glittering silver, as he held the jet pin before himself. He inhaled, then breathed flames so hot that they were white.

Donovan schooled himself to remember what Quinn had taught him about taking dragonfire, knowing that he'd soon be exposed to another assault of it. What Quinn managed on instinct, Donovan had to prepare himself to endure.

Maybe it would become intuitive in time.

Donovan had given the two scales to Sara—the one that had held the Dragon's Tooth and the one of his own—she offered them to Quinn. He heated them with his white-hot dragonfire, fusing them together in the right configuration. He worked like a jeweler to join the silver setting of the brooch with the gold of the scale. He was hampered without his tools, but he made deft use of his talons. Quinn's dexterity and skill impressed Donovan, as always.

Alex watched with equal fascination, sheltered by Donovan from the heat. He offered his talon to her when Quinn was done, coaxing her closer.

She came, her eyes shining with her trust.

And maybe something else.

Quinn lifted the new scale, the jet shining brightly in its new setting. He tested the fit, then heated the back of the makeshift scale with a fiery blast of dragonfire. Donovan barely had time to catch his breath before Quinn pressed the glowing scale against his chest.

"Alex!" Quinn commanded, and she understood. She put the palm of her hand on the jet, replacing Quinn's claw, and pushed the scale hard against Donovan's flesh.

The pain was searing. Firestorm and dragonfire burned together to repair his armor. The new scale could have been a brand. It burned deep, sending a stab of pain through Donovan.

Donovan tipped back his head and bellowed as the heat cut straight to his marrow. The fire incinerated his old pains and injuries, even those that had left scars upon his heart. It cauterized the wound of Olivia's deception. It knit his flesh and burned away the detritus and left the image of Alex seared onto his very soul.

Donovan ached for the mistakes he had made and the grudges he had nursed. He regretted the fate of Delaney and he mourned his own error in trusting Olivia. He had erred but he had learned.

He felt Alex take a tear from his face with a gentle fingertip. It glimmered on her fingertip. It sizzled as she placed it at the root of the new scale. The heat within him burned brighter as the tear ran around the lip of the scale. He felt Alex lean close. She brushed her lips across the jet.

"Be invulnerable, Warrior," she whispered, the fan of her breath cooling his injury. He looked down and saw her smiling up at him. "We've got to kick some *Slayer* butt."

Donovan wanted to feel more than the brush of her lips against his skin. He shifted shape again and caught her close, thrilled that she had chosen to help him. The *Pyr* shifted in unison and applauded. Rafferty shook Quinn's hand as Donovan kissed Alex, and the others hooted at Quinn's success.

The white radiance that had shot through his veins had clarified his vision and made obvious to him what he had to do. Donovan was going to win the heart of his mate, no matter what the price.

The first step was to get the Green Machine running.

Chapter 19

The black Lamborghini slipped through the rain-soaked streets of Chicago like a panther on the prowl. The low thrum of its engine echoed the night pulse of the city. Its windshield wipers struck a rhythmic beat, as insistent as the raindrops beading on the hood.

It was more than the rain that gave the driver chills. There was a portent in the wind, the scent of trouble. He wasn't entirely certain whom he'd meet before morning's light.

Or what result the night's adventures would bring.

Nevertheless, it was time.

Erik followed his opponent's scent to a part of the downtown that was being re-gentrified. He parked in front of a chic new bistro, ignoring the valet and the NO PARKING signs. He got out of the car, leaving its engine idling, just as two men stepped out of the restaurant. The rain fell on the shoulders of his black leather jacket but he stood silent, watching.

The men chatted as they paused under the bistro's red awning, taking shelter from the onslaught of rain. They fastened their coats and turned up their collars, reviewing the meal they'd enjoyed. The one Erik didn't know frowned at the Lamborghini, then lifted his gaze in search of a cab. He lit a cigar with care.

The other met Erik's gaze without surprise. His pale eyes lit with anticipation and he seemed to almost smile.

Erik tossed his challenge coin. The Olaf Tryggvason penny glinted as it flew through the falling rain. Boris snatched it out of the air, stepping out from beneath the awning into the rain to do so. His smile flashed as his hand closed over the coin.

"Took you long enough," he gloated in old-speak.

"Now," Erik replied.

He had no interest in small talk, no inclination to be delayed. He pivoted and got back into his car, revving the engine before he pulled away from the bistro. Boris made his excuses to his companion—who looked bewildered by his departure—then hauled open the passenger door.

He got in, smelling of cologne and brandy and wet cashmere, and slammed the door. He stared straight out the windshield, still using old-speak. *"The docks,"* he said, as if giving directions.

It was his choice and he'd made a good one.

"The docks," Erik agreed, and squealed the tires as he pulled away from the curb.

It was midnight when Donovan watched Alex turn the key in the ignition of the Green Machine. The engine sputtered, then started. It idled beautifully and when she touched the accelerator with more force, the engine purred like a kitten.

"It works!" she cried, her eyes alight.

The *Pyr* shouted as one. They cheered and laughed, high-fiving each other, triumphant in their success. Donovan was so exhausted that he thought he'd sleep for a week. Quinn looked worn-out and Donovan knew he should summon some more dragonfire for his friend.

Maybe in a few minutes.

"I love stealing the moment," a man said from the driveway.

Donovan spun to find a stranger standing just beyond the *Pyr* perimeter mark of smoke. He knew he wasn't the only one to take the new arrival's scent and to smell the darkness emanating from him. He was slick and expensively dressed, confident and smooth.

"Jorge," the blond *Slayer* said. He grinned at their surprise and shoved his hands into his pockets. "Trick or treat."

Donovan realized belatedly that it was Halloween.

Rafferty swore and Donovan immediately saw why. Jorge wasn't alone. He was accompanied by a foe Donovan had never expected to see again.

Magnus.

That *Slayer* stepped out of the shadows, looking as virile and confident as ever. He hadn't aged a day since their last exchange and still looked smooth and sleek, the image of a successful man in his fifties.

"Surprised?" Magnus asked, turning to Rafferty. "How hale you look, my old friend." He chuckled, and Donovan knew Magnus had noticed how tired they all were. The arrival of the *Slayers* had been perfectly timed to find them at their weakest.

It wasn't a coincidence.

Delaney started to moan and twitch when Magnus spoke. Sloane put a hand on his shoulder, even as he watched the new arrival. Delaney wasn't visibly reassured. Donovan understood then that Magnus had been partly responsible for Delaney's change.

"I was afraid of this," Rafferty said with concern.

Magnus cocked a finger at Rafferty. "We have unfinished business, you and I. All that hoard, so carefully gathered, lost in one night. I've never gotten over the shock."

"I thought you were dead," Rafferty said.

"I know you did. But we *Slayers* are somewhat difficult to kill." Magnus smiled. "We came, actually, to extend an invitation to the rest of you. We thought you might want to join the winning team, while there's still time."

"I'll never become *Slayer*," Quinn said, spitting the words.

"Not a chance," Donovan agreed with heat.

"Ditto," said Niall and Sloane in unison.

"It doesn't matter what you want," Magnus whispered. "Not if we take you alive." He whistled then and Delaney started, like a dog called to obey. Delaney's eyes turned darker again, and he began to fight against Sloane and Niall, to try to regain his freedom.

"Leave him alone!" Donovan roared.

Magnus chuckled. "He's the least of your worries. Listen."

There was a low rumble, the sound of shackles falling and heavy doors being thrown back on their hinges to collide with walls. Donovan heard locks tumbling, although he couldn't see anything. The shadows seemed to be getting darker beyond the driveway, as if the light were being extinguished.

"The earth moans," Rafferty murmured, clearly as puzzled as Donovan.

"The fire flickers," Quinn added.

"The wind dies," Niall said, scanning the sky.

Sara raised her hands to her mouth. "The dark academy is opened," she whispered, her voice filled with dread.

Donovan caught his breath as the darkness of the forest beyond the drive took on shapes. He saw figures silhouetted there, twisted shapes that seemed to absorb every increment of light.

"Meet part of the team," Magnus said amiably. He gestured to the approaching shapes. "Maybe you'll see some familiar faces."

"My father," Sloane whispered in shock as one figure stepped out of the shadows. "But not." He rose to his feet and stared.

The shapes kept coming closer, men with fathomless hollows where their eyes should have been. They were *Pyr* with no spark of the divine in their hearts.

They were opponents who did not bleed.

"My twin brother," Niall said as he recognized one. "Or a travesty of what he was."

"Three of my brothers," Quinn said grimly. He paled. "Or what the *Slayers* did to their bodies."

"My grandfather," Rafferty murmured, his voice breaking. He turned to Magnus. "What evil is this that you do?"

"In a war, every weapon must be put to use," Magnus said with a smooth assurance that made Donovan want to injure him.

"Going to hide behind your smoke?" Jorge sneered at the shocked *Pyr*. "Or are we going to solve this, for once and for all?"

"We can take them," Rafferty muttered. "We have to."

Donovan was already pulling on his gloves. "The smoke forms a wall six feet out from the garage doors," he told Alex. "The barrier runs all the way to the wall adjoining the front door. They cannot cross it. Don't believe anything they say otherwise." He gave her a hard look. "All you have to do is stay on this side of it. Promise?"

She smiled a little, her eyes shining with that familiar determination, and he knew there would be no guarantees. "No. I won't promise because I'll do whatever I need to do."

"To protect the Green Machine?"

"That's not the only thing worth defending," Alex said. She laid a hand on his chest, right where the new scale still ached. The admiration in her eyes stole his breath away.

"Be careful," she whispered.

"I always win," he assured her in a low voice, then smiled. "And now I have more motivation than usual."

She smiled, just as he'd hoped. "Hotshot."

"That's it." He kissed her, hard and quick, before she could argue, then nodded once at his companions. They looked as resolved as he was. At his nod, the *Pyr* ran toward their opponents and shifted in unison. They flew through the barrier of their own smoke as the *Slayers* and their minions shifted, too.

It was the fight Donovan had been waiting for.

*   *   *

Erik parked the car on a darkened pier. It was an industrial space he had rented before, to moor a pyrotechnics barge and set up fireworks for their timed display. On this Halloween, it was dark and deserted, the lake beyond it reflecting the lights of the city. The rain fell on the car in a persistent patter, making the dock look slick and black.

Once again, Erik had the sense that more could happen on this night than he expected. It wasn't a feeling he liked and he was determined to get this battle behind him as soon as possible.

Boris didn't share his urgency. The *Slayer* turned Erik's penny in his hand, then slanted Erik a smile. "You've no idea how long I've waited for this."

"As long as I have, more or less." Erik wasn't interested in conversation, even though Boris seemed to be in a thoughtful mood.

"Only one of us will survive," Boris mused. "Winner take all."

"Those are the stakes," Erik agreed curtly. He reached for his door, but Boris suddenly clutched his arm. Erik saw the talons on Boris's hand—dragon talons on a human hand—then looked at his companion in surprise. He wasn't accustomed to seeing *Pyr* or *Slayer* linger on the mingled state between forms. Boris's smile gleamed, his teeth more jagged and numerous than they should be in his human form.

"How allied with the humans are you?" he murmured, his words low and persuasive. "How much will you do to let them live?"

If Boris thought Erik would be impressed by his ability to hover between forms, he could think again.

"There's no one to do your dirty work for you," Erik said, letting himself shimmer on the cusp of change. "Are you going to have to get your talons dirty, Boris?"

Erik didn't wait for an answer. He exhaled fire, still in

human form, and felt Boris's shock as the flames licked his skin. The cashmere coat smoldered, then began to burn.

Boris snarled. He lunged for Erik, talons extended. Erik opened his door with one claw, and seized Boris by the throat with the other.

He flew high, shifting as soon as he was out of the car, and carried his opponent far above the city. Boris changed form as well, his urgency evident in his failure to fold away his clothes. The burning cashmere overcoat fell to the wet pavement, followed by Boris's suit.

Erik was momentarily distracted by this unexpected concession. Were the old stories true? It was said that if a *Pyr* or *Slayer* lost his garments while in dragon form, he would be unable to shift back to human form. Erik had always thought it was a myth but was ready to find out.

At Boris's expense.

Erik pivoted in midair and spewed dragonfire across the falling garments. Boris growled and snapped, trying to stop him, but Erik was undeterred. The coat burned; the suit burned; the silk tie danced as it fell toward the ground and the flames devoured it. The shirt burned, as did the socks and shoes and underwear.

It was all incinerated, a smoking pile of executive wear on the dock. Erik's penny rolled free and spiraled to a glimmering halt half a dozen feet away from the burning garments.

Boris roared in fury, summoning the strength to slither free of Erik's grip. Erik guessed that the *Slayer* believed the old stories were true.

"Wyvern spawn," Boris raged. "How dare you?"

"All in the interests of investigation," Erik taunted. "Only one of us will walk away."

"I bet on it being me," Boris replied.

They circled each other in assessment—one onyx and pewter, one ruby red and brass—then leapt at each other, locking claws in the time-honored choreography of dragon battle.

They were both old, both strong, both experienced.

And they both had everything to lose.

In Minnesota, the *Pyr* locked claws with their *Slayer* opponents and with the captive converts. Rafferty flew directly to his grandfather—or what that old *Pyr* had become—and searched his gaze for a spark.

"Gone!" Rafferty cried with pain. "They stole his soul!"

"Released it," Magnus confirmed mildly. "They have all been converted to fighting machines of maximum efficiency."

"They are abominations!" Rafferty roared. The ghoul attacked him with vicious strength, and Donovan knew the moment that his mentor fought for more than his own defense.

"We have to kill them," Quinn shouted. "It is the only dignity we can do them."

"Dismember and burn," Donovan cried.

He saw Rafferty weep as he fought the *Pyr* he had loved with all his heart and soul. Magnus attacked Rafferty from behind as he fought, doing his best to set the odds high against his former opponent.

Quinn was set upon his three brothers. Donovan leapt to help. He exhaled dragonfire on his friend and locked claws with the largest of the three. Quinn sparkled with the influx of energy, then swung his tail at his brothers with new force, breathing fire as their scales scorched and burned.

They fought on with fearsome determination.

Niall engaged with his twin and Sloane fought his own father. Donovan knew himself how hard it was to separate memory from the truth of what these *Pyr* had become, how hard it was to strike a killing blow to something that so closely resembled a loved one.

He feared then that the *Pyr* might lose.

Donovan fought against Jorge, doing that *Slayer* injury so quickly that he feared a trick.

Then he heard what he had missed. Delaney yowled and

Jorge chuckled. "The darkness isn't that easily dispelled," Jorge said. "The charm is planted deep."

Donovan noticed that Magnus was murmuring a low chant, even as he fought Rafferty.

"Don't call him back to the darkness!" Donovan shouted, and struck Magnus with his tail.

Rafferty took a blow from his own grandfather, one that sent him tumbling through the air, but Rafferty pivoted and raged back at his opponent.

Magnus didn't miss a beat of his chant.

Delaney raised his head slowly. His cold gaze fixed on Donovan and once again, the light had been doused to a flicker.

The *Slayer* shadow was winning because of Magnus's song.

Donovan targeted Delaney and made to lock claws. Delaney ducked his grip, seizing Donovan's back claws instead. He snarled and gnawed on Donovan's leg. Donovan struck Delaney with his tail, then shook off the *Slayer*'s grip. Donovan wasn't fighting to kill: he needed to capture Delaney again so that Sloane could heal him.

But Delaney fought as though possessed. He dove at Donovan time and again, biting and tearing. The metal claws Quinn had made for Donovan were lethal, but he used them sparingly. He tried not to cause permanent damage.

Delaney was still in there.

Somewhere.

Donovan had seen the truth in his eyes. The firestorm had brought him back toward the light and Donovan was sure Delaney could be completely healed.

For that, he had to live.

"Look what we will do to all of you," Jorge gloated, obviously noting Donovan's dismay. "We can turn you all *Slayer*, and make you subject to our will. You will fight until the death for a cause you don't even embrace."

"Never!" Quinn bellowed, his white-hot dragonfire

dispatching one of his brothers. That shadow dragon fell and
burned to ash on the pavement. Quinn raged after a second
brother, snatching him and casting him against the stainless
steel shutters of the house. There was a crash as he hit, and
he had time to moan before Quinn hovered above him and
breathed dragonfire.

"Window damage in spare bedroom number three,"
Oscar said, his voice faint behind the shutters.

"We have to incinerate them," Sloane shouted.

"We have to let the wind disperse them," Niall agreed,
then grunted as his father slashed his belly open. Niall's
blood flowed, but he fought on.

Quinn's fallen brother, his scales alight with flames, leapt
from the roof with fury and attacked Quinn. The other brother,
still uninjured, assailed Quinn from the opposite side.

Meanwhile, Delaney struck with fury and bit deep.
Donovan breathed fire at him and struck him hard across the
face. Delaney fell back only for a moment. He came after
Donovan once more and Donovan hailed blows upon him.

It made no difference. Delaney rose once more, and
locked his gaze upon Donovan's chest. He leapt toward
Donovan, claws outstretched, and embedded his talons in
Donovan's chest.

Donovan screamed as much in frustration as in pain. Delaney gouged at Donovan's chest, as if trying to dig out the
gem Quinn had just embedded there. Donovan wouldn't part
with Alex's talisman that easily. He shredded the former
Pyr's back, ripped him free, and cast him on the ground.

Donovan made to leap after his cousin and trap him, but
Magnus struck Donovan from behind. Donovan tumbled,
startled, and Delaney leapt skyward after him. Delaney
buried one claw in Donovan's chest, then opened his mouth
to bite at Alex's jet talisman.

He froze, as if confused. That blank gaze was fixed on
Donovan's chest with curious intensity. Donovan saw the
flicker of light in his doubt and dared to hope.

"Get it!" Magnus bellowed. "Get the Dragon's Tooth!"

Donovan knew what the problem was. "The Dragon's Tooth is gone," he said to Delaney. "Your quest has failed. You battle for nothing, or for nothing that can be won."

Delaney shook his head.

"They've given you an impossible task, Delaney. Come back, my brother, come back to the light. You felt the firestorm. Surrender to me and be healed."

Delaney loosed a scream of anguish and had a convulsion. It was as if demons battled within him for supremacy. Donovan almost lost his grip on the writhing snake Delaney had become, but he wasn't going to lose his brother again.

Donovan locked one rear claw around Delaney's neck to hold him down. He kept talking to him, kept urging surrender, and gradually the convulsion ended. Delaney shuddered and fell still.

What had happened within him? Which side had won? Donovan didn't know and he wasn't going to guess.

What he needed was a shackle, one strong enough to keep a dragon captive. He looked up in time to see Sloane slash at his father so that his wings fell in tatters. The older dragon didn't bleed, but he tumbled toward the earth.

"Did you have to make work for me?" Sloane muttered, then landed beside the fallen Delaney. "All I need is physical damage to heal along with the psychological."

"He's not dead," Donovan said. "That's a start."

The copper and emerald green dragon appeared to be unconscious, which Donovan thought was a blessing. Sloane leaned closer to examine the former *Pyr*'s injuries. At that same moment, Peter's son came running out of the garage.

"No!" Jared bellowed, pointing at something behind Donovan and Sloane. "Don't hurt my dragon!"

"Jared, stop!" Alex shouted, and lunged after the little boy.

When they both crossed the smoke barrier, Donovan's heart stopped cold.

* * *

Erik fought hard early, wanting to secure his early advantage. He didn't trust Boris as far as he could throw him, and didn't doubt that the leader of the *Slayers* had a trick or two in his arsenal.

Boris, after all, seldom engaged in physical work. Erik should be able to overwhelm him, if he came out strong.

They rolled across the sky, claws locked together and tails slashing. Erik landed a blow on Boris's back with his tail, and simultaneously tore at Boris's chest with his back claws. He flung Boris across the sky and into an electrical billboard. Sparks flew as part of the display shorted out and smoke rose from the *Slayer*'s bruised and fallen form.

Boris straightened with a snarl and leapt after Erik, his red feathers streaming like flames. He caught Erik by the wings and hurled him into the darkened window of an office building. The glass cracked noisily and Erik fell, dazed from the blow.

He glanced up to find Boris breathing smoke.

The dragonsmoke unfurled toward Erik and he retreated warily. Smoke sought weakness and multiplied that weakness. But Boris's smoke did more than that: it tracked Erik. It followed him, pursuing him no matter how he changed course.

Until finally it touched him. Everywhere the dragonsmoke contacted Erik, it burned. It was a brand touched to his flesh, a burning weapon that eased beneath his scales, seeking weakness it could exploit.

Erik couldn't evade it and he couldn't outrun it. He heard Boris chuckle even as the *Slayer* breathed an endless tendril of dragonsmoke. Erik felt the smoke stealing vigor from his body, wearing him down, weakening him with pain. He struggled and twisted, knowing one target it sought.

He had one misshapen scale, one lost scale that had grown back, thick and unnatural. Erik didn't doubt that the smoke would writhe beneath it. He flew away from the smoke and it followed him with leisurely persistence. It caught him again, winding around his ankle to hold him captive, rising like a cobra before him, stealing the strength with its furtive touch.

Erik looked beyond the smoke to Boris and was shocked. The *Slayer* became larger and brighter, his eyes shining with triumph as his smoke tormented Erik.

The smoke wasn't just stealing Erik's strength: it was giving that vitality to Boris. It was a conduit between the two of them, cheating Erik to fuel Boris. Boris would see Erik sucked dry, a shell of his former self.

Given new strength by the realization, Erik snarled in his turn, pivoted, and dove toward the lake. The smoke pursued him but Erik knew how to lose it. He plunged into the lake's icy depths, refreshed by the cold and free of the smoke. He looked up to see it gathering on the surface, ready to ensnare him when he emerged. Boris would be larger and stronger yet.

Erik had to make his kill while he could.

Alex snatched up Jared and pivoted immediately to return to the garage.

No luck. Jorge landed in her path. He was beautiful in dragon form, all glittering topaz and gold. His eyes remained the same cold, cold blue. He smiled smugly and Alex wanted to deck him.

"Auntie Alex?" Jared whispered against her throat.

"Just hang on," she told her nephew. "We'll get out of this."

He whimpered and looked back at Sloane. Alex was thinking about the distance to Donovan's Ducati, parked outside the garage, and wishing she had the keys.

Then Magnus landed between her and the *Pyr*, effectively sandwiching her between two *Slayers*. He, too, seemed content to smile at her hungrily and bide his time.

"I love a good dragon fight," he murmured to Alex as if they were spectators at a sporting event. She bit back a rude reply. Delaney lay injured beside her and Alex didn't know whether to trust him or not.

Then she saw that the trickle of blood from his wounds was red.

Meanwhile, Sloane had glanced over his shoulder, following Jared's gesture. A larger and darker version of Sloane approached quickly, his talons extended and his teeth bared. He was a broken and burned version of the *Pyr* he must have once been, and one bent on slaughter. Sloane roared in pain as his father fell upon him.

Sloane rallied and struck his father hard with his tail. They fought viciously for several moments and Jared cheered for his dragon. The *Slayer* fell, but Sloane didn't rush in to make the kill. Instead, he studied the fallen *Slayer*. Alex saw Sloane's hesitation—evidently there was enough familiar in the *Slayer* that Sloane couldn't strike the final blow.

"Kill him!" Donovan commanded.

Sloane shook his head mutely just as his father rose again. The *Slayer* breathed slowly, fixed his gaze upon his son, and Alex was sure that the darkness of his eyes became more intense.

"Join us," he urged with quiet force, and Sloane averted his gaze.

It wasn't a time for doubts. Donovan attacked the ghoul that had been Sloane's father before he could say more. He carried the *Slayer* high above the ground, then used his steel talons to cut off his claws. Jared watched with fascination, but Alex looked away. She'd seen this show before.

Sloane's father struggled and screamed, but even he must have known that his wings weren't fit to save him if Donovan let him go. Donovan dismembered Sloane's father just as he had destroyed his own. He wore the same expression of regret.

When the pieces fell sizzling to the driveway, Sloane turned his dragonfire upon them, committing his father to ash and oblivion. Donovan landed beside him and added his dragonfire to finish the task.

Alex saw that Sloane's face was wet with tears, and understood that the deed had not been easy for him. The spark of the divine had been extinguished in his father, so there was no choice.

That couldn't make it any easier to do.

Which was presumably what Magnus and the *Slayers* were counting on.

When the ash stirred in the wind, Donovan surveyed the scene. Magnus chortled and waited. Donovan had obviously assumed that Alex had returned to the garage, and she knew the moment he discovered he was wrong.

"Shit," Sloane said.

Donovan looked grim. He scanned the area, checking for allies and casualties. Magnus gave him time to look. Alex saw that Rafferty had fallen—Donovan's mentor was bleeding and unconscious on the pavement. There was no sign of Rafferty's grandfather, which she assumed was a bad sign.

Niall was still battling the *Slayer* that had been his brother, but his brother was winning. Quinn was fighting against two of the *Slayers* created from his older brothers, one of which was blackened from dragonfire, his exhaustion showing. Sara stood in the shelter of the garage, her gaze fixed on Quinn.

Donovan seemed to note all of this, then eyed Magnus. Alex knew he was assessing the *Slayer*'s strength. Could he see that Magnus was still missing the same scale he'd been missing all those centuries ago? The light wasn't good, but Alex didn't want to shout what she could see.

Too bad humans and their *Pyr* mates couldn't exchange a private kind of old-speak. She tightened her grip on Jared, who—for once—didn't seem to mind being hugged.

Magnus smiled with confidence as he addressed Donovan. "Care to reconsider your choices? We'd love to have you on our team."

"Never," Donovan seethed. Alex knew he'd die fighting rather than surrender to evil.

She just wished it didn't look as if things could end that way.

Delaney felt despair. The darkness had come from nowhere, dragging him back to its depths like a malevolent monster of the deep. A whistle and a chant, both of which he had been taught to remember forever, had undone him.

Despite the power of Donovan's firestorm, Delaney feared he would never be healed.

He felt the presence of Donovan's mate close beside him.

He listened to Magnus and Jorge, heard Donovan's frustration, and understood the situation. He wasn't going to let Donovan lose what was precious to him.

Delaney didn't care what price he paid to secure the future of Donovan's mate. His own future wasn't worth living, not with this dark stain placed upon his heart, not with this charm that he couldn't deny. He wouldn't be a *Slayer* pawn forever, commanded to injure those he had cared for. He couldn't imagine a better cause for sacrifice than Donovan's future.

Little did he know that making that choice was the key to finally erasing the stain laid upon his heart.

"Isn't this interesting?" Magnus murmured as he locked claws with Donovan. "You saw that my treasure was lost and now I can return the favor."

"Don't touch my mate!" Donovan spun in the air, fighting Magnus as they turned together. Their tails entwined and he was startled by Magnus's great strength.

Jorge snatched up Alex and Jared, when Alex might have run into the garage, laughing as he held them above the ground.

"I don't have to touch your mate to kill her," Magnus said with a smile. "Although it might add to the fun."

Rage filled Donovan, a fury at the crimes of the *Slayers* and their quest for victory at any price. They would break any taboo or twist any soul to their purpose. They would destroy and devour and never regret a bit of it if their own ends were served. What would be left of the planet if they won? The anger threatened to consume him; then he remembered Alex's trick.

He deliberately used his anger to fuel his desire for justice. He battled ferociously against Magnus, letting his fury over the *Slayers'* treatment of Delaney fill his veins. He cast Magnus against the pavement, heard a bone crack, and watched Magnus take flight again.

They locked claws, spiraling through the air in their struggle for supremacy. Donovan thought about Alex's ordeal, how Boris and Tyson had let her watch them eat Mark alive. He thought about her nightmares and her fears and the very real chance of her being committed to a mental hospital.

The injustice made him livid.

"More," whispered the Wyvern in old-speak.

Donovan thought about Magnus manipulating Olivia, about Boris fighting Erik, about Tyson stalking and attacking Alex. He thought about the *Slayers* attacking Peter and his family, about Boris deceiving Mr. Sinclair, about a thousand acts of unfairness both big and small. He let his heart fill with the darkness that was *Slayer*; he let himself despise it; then he used it against his opponent.

And with the crescendo of rage, Donovan felt a resonance grow within him. He felt an accord with Gaia, that he was not just a part of the earth or an inhabitant upon it, but that he was her instrument.

The elements of the earth were his weapons of war.

He was the Warrior.

Donovan roared as Gaia fed his triumph. The earth bellowed and shook and heaved. Hail fell from the sky like arrows of ice, the second weapon beneath his command. Rock projectiles took flight and pummeled the dark opponents of the *Pyr*, the third weapon in Donovan's arsenal. Magnus shouted with frustration, recognizing that a greater force had joined the fray.

Just when Donovan was sure they'd win, an unknown dragon came over the roof of the house.

"Who's that?" Alex cried, hoping to distract her captor. Jorge looked but he didn't loosen his grip.

Pyr and *Slayers* stared at the new arrival with shock.

He was the color of anthracite, a thousand hues of silver, gray and black, his scales gleaming in the starlight. He seemed primitive compared to the other *Pyr*, more reptilian.

"He looks like a dinosaur," Jared whispered.

"*Pyrannosaurus rex*, maybe," Alex replied.

"I wonder whether smart women taste better," Jorge mused. Alex ignored him.

Sara had been right. This was the fighting dragon that had grown out of the Dragon's Tooth pearl they'd planted. No wonder he looked so old.

"He has no scent," Sloane murmured. "Which side is he on?"

"We're always ready for converts," Jorge said.

"So, you figured out the secret of the Dragon's Tooth," Magnus mused, his voice dark. "To think that there were once a hundred such teeth, simply waiting to be put to use. To think we could harvest an entire *Slayer* army if we simply retrieved them."

"You mean you lost the other ninety-nine?" Donovan scoffed. "Remind me never to trust you with anything important."

"I had them all!" Magnus bellowed.

"So, Olivia coaxed the others out of you?" Donovan said. "Did she even know their power?"

"That stupid woman had no idea what she asked of you," Magnus said, seething at the memory. "Much less what sacrifice she asked of me." He turned a bright glance on Rafferty. "It was his fault that I lost them all. It was always his fault."

Out in the driveway, Rafferty lifted his head, his eyes glimmering. Alex was surprised when he began to hum.

So was the new arrival, who turned as if entranced by the music.

"It's the same song Rafferty sang when we planted the tooth," Sara murmured from a safe vantage point inside the garage. "I remember it."

So did the new arrival. Alex held her breath. Would the song infuriate him or persuade him to take the *Pyr* side?

Erik erupted from the lake like an arrow loosed from a bow. He sliced through the smoke and spiraled upward, targeting Boris.

The startled *Slayer* took the brunt of Erik's blow in his chest. The force of impact sent them both spinning through the air.

Erik wasted no time on formalities. He ripped open Boris's chest and bit the *Slayer*'s neck. Black blood flowed over ruby red scales as Boris screamed in pain.

Erik thought of Louisa, killed by *Slayers*.

He thought of the son Louisa had borne him, Sigmund, turned *Slayer* at Boris's behest.

He thought of the Wyvern, tortured at Boris's command.

He thought of the wickedness done by his opponent, and shredded Boris alive. He ripped his scales and tore his flesh, ignored the screams as the blood ran. He ravaged Boris's body, turning it into a wreckage of its former glory.

When Boris ceased his screaming and struggling, Erik flew high over the city of Chicago. He dropped Boris, then flew beside him, loosing an endless torrent of dragonfire on the *Slayer*'s body. The brilliant scarlet feathers that trailed behind Boris burned to cinders. The ruby red scales darkened to black. The brass edges of the scales darkened and the leathery wings curled into impotent wisps.

Boris hit the pavement with a resounding thud and moved no more. Erik checked that he'd left no detail unattended. He wanted Boris to remain dead.

Boris had been struck with dragonfire.

He'd fallen to the earth.

The cold wind off the lake touched his broken body.

The rain fell upon his stillness.

All four elements had been accounted for. A dark puddle of blood spread beneath Boris, mingling with the rain and glistening like an oil slick.

Boris had played his last trick. He was dead, or so close to it that the difference was immaterial. Erik hovered, watching his opponent's fallen form with suspicion.

But Boris didn't stir.

The wind did. It burst forth suddenly, setting the litter on the dock to whirling. The wind tasted dark and ominous, and Erik turned his attention to it.

Something was wrong. There was an unnatural disturbance in the forces surrounding the earth. The north wind hinted at where the trouble had occurred.

Minnesota.

With one last lingering look, Erik abandoned Boris's corpse, turned in midair, and streaked north at lightning speed to help his fellows.

Erik didn't see Boris rouse himself long moments later. He didn't see Boris slowly drag his burned and battered body across the wet pavement toward the detritus of his clothes.

Erik didn't see Boris, hatred in his eyes, deliberately pick up the penny in his talons and lock his fist around it.

Erik didn't see Boris change back to human form, see him bleeding and bruised, wearing only the undershirt he had managed to hide away. He didn't see Boris lean his forehead on the ground, gathering the last shards of his strength.

Erik certainly didn't see Boris crawl away.

If Erik had witnessed any of this, he would have been far more worried about the future than he already was.

He had never believed that the legendary Dragon's Blood Elixir truly existed. Seeing Boris rise from the ashes of destruction and cheat death would have changed Erik's thinking.

But Erik was gone.

Chapter 20

Nikolas had been enchanted too long.

The world was so different that it bore little resemblance to the one he knew. The earth sang a variation on the song he understood—her tune was more angry than it had once been. The wind carried different scents than the ones he had known. The water in the lake beyond knew nothing of the Mediterranean that he so loved.

But the dragonfire was the same.

He knew it and he recognized his own kind. He knew that even if much had changed, some things had remained constant. He sensed valor in the lapis lazuli and gold dragon to his right, and respected the unknown talisman on that one's chest.

He sensed evil in the jade and gold dragon to his left and felt the relentless darkness of that one's selfish heart. He did not understand the shadow dragons, the ones that were neither dead nor alive, but he felt an abhorrence of them.

Then he heard the song that had coaxed him to awaken, a song as old as the earth herself, a song that roused a rhythm in his blood and reminded him that he was again alive. It was a song that awakened his commitment to justice and his pledge to use his abilities for the cause of right.

He had been born to fight, and reborn to fight again.

Nikolas raged after the jade dragon, fighting with vicious fury. The lapis lazuli dragon joined forces with him and they assaulted the jade dragon from both sides. The old dragon did not surrender the fight easily, but battled with surprising vigor.

Meanwhile, the topaz and gold dragon held the woman and child captive. His wings flapped, and Nikolas knew he meant to kidnap the pair and hold them hostage. The woman screamed.

The jade dragon locked claws with the lapis lazuli one, keeping him from going to the woman's aid. One of the shadow dragons left the sapphire dragon to assail Nikolas and Nikolas met his assault with fury.

How dare they endanger a woman and child?

The fallen dragon, the copper and emerald one, roused himself suddenly in the woman's defense. He attacked the topaz dragon with unexpected force. The woman squirmed free as the pair fought. They looked like vicious snakes knotted around each other, blood running red and black over their scales.

The woman and child ran back into the shelter where another woman waited. Nikolas was relieved. A dragon battlefield was no place for humans.

Chaos reigned, but Nikolas sensed that it was under the command of one of the *Pyr*. He surveyed them and identified the lapis lazuli dragon as the source of power. He wore a badge upon his chest, a mark of black and red. He was a veritable fighting machine and Nikolas felt the earth answer his summons. Hail sliced through the sky, rocks flew, and the wind swirled in a maelstrom beneath his command.

He was magnificent, a leader of warriors and one whom Nikolas could respect. He committed himself to the lapis lazuli dragon's side. They fought together and he followed his leader's strategy, destroying those who were neither dead nor alive.

The opal dragon sang, changing his tune.

There was a rumble as the earth parted, leaving a chasm across the land. Nikolas instinctively seized the jade dragon when he halted in surprise, then cast him into the abyss. Hail fell down upon him, leaving wounds everywhere it struck. The copper and emerald dragon dispatched the topaz dragon after him.

The lapis lazuli dragon then cast others in the abyss, the others who were neither dead or alive. The shadow dragon fighting the amethyst and platinum dragon screamed and streaked skyward. His opponent landed, breathing heavily, as he watched the shadow dragon go. The shadow dragon Nikolas had fought followed suit, flying high over the trees and fading from sight.

Nikolas wondered where they would go.

And when they would be back.

Three dragons—sapphire and steel, tourmaline and gold, amethyst and platinum—stood on the lip of the chasm and breathed dragonfire into the pit in unison. The sapphire dragon's fire was white-hot and burned clean. Nikolas lost sight of the jade and topaz dragons in the flames.

When the pit was full of the ash of the dragons who were neither dead nor alive, the opal dragon's song changed ever so slightly. Its tune made Nikolas nostalgic for past glories. The earth shut with a groan, trapping the fallen within her darkness.

The lapis lazuli dragon landed close before Nikolas, assessing him. "You're the Dragon's Tooth," he said.

"I am but one of many, one of an army enchanted. Old tales have their roots in truth," Nikolas said, allowing himself a smile. "I have slept long and now I am prepared to fight."

He held the gaze of the lapis lazuli dragon and by some

unspoken agreement, they shifted shape in unison. "What were they? The undead ones?"

"Dead *Pyr* who had not been exposed to all four elements," said the man who had been the copper and emerald dragon. He shuddered, as if he knew too much of this. "*Pyr* who were enslaved by the darkness of the *Slayers*." He and the auburn-haired man shook hands and Nikolas saw the physical similarity between them.

"*Slayers*," Nikolas had not heard this term before and he repeated it again. "Are they not *Pyr*?"

"They were *Pyr*, but now are *Slayers* bent on destroying mankind," said the one who had sung to the earth.

"The dark ones," Nikolas said with a nod. "There was always darkness, but in my time, it had no such name."

"Donovan Shea," the auburn-haired *Pyr* said, offering his hand. "Welcome."

"You are the Warrior foretold," Nikolas said, acknowledging a truth that was obvious to him.

Donovan inclined his head in agreement.

"Nikolas of Thebes," he said, liking the strength of the other warrior's grip. "And where am I welcomed?"

"The United States of America," Donovan said. "Two thousand and seven years after the birth of Jesus Christ."

"Where? Who?" Nikolas asked in confusion.

Donovan laughed. "You've slept many thousands of years. We'll help you."

Nikolas felt relief at this, and a measure of excitement. He watched the dark-haired man who had been the sapphire dragon stride closer. The opal dragon became an older man, one who moved with purpose as befit one who sang to the earth.

"Quinn Tyrrell," Donovan said. "The Smith. And Rafferty Powell."

Beyond the men was the shelter protected by dragon-smoke and occupied by the women. One set down a child, who ran toward the *Pyr*.

"Sloane Forbes," said the dark-haired man, scooping up the boy with one arm as he offered his hand with the other.

"My dragon," the boy said.

"Apothecary," Sloane corrected, then arched a brow as he considered his fellows. "With a good bit of work to do."

"Niall Talbot," said the fair man who had been the amethyst and platinum dragon. He had a head wound that obviously concerned Sloane but spared a glance at the sky, as if seeking some sign of his departed opponent.

An onyx and pewter dragon spiraled out of the sky just then, angling his flight to land before them. Nikolas bristled, prepared to defend the *Pyr* if necessary.

Rafferty shook his head as he noted Nikolas's response. "Erik Sorensson, leader of the *Pyr*." He smiled. "You need fear only the sharpness of his tongue when he is displeased."

"Oh, I have known many such leaders in my time," Nikolas acknowledged, and they all chuckled.

"Boris is dead," Erik said by way of greeting, and a ripple of shock passed through the *Pyr*.

"Boris Vassily was the leader of the *Slayers*," Niall told Nikolas, and he nodded his approval along with the others.

"You're sure?" Rafferty asked, eyes gleaming.

"Absolutely." Erik nodded with conviction. "His body was exposed to the four elements." Erik's gaze landed on Nikolas and his eyes narrowed. Donovan introduced them, and Erik smiled slightly as they shook hands.

There was nothing, in Nikolas's experience, better than a battle ended well, and the company of comrades in arms. He was ready to celebrate in the traditional manner, more ready than usual, given that he'd spent several millennia enchanted.

He glanced toward the two women who stepped out of the shelter, unable to decide whether the tall, dark-haired one or the delicate blonde was more attractive. Donovan and Quinn bristled as one, though, and Nikolas knew he would have to look elsewhere for that particular pleasure. These women were claimed.

It was reassuring how few things had changed.

Donovan was raging with desire and impatient with details. He wanted to celebrate victory with Alex. They had a whole night to share before her meeting, and he knew how he wanted to spend it. He wanted to talk to Alex.

He wanted to make love to her.

He wanted to settle the questions that were outstanding between them, the questions about their future together.

He wanted to do it alone.

"Alex should be clear for her meeting tomorrow," Erik said.

"I'll be with her," Donovan said flatly, and Alex leaned against him. He pulled her close against his side, and tapped his toe with impatience to leave.

Sloane considered Delaney. "What happened there? Are you back on our side or not?"

"I don't know," the *Pyr* said with a shake of his head, and Donovan felt sympathy for his brother. "It's as if the shadow and the light are at war within me. I can't tell who will win."

"That whistle of Magnus's gave the shadow the upper hand," Alex guessed.

"Never mind his chant," Sloane added.

"It triggered something I couldn't fight. How do I get rid of that?" Delaney asked with fear. "Will they always be able to get my attention that easily? How can you all count on me? How can I count on myself?"

"I have the treatise," Sloane said. "Come with me to my lair and I'll try to heal you."

"I don't think it will be easy," Delaney said, looking despondent. "I don't think I'll ever be right."

"Nothing worth doing is ever easy," Donovan said, and when his brother looked at him, he smiled. "Thank you for helping Alex. Even under Magnus's spell, you proved that I could count on you." Donovan sensed that Delaney drew strength from his conviction. "Anything you need from me," he said, "anything, anytime, you just let me know."

"Thanks." Delaney straightened. "I want to beat this. I *need* to beat this."

"I think you've made a good start," Sloane said. "A self-less choice, like the one you made, is a step away from the darkness."

"How many were there in the academy?" Erik asked.

Delaney shuddered. "I'm not sure. We were isolated from each other."

"There could be an army of ghouls," Rafferty said.

"More even than we battled tonight," Quinn added grimly.

"How many *Pyr* have died and not been exposed to all of the elements, over the history of our kind?" Erik uttered the question in all of their thoughts. No one had an answer and no one liked the prospect of meeting more like those they'd defeated.

"I dislike the fact that Magnus has returned," Rafferty said. "And that he had a minion."

"We defeated them both," Sloane said.

Rafferty shook his head. "I have thought Magnus defeated before. He has old knowledge, which was arcane even when I was young. It was even said that he possessed the Dragon's Blood Elixir—"

"Which does not exist," Erik interrupted sharply. "Magnus lies about such myths to impress his minions."

"And he is not one to be satisfied with a single minion. I will wager that he has trained more *Slayers*."

The future looked more grim than Donovan would have liked. "It has to be worth something that we've fulfilled the prophecy of two firestorms," he said.

"Something, but not everything." Erik cleared his throat and nodded at Nikolas. "I can teach you what we know, if you'd like to be my guest in my lair. With any luck, you'll have lore to share with us. We're going to need every asset we can find."

Nikolas frowned. "What about the others?"

"What others?" Erik asked. All of the *Pyr* looked puzzled.

"There were a hundred of us imprisoned by that curse. Where are the others? If you seek an army, there is an enchanted one that can be awakened."

The *Pyr* exchanged glances.

"I would wager that Magnus knows," Rafferty said.

"And that he won't tell," Donovan concluded.

"What about his old hoard?" Sara asked. "He said he had collected them all."

"I wonder," Rafferty mused. "Is it lost or hidden?"

"You could ask the earth," Donovan suggested.

His old mentor nodded. "I can, although one can never predict when she will answer."

"Were you all *Pyr*?" Erik asked Nikolas with excitement.

"We all were dragon warriors."

"But *Pyr* or *Slayer*?"

Nikolas shrugged. "There are shadows in the hearts of all men. We did not divide into two camps as you have done. There were those I would trust and those I would not." Donovan wondered whether he was the only one who heard the echo of Sophie's prediction in Nikolas's words.

"Do you think you could tell the difference between teeth, should we find the hoard?" Erik asked.

Nikolas shrugged. "I cannot say. I have never seen these teeth."

Before Erik could respond to that, a sweet wind began to blow. It swirled over the trees, smelling like sunshine and summertime.

"Look!" Jared shouted from Sloane's shoulder, and pointed high.

It was the Wyvern. Donovan watched her descend, her white feathers swirling. He was always struck by her delicacy, how she could have been made of spun glass. He felt the usual wonder in her presence, but there was one even more awed.

"A miracle," Nikolas muttered, and fell to his knees. He bowed his head and touched it to the pavement, his hands spread before him in supplication.

He was the one.

The thought echoed in Sophie's mind with utter conviction. One glimpse of the new *Pyr*, with his rugged masculinity and dark good looks, was enough to tell her of his origin.

And his destiny. He alone was old enough to enter the dark academy and survive.

There was something else about him, too, something that made her afraid to look directly at him, something that made her flutter her feathers a little more as she landed.

There was something about him that made Sophie feel shy.

She was afraid that she knew exactly what it was.

Rafferty was intrigued. Sophie shifted shape and strolled toward them, her sheer dress swirling around her ankles. Nikolas didn't move and she didn't seem to notice him.

Rafferty didn't believe that for a minute, but he still didn't know what was going on.

"Two destined firestorms concluded with success," he said when Sophie drew near. She nodded, indicating that she already knew as much. "And a Warrior upon our team."

"One more to go," Erik said, his exhaustion clear. "Whose will it be, Sophie? Or are you not going to tell us?"

"A prophecy, maybe?" Donovan said with a smile.

"You already know," Sophie said softly, and looked at Rafferty.

He felt a jolt when her gaze landed on him and knew that the time to tell of his dream had come.

He counted the destined trilogy off with his fingers. "Smith and Seer. Warrior and Wizard." Rafferty slanted a glance at Erik. "That leaves King and Consort of the high three."

Sophie nodded approval, her gaze moving between Rafferty and Erik.

Erik's eyes narrowed. "Assuming you know who is to be King."

"You lead us," Rafferty noted. "It will obviously be you."

"I lead with less success than I could hope," Erik said. "My mistakes have led us to our current compromised situation."

"Perhaps your firestorm will transform you," Sloane suggested.

"But I've had my firestorm." Erik looked grim as Sophie watched him. "And the product of it is the *Slayer* who provides the learning they use against us." He dropped his hand onto Rafferty's shoulder. "It is said that the true King reveals himself when his presence is necessary. That may not be me."

Rafferty's heart leapt. His firestorm. Could it be true? Would he be next? He cared less about the fated role of King and leader than he did of having a mate after all these lonely centuries. He looked at the Wyvern, but she simply smiled at him, revealing nothing.

"The eclipse is in February," he said, recognizing that Erik was letting him take the lead. "Then we will know for certain."

"Indeed we will," Sophie said, then turned her turquoise gaze on Jared. The little boy was wide-awake despite the hour.

She smiled at him and touched his cheek. "I am sorry, but you must forget all of this," she murmured. He looked as if he would argue, but she ran her fingertip across his mouth. "It is for the safety of all of us. Do you not want your dragon to be safe?"

Jared nodded. He surveyed all the *Pyr* quickly, as if trying to secure them all in his thoughts. He held on tightly to Sloane, who told him not to be afraid.

Then Sophie leaned closer.

"Close your eyes," she whispered. "And forget." On his forehead she planted a kiss, one that shimmered silver on his skin.

When it faded, Jared was asleep on Sloane's shoulder. Sloane passed the little boy to Alex, who carried him into the house, Donovan fast behind her. They looked right with a small boy in their care, although their son would have red hair.

Rafferty watched them go, pride swelling his heart at what his student had become.

"You glimpsed the Warrior in him," Sophie said beside him.

"I thought so."

"You believed in him, and that was the key." She slanted a smile at him. "Remember, Rafferty, the Great Wyvern works in mysterious ways." She held his gaze as she faded away, disappearing as surely as if she had never been present.

But her last words echoed in Rafferty's thoughts, tempting him to believe that nothing would proceed as they anticipated.

Too bad he didn't know whether that was bad or good.

Something had changed in Donovan. Alex could feel the transformation he had undergone. He exuded new power and authority; his eyes were brighter and his manner more intense.

She understood that he had become the Warrior.

What happened to the Wizard after that?

He caught her hand in his, the white heat of the firestorm making her mouth go dry. She wanted him as badly as she had the first time she'd glimpsed him—no, even more than that. She would never have believed it possible that desire could burn with such ferocity, that she could find such pleasure and still be hungry for more.

She'd never imagined that one man, especially a man with Donovan's powers, could have eliminated her nightmares. But she hadn't dreamed of dragons the night before.

Donovan had given her that gift. He'd taught her that not

all dragons were to be feared, that she wasn't powerless against him and his fellows. Her heart beat a little faster when she left Jared's room and found Donovan waiting in the hall.

He glanced up, and their gazes locked. Even at a distance, the man could set her to simmering. They stared at each other for a potent moment; then Donovan came to her side.

He smiled down at her, and his crooked grin and the way his hand caught hers combined to shake her world. He glanced at their interlocked fingers and the glow that emanated from that point. "Still getting hotter," he said, his eyes gleaming. "The firestorm is relentless."

"I guess it doesn't want to be cheated." Alex ran a fingertip over his tattoo, unable to keep from touching him. Sparks shot from beneath her hand. She thought more about babies and long-term commitments than she ever had before.

Maybe other options were possible, too.

Donovan watched her so carefully that Alex was sure he could read her thoughts. "No," he said softly. "The firestorm won't be cheated."

Alex heard the consideration in his tone and met his gaze. She thought about having Donovan in her life for the duration and liked the concept a lot. She could even wrap her mind around the notion of having his child—a little red-headed boy who would be full of energy and enthusiasm.

Would he have green eyes or brown? Genetics said brown would dominate, but Alex had a feeling that Donovan's child would favor his father in more ways than one. She imagined the three of them together, and her chest tightened just a bit.

"You look stronger and bigger," she said, trying to change the subject.

He trailed a finger down her cheek, leaving a trail of fire that stole Alex's breath. He smiled slowly, looking like trouble and temptation in one tasty package. "That's your alchemy, Wizard."

"What happens to the Wizard once the Warrior is transformed?"

Donovan studied her and spoke very softly. "That's up to the Wizard."

His slow kiss left her sizzling and breathless; she was trapped against his broad chest and unwilling to be anywhere else. His eyes were glittering when he lifted his head, and their hearts pounded in unison. Alex had to narrow her eyes against the brilliance of the firestorm, its light burning hot and furious between them.

"Don't we have a triumph to celebrate?" Alex whispered. "In the traditional way?"

Donovan smiled. "It might be a shame to end this," he mused, playing with the sparks that danced between their fingertips.

"And sating the firestorm is a big commitment," Alex agreed, her heart leaping. "Babies and dragons, fighting *Slayers*, saving the world." She shook her head, pretending to be daunted, but Donovan wasn't fooled.

He arched a brow. "Don't tell me you're afraid?"

Alex met his gaze. "I'm not afraid of anything. Not anymore."

"No more nightmares?"

"No. Thank you."

His smile flashed. "The least I could do."

"What about you? Are you ready to face your dragons?" Alex watched Donovan, noting his stillness, and knew she had his undivided attention. "We could satisfy the firestorm."

Donovan gave her such an intense look that Alex knew he'd already made his decision. He uttered a single word with such conviction that Alex had no doubt of his feelings. "Yes," he said with resolve.

She stretched and brushed her lips across his, feeling the leap of his heart beneath her hand. "Let's celebrate success," she whispered. "By leaving the condoms on the nightstand tonight."

"Are you sure?"

Alex fixed Donovan with an intense look of her own. "Yes."

He didn't give her a chance to say anything more.

Archibald Forrester was in a bad mood. Not only had he spent the entire week in the hospital, thanks to his emphysema acting up again, but some fool had stolen his car. His body might be healed but he was as mad as hops. The police had found the burned-out wreckage on the outskirts of town, and Archibald couldn't imagine what the world was coming to.

Worst of all, it was Thursday. He'd finally persuaded Berenice to go to the dance at the Legion with him on Saturday night, but without a car, he wouldn't be able to pick her up. She would decline to go with him, again, and he'd have to start over his campaign to win her favor. Again.

Archibald wasn't getting any younger.

His mood hadn't improved—and his impatience hadn't mitigated—when the nurse found some reason to avoid taking him downstairs on time.

Archibald wasn't dead yet, though. He got into the wheelchair the intern had brought and piled all of his documentation and belongings on his lap. The sooner he got out of the hospital, the sooner he could figure out how to get a car by Saturday night.

He'd just wheeled himself into the hall when the nurse called after him.

"Oh, I'm sorry, Mr. Forrester," she said, then grabbed the handles on the wheelchair and pushed him forward with greater speed. He didn't acknowledge her, but she didn't seem to mind. "Do you have your charts? Good. I just got caught up talking to your grandson."

Archibald raised a brow, but said nothing. He wasn't senile yet, either. His only grandson lived in Atlanta and his wife had delivered triplets less than a month before. Archibald doubted that Roger had made the trip to

Minneapolis, and knew that if he had, he wouldn't have wasted time chatting to nurses when he could have talked to him.

Archibald knew an excuse when he heard one. He folded his arms across his belongings and let himself be pushed toward the elevator in silence.

"Such a charming man," the nurse said, clinging to her lie. "Here. He brought you a card."

She handed Archibald an envelope. He fingered it with suspicion. If it really was from his grandson, and if he had really been on this floor of this hospital five minutes ago, wouldn't he have brought the card to Archibald himself? It was fat, as if it contained more than a card.

Was it a trick? He hated practical jokes, always had.

"Go ahead and open it," the nurse chided as she backed his wheelchair into the elevator. "Get-well cards don't bite."

That was true enough. Archibald opened the envelope and pulled out the card. It was attractive, not too fussy, and stuck to the basics. *Get well soon* was written across the front. No flowers—they had always made him think of funeral homes—but a cartoon of a dog.

He opened the card and something metallic fell to his lap. There was no verse, just a handwritten note.

Mr. Forrester:
   Thanks for the use of your car. I'm sorry for the result, and also for the fact that I couldn't get another taupe one.
   Maybe the navy is more "you."
   I told the dealership you'd stop by to do the paperwork for the license plates.
   Take care—
   D.
   P.S. I left something for the insurance in the glove box.

The metal that had fallen to his lap was a pair of keys: Buick keys on a WWII vet key ring. A license plate number was written on a separate hang tag on the key ring, and that tag also had the name of a Buick dealership in town.

Archibald read the note again. He wasn't illiterate, either. His grandson's name was Roger, which certainly did not start with a D.

The nurse wheeled him through the exit, into a perfect, sunny fall day. He immediately spied a navy Buick in the short-term parking lot. It was the new model he'd been eying, and the dealer license-plate number matched the one on the tag.

"There," he said, as if it were truly his car.

The nurse took him right to the driver's-side door, and he stood beside it, trying not to admire it too openly.

"New car?" she asked.

"Yes."

"It's beautiful." She was pretty, this nurse. She smiled at him, and the sunlight danced in her hair. "I think you look good in navy. It'll make your eyes look more blue."

Archibald snorted, pleased although he tried to hide it. "Thank you for your help," he said.

She shook a playful finger at him. "Let's not be seeing you again too soon," she teased. "As charming as you are, I'd rather you were healthy."

Archibald nodded agreement, and she headed back to the hospital, pushing the wheelchair.

He looked at the car again. It was a fine piece of machinery, painted a metallic navy blue that glistened in the sun. Was this a trick? Some kind of *Candid Camera* setup? He couldn't see any cameras, but he wouldn't make a fool of himself anyway.

He turned the key in the lock and his heart skipped when the door unlocked, then opened with nary a squeak. He got in, savored that new-car smell, and—still skeptical—leaned over to open the glove box.

The receipt for the car was there, and it was marked PAID IN FULL. The paperwork for the license plates was there, with a business card clipped to it for the car salesman. There was an envelope with his name on it, addressed in the same handwriting as the card.

He opened the envelope to find twenty new hundred-dollar bills.

For the insurance.

It seemed that the world was a better place than he'd come to believe.

Archibald exhaled and looked around, seeing the day with new eyes. He didn't know who had taken his car and wrecked it, but that person had done the right thing and that was good enough by him.

Archibald turned the key in the ignition and liked the sound of the engine. He ran his hand across the brand-new upholstery and couldn't help but smile.

Wait until Berenice got a look at this.

Alex was locking the Green Machine into a temporary garage late Thursday afternoon when she heard the distinctive roar of a Ducati. She turned and waited, her buoyant mood made even better with the promise of Donovan's arrival.

He turned the corner and slowed the bike as he approached her, opening the visor on his helmet. He looked long and lean and sexy, his wicked smile doing dangerous things to her pulse. He was James Dean and every other hunk movie star rolled into one package.

And he was smiling at her.

"Hey gorgeous," he said as he came to a stop. "Going my way?"

It wasn't a joke. Alex felt gorgeous in his presence, sexy and feminine as she never had before. She was happy when she was with Donovan, too, and she loved how he had helped her.

Having him in her life was worth fighting dragons.

"Depends," she said, sauntering over to the bike. "Where are you going?"

"How was the meeting with Mr. Sinclair?" he asked instead.

"Amazing!" Alex couldn't hide her enthusiasm. "He's bringing in a technical consultant tomorrow to go over the Green Machine and he took at least a hundred pictures. He has that team already lined up for a strategic partnership and half of them are coming in for the weekend. Everything is a go!" She flung out her hands, still unable to believe how well it had gone. "We drove all over the place and he talked on the phone the whole time. The man seems to know everybody."

"So, it's happening." Donovan nodded approval.

"It's happening," Alex agreed. "I couldn't have managed it without you and the *Pyr*. Thanks." She would have kissed him but he was still wearing his helmet. She laid a hand on his arm instead and he put his hand over hers.

Even without the spark of the firestorm, it was pretty electric.

"So how about us?" he asked.

"Us?" Alex felt her heart skip.

"Us." Donovan gave her a hard look, one that made Alex's mouth go dry; then he looked away. "We have an outstanding bet to settle," he mused. "There was a bottle of champagne riding on who could hold back the longest, and it seems to me that we should confirm who's buying."

"It's not just about sex," Alex whispered, and Donovan shook his head with force.

"No, it's not. It's about celebration."

"It's not just about proving that you're alive, either."

Donovan pulled off his helmet and got off the bike, then took her hand in his. "The firestorm is about love," he said, his voice husky. "It's about finding your destined mate and falling hard enough that you worry about that person before you worry about yourself. It's about finding strength in your own weakness." He bent and brushed his lips across her knuckles, launching a wave of desire that nearly took Alex to her knees.

He looked at her, a wicked glint in his green eyes as he put her hand over his chest. She knew he had a new mole there, a mole that marked the contribution of her talisman. She was fiercely proud that she'd been able to offer something to make him safe.

No matter what happened.

"The firestorm has just drawn us to where we needed to be, Alex," he murmured, his eyes filled with promise. "I love you, and half measures just aren't going to be good enough."

Alex couldn't think straight about what he had said. Not yet. Not when his words were what she most wanted to hear.

"Dragon babies," she said, liking the sound of it more and more.

"There will be a child, and he'll be our son. No matter what happens between you and me, I'll take care of him."

"I know."

Donovan frowned down at her hand. "I know you aren't crazy about dragons, and if being with me is too much for you, I'll understand. . . ."

He was giving her the choice. Alex was humbled and thrilled.

"I'm not crazy about *Slayers*," she corrected. "But I think I'd like to have a good dragon of my very own." She wrinkled her nose at him. "Just in case."

His eyes twinkled. "Insurance?"

"Like a dragon's tooth in the garden, but better."

Donovan smiled a slow crooked smile that made her pulse go crazy. Alex knew that she'd never get tired of this journey of discovery. "We can't go to my apartment. It was trashed by the *Slayers*—"

Donovan put a finger over her lips, his touch making her mouth go dry. Alex felt her heartbeat synchronize with his and watched his eyes darken with desire. "You asked where

I was going. I've got an appointment to look at real estate tomorrow."

"Real estate?"

"I'm thinking I need a real lair, not just somewhere to leave my hoard, and that I need it in Minneapolis-St. Paul."

"Someplace with a dangerous downtown vibe?"

"Someplace with good schools." He smiled at her. "I'd like you to come along, since I'd like for us to share that lair."

"I'd like that, too." Alex leaned closer, knowing it was time for the truth. "I love you, Donovan Shea," she whispered, her voice low. She saw his grin flash before he kissed her.

"We should keep it legal," she teased moments later. "Seeing as we're in a public place."

"I can fix that," Donovan said, handing her the second helmet he'd brought. "Just don't tell me what kind of lingerie you're wearing."

"White lace, of course," she said as she got on the bike, and he groaned. She put her arms around his waist. "I think I might start a collection. For luck."

"There's more than luck at work between us," Donovan said, and revved the bike.

At the sound, Alex had an idea. "What do you think about driving the world's first and most environmentally friendly motorcycle?" she said, and Donovan laughed.

"I wondered how long it would take you to think of that," he said. "I've already warned the others that you'll be converting their vehicles. Quinn volunteered his pickup truck to be next."

"That reminds me," Alex said, leaning closer as Donovan took a curve. "There's one more thing we need to make right."

"What's that?"

"Three words."

"Archibald Forrester's Buick," they said in unison.

Donovan grinned. "I took care of that this afternoon."

"What did you do?"

"Made things right. Besides, I think navy will suit Archibald better than taupe."

Alex laughed and kissed him again. "Thank you. I was worried about him losing his car."

"We had to fix it, and I needed something to do during your meeting." His expression turned wicked, and Alex's heart skipped at the sight. "Because we've got other fires to light tonight."

Alex wasn't going to argue with that.

AUTHOR'S NOTE

When I first proposed this story, I had Alex's prototype car use water as fuel. By the time I sat down to write the story, I was beginning to wonder how I would make that sound plausible. But in August 2007, there was a story in the news—what perfect timing!—about a cancer researcher named John Kanzius in Erie, Pennsylvania, who inadvertently discovered that salt water will burn while exposed to radio frequencies. His results have been confirmed and are the focus of research.

So, while Alex is ahead of her time, the Green Machine isn't that implausible.

Read on for a sneak preview of the next
book in Deborah Cooke's Dragonfire series

KISS OF FATE

Coming from Signet Eclipse in February 2009

Chicago
February 2008

The *Pyr* gathered at Erik's lair for the eclipse.

Erik's lair was in a warehouse that had been partly converted to lofts. It was large and industrial and in a lousy part of town. Rafferty wondered who would see the high council of dragons on the roof of the building and what they would make of the scene. The idea made him smile.

Rafferty was older than all the others, but he never got bored of the world and its charms. As usual, he was optimistic that this time the firestorm would be his, but he couldn't resent the good fortune of his fellows.

The Great Wyvern had a plan for each of them; Rafferty believed that with all his heart and soul.

And he would wait his turn.

While he waited, he did his best to facilitate the firestorms of his fellows.

The company stood on the roof, watching the moon slip into the earth's shadow. It took on the hue of blood, casting the earth in surreal light.

"Quickly," Erik said with more than his usual impatience. "The full eclipse will last less than half an hour this time." Rafferty understood Erik's concern; this was the third of the full eclipses, three in a row before the final battle between *Pyr* and *Slayer*. After this eclipse, the die would be cast and the battle for power over the planet's fate would begin in earnest.

Rafferty wasn't looking forward to that.

Meanwhile, the *Pyr* shifted shape in unison. For this eclipse, they were joined by the two most recent human mates, both of whom were pregnant. Quinn, the Smith, was scaled in sapphire and steel; his mate, Sara, the Seer, stood petite and fair at his side. Donovan, the Warrior, took his lapis lazuli and gold dragon form, while his tall and dark-haired mate, Alex, the Wizard, looked on. Theirs were two strong partnerships that had been made at this vortex of change.

This would be the third, if the *Pyr* could make it work.

Erik turned to an onyx and pewter dragon, while Rafferty became an opal and gold dragon. Sloane and Niall brought Delaney and kept him between them, although Rafferty believed that it was Delaney who was most worried about what might happen.

After all, the spark in Delaney's eyes was much brighter. Rafferty believed that Sloane's treatment was working and that the darkness inflicted upon Delaney was steadily diminishing.

Sloane changed form, his tourmaline scales shading from green to purple and back again, each one edged in gold. Niall, meanwhile, became a dragon of amethyst and platinum. Delaney changed to an emerald and copper dragon. Nikolas of Thebes, new to this ceremony, shifted to a dragon of anthracite and iron, then hung back to quietly observe.

Erik murmured the ancient blessing once they were all in dragon form. Rafferty watched Erik spin the Dragon's Egg, saw the moon's light touch the round dark stone. Gold lines appeared upon its surface almost immediately, prompting a startled gasp from both Alex and Nikolas. Rafferty watched hungrily as the gold lines triangulated a location.

Would this be his chance? The Dragon's Egg glistened as Erik leaned closer to read its portent.

"London," a woman's voice said from behind them all. Rafferty pivoted to find the Wyvern lounging against the fire escape, still in her human form.

He doubted that he was the only one surprised to find her there. Sophie was wearing a long white skirt that floated around her ankles. Her long blond hair was loose and flowed down her back. She looked like a graceful swan, or perhaps like one that was made of glass.

How did she keep herself from shifting shape under the eclipse's light?

She smiled as she regarded them, smiled so knowingly that Rafferty wondered if she had heard his thoughts.

She strode closer and crouched down beside the Dragon's Egg. "Why don't we ask it to tell us something we don't know?"

"I do not have your skill, especially as you choose not to share it," Erik said in old-speak. His irritation was clear, but Sophie's smile never wavered.

"Listen," she bade him in old-speak, the single word resonating in Rafferty's chest. She murmured a chant. It was short and wordless, either a string of sounds or a language forgotten. It sounded old to Rafferty. Potent.

She repeated it, and Erik echoed the sound. She nodded approval and beckoned to him. Erik leaned over the Dragon's Egg at her urging and the two of them chanted in unison.

Then Sophie blew on the dark globe of stone. The golden lines disappeared immediately, as if lines blown from the sand, and a woman's face came into view. It was as if she swam to the surface of a lake, her hair streaming back and her eyes closed.

Then she opened her eyes and looked directly at Erik. Even from his position, Rafferty could see that her eyes were a glorious blue. The hair that flowed around her face was wavy and chestnut brown, and billowed as if she were underwater.

When she simply stared at Erik, the Wyvern blew on the Dragon's Egg again.

"My name is Eileen Grosvenor," the woman said, her words clearly enunciated. She paused, as if to think. "At least, that's what they call me this time."

She lifted a fingertip toward Erik and he lifted a talon, seemingly against his own volition. When his talon was over the Dragon's Egg, a spark danced between it and the woman's finger.

He recoiled in shock. "Louisa!"

"Yes," the woman murmured, as if remembering something she had half forgotten. "Yes, I have been called that, too."

Erik stared at the Dragon's Egg in shock and took a step back.

Untroubled by his response, the woman smiled a brilliant smile, one that lit the Dragon's Egg from within. Then she seemed to take a deep breath, closed her eyes, and disappeared as if sinking to the bottom of a lake. Her hair flowed around and over her before the ends flicked out of sight.

Erik gave a cry and seized the Dragon's Egg just as the moon peeked out from the earth's shadow. The stone turned black again, reverting to its usual smooth orb of obsidian stone.

"How can this be?" he demanded of the Wyvern.

Sophie straightened and smiled as the _Pyr_ shifted back to human form around her. She gave Delaney a hard look, then nodded once at Sloane. "You are half done," she said. "Do not falter."

By the time Sloane had nodded agreement, Sophie had turned and walked to the lip of the roof. She lifted her arms over her head, laughing as the wind teased her skirts, and leapt.

Rafferty was the first to reach the edge. Even having guessed what he would see, he was still surprised.

Far below a white dragon soared, her feathers flowing behind her. She glinted in the changing light, reflecting and refracting the hue cast by the moon, like a dragon carved of crystal. She ascended and turned a tight curve over the roof, leaving the *Pyr* staring after her with awe.

She flew straight up, then abruptly disappeared. The sky was clear and there was nowhere for her to be hidden. She had simply vanished, as suddenly as she had appeared.

"I hate when she does that," Donovan muttered. Rafferty didn't agree, not this time. No matter how often he saw her, he found that Sophie's appearance gladdened his heart. He realized what a gift it was to have her among them. He felt as though there was a greater force on their side, on the side of right, and he was touched by her beauty, as well.

He found Nikolas beside him, the other *Pyr*'s dark eyes wide with astonishment. "She is real, then," he whispered. "I thought that I had dreamed her presence before."

"She didn't stay long enough to be introduced. Her name is Sophie," Rafferty said. "She is the Wyvern, a prophetess who has skills far beyond our own."

"I know who she is," Nikolas murmured, seeking some sign of her presence.

"Her prophecies only count if you understand them," Quinn noted, and Sara smiled.

Nikolas nodded though, his awe undiminished. "If we do not understand, then we are not worthy of the prophecy," he said stiffly. "Praise be to the Great Wyvern that such beauty exits." He put his hand over his heart and bowed his head in an attitude of prayer.

Erik was still staring into the Dragon's Egg, his features pale. "Louisa," he whispered, raising his gaze to meet Rafferty's. "It can't be true."

But Rafferty knew that it was, no matter how Erik might wish for it to be otherwise. He decided then that Erik might need his help.

"Stay with me in my lair in London," he said. "We'll find your firestorm together."

In the burn ward of a major hospital, the patient known as John Doe felt the tug of the eclipse, as well.

He awakened, stiff and groggy, his body determined to heed the ancient call. He knew what would happen instants before it did, knew that the sedative would keep him from effectively controlling his primal urges. He tore bandages from his hands and the IV needle from his arm, flinging himself off the bed in the nick of time. No sooner had his bare feet touched the cold linoleum than he shifted shape.

Mercifully, he had arranged for a private room.

With a swing of his mighty tail, he shattered the tinted window. Before the nurses could arrive, he launched himself through the broken glass and took flight over the city. He had not recovered his full strength, but Boris Vassily had learned to make the most of whatever he had.

He whispered to the wind and the sky and listened to the tales they told. He asked one question of the moon and heeded its response. Anger boiled within him as he understood with perfect clarity who would feel the firestorm this time.

There would be no happy ending if Boris had anything to say about it.

And he did. The ruby red and brass dragon he became was less splendid than he had once been. His trailing red plumes were gone, his body as scarred in dragon form as it was in human form. He could not bear to look at himself, for he had once been the jewel of his kind.

He knew where to lay the blame. The *Pyr* responsible for his scarred self was none other than Erik Sorensson, none other than the *Pyr* whose firestorm would not proceed without interruption.

The time for recovery was past.

The time for vengeance had arrived.

But there was one small detail to be resolved first. Boris sought the address he knew so well, the address where the payments had gone. He wheeled through the sky toward the luxury condominium, and his nose told him that the plastic surgeon he had retained—the one bribed to overlook any physiological oddities in his anonymous patient—was home.

What a perfect night for a house fire.

Boris landed on the terrace that overlooked Lake Michigan and confronted the good doctor thought the sliding-glass door. The doctor put down his glass of champagne and turned at the sound of Boris's arrival, alarm and disbelief mingling in his expression.

Boris reared up, letting the doctor see his scars, willing him to make the connection. The surgeon's eyes widened in horror; he dropped the glass and backed away with his hands held high.

That was when Dr. Nigel Berenstein understood that he would never collect the bonus payment for successful completion of the surgery.

Boris laughed, kicked his way through the sliding-glass door and loosed his dragonfire.

He took great pleasure in the way the plastic surgeon's skin crackled as it burned, inflicting damage beyond the ability of any human doctor to repair. He let the doctor experience the fullness of the pain, let him see what he had become, then fried the life out of him.

Humans were such a feeble species.

Boris left the apartment ablaze, knowing the fire was his ally in destroying signs of his presence. Pesky details resolved, he turned his attention to a matter of greater import.

He was going to enjoy thwarting Erik's firestorm.

It would be the credential he needed to ensure that Magnus didn't steal the leadership of the *Slayers*.

                    *   *   *

In a London hotel, Eileen Grosvenor awakened with a start. She sat up and looked around the bedroom, shocked to find it exactly as it should be.

Instead of filled with water. She'd dreamed of swimming underwater, swimming so far underwater that she might have been a fish. It had been wonderful; she'd felt strong and agile, the muscles in her body moving in perfect concert.

There had been light. A warm light, like that cast by a candle. She'd moved directly to it, unable to resist its allure.

She closed her eyes and again saw the face of the man who had been bent over the surface of the water, looking down at her. She remembered raising a finger and seeing him reach out with one hand. She saw again the spark that had leapt between their fingers, illuminating the surface of the water.

There was something in his eyes that melted her heart. A memory of pain, or of some old injury. Eileen had been sure that she could heal him, even though he was beyond the water and she was beneath it.

Maybe it was a portent. Maybe she was finally going to meet a man worth the trouble. She'd certainly know him again if she saw him. She focused on his image, sharpening it in her thoughts. Oh, yes, she'd recognize him anywhere.

Maybe it was just a silly dream, brought on by the stress of being away from home.

The dream made Eileen happy, though, made her feel strong and sexy and optimistic. She had a strange, irrational conviction that she was going to meet the man of her dreams, so to speak.

That didn't sound like Eileen, the ultimate pragmatist. She scoffed and got out of bed for a drink of water. Eileen was standing in the bathroom, drinking, when she saw in the mirror that her hair was wet.

And there was a piece of water lily tangled in the ends.

But Eileen didn't swim; she never had. She had a fear of the water, one she'd struggled to overcome because it was without any basis in her history. She certainly didn't swim in hotel rooms that didn't have ocean access.

Eileen met her own gaze in the mirror, seeing her surprise and confusion. If her hair *was* wet, then it couldn't have been a dream, could it?

What had just happened to her?

And why?

About the Author

Deborah Cooke has always been fascinated by dragons, although she has never understood why they have to be the bad guys. She has an honors degree in history, with a focus on medieval studies, and is an avid reader of medieval vernacular literature, fairy tales, and fantasy novels. Since 1992, Deborah has written more than thirty romance novels under the names Claire Cross and Claire Delacroix.

Deborah makes her home in Canada with her husband. When she isn't writing, she can be found knitting, sewing, or hunting for vintage patterns. To learn more about the Dragonfire series and Deborah, please visit her Web site at www.deborahcooke.com and her blog, Alive & Knitting, at www.delacroix.net/blog.

Also Available

THE FIRST NOVEL IN THE DRAGONFIRE SERIES

KISS OF FIRE

by DEBORAH COOKE

For millennia, the shape-shifting dragon warriors known as the Pyr have commanded the four elements and guarded the earth's treasures. But now the final reckoning between the Pyr, who count humans among the earth's treasures, and the Slayers, who would eradicate both humans and the Pyr who protect them, is about to begin...

When Sara Keegan decides to settle down and run her quirky aunt's New Age bookstore, she's not looking for adventure. She doesn't believe in fate or the magic of the tarot—but when she's saved from a vicious attack by a man who has the ability to turn into a fire-breathing dragon, she questions whether she's losing her mind—or about to lose her heart...